GW00360135

A Certain Splendour

A Certain Splendour

CAROLA SALISBURY

WORDSWORTH EDITIONS

The paper in this book is produced from pure wood
pulp, without the use of chlorine or any other substance
harmful to the environment. The energy used in its
production consists almost entirely of hydroelectricity
and heat generated from waste materials, thereby
conserving fossil fuels and contributing little to the
greenhouse effect.

First published by Century Publishing Limited

This edition published 1994 by
Wordsworth Editions Limited
Cumberland House, Crib Street, Ware,
Hertfordshire SG12 9ET

ISBN 1 85326 506 3

Printed and bound in Denmark by Nørhaven

PROLOGUE

London – June 1916

The day the telegram arrived began like any other: I made myself some tea, and while the kettle was boiling fed my two goldfish, put some crumbs out on the kitchen windowsill for the birds, brushed my rather unaccommodating hair, decided what I would wear that day and changed my mind twice. I also made some toast.

Keeping strictly to my morning schedule, I took my tea and toast into the sitting-room and curled up in the button-back chair in front of the empty grate – it was high summer and a heatwave – beneath the chimneypiece where were set my favourite photographs. There was one of Father, looking terribly handsome in a yachting cap, with his neat beard and a cigarette between his lips at a jaunty angle. We always – *everyone* always – said that he and King George and the Tsar of Russia were practically interchangeable in appearance, but that Father was much the most handsome! Next to it was a photo of me taken in Malta five years ago, standing on a balcony overlooking the Grand Harbour with 'a certain person' by my side – not talking, just looking at each other. The years have gone by, I have shed an ocean of tears and nothing can ever be the same again, but I remember as if it were happening now exactly what I was thinking at the moment the photograph was taken – a thought which has warmed and comforted me through the many long dark days between.

I nibbled at my toast, sipped my tea. Half-past eight and time to leave. I brushed the crumbs from my lap, rose to my feet and went to get ready.

And then the doorbell rang. . .

Still in dressing-gown and slippers, I went to answer it, and remember feeling rather puzzled because tradesmen did not usually begin their calls so early. My landlady, Mrs Slyte, usually coped with that side of things, but she was in bed with a summer cold; I had taken her a hot lemon and whisky the night before and given her firm advice to stay right where she was until her temperature went down.

In the event she nearly beat me to the door as she came out of her flat on the ground floor, shrugging a dressing-gown over her shoulders, her hair tousled.

'Who can it be?' I asked, my hand already on the door-handle.

'It's a telegraph boy,' she said in a tight voice. 'I saw him pass the window.'

I looked into her eyes and saw the agony there. A widow, she had an only son of just nineteen – and he was serving over in France, a private soldier fighting in the trenches.

I opened the door. . .

'Telegram, missus,' said the boy, holding out a buff-coloured envelope. 'For Miss Dangerfield – Miss Faith Dangerfield.'

'Oh, thank God!' breathed Mrs Slyte. 'Thank God.' She gave a sob.

I took the envelope from the boy and slit it open. There was never any doubt in my mind as to what I should find there, nor was I mistaken.

Through the sudden tears, I saw the prim handwriting of some Post Office clerk who had been delegated to score a knife wound across my life:

'THE SECRETARY OF THE ADMIRALTY REGRETS TO INFORM YOU. . .'

MALTA

June 1911

ONE

My routine aboard the *Gloria* when we were in harbour was as follows: Annette my maid woke me at nine, sometimes later if I had been out to dinner or to a party, or if we had been entertaining aboard. She drew back the curtains and opened the door leading out on to the poop deck, which was my private verandah where I could gaze out upon the passing scene. And then she gave me my breakfast tray of tea and toast.

That morning she said, 'There's a message from the harbour-master, ma'am. The flotilla's been sighted and he reckons they'll be here about ten.'

'Good,' I replied. 'Oh, Annette, no one can make toast like you. How do you do it?'

She went pink with pleasure. A little Cockney waif I had originally encountered during charitable work in London's East End, she had responded well to my tuition and become a most excellent lady's maid – a competence which would provide her with a good living for the rest of her life. The name Annette was of my own devising: her real name was, as I recall, Effie. Or it may have been Bessie. Certainly something irremediably lower class.

'Run my bath, please, Annette,' I said. 'I must be ready to receive my father when he enters harbour. Will you please also ask Captain Jaggers to dress the yacht overall for the flotilla's arrival?'

'Overall, ma'am?' She looked puzzled, poor little thing; the niceties of maritime protocol were still beyond her.

'The flags, Annette,' I said, amused. 'The pretty signal flags that are strung right over the yacht from front to back, over the masts, for festive occasions. It's rather like – well – putting up holly and mistle-toe for Christmas. Don't worry – just ask the Captain to dress over-all – he'll know what you mean.'

'Yes, ma'am.' She bobbed a curtsey and left me.

Still amused and in a curiously euphoric mood, I slid out of bed and shrugged into a peignoir, then took my tea and a piece of toast out on to the poop deck. The sun was well up, but the stark white canvas awning above my head had been rigged by the sailors since dawn, and a refreshing light breeze blew across the placid waters of Malta's Grand Harbour. I sipped and I nibbled. From the Valletta quay, a boat propelled by a muscular youth in a red vest made its way across the harbour in herringbone patterns, shaping course towards the row of grey battleships on the huge buoys in midstream, and then pointedly going somewhat off-course so as to pass close by *Gloria*'s stern – and me.

' 'Allo!' He waved, the lad in the red vest.

'Good morning.' I waved back. There was a little dog – a wire-haired terrier – standing guard in the bows of the boat. He wagged his tail frantically and barked at me as they passed on their way.

My pleasure at the beautiful day oddly heightened by this fleeting encounter, I drained my tea-cup, tossed the remainder of my toast to the scavenging seagulls and went to take my bath.

A day like any other in my very sheltered and immensely pleasurable life – but one which was to mark a watershed in my greatly indulged existence, so that nothing which came after was quite the same, and what had gone before gradually began to take on a new flavour, as if remembered through an entirely different set of senses.

*

My name is Faith Anne Dangerfield. My mother died when I was an infant. She must have been a very splendid person, for my father loved her desperately, and I am quite sure he was never the same man again when she had gone. He said often that I greatly resembled her in many respects; in any event, he quite unashamedly spoilt me beyond belief.

Father was the second son of Claud Dangerfield, who had been successively the Chairman of the Stock Exchange, Lord Mayor of London and a peer of the realm – in that order. My grandfather died before I was born, leaving his fortune equally divided between his widow and two sons, and his title of course to the elder. Father, who had chosen the Navy for his career and was thoroughly determined to emulate Nelson in any future war upon which Britain and the Empire might be engaged, was a darling of that greatly demanding

12

Service. His dash, his style, his sheer professionalism endeared him to the more discerning – though by no means all – of his professional superiors; while the tremendous wealth lying at his disposal – which he dispensed freely, generously and totally without any 'side' or conceit – gave him independence from the normal strictures of Service life. For instance I, being now twenty-four, motherless, unmarried and something of a handful, might have been a source of anxiety to him; however, his wealth made it possible to set me up in luxurious villas in Alexandria, Plymouth, Kingstown or wherever he was stationed. And we also had the *Gloria*, a steam yacht of 1,665 gross tonnage which was scarcely less luxurious and commodious than our family town house in Park Lane and in which I – for want of a better term – 'followed the fleet' when Father was in home waters or in the Mediterranean. . . as I was doing at that time.

Presently bathed, dressed in a white gown of sprigged Irish linen and wearing a magnificent cartwheel hat which I had bought in Paris earlier in the season, I went out on to the boat deck with my binoculars to await the arrival of my father's flotilla of six deadly little motor torpedo-boat destroyers – the latest pride of the Royal Navy, devised by brilliant Admiral 'Jackie' Fisher whom I adored. Named *Havoc, Hornet, Hasty, Hecuba, Hengist* and *Horsa*, and only half the length of *Gloria*, they each carried torpedoes and other armament and were capable of achieving the then unheard-of speed of 28 knots. As commander of this crack flotilla, carrying his flag in *Hecuba*, father had currently been engaged upon manoeuvres in the wine-dark seas between Malta and the North African littoral, and – a piquant situation – the flotilla had lately joined up with the *Darmstadt*, a light cruiser of the Imperial German Navy, and had been conducting manoeuvres with her around Sicily. I looked forward with lively interest to hearing Father's account of the cruise, for the manoeuvres had been of his own devising; he it was who had persuaded the Admiralty that the Royal Navy's most likely enemy should be made aware of the deadly power of the new torpedo-boat destroyers. In Father's phrase, 'Give the Kaiser and his admirals food for thought and a few sleepless nights!'

Charles Knight was already on deck. Knight was Father's social secretary and incidentally mine. A civilian, thirty-ish, the son of an impoverished Devon clergyman, he was everything a social secretary should be: neat, efficient, attentive, full of quiet charm. And also very presentable – China-blue eyes, curly hair, boyish.

He greeted me formally as always. 'Morning, Miss Dangerfield. I trust you slept well?'

'Exceedingly well, Knight, thank you. Any sign of the flotilla yet?'

'I think so, ma'am.' He pointed to the north, straight out of the entrance to the Grand Harbour. 'See that smudge of smoke on the horizon? That will be the *Darmstadt*'s funnel smoke, without a doubt.'

'Yes, I can see it.' I trained my binoculars.

'Ma'am, regarding the ball on Saturday. . .'

'Oh, yes. We could profitably fill in time until the flotilla arrives by working on the guest list. Will you have them bring a pot of coffee, please?'

Presently, seated side by side in deck-chairs, sipping the *Gloria*'s justly famous special blend of coffee, we set to work – Knight with his notebook on his knee, pencil poised.

He cleared his throat. 'Ma'am, first I would like to query your suggestion of holding the ball on Saturday. The Commodore will undoubtedly wish to play polo late on Saturday afternoon, as usual. . .'

'My father will wish *not* to play polo next Saturday,' I replied firmly. 'This is my ball and he will grace it with his presence from first to last.'

My companion nodded and made a note in his book. I think I detected the beginnings of a grin crinkling the corners of his mouth.

'As for the programme,' he said, 'I understand you propose a buffet tea at 3.30 pm with dancing, held on the boat deck. This to be followed by a formal dinner in the main saloon at sunset. Dancing until dawn, with eggs and bacon served from 4 am. Boats and carriages at 8 pm?'

'Correct,' I said. 'Did you manage to secure the Royal Marine orchestra from Fort St Angelo?'

'I did, ma'am. And right from under the nose of the Governor's lady, who wanted them for a reception she's giving for the Italian chargé d'affaires.'

'Splendid,' I said. 'If she is holding a reception on the same evening, she will not be coming to my ball, and I shall be spared the tedium of listening to a diatribe on her latest aches and pains. Now, with regard to the guest list. We ought to get the invitations away this morning, for Saturday is rather short notice. Suggest some names, please!'

I relaxed, sipped my coffee, gave an occasional glance towards the burgeoning smoke-cloud on the horizon and listened while Knight read out the names of my guests – as proposed by him. The list was quite impeccable; as social secretary, there was none to match him. Admiral Freakley, C-in-C Malta and his lady led the list, of course. Then the Governor and *his* lady (who would not be accepting, thank heaven). Captains of major warships present. A good sprinkling of young and amusing lieutenants to leaven the former rather heavy dough. Ladies – dowagers with their pretty daughters, a few un-attached ladies of maturity and distinction, single or widowed. . .

'Mrs Chalmers. . .' I caught the inflection in his voice; it was almost but not quite a question.

'I think not.'

'Ma'am, you owe her the return for her dinner-party.'

'I know.' I sulked into my coffee cup.

'You will recall, ma'am, that Mrs Chalmers has a standing invita-tion to come aboard any time.'

'Not from *me*.'

A silence passed between us like the wraith of smoke that was beginning to fill the northern horizon: intangible yet all-pervading.

'All right,' I said at length. 'Include Mrs Chalmers.'

'Yes, ma'am.' He continued with his list.

Natasha Chalmers was a widow. In my uncharity, I dubbed her a 'professional widow', a 'merry widow'. Bereaved in her late twen-ties – her late husband having been a millionaire American banker – she was reputed to have been a lover of – among many others – the late King. Rich and ostentatiously so, she lacked only one thing: a permanent attachment. And I was thoroughly convinced that she had set her cap at my father to fill that role. Why else, I asked myself, was she always at polo to cheer him on? People like Natasha Chalmers held a rough sport like that in no regard. And there was the recent occasion at Government House when, stepping outside for a breath of fresh air after a particularly breathtaking waltz, I had surprised Father and that woman in an embrace on the terrace.

A mild flirtation, perhaps: the attraction of a still handsome and dashing naval commander for an unquestionably fascinating woman some years his junior. Better it went no further. I neither liked nor trusted the fascinating Mrs Chalmers!

*

15

The flotilla and its consort, the high-sided cruiser with its four towering funnels, were soon over the horizon and presently steaming into harbour in line-ahead, Father's *Hecuba* leading. As the TBDs approached their line of buoys, *Hecuba*'s mast blossomed a hoist of flags that signalled the flotilla to moor together – that is to say, as near simultaneously as possible. It was a tricky manoeuvre, for even a tiny margin of human or mechanical error could upset the apple-cart, as I had witnessed several times.

The crew of the *Gloria* were all up on deck to see their owner's arrival, watching with critical and professional eyes. Captain Jaggers was at my elbow, treating me to a commentary on the finer points of the manoeuvre.

'See, ma'am, how the Commodore's brought *Hecuba* in line and within a couple of feet of the mooring buoy. And now he stops. There's mastery for you! The buoy-jumper – see? – he's naught to do but step on there and make fast with the steel wire rope. Now the anchor chain goes over with a shackle on its end, to make the final attachment. Brilliant piece of seamanship!' The Captain of the *Gloria* was one of Father's most fervent admirers – and there were many.

'The rest don't seem to be doing quite so well,' I remarked. 'Number four in line, for instance.'

'Oh, dear me no!' confirmed Jaggers. 'What's happened, see, is that she approached too fast, was obliged to reverse engines too vigorously – and now she's backed off from the buoy. She'll have to try again. The whole manoeuvre's spoilt.'

'Isn't that *Hasty*?' I ventured. In truth they all looked alike to me, and I could never remember the large pennant numbers emblazoned on their sides.

'*Hasty* it is, ma'am. Young Lieutenant Jobling. Hasty by name and by nature. That lad has much to learn.'

'Poor Mr Jobling,' I murmured. 'And you're quite right about him. Hasty in every respect.'

'Beg your pardon, ma'am?'

'Oh, it was nothing, Captain.' I smiled to myself.

*

The flotilla having moored – *Hasty* included – and the German cruiser having taken a place among the big ship moorings, a boat put out from *Hecuba* and shaped course towards us. Using my binoculars, I had no difficulty in picking out the tall and commanding figure of my father, standing in the stern sheets. He was splendid in his all-white tropical uniform, with the splash of medal ribbons at the breast, the broad gold stripe of Commodore on his epaulettes.

And he was not alone in his glory. There was another officer with him: a much younger man, though scarcely less impressive as to height and bearing. Dark as my father was fair, deeply bronzed by tropic suns, wearing as much 'fruit salad' as Father, though less gold lace, he had power to excite the eye and the imagination, having the looks of a corsair or a buccaneer. And he was a complete stranger to me.

Father was piped aboard, Service fashion, by the bosun's mates and came straight aft to the quarter-deck where I awaited him. The 'corsair' followed at his heels.

'Dearest Faith, how are you? What have you been doing with yourself these last weeks? Have you been terribly bored without me?' Father embraced me in the warm, loving manner that had made a delight of my childhood and recompensed me for the lack of a mother. I kissed his cheek. Over his shoulder, I saw the dark man staring evenly and expressionlessly at me.

'Faith, I want to present Lieutenant-Commander Jack Cummings, my new First Lieutenant who joined us in Augusta. Cummings will be to all intents in command of *Hecuba*, leaving me free to direct the flotilla.'

'How do you do, Commander,' I said, offering my hand to him.

'Miss Dangerfield.' He bowed stiffly. His hand, which I could feel quite distinctly through my lacy glove – the firm texture of it, the coolness – lingered in mine for only a shade longer than propriety permitted. His eyes were of the deepest blue and quite inscrutable.

'Cummings brought us to the buoy,' said Father. 'Neatly done, didn't you think, Faith?'

'Excellent,' I responded. 'You're very skilful, Commander.'

'That young idiot Jobling!' snorted Father. 'I'll burn the seat of his trousers when I see him. Thank heaven the Germans didn't notice it.' He chuckled. 'The *Darmstadt* was too busy with her own troubles to criticise our performance. She got to her buoy on the third shot, would you believe?'

'I don't think you should be too hard on Mr Jobling, Father,' I said. 'What he lacks in application, he more than makes up for with enthusiasm.'

'You may be right at that, my dear,' conceded my parent.

'Miss Dangerfield.' Cummings' voice was deep, with a harsh edge of command and I felt my hackles rise upon his so addressing me. 'I would point out that enthusiasm is not enough in the modern Navy. It may have served us well in Nelson's time, but in this the twentieth century, the tools we have to hand, the precision instruments in which we go to sea and train ourselves to make war, are not to be mastered by mere enthusiasm but by *professionalism*!'

The blue eyes blazed and I saw in the instant that behind the romantic mask of the corsair there lurked an opinionated man, a bigot perhaps. A martinet, certainly. I suddenly felt unaccountably sorry for poor Dickie Jobling and his broad, carefree grin that eased him through most of his shortcomings.

'Very true, very true, Cummings,' interposed Father. 'And now – the sun being nearly over the yardarm – let's have a drink. Ring the bell for the duty steward, would you, please, Faith?'

'It's a little early for me, sir,' responded Cummings. 'With your leave, I will abstain.'

'As you will, as you will,' Father replied. 'And you, my dear?' addressing me.

Now, I greatly disapproved of some of my father's drinking habits. The sun was by no means 'over the yardarm', for it wanted all of three-quarters of an hour till noon. Nor am I given to tippling at midday; but the stuffy and puritanical manner in which the martinet (I could no longer think of him as a swashbuckling corsair) had made his declaration, drove me to cast aside my normal habits.

'I think I should like some champagne, Father,' I declared. 'To celebrate your return and as a foretaste of the ball, which I am giving in your honour on Saturday.'

'That will be nice,' replied Father. 'After the polo, of course?'

'After, before and *during* the polo!' I retorted, with one eye on Lieutenant-Commander Cummings.

Let him see that *I* could play the martinet, also!

*

We had luncheon *à quatre*: Father, the egregious Cummings, Charles Knight and I, in the delicious coolness of the quarter deck, under the shade of the stark white canvas awning.

I had arranged for the fish course to be lampuki – the delicious mullet-type delicacy that is curiously peculiar to the seas surrounding Malta and is regarded as a great treat by the islanders (and also

18

by my father) for it swarms for only a short season in the year.

'I put it to you, Cummings,' said Father, 'that if one could open a restaurant in Soho and serve lampuki all the year round, one would make a fortune. I'd wager a thousand guineas on it, blessed if I wouldn't. What do you think, hey?'

'It's very excellent, sir,' declared the other.

I turned to Charles Knight, for something had been troubling my mind. 'I've been very remiss,' I confessed, 'not to have asked you to invite Miss Dearing to my ball. Please do include her in the guest list. And forgive my lapse.'

He coloured slightly and looked very pleased. Angela Dearing and he had an unofficial engagement, which was scarcely likely to come to fruition in the foreseeable future, for Knight had nothing but the modest salary that Father paid him; she, a poor little mouse of a thing with no fortune, was companion to an aged dowager of the Maltese aristocracy – and if Lady Borg paid her anything over her board and keep (which I doubted), there could not have been enough to put aside any savings.

'You are very kind, ma'am,' murmured Knight.

Father was talking politics and strategy: 'Malta is the key to our Eastern Empire,' he declared, 'and will remain so until well into the twenty-first century, when the aeroplane will supersede the ship as the major factor in both warfare and commerce.'

Cummings looked evenly at his superior and seemed to me to wish to take strong issue with Father's sweeping declaration; instead he satisfied himself by saying, 'That's a very surprising thought, sir. Do you think that the aeroplane will ever be perfected to a degree beyond that of a plaything for extreme eccentrics? One has heard of course that the Navy is beginning to take aviation half-seriously.'

'More than that,' responded my parent. 'I have to inform you, my dear Cummings, that there is already a force in being and that they are training naval pilots at some place in Kent. Now – what do you think of that, hey? From every report I receive, it's certain that the Service is vastly interested in aerial developments. I'll wager a thousand guineas that we shall have developed the aeroplane into a fighting arm within the next decade. What do you think of that?'

'I am overwhelmed, sir,' responded Cummings. And he said it in a cool, flat voice that seemed – to me, at least, who had decided that she had the measure of the man – to exhibit a total disbelief. Father appeared not to notice, but scooped up the last of his lampuki and chewed it with a certain reverence.

During the silent hiatus that usually accompanies the serving of another course (in this case curried chicken), I essayed to engage the Lieutenant-Commander in light conversation, he being seated on my right.

'Do you know Malta well, Commander?' I asked.

'Not well, ma'am,' he responded, fixing me with his disconcerting blue glance. 'Indeed, scarcely at all. I've only put into here during my passages from England to the China station, where I've spent most of my naval career.'

'I must interject that Cummings most gallantly disported himself during the Boxer uprising,' said Father. 'He was present as naval attaché at the siege of the legation quarter in Peking, for which action he gained his Distinguished Service Order.'

I made no comment upon that, nor did Cummings, but he continued, 'I should very much like to explore the island.'

'Two islands,' interposed Father. 'There's also Gozo – not to mention bits and pieces of small islets. If you want a guide, you could hope for no one better than my daughter, who is what one would describe as a 'Maltaphile'. I don't suppose there's an Englishman or woman alive who knows his or her way around Malta like Faith. Indeed, I'd wager a thousand guineas on it, so I would!'

Neither Lieutenant-Commander Cummings nor I made any comment upon that observation and implied suggestion.

Over the dessert (*pêche Melba*), the conversation turned to naval matters again and I split the discourse by addressing myself quietly to Charles Knight on the subject of my coming ball. We discussed the menus for tea and dinner, the dance programme (the Royal Marine orchestra was always most accommodating as to programmes and its repertoire was seemingly endless), and the shipboard arrangements whereby those ladies who found the strain of round-the-clock dancing too arduous, might rest in quiet cabins for an hour or so; just as the gentlemen could retire to the lesser saloon and put their feet up over a brandy and seltzer if they were so inclined.

Over coffee and brandy, Father said, 'Knight, I have to return to *Hecuba* within the hour, and there are matters – private business matters from London – that I must discuss with you. Shall we take our coffee and brandy to my cabin and wade through the quite appalling amount of paperwork that seems to have accumulated?'

They departed, leaving me alone with Lieutenant-Commander Jack Cummings, DSO, RN.

'I understand, ma'am,' he said 'that the conventional mode of private transport in the islands is by carriage?'

'That is so, Commander,' I replied, 'though one can hire livery horses for riding. My father and I have a small stable of hacks and polo ponies near Valletta, and you are very welcome to take your pick at any time.'

'Very kind, very kind, ma'am,' he responded. 'Unfortunately, the competence of horse riding is not within my compass. I shall have to explore Malta by carriage.'

'We don't own a carriage here,' I said. 'It's scarcely worth the trouble, for they're available for hire on any street corner in the towns and villages.'

The stewards cleared away the coffee things; my companion and I had declined more brandy. I directed my gaze to a large harbour boat crammed with people which was being ferried across the Grand Harbour from the direction of the dockyard to Valletta quay. It looked like a wedding party: everyone dressed up and very jolly, singing.

'I think,' said the former corsair presently, 'that I will hire a carriage and take a look around Malta. Later this afternoon. In the dog watches.'

'You would be well advised to go when the sun's down,' I replied. 'It can be cruelly hot in the afternoon.'

'Where would you suggest I go?' he asked.

'From here,' I mused, 'I would say probably south.'

'South.'

'To Marsaxlokk.'

'Marsaxlokk. . .ah.'

'Yes, that would be a modest way of introducing yourself to the island.' I found myself speaking swiftly and without pause – as if to prevent him from interjecting a question which I sensed would inevitably come. 'Valletta itself, and Mdina, are worth a day's exploration each. Yes, I would suggest you have yourself driven down to Marsaxlokk for your introduction to the real Maltese countryside.'

There was silence for a moment and I took a deep breath before continuing my peroration.

He forestalled me: 'Miss Dangerfield, ma'am. . .'

'Yes, Commander?'

'I wonder if, following upon your father the Commodore's suggestion, I might trespass upon your goodwill and invite you to accompany me to this place? To Marsh. . .'

'Marsaxlokk.'

'To Marsaxlokk.'

He grinned broadly – almost as if, sensing my discomfiture, he was trying to say, 'Don't worry – I'm not such a bad fellow after all. I neither bite, nor swallow pretty young women alive.' It was a curiously boyish grin, that of a cheeky urchin. A fresh light upon this curiously changeable man: from corsair to martinet, from martinet to gamin; I was quite disarmed.

'Why, of course, Commander,' I replied. 'With the greatest of pleasure. Thank you.'

*

Our horse clip-clopped down a shining black road shaded with dusty palms, the dainty carriage with its fringed awning gently swaying over the ruts – out of Valletta and into the sunlight of a village street.

We did not speak as we skirted the complex of inlets radiating from the high-walled city: forests of yachts' masts in Pieta and Msida; Marsa, with the blue immensity of Grand Harbour as its backdrop. Once beyond Tarxien we were out in the open countryside, trotting the rutted lanes that sliced between fields of tomatoes and sweet-corn. A bare-footed boy waved to us from his perch on the top of a well, about which plodded a blindfolded donkey turning a water-wheel.

The road came out from between drystone walls on to a plateau set with whirring iron windmills – and here all Malta was laid out before us: hill succeeded hill in the heat haze of the late afternoon, to an horizon of blinding cerulean blue speckled with the white sails of distant yachts; the compact shapes of hilltop villages standing like pieces of cut-out scenery in a child's toy theatre, crowned with the domes and towers of noble basilicas.

I pointed to the hooked fingers of a wide bay, where toy ships lay at anchor, their sides streaked with rust.

'Marsaxlokk,' I said. 'Soon be there.'

Cummings nodded.

He was wearing a civilian tropical suit of white linen and a straw boater, looking for all the world exactly what he was: a naval officer sightseeing ashore.

'Is there somewhere we can have a collation?' he asked.

'There's an excellent little restaurant overlooking the harbour,' I replied. 'Very plain and simple. Typically Maltese. The lady who keeps it is a very great friend of mine. She would make us most welcome.'

'Then let us go there,' he said, 'unless you are in a hurry to return?'

'No. As you possibly know, my father and the Captain of the *Darmstadt* are dining ashore with the C-in-C – where the conversation will inevitably be confined to a post-mortem on the manoeuvres. By the way, Commander, how *did* the manoeuvres go?'

He did not answer for a few moments. 'Pretty well on the whole, I would say,' he replied. 'There are a few snags that we discovered in the process of executing complicated movements at high speed under conditions of attack. But we shall get them ironed out . . . in the end.' He looked out over the tiny fields bounded by low walls, where men and women were bowed over their tasks amongst the crops. I received the distinct impression that he could have said very much more – but had no intention of confiding in me. And I wondered if there was anything seriously wrong.

*

We climbed down to the water's edge, clambering over ancient rocks to where a group of small naked boys were swimming in the shallows. Cummings tossed them a coin. One could see it glinting, silver and dark, silver and dark, all the way down to the sandy bottom where it lay until it was snatched up by the fastest of the swimmers.

'I used to swim as a boy in Plymouth harbour,' said my companion, 'but even when the fishing fleet was at sea, the water was never so clear as this.'

'Are you a Plymouth man, then?' I asked.

He nodded. 'Devon born and bred.'

'Naval family?'

'My father,' he said, looking out across the still waters of the bay, 'was a naval stoker all his working life. Once he was promoted to leading stoker – until they took his badge away for fighting on the mess-deck. He never lived to see me become an officer.'

The suddenness, the unexpectedness of his announcement, the sheer outspokenness of its delivery held me silent and confused. He glanced at me sidelong; there was amusement in his face but it did not reach his eyes, and his lips were more mocking than smiling.

'Yes, Miss Dangerfield, ma'am,' he said. 'As you had no doubt already perceived, I am not a gentleman.'

My chin went up at that. 'I had perceived no such thing, sir,' I countered – and with truth, 'but had accepted you – and still accept you – as you first presented yourself: a gallant and distinguished naval officer and . . . by that definition a gentleman.'

'You are very kind,' he said. But his eyes – those deep blue eyes which contrasted so forcibly with the bronze of his complexion – were still wary.

'Kindness scarcely comes into it, Commander,' I replied.

We threw more coins to the boys, but the carefree lightness which had accompanied our arrival in the bay, the feeling of rapport that had been ignited between us might never have been. We strolled on a little further by the whispering water's edge while up above, on the road, our carriage followed us at walking pace. I then determined that, upon some pretext, I would renege on my acceptance of his suggestion of a meal, and ask to be driven back to Valletta as soon as decently possible.

But upon what pretext? There had to be one – for to declare out of the blue that I wished to be taken back might – almost certainly would – be interpreted by him in the most unfortunate light. He might even think – horrors! – that I was rejecting him because of his social background.

And then, in the curious manner that he had, Jack Cummings changed all this: my uneasy mood, the constraint that lay between us, my uncertainty as to how to extricate myself.

'I am so hungry,' he said. 'I confess to you, ma'am, that I could eat a horse. And you?'

He was looking straight at me with that broad, oddly lopsided, boyish grin. And in that moment, all was as right as a trivet between us.

'Yes, I am,' I confessed. 'It's past seven, and I declined my tea because of the appalling heat of the afternoon.'

'Shall we partake now?'

'Why wait?'

He waved to our driver and helped me up the broken rocks to the

24

road. Presently we were bounding along at a spanking pace, face to face in the carriage and smiling companionably at each other.

In this up and down manner – this moving from sunlight to shadow, from constraint to amity – was the relationship between myself and this very complex man fated to continue, did I but know it.

*

'Mees Dangerfield! – how nice to be seeing you again!'

The proprietress came bustling out of the kitchen as we entered the restaurant, which was a low and rambling, paint-flaked Victorian building on a cliff above the shoreline, with a wrought-iron balcony that looked out across the bay.

'Hello, Mrs MacIntosh, how are you?' We shook hands and the affectionate little woman gave me a hug and a kiss on both cheeks. 'This is Commander Cummings.'

'Hello, sir. A very great honour, I'm sure.' She gave Cummings a most appraising look and her hands went instinctively to her grey hair, touching it quite unnecessarily into place. She also stole me a quick glance and I saw approval there – to my amusement. Mrs MacIntosh, mother of six and grandmother of twenty-three at my last count, was, like all Maltese matrons of her age, an inveterate romantic and matchmaker.

'You are eating, Mees Dangerfield?'

'We thought so, Mrs MacIntosh. Are you very busy?'

She spread her hands to encompass the tall room with its white-washed walls and the chequered-tile floor scrubbed pale. None of the half-dozen or so tables was occupied. 'An hour, two hours and I shall be turning them away,' she said. 'Eat now, Mees Dangerfield and be happy.' She bustled away in a flurry of black bombasine and flowered apron. 'Sit where you like.'

'I omitted to mention that there is no choice of menu,' I murmured. 'One has what Mrs MacIntosh has decided to cook on the day. The same goes for the wine – it's the red wine that's grown, trampled, fermented and bottled in the local village . . . and none other.'

'Nice to be free of decisions,' he replied.

A young girl whom I knew to be named Maria, one of Mrs MacIntosh's grand-daughters, brought a flagon of wine and laid it before us. She smiled shyly when I addressed her. As she went back through the kitchen door, one could see three more dark-eyed young faces peering in at us in contemplative curiosity.

He poured the wine.

'What are the flotilla's plans in the near future?' I asked. 'More manoeuvres?'

'Yes, quite soon,' he answered.

'To . . . iron out those snags you discovered?' I essayed, watching him over the rim of my wine-glass.

'Among other things – yes,' he replied. But was not to be drawn further.

The return of our hostess filled the silence that followed. She came bearing a covered dish, followed by two of her smaller grand-daughters who were carrying warm plates and sauces.

'Is very hot,' declared Mrs MacIntosh. 'Omelette with herbs. Fresh cooked. *Very* hot!'

'It looks delicious,' I declared as she served me.

When we both had laden plates, our hostess stood back regarding us – and her culinary handiwork – with approval and pride in that order. The little girls clung to her skirts and stared at us, huge-eyed.

We tasted and tried; I had never known such an omelette and told her so. Jack Cummings did likewise. As the trio were departing back to the kitchen, he pointed to a faded photograph of a severe-looking gentleman in a peaked cap that hung on the wall near our table.

'Mrs MacIntosh, who is the naval gentleman?' he asked.

Her face was all joy. 'Why, sir, is my husband, the late Petty Officer William Hamilton MacIntosh, Royal Navy,' she declared with tremendous pride. 'A very fine gentleman and husband and father of his children, and is certain that the angels bore him straight up to heaven. Will you be wanting some more wine?'

We declined more wine and my companion smiled. 'Another naval family,' he commented, adding in a bland note that quite dismissed the awkward small exchange we had had down by the water's edge, 'Were there any other seafarers in your family, ma'am – apart from the Commodore?'

I shook my head. 'The Dangerfields, despite the eponymous sur-name, have not been famous for their derring-do,' I told him. 'Not the males of the line, at any rate. The females certainly were involved in the danger of childbearing in fairly large numbers. But, no, until my father came along the male Dangerfields had largely been concerned with the arduous business of making money and winning civil honours – at which they were uncommonly successful.'

'You were brought up in very wealthy surroundings, I would guess?'

'Yes. I have never known what it is to be denied. Indeed, until I was quite old – sixteen or more – my life had been so sheltered and cocooned against the realities of the world outside that I didn't even know that denial existed.'

'Were you happy? Were you always happy?'

'No.' I looked down at my plate.

'Tell me about it,' he suggested quietly.

So – I told him. . .

*

There was the big house in Park Lane, Mayfair, and the even bigger Elizabethan mansion in Suffolk where I had my pony Bimbo. There was the Paris *hôtel particulière* that had once belonged to Philippe d'Orléans, who had voted for the execution of his cousin Louis XVI and had himself perished on the scaffold – this must have been perfectly visible from the window of my nursery, that looked out across what is now the Place de la Concorde. The maids used to frighten me by recounting how d'Orléans' ghost haunted the rooms facing the square, and his sighs could be heard (*'Ses soupirs, Mam'selle Faith – avec clarté, bien!'*) on the anniversary of his death. Despite this, I loved the Hotel d'Orléans best of all the family residences, for it was there that my grandmother lived and I would visit her in the spring and in the autumn, when Paris is at her best. Grandmama would take me to the theatre, the circuses, the parks and the *hippo-dromes* at Auteuil and Longchamp – which I loved most of all; and so did Grandmama who, though half French, was also half English and expressed the fact that she was 'a bit fond of a flutter on the gee-gees'.

Paris, then, despite the shadowy presence of Philippe d'Orléans, was a delight. For three or four months of the year, before I was sent away to the exclusive boarding school for young ladies outside Bath, I was happy because of Grandmama and for being with her – the nearest to a mother I had ever known.

The rest was mostly a desert. . .

I had no friends of my own age in either London or Suffolk. In both establishments I was taught by resident governesses, both of whom I detested and who detested me in return. Winters I spent in

27

London, summers – apart from three weeks at our seaside villa in Frinton – I wandered around the formal gardens of Mondisfield Hall by myself, or rode Bimbo under the stern and disapproving eye of my father's head groom.

My only other delight – and it came infrequently and lasted so short a time – was when Father came home from sea.

In Suffolk there was always a telegram announcing his arrival and the time of his train and giving instructions that I was to be brought to meet him at Newmarket Station. Then would follow a day or two of nerve-racked suspense: supposing he was delayed, supposing his ship was called to sea again at short notice? The latter had happened many times. More often than not my fears proved to be without foundation, and Joris the coachman and I would clatter off to Newmarket in the dog-cart to greet the tall figure in tweeds who emerged from the carriage and held out his arms to me.

As I grew older, I came to realise that my father was a lonely man, and later still I became aware that my mother's death had left an emptiness in his life that nothing and no one – not even I – would ever replace. He fought against loneliness and nostalgia for times past – how hard he tried, I became more increasingly aware as sensibilities were sharpened by experience. For instance, he would never permit paintings or photographs of my mother to be displayed in any of the residences, though once when rummaging in a drawer in the library in Park Lane, I came across a sheaf of photographs showing him with a beautiful woman with my colouring, my eyes, my hair . . . and I knew her for my lost mother.

I never spoke to Father of my find, but kept my own counsel.

My three years at boarding school were a half-life. I made a few friends, but always among half-life creatures like myself: the only children, the orphaned, the offspring of the so-very-rich that their lives had been bounded like my own by a gilded pale.

Only when I was free to follow my father's flotilla in the *Gloria* – I told Jack Cummings – and to act as his chatelaine in the various houses that he rented ashore in distant stations, did I become fully alive. This now, I told him – my present existence – was the happiest I had ever known.

'But even now,' I confided (and heaven knows, I had never admitted such a confidence to anyone else, and scarcely even to myself before then), 'even now, it's all overshadowed by the events of my childhood: the loneliness, the lack of affection, the sheer uncaring attitude of the governesses and servants who really brought me up. The loss of my grandmother, worst of all. And the fact that I saw so little of my father.

'There, you see, Commander,' I added as lightly as I was able, for I was by then very close to tears, 'you have succeeded in making me feel sorry for myself. Aren't you ashamed?'

'I accept the gentle imputation,' he murmured.

When the next course was brought – the inevitable lampuki, grilled, with a spicy tomato sauce and sweet potatoes – we ate in silence for a while and then he said: 'It's always been my view that the human mind has only a limited capacity for happiness, and that material good fortune, good health, good luck, success as the world reckons it . . . none of these things greatly affects the balance of one's happiness, nor one's inner capacity for making the best of one's life.'

'That is a very idealistic philosophy,' I observed.

He shrugged. 'On the other hand,' he said, 'I'm as cynical as the next man when the spirit moves me. Such wise saws as: "You can't buy money with happiness" and "Money doesn't make for happiness, but it allows you to be miserable in comfort" strike me very forcibly sometimes, and I am sure that they contain a grain of truth.'

'Does money or the lack of money make a very great difference in your life?' I asked him. 'Or has it ever?'

He thought for a few moments and said: 'When I was a child, the material things were greatly lacking in my life. But I don't think that if I had had your material advantages, I would have been any happier than I was. That was because, perhaps, I had – have – only a limited capacity for happiness. Which brings me back to my original thesis. But as for myself, I am too close to judge.'

Our eyes met; neither of us looked away.

'Tell me about it,' I said, 'and let me be the judge.'

So he did. . .

*

He was the seventh child of a family of twelve. Twelve small heads bowed in Grace around a scrubbed table in a two-bedroomed slum in Plymouth: sometimes huddling, barefoot and enraptured, on the lovingly-whitened front step, to see coloured rockets blossoming in the night over the Sound, from the anchored fleet on Trafalgar Night. Candled birthday teas twelve times a year, with freshly home-baked bread and – for a treat – plum jam. Church every

Sunday, all marching in pairs in their mother's wake: the wonder of the stained-glass windows and the haloed saints, the liturgy, the hymn-singing, the need to nudge the younger siblings when they nodded off over the rector's sermon. A young life compounded of desperate poverty and yet a limpid wonder at the beauty of familiar things. By the time Cummings had arrived at this part of his narrative, I had formed a very clear idea of his capacity for happiness.

There was the father, who came home from sea; whose every return presaged, in due course, yet another mouth to feed. His offspring held him in awe, for was he not the terror of the dockland public houses? And when he returned to sea, a great sigh of relief went up from the neighbourhood. Yet in his home the big stoker was meekness itself, obedient to his tiny wife and gentle with the little ones, even if given roughly to instruct the older boys in the art of fisticuffs – holding, as he did, that a man must learn to defend himself in this hard and unaccommodating world.

Without any false modesty, Jack Cummings told me how it was the parish rector who, espying more than usual brightness in the stoker's seventh child, contrived his entrance in due course, to a local grammar school, and even solicited the fees from a titled Devon philanthropist. Young Jack prospered mightily at school and presently joined the Royal Navy as an ordinary seaman – possibly the only one of that rating in the entire Fleet who could compose Greek and Latin verse and was familiar with the calculus, as he observed with a chuckle.

Of his further advancement, he was vague and non-committal; but it did not require much imagination on my part – knowing the Service as I had come to do while following my father around – to perceive how difficult it must have been, and how extraordinarily outstanding the man, to have won his way from the lower deck to his present eminence.

His story faltered and died over the dessert of black grapes and peaches. He had told me enough, his attitude said; the time had come for my promised judgement.

'It seems to me. . .' I began.

'Yes?'

'It seems to me that your thesis appears to be proven – entirely on the evidence of your own childhood. You were greatly deprived of material things. . . yes. But you were happy. Given everything else – your mother, who was obviously a wonderful woman. . .'

'She was a saint,' he said simply.

'As you say. And given also the company of your brothers and sisters, one wonders if you could possibly have known any greater happiness if you had also enjoyed the material advantages that I enjoyed for example. And yet. . .'

'And yet . . . what, Miss Dangerfield?'

'Speaking for myself, I now question if the unhappiness of my own childhood did not – does not still – lie in myself. So that even if I had known my wonderful mother, and shared with a large family of brothers and sisters, I would still have been spoilt and discontented because it is in my nature to be so.'

He was very blunt with me: 'I don't know you well enough to comment, Miss Dangerfield,' he replied.

I felt curiously quenched. Perhaps I had been looking to him for some reassurance that I was not – as many might have thought, including myself – merely a spoilt only child whose many faults could be traced back to a lack of affection. If so, I was clearly looking to Jack Cummings in vain.

Perhaps, I told myself, I had not expressed matters very well, and he had not appreciated that, my father apart – to whom I was devoted, who was the overriding image of strength and stability in my life – I had never before reposed my confidences in any other man. At the age of twenty-four, this was the first time I had put the tip of my toe over the dividing line that separates the sexes; for it could be said that my emotional life had been lived only through my father . . . and through the reading of novels.

All in all, I felt deflated and rather disappointed with my attempt.

We left soon after. Mrs MacIntosh and the selection of daughters and granddaughters who helped her in the restaurant and kitchen, gathered at the door and watched us being carried away: waving at us until we rounded the bend in the road and they were shut from our sight by the drystone walls that enclose the fields of Malta.

*

We parted company at the foot of the *Gloria*'s accommodation ladder. He handed me out of his ship's boat which had put out from *Hecuba* to bring us off shore, raised his hat and wished me a good evening. With no more than the briefest of thanks for my outing, and with no thought to invite him aboard for a night-cap, I bustled up the ladder with my heart pounding most unaccountably. Nor did I

31

wait on deck to see him being carried on towards the line of sleek TBDs at their mooring buoys; but went straight to my cabin and, throwing myself down upon my bunk, stared up at the ceiling with arms pillowed behind my head – thinking over my encounter with the strange man who had so unexpectedly entered my life only a few short hours before, and of the quite disturbing impression he had made upon me.

Was Jack Cummings really the corsair I had first taken him to be? I remembered that, apart from being wildly swashbuckling and romantic, the corsairs of old – the Barbary pirates – were also cruel and merciless.

It seemed to me that he was capable of cruelty and might, given certain circumstances, be entirely lacking in mercy.

Then why, I asked myself, did I find certain aspects of the man so compulsively attractive?

It was all very odd.

TWO

The rest of my week was taken up with preparations for the ball and I saw nothing more of Jack Cummings, save for one occasion when he was taken ashore and passed across the stern of the *Gloria*. I waved to him and he waved back, but he was too far away for me to gauge his expression. I returned to perusing the cards of acceptance and refusal (the latter being few) which had just arrived aboard.

It was on that same morning – Thursday – and shortly after the fleeting encounter with Cummings, that Charles Knight – coming out on to the poop deck where I was sitting, to collect and collate the cards for his guest list – asked if he might have a few words with me in the strictest confidence. He looked worried and I had a slight but distinct frisson of foreboding.

'Is it concerning Miss Dearing, Knight?' I asked, thinking that there might have been a lovers' quarrel in which he hoped for my intercession.

'No, ma'am,' he replied and actually smiled, but the smile soon vanished. 'It concerns . . . it concerns the Commodore, ma'am.'

'Sit down,' I said, indicating the deck-chair opposite. 'What is it that you have to say to me concerning my father – and why in confidence?'

'It *must* be in confidence, ma'am,' he replied, 'and I ask your word on it, otherwise the matter must end here.'

'Must it, now – *must* it?' I was not used to being so dictated to by paid staff, even though I was prepared to give a fair amount of leeway to the admirable private secretary who was, after all, a gentleman. It was this last consideration, coupled with the fact that I liked him and he really did look most concerned, which led me to give him my word that whatever he had to tell me and whatever passed between us would be in confidence.

He looked greatly relieved.

'Well, then,' I said encouragingly. 'You have the floor, Knight, so speak on.'

'Ma'am, I am concerned about the wisdom of some of your father's business transactions!' he blurted out, with a swift glance over his shoulder as if worried about possible eavesdroppers.

I could have laughed in his face. 'My good man, my father *has* no business transactions worth a mention,' I declared. 'He's a naval officer, not a business man.'

Knight fidgeted in his chair. 'That I know, ma'am,' he said, 'and I confess that I am not privy to all his dealings, but I can assure you that the Commodore invests a great deal of money in Stock Exchange speculations. And not wisely – not wisely at all, I'm afraid.'

'How do you know this?' I asked.

'Upon his return from manoeuvres, the Commodore and I retired to his cabin after luncheon, as you will remember, ma'am. It was then that he dictated to me several letters to various associates in the City, and also to his elder brother Lord Dangerfield. The letters in question were all apologies for his bad judgement in advising them to buy into San Francisco Securities. In the case of Lord Dangerfield, the Commodore cited the loss incurred as . . .' here he swallowed hard and looked at me in considerable trepidation '. . . *a quarter of a million pounds!*'

I remained unmoved, clearly to his astonishment.

'Did – did you hear me aright, ma'am?' he faltered.

'Yes, Knight. I heard you,' I replied.

'But. . .' He was quite nonplussed.

I determined to put the poor man out of his agony. 'Mr Knight,' I said, 'do you know how much my grandfather – the first Baron Dangerfield of Heathfield and Channock – left in his will, to be shared equally between his widow and his two sons?'

'I – I do not, ma'am. It . . . it was a little before my time.'

'Then I will tell you. The sum total involved was seventeen million pounds.'

His eyes opened wide. 'That . . . that is a great deal of money, ma'am,' he breathed.

'Furthermore, upon my grandmother's sad demise her third share reverted to her two sons. You are a man who juggles readily with figures and will not need me to tell you – give or take a few million – how much my father and uncle have inherited in the last twenty years.'

34

'That I do not, ma'am,' he replied. And looked very quenched.

I smiled at him, poor man. 'You see, Knight, a quarter of a million to such men, is . . . well, almost picayune. With such fortunes as theirs, they might well win or lose what most folks would regard as inconceivable sums without turning a hair.'

He shuffled in his chair again. Clearly, something was still worrying him.

'I see that, ma'am,' he said at length, 'but. . .'

'There are no "buts", Knight,' I interposed. 'As far as you are concerned, there the matter ends. I thoroughly understand your motives in bringing the matter to my attention. You have worried about it and wisely you have slept on it. In the end, you conceived it to be your duty to warn me about my father's – how would you have put it? – wild extravagance? Headstrong folly?'

His face was an agony. 'Your family, ma'am – the Commodore. . . you yourself – have been so kind to me. I owe everything to you. Not merely duty, ma'am, but gratitude and affection, yes – affection – have led me to bring this matter to your attention.'

My heart went out to him – this honest and faithful man! I said, 'Mr Knight, I understand it all now. You had hoped that, armed with your information, I would tactfully put it to my father that he must curtail his gambling. Oh, he gambles on everything, I know well, and not only on the Stock Exchange. It runs in the family, he has it from my grandmother. Am I right?'

He nodded. 'I had hoped for something of the sort, ma'am,' he admitted. 'It is not my place to remonstrate with my employer.'

I reached out and patted his arm. 'Don't worry,' I told him. 'At an early opportunity, I will bring up the subject with my father and let him know my views on the evils of excessive gambling (not that he has not heard them from my lips on previous occasions). And you need not worry – he will never know that I heard the story of the San Francisco Securities disaster from you. I shall respect your confidence.'

He looked at me in some puzzlement, as if I had uttered an irrelevancy. Then he said, 'If I may be permitted the observation, Miss Dangerfield – knowing you, I would never dream you would do otherwise.'

*

It so happened that, on the afternoon of the ball, I had a chance to search out my father on the matter that Knight had raised. I was ready in my new white satin gown by Worth, and Annette had dressed my hair up and around a silver and diamond tiara – a twenty-first-birthday present from Father – when there came a knock on the cabin door.

'Need your help, my dear,' Father informed me. 'My dashed valet's disappeared and I've made six attempts to fasten my bow-tie. If you'd be so kind. . .'

'Come in darling,' I said indulgently. 'It won't be for the first time, nor for the last.' I turned to Annette: 'Run along and fetch a pot of tea for us, please.'

'Champagne would be more amusing,' declared my sire.

'A pot of tea for one and *one* glass of champagne then, Annette.'

'Yes'm.'

'You're very firm with me,' he said as I addressed myself to my task. 'It's one thing to be forbidden my polo, but when one's daughter dictates one's intake of champagne. . . Tch!'

'Keep still!' I chided. 'How do you expect me to fasten this wretched thing when you're whirling like a dervish? Besides, Father, we have a long night ahead and you will be fit for nothing if you start tippling at three in the afternoon. *And* you had a bottle of claret with luncheon – not to mention a large brandy afterwards.'

'I'll wager you,' he began, 'that I could drink the clock round. *And* dance all night. *And* still be as fresh as a daisy at four bells o' the morning watch, when boats and carriages are called. *And* I'll wager a thousand guineas that there's not a young officer in my flotilla who could do likewise. What d'you think of that, hey?'

'Sheer boasting!' was my comment as I executed the last part of the manoeuvre, which was to pull all four ends of the white bow simultaneously. As I did so, his mention of a wager prompted me to a subtlety.

'Thank you, m'dear,' he said, eyeing his reflection in my dressing-mirror. 'Very nice.'

'Heard from Uncle James lately?' I asked casually.

'Ha!' he replied. 'Had a letter waiting for me from the noble lord when we arrived in the other day. Dear Jamie's none too pleased with his little brother. Oh, no.'

I thought I was on the trail. 'Why, Father?' I asked, still as offhand as you please.

'Had this hot tip from a financier wallah when we put into Genoa the other month. Italian chap, of course – met him at the civic reception they gave to the Fleet. He told me that San Francisco Securities were very hot mustard, so I passed on the tip to Jamie and a couple of other chaps. 'Fraid the other chaps lost their shirts, and Jamie was none too happy. Very bad loser, my brother. Always been the same, ever since he was a young boy. Could never bear to lose at marbles. And you've seen the way he acts up over a friendly game of croquet.'

'Did you lose anything on the transaction, Father?' I asked.

'About the same as Jamie.'

'But you're a good loser, aren't you?'

He shrugged. 'One can't win all the time, m'dear. Gambling's a mugs' game, but if a feller's shrewd he can usually break even.'

And that was my father's philosophy, the same that he offered me every time I tackled him on the subject. I only hoped that he was right; and thanked heaven he had virtually unlimited means with which to protect himself.

'And by the way, young lady,' he said, an amused, wry twinkle in his blue eyes, 'I'm expecting a bit·of good news this evening!'

'Oh, Father, your promotion has come through!' I cried. 'They've appointed you Rear-Admiral!'

He put his finger to his lips. 'I'm saying nothing,' he declared. 'Saving it for the auspicious moment, that's what. And I'll lay a thousand guineas every ship in the harbour will be dressed overall tomorrow morning when the news gets round.'

He would be drawn no further and Annette's return with the tea and champagne precluded any more probing on my part.

I had not greatly advanced my influence over Father's gambling obsession; but at least I knew that he was quite open and above board about it – no secrets there, nothing held back. Charles Knight had raised a bogey where none existed; but he had done it for the best.

*

Knight had so stage-managed the arrangements that the first guests to arrive would be the commanding officers of the TBD squadron – all of them, with the exception of Jack Cummings who had not yet arrived, were lieutenants; all well under thirty and most of them, Dickie Jobling included, under twenty-five; as handsome, dashing, gallant, gay and amusing a handful as would make any party go with a swing. I greeted them on the quarter-deck. I was on easy, first-name terms with them all and they had brought me flowers and claimed a kiss on my cheek.

'Now, listen, gentlemen. . .' I began in all seriousness.

'*Ma'am!*'

'Atten-*shun!*'

'Ma'am is about to speak!'

'*Silence in the ranks!*'

They faced me in line, stiffly to attention, a row of broad grins. My resolve faded and it was as much as I could do to keep a straight face.

'You may stand at ease,' I said. 'Seriously, gentlemen, I look to you to ensure that all – *all* – my lady guests have a marvellous time. I don't want to see you dancing only with the pretty young un-attached girls. . .' (a concerted groan greeted this injunction) 'nor do I expect to see you all lounging in the buffet when the orchestra is playing the Valeta, the Waltz – or even the Polka, a very jolly dance which I should have thought you would thoroughly enjoy.' (More groans.) 'Only to leap to your feet when you hear the abominable sound of Ragtime! (There followed loud cheers.)

I may have seemed to be wasting my time, but I knew very well that despite the high spirits, they were all gentlemen to their finger-tips, with the grave, unselfish courtesy that the seafaring life seems to instil in a young man. I was certain that there would not be a lady among my guests that evening – be she so old, so alone, so unblessed by illusory beauty – who would not be treated by them as if she were a fairy-tale princess.

I directed them towards the buffet and went up on to the boat deck to see if I could espy the approach of more guests. I was not alone for long.

'And how are you, Dickie?' I asked, turning to face him.

Dickie Jobling grinned, mischievous green eyes dancing in his bronzed and freckled countenance. In his tropical white mess-kit, he looked for all the world like a boy at his first grown-up dance.

'The first of the month has come and gone, Faith,' he intoned with a solemnity that was quite out of kilter with his expression.

'Oh, Dickie, must we go through the ritual so frequently?' I begged him. 'Would not one proposal followed by one refusal, say twice annually, be quite sufficient?'

'There may be occasions when we shall not meet twice a year,' he said. 'That's what we agreed: first time we meet after the first of the month, every month. You were party to the agreement; don't deny it, Faith!'

'True,' I said. 'I can only say you must have made the proposition while I was not listening and it went through on the nod.'

'That's a poor defence. We will continue.'

'Very well.'

He took hold of my right hand, which I did not withdraw.

'Miss Dangerfield – Faith,' he began. 'It may not have escaped your notice that, since I have known you, I have come to esteem you greatly. . .'

The trouble was that he was such an exceptionally nice person. The kind that any woman would have been proud to have and to hold – as, indeed, I was half-proud to be the object of this half-joking, half-serious monthly ritual. It was as if, being unable to win my acceptance by conventional means, he was trying to laugh me into marrying him because of his infectious drollery. And he really was very droll.

'. . . furthermore, my aged father. . .' he was saying. And then he forgot his lines.

'Has pledged to settle his overdraft,' I prompted him.

'Has pledged to settle his overdraft on me, plus the mortgage of the family town house in Upper Brook Street. . .

'Oh, Faith, Faith – it's no use, is it? I'm out of luck again, aren't I?'

'You're out of luck again, Dickie. I'm sorry, I really am.'

He shrugged. 'I shan't give up all that easily, Faith. Unless the flotilla's ordered to another station, you'll have me asking again next month!'

To change the subject, I said, 'That wasn't a very impressive performance you put on the other morning, Dickie.'

'Oh, you mean when we came to the buoy? No, it wasn't.'

'Did my father tick you off?'

'No, but Cummings did.' He glowered like a small boy who has been slapped for dipping his finger into cook's pudding mixture. 'Interfering blighter. Confounded upstart!'

My sympathy for Jack Cummings was such that I had no wish to be led into the particular line of thought that Dickie Jobling was indicating. Instead, I said, 'Well, you had only yourself to blame.'

'True enough,' he admitted. 'I ordered the midshipman to bring us to the buoy. Heavens, unless these youngsters have their noses pushed hard against the grindstone, they'll never learn anything!'

I stared at him. 'Do I have it right, Dickie?' I asked. 'It was your midshipman and not you yourself who was giving the orders to bring *Hasty* to the buoy?'

'Yes,' he said.

'Did you tell Cummings this when he ticked you off?'

He eyed me uncomprehendingly. 'Of course not,' he said. 'It would only have blotted the lad's copybook and anyhow, the responsibility stops with me.'

I smiled at him. 'You really are a very nice person, Dickie.'

He coloured up alarmingly. 'Oh, it's all a lot of rot, really,' he mumbled. 'Let's talk about something else.' He brightened. 'About you and me, for instance.'

We had talked about 'you and me' before, and that was a tricky and meandering road well-laid with traps and pitfalls which I had no intention of journeying again. Fortunately I was spared by the approach of a naval barge which was shaping course for our companion ladder. The White Ensign and a distinguishing flag at the mast announced the quality of its passengers.

'Here come the Admiral and his lady,' I said, gathering up my skirts. 'I'll see you later, Dickie.

*

'Miss Dangerfield! Divine child! So pretty, so pretty!'

Lady Freakley, the Admiral's lady, was built of a material – both physically and spiritually – that was more suited to the eighteenth century than our own. She was large in almost every way: towering half a head above her spouse, with arms like hams that terminated in hands of unexpected smallness and delicacy. It was with her gloved right hand that she now stroked my cheek as she delivered what had become her customary greeting whenever we met. And the large and commanding eyes that gazed at me from behind the veil encompassing her enormous picture hat – decorated with surely a whole aviary of birds of paradise – were majestically assured beyond all pretence and affectation.

'So nice of you to come, ma'am,' I said. 'Hello, Sir Jasper.' I extended my hand to the diminutive sea-dog who represented the long arm of British sea power in and around the Maltese islands of the Central Mediterranean.

'Your servant, ma'am!' Admiral Sir Jasper Freakley had a voice like a corncrake. Furthermore, according to naval legend, its rasp was capable of carrying from the verandah of the Royal Yacht Squadron across the Solent to Lymington, as had been proven during the first Cowes Week of the present reign. Sir Jasper ran his appraising eyes over my Worth frock; he was very much the ladies' man.

'Come, my dear Miss Dangerfield,' said Lady Freakley. 'We will leave the gentlemen' – she beamed at Father and her spouse – 'to their deliberations, while we have a cup of tea and a gossip.'

This suggestion, carrying as it did the overtones of a royal command, relieved me of the burden of greeting every one of my guests as they came over the side. However, the ever-present Charles Knight quietly slipped forward to do the honours on my behalf without any prompting. Minutes later, Lady Freakley and I were sitting in the privacy of my poop deck, sipping tea and exchanging confidences; at least, I listened while she confided.

'My dear, have you met Captain von Schleicher of the *Darmstadt*?' she asked and without waiting for a reply: 'I am of the opinion that, in addition to his duties of a purely nautical nature, he is also a spy for the German Emperor. I presume that he is on your guest list for this event?'

'Yes, he. . .'

'Quite so, quite so. One is obliged. I entertained the fellow to dinner at Navy House the other evening, along with your dear father and other officers. I must say, my dear, that I felt inclined to count my spoons after the Herr Kapitan had departed. *Shifty*, my dear, most incredibly *shifty*. But then, that is how all Germans strike me. I was never entirely at my ease with the late King, who retained so much of that appalling accent, no doubt from his father. King Edward, as I know to my cost, was not to be trusted alone in a room with a woman, be she married or single, for longer than it takes to greet a guest in the hall. Did I observe you talking to young Mr Jobling as we approached?'

'Yes, as a matter of. . .'

'Excellent young man! One of the Norfolk Joblings, you know. The father, though a commoner, is heir to the marquisate of Dewsberry, and will succeed unless a whole string of highly unlikely marriages and births intervene. There is also money on the mother's side, for she was one of the Vanhollands of New York, who own

41

more of that city than would be considered modest in more stylish society. Does he have aspirations towards you, my dear?'

'Lady Freakley, I. . .'

'I thought so. Despite his prospects, I would not advise it. He is of a physique that will speedily run to fat as soon as he resigns his commission and takes up the life of a landed nobleman – as presently he will when he succeeds his quite elderly father.'

'I'm most grateful for your advice, ma'am, and I. . .'

'One is a little worried about your dear papa. Oh, I know you will say that he is happily absorbed by the interests of the Service; but a woman of experience – such as myself – is very conscious of the gap of loneliness in his life; a gap, my dear, that you for all your filial affection are unable to fill. In short, dear Miss Dangerfield, one is conscious that your papa is in need of. . . yearns with all his being for . . . a *consort*.'

'Lady Freakley, I'm sure that my father. . .'

'And not only as balm and consolation for the lonely heart, but also as a social asset. Your father, my dear, is destined greatly to advance in his career. The senior officers of Sir Jasper's generation – those who have borne the torch of Nelson's fame, if I may be permitted to fanciful expression – look to your papa and his like to carry forward that torch through the twentieth century. Such men – the torchbearers – need the help and support of good, sound women. An admiral's career, my dear, is determined as much by his performance in his wife's drawing-room as by his manoeuvres at sea.'

'I wonder, Lady Freakley,' I began, 'if you have any news of. . .' Prompted by her remarks, I was eager to learn if Father's promotion to admiral was in truth imminent. But her ladyship was not to be diverted by questions from the floor of the House; she was off on another tack but, as quickly became apparent, was still pursuing the same end.

'I am greatly pleased with Mrs Chalmers,' she declared. 'Though one has to admit, in all sincerity, that one was not much taken with the lady on first acquaintance. There is something about the manner and bearing of widows – *very* rich widows – that puts one in mind of predatory peahens dolled up in peacocks' plumage and can be quite insufferable. Mrs Chalmers, on closer acquaintance, I find to bear the burden of her wealth quite lightly and without affectation. A very kindly, sincere person, she is a great help and comfort to me in all the many calls upon my person, my time and my purse. Last

week she assisted me with my fête and garden party in aid of the
Naval Orphans Fund (I know that I could have counted on your
support also, my dear, but you were at sea at that time). She has also
placed one of her carriages entirely at my disposal – a tremendous
boon, since we have no stabling at Navy House and indeed the
Admiralty allocation of expenses does not run to the maintaining of
carriages, more's the pity.'

'Mrs Chalmers sounds a . . . a very fine person, ma'am,' I said.
And not only was I permitted to make the observation, but my
companion maintained a watchful silence, as if waiting for me to
enlarge upon it.

Presently, my not being forthcoming, she prompted me: 'Make an
eminently fine naval wife, don't you think, my dear?'

In the event, I was saved from having to answer her barbed
question by the arrival on board of the very person under discussion.
Lady Freakley pointed with her parasol.

'Why, there is Mrs Chalmers now. And people are coming aboard
in droves. My dear, I've monopolised you long enough. Let us go
and join your guests.' She tapped me on the arm as we left the poop
deck. 'I think we have covered some interesting ground in our little
discussion, and one has arrived at some very thought-provoking
conclusions, don't you agree?'

'Yes, Lady Freakley,' I replied meekly.

What else could I say?

*

The buffet tea still continued, but was largely disregarded; most of
the guests seemed to be occupying themselves with champagne,
already no doubt with the intent of fortifying themselves against a
long night of dancing and gaiety.

The quarter-deck, whose awnings had been colourfully augmented by every national and signal flag in the *Gloria*'s locker, was a
scene of brilliant animation when Lady F. and I ascended there. The
costumes of the ladies, the officers' uniforms – naval white and gold,
the elaborately embroidered blues of the diplomats, occasional
splashes of military scarlet – fairly bedazzled the eye and heightened
the senses. From above, on the boat deck, came the strains of the
Royal Marine orchestra playing a selection from *The Girl of the
Golden West*. And the late afternoon sun played like liquid silver upon
the wrinkled wavelets of the Grand Harbour.

'Miss Dangerfield. How nice!'

I turned to regard the object of our late – Lady Freakley's late – discourse. Mrs Natasha Chalmers wore a silk surtout over her ball-gown of *tissu d'or*, and still retained her very becoming hat trimmed with golden roses. In the subtle, airy shade of the awnings, the muted sunlight displayed the perfection of her skin (and also, I thought, uncharitably, the artistry of her maquillage). But there was no doubt about it; one had to admit that the woman was a raving beauty, with her wild-rose-and-snow complexion dramatically enhanced by the ravens'-wing sable of her hair, eyebrows and unbelievably long lashes.

We touched hands. 'How beautiful you look, Mrs Chalmers,' I said with complete sincerity.

She smiled, but only faintly; clearly my compliment was familiar to her ears and my turn of phrase not particularly original.

'My dear,' she said, 'I should like to introduce Mr Glendon Hawick.' She indicated a tall man standing at her elbow.

'How do you do?'

'How do you do, Miss Dangerfield. A lovely yacht you have here. I should like to make a painting of it some time.'

'Mr Hawick is a painter, architect, designer – everything you could imagine in the field of artistic creation,' declared Mrs Chalmers, turning her burning green-eyed, long-lashed gaze upon her companion. 'We met last year in Boston, when I was over in the United States. At present he is completely redesigning my house in Sliema. You must come and see it . . . soon, my dear.'

'How exciting,' I commented. 'In what manner are you redesigning the house, Mr Hawick?'

'After the manner of a Roman villa,' he replied. He was quite extraordinarily good-looking in a heavy, florid sort of way that I have never much admired, with butter-yellow hair drawn across a wide brow, lustrous dark blue eyes, a heavy moustache and very white teeth. 'A re-creation of the Emperor Tiberius' villa in Capri. An exterior of cool fountains, gesticulating statuary of stark white marble, murmuring cypresses, with the music of eerie flutes seeping through the gardens in the moonlight.'

'The music comes from a concealed gramophone,' supplied Mrs Chalmers, which won her a slight frown of annoyance from Mr Hawick who then seemed disinclined to continue his peroration.

'How very noble of the Commodore to have foregone his Saturday

44

polo on account of your ball,' said Mrs Chalmers with a touch of . . . was it slyness?

'Not so *very* noble,' I replied tartly, 'for after all the ball is in his honour. Ah, here is my father now.'

The orchestra had turned to airs from *Naughty Marietta*, as the object of our brief exchange came towards us. He was in very good spirits and humming to the music. His eyes lighting upon Mrs Chalmers, gave a knowing twinkle which had been familiar to me since childhood; in such a manner did he regard one of his favourite cigars when, having taken it out of the humidor, he would roll it between his fingers, holding it to his ear, listening to heaven-knew-what arcane harmonies.

He greeted that woman with a kiss on the cheek, nodded brusquely to the American artist whom he appeared already to have met and patted my arm.

'Marvellous party, my dear,' he said. 'What time does the serious business of the evening begin?'

'The champagne has already begun to flow in preference to tea, Father,' I replied. 'Those with a taste for the *thé dansant* have been indulging their curious craving on the boat deck since the orchestra began to play. The ball proper will open at 7 o'clock when you and I take the floor with the opening waltz. And formal dinner will commence at sunset.'

He put his arm round my waist and drew me to him. 'That's my little girl,' he declared. 'Dash me, I'll lay a thousand guineas that my Faith could run the Admiralty a blessed sight more efficiently than their Lordships themselves, indeed I do. What do you say, Mrs Chalmers, ma'am?'

'Faith is a treasure and I am quite besotted with her,' responded the lady. 'She has promised to visit me next week, to approve of my refurbished surroundings. I hope to be able to persuade her to accompany me to my residence in Taormina for a few days, furthermore.'

'Capital idea, capital!' cried my father. 'Faith, my dear, the two of you shall sail to Sicily in the *Gloria*, and I will try to arrange next week's flotilla programme so as to put into Taormina while you are there.'

'And I will give a ball,' interposed Mrs Chalmers, eyes gleaming. 'Dear Faith will help me to arrange it.'

Trapped! I suddenly felt trapped. In a few short phrases, that

45

woman had contrived to give Father the impression that the two of us were intimate friends, whereas until a few moments ago she had never before called me by my Christian name. And now – now I was seemingly committed to sailing with her to Taormina. For a stay at her no doubt palatial residence in that exclusive Sicilian resort.

She was looking keenly at me, Father was looking at me, Mr Hawick was looking at me with one eyebrow slightly raised. What I said or did next would commit me, one way or the other; either I would accede to being Mrs Chalmer's bosom friend, or I would reject her with or without the 'cut direct'.

It was then, seeking for a diversion, that I saw an imposing figure in naval uniform: blond and bearded, with close-cropped hair and sporting a monocle. His epaulettes were unfamiliar and he wore a galaxy of decorations that I could not place.

'Why,' I exclaimed, 'that must be Captain von Schleicher! What will he think of a hostess who so badly neglects him that she does not greet him upon boarding? Do please excuse me, Mrs Chalmers, Mr Hawick. See you later, Father. Don't forget the first waltz!'

Saved – or, rather, reprieved. . .

*

A less likely candidate to steal Lady Freakley's silver spoons than the Captain of His Imperial German Majesty's cruiser *Darmstadt*, I have never met, nor was there the slightest shiftiness in his manner. When I introduced myself, I was greeted with a heartening smile, a click of the heels and a kiss of the hand – all done without any 'side' or pomposity. And he had the merest trace of an accent, which personally I found most pleasing.

'This is most elegant, Miss Dangerfield,' he said. 'Truly, the kind hospitality that the Royal Navy and the people of Malta have extended to the *Darmstadt* is beyond all praise, leaving one speechless for thanks.'

During that very pretty speech, I examined him. Younger than Father by five years or so, he had the same quality of *watchfulness* that lightly overlaid an essentially bland and cheerful manner. He smiled a lot – as did Father – and like my sire he smiled with his whole face, eyes and all. It struck me very forcibly that von Schleicher would be a good man in a tight corner. I wondered if, like Dickie Jobling, he had delegated to a junior officer the task of bringing his ship to the buoy – at risk to his own personal reputation, if not his career. He looked the sort.

'I should like to return the hospitality, ma'am,' he said. 'Upon our return from the next round of manoeuvres, I will issue invitations and you shall be my guest of honour.'

In the face of such gallantry I might well have slipped into a little bland flirtation, but I had no such intent on this occasion. Here was an opportunity to sound out the edges of a mystery that was beginning to take shape in my essentially probing mind.

'Did the last manoeuvres go well, Captain?' I asked.

'Well enough,' he replied – but after a perceptible pause of several seconds. 'Exercising at sea seldom goes entirely according to plan: "Man proposes; God disposes".'

'Were you impressed by the performance of our torpedo boat destroyers?'

He gave me a shrewd glance. 'Ah,' he said, 'I think that you have come – a pretty little bird of Paradise – to perch upon the shoulder of this old albatross and search out his secret thoughts.' The imputation was delivered with a good-humoured smile that absolved it of any offence.

'I am curious to know what the Imperial German Navy thinks of my father's latest plaything,' I admitted, as good-humoured as he.

'It is . . . a very dangerous plaything,' was his answer. And I thought that, with those words, he was approaching the very nub of the mystery which Jack Cummings had shied away from sharing with me.

'Dangerous – to whom?' I asked, drawing a bow at a venture as the saying is.

Again that smile and I knew I should never draw him out. 'Shall I say that what I have seen during the manoeuvres leaves me with an open mind as to how I might answer your question?

'And now, ma'am,' he added, 'I must go and pay my respects to the Commodore, who is gesturing to me. I trust that I may request the pleasure of a dance later in the proceedings?'

'Delighted, Captain,' I replied, acknowledging his bow and click of heels.

Drifting through the throng of guests on the quarter-deck; in and out of the parakeet chatter, nodding here, exchanging a word there, I allowed half my mind to dwell upon the German officer's response to my probings, while the other half acknowledged that my present wandering had only one end: to find the man I sought – he whom, if

47

I were honest with myself, I had been seeking ever since the first of my guests arrived on board and he had not been with the other officers from the flotilla. I even acknowledged that I had been watching and waiting, waiting and fretting, while I had been talking to Dickie and to Lady Freakley.

And then – I saw *him*. . .

His back was towards me and he was talking to Charles Knight and his intended Angela Dearing. There was no mistaking his broad back and shoulders, the gleaming darkness of his hair, the strength of the bronzed hands clasped lightly behind his back.

'Hello, Miss Dangerfield.' It was Angela Dearing who saw me first.

He was next to turn and as we exchanged pleasantries I told my sane sensible self that this was quite absurd. I have only met this man once before and part of the time I quite disliked him. It is ridiculous that the only thing I really remember of the days between is the time when he passed by the yacht in his ship's boat and we waved to each other. Almost a week has gone by since then: I have been up to my eyes in arrangements for this wretched ball, I have talked to innumerable people, written several letters, ate, slept, dreamed, lived the days through. Yet that passing encounter, that brief wave is all that carries any significance throughout all those empty hours.

It *is* ridiculous – and I must dismiss the thought.

'I thought you were not coming,' I said.

'A sheaf of important signals arrived from Admiralty,' he replied, meeting my gaze unwaveringly. I willed myself to look away, but could not. 'So I had to stay behind and decipher them,' he added.

'Have you been busy this week?' I asked.

'Pretty busy – and you?'

'Oh, the ball and all that, you know.'

'I like your frock.'

'Thank you.'

'I wondered if. . .'

'The weather's been. . .'

'I'm sorry,' he said.

'No, please go on.'

'I wondered,' he said, 'if you would care to come to the Blue Grotto with me tomorrow? You know it, of course?'

'Well, it so happens that I have never been to the Blue Grotto.'

48

'Obviously I have not, but I've picked it out on the chart and there is a Navy sail-boat available to take us there. Just the two of us. You can crew a whaler, I hope?' Anxiously.

'Oh, yes – yes!'

*

Four bells of the second dog-watch marking the hour of 7 pm was the signal for the conductor of the Royal Marine orchestra to bring down his baton and draw forth from his musicians the magical strains of *The Beautiful Blue Danube*. I gathered up the hem of my skirt and laid my hand on Father's arm. We smiled at each other, then drifted away across the deck as smoothly as you please, watched by the circle of guests lining the rails and the super-structure.

Three turns of the floor and then we were joined by the rest. The ladies, having retired earlier to remove their hats and attend to their maquillage, in some cases to change their frocks, brilliantly comple-mented their partners who were mostly in uniform. Mindful of my duties as hostess, I watched around as Father and I circled and was delighted to see that the flotilla officers, obedient to my 'orders', had each taken a mature lady for a partner in this, the first waltz. In-deed, it was the young and pretty ones who still lined the rails as 'wallflowers' – and none too pleased did they look.

Lieutenant-Commander Cummings – Jack – was dancing with Mrs Chalmers; *I* was none too pleased to see *that*. Furthermore, he was obviously amusing her with small talk; she was looking up into his face and smiling most winningly, with a deal of eyelash work. How I hated that woman, I decided.

The *Blue Danube* ended with a clash of cymbals and we applauded.

'More champagne, I fancy,' said Father. 'It's deucedly hot work.'

My eyes flickering towards Mrs Chalmers and the tall figure at her side, I said, 'Good idea, I'll come with you.'

Deliberately turning my back to the floor, I stood at the buffet sipping my champagne. And waiting. While I waited and the orchestra played on, I had the notion to sound out my father, who was standing with glass in hand smilingly regarding the passing charivari. He looked so handsome, so much the brilliant naval commander, every inch, that I could have hugged him from sheer pride.

'Father. . .'

'Mmmm? Yes, m'dear?'

'Father, Commander Cummings tells me the reason he was late was because he had to stop and decipher some important Admiralty signals.'

'That is so, that is so. And?. . .'

'Well, Father, I wondered if one of those signals might concern . . . well – you-know-what?'

He twinkled at me. 'To which "you-know-what" are you referring, my dear?' he asked blandly.

'Oh, Father, don't be such a maddening tease! You know perfectly well what I'm referring to.' I looked over my shoulder, both ways, to make sure I was not being overheard. 'Your promotion,' I whispered.

'Oh, *that!*' He stroked his beard and looked at me with irritating coolness. 'I shall be making an announcement at the end of dinner in all probability. 'Fraid you'll have to bear yourself with patience until then, my dear.'

I pulled a long lip. Knowing Father, there was nothing more to be got out of him and I took another sip of my champagne.

And then the music stopped. There was a patter of applause, a cacophony of conversation. Many footsteps were approaching the buffet. I did not turn, my five senses straining for an intimation of *his* approach. In the event, I think it was a little of my sixth sense, functioning out of time and place, that perceived his coming; almost before I heard his voice, certainly before he laid a hand on my arm, I knew that he was standing slightly to one side of me and outside the compass of my gaze.

'May I have the pleasure of the next dance, Miss Dangerfield?'

'Of course, Commander.'

A moment passed.

'Cummings, my dear fellow!' It was Father. 'A word in your ear. Regarding that signal from the Commission and Warrant Department – walk with me as far as the fo'c'sle and clarify the issues in my mind if you will.' He nodded to me. 'Have no fear, dear Faith, I shall return him safely in good time for the next dance but one.'

They were gone, with only a backward glance from Jack Cummings. I was alone in that thronging crowd around the buffet.

But not quite alone. . .

'Got you, Faith! I claim my dance. And I've made representations

50

to the conductor of the orchestra to play a request. Now, what do you think of that?'

'You are never lacking in enterprise, Dickie,' I conceded.

The orchestra struck up. The catchy, tricky and – to me – essentially cheap rhythm of the ragtime nevertheless had power to make one's feet go tap-tap. 'But I can't ragtime, Dickie!' I protested.

'Only because no one's ever showed you how!' he shouted above the din. 'Come on – just you follow me. And keep watching what I do.'

I was surrounded by whirling, jigging couples. Dickie, who more often than not was scarcely holding me at all but flinging his arms about, crossing his hands with his knees and acting quite independently of my tentative efforts, seemed to be the star of the floor. All eyes appeared to be on us and I redoubled my efforts to emulate my partner's gay abandon.

Presently, what he was doing and what the orchestra was playing seemed to make sense in my mind and I began to find myself becoming part of them both.

'That's the ticket, Faith!' cried Dickie. 'You're getting the hang of it. You're a natural-born ragtimer!'

Presently, and none too soon for me, the jangling rhythm ceased and he took my arm to lead me off the floor. 'By jove, Faith, you've really got the knack,' he enthused. 'That's worth a glass of champagne, bless me if it isn't.'

'Not for me, Dickie,' I protested. 'There's a long night ahead. Fetch me some iced fruit punch, please, there's a dear.'

He brought the punch. Somewhere between his handing it to me and my taking it, either one or both of us fumbled the glass which fell to the deck, spilling sticky red stain everywhere as it went – including the skirt of my white satin gown.

'Oh, golly, I'm sorry, Faith!' cried Dickie. 'What a clumsy ass I am! Can it be dabbed off, or something?'

'No, it can't!' I retorted, with only a little more irritation than I would have wished to show. 'I'll have to go and change.'

'It doesn't show very much.'

'Of course it shows – don't be ridiculous!'

'Faith, I'm so sorry, I really am.' And he did look most contrite.

'Don't worry, Dickie,' I said. 'It was as much my fault anyhow.' And I went down to my cabin to change.

*

51

There was no sign of Annette. Along with many of the servants who had the opportunity, she was watching the dancing from the bridge. I rummaged around in my wardrobe and finally settled for a very pretty gown in kingfisher blue organdie, sewn all over with dark blue sequins. It suited me very well and now I wondered why it had not been my first choice for the evening.

I was looking at myself, back and front, in the cheval glass, when I heard a man's voice coming through the part-open porthole giving out on to the poop deck — my little poop deck.

'Natasha, my lamb, you can't go through with this goddamned crazy idea! Not after all we've been to each other.'

Another voice. A woman's voice. *Her* voice. . .

'I have no intention of keeping you any longer, darling. You're quite sweet, but you mustn't look to me as your provider for life.'

'What's Dangerfield got to offer, for Pete's sake? Hell, you've got all the money you need! Between you, you could buy up half England. Is that what you're after?'

Choked with horror and indignation, I heard Mrs Chalmers's bland drawling reply: 'You've got it quite, quite wrong, my dear. Myles Dangerfield has everything that money *can't* buy. Social position, power, the automatic introduction into the highest of high society. My late unlamented husband and I lived such rackety lives together that we were dropped from the Buck House garden parties by the old Queen. And when I had my *p'tite affaire* with You Know Who, His Majesty's representative declined to accord me a voucher for the Royal Enclosure at Ascot — nor did You Know Who dare to raise a murmur in protest.

'Myles Dangerfield can win me back all those perquisites, you see . . . and more. They are going to make him an admiral; with that will undoubtedly go a knighthood and later a peerage. If we go to war with Germany — and everyone *says* we shall — he will be the twentieth-century Nelson who leads the Fleet to a latter-day Trafalgar. It will be fame and glory all the way and he will be buried in Westminster Abbey.' She laughed. 'And in the fullness of time they will bury me alongside him, I shouldn't wonder.'

He joined her in laughing at this sally; the two of them were crowing over her triumphant jest, while I stood shaking with an emotion that went close to tearing me apart. I had to bite my lip to prevent myself from screaming out loud, and drive my fingernails into the palms of my hands to quench the hurt within.

Presently, their wicked mirth having subsided, the American said; 'But you haven't landed the big fish yet, Natasha honey. And there's a great big stumbling-block in the way. I refer to the daughter.'

'That spoilt whey-faced brat!' She almost spat out the invective and I flinched as though I had been struck across the mouth.

'She doesn't like you, baby. If ever I saw jealousy and resentment written plain on a human countenance, it was there tonight. Oh, it was there in spades!'

I hung upon her response, breathless with suspense, sick with trepidation. Then it came, prefixed by a gentle assured laugh and delivered in a voice that was sweet-sour like honey and vinegar mixed: 'Little Miss Reptile will dance to *my* tune, or find herself cut off with a penny,' she said. 'I have already laid the ground-bait for us to be girlie-girlie pals, and if she's smart she will swallow what passes for her pride and accept my olive branch. If she does not – if she kicks over the traces – I shall let her go right ahead and destroy herself; I will nobly offer to withdraw from the situation rather than come between an honourable man and his spoilt, hysterical chit of a daughter.' She laughed again, a throaty, confident sound. 'I think I can predict Myles' reaction to *that*!'

'I really think you're going to make it, Natasha,' declared Hawick, 'I really do. And when you've landed the big fish, I hope you won't forget me entirely.'

I knew, without seeing it, that the brief silence which followed was filled by her leaning forward and bestowing upon him an un-hallowed kiss; her small gasp of passion, followed by another silence, seemed to mark a kiss returned and I winced with distaste.

'Don't worry, darling,' murmured Mrs Chalmers huskily. 'When the rose petals and the rice have all settled, I shall still find time for you. Now let us go and rejoin the party before we are missed.'

*

Careless of my frock and my carefully dressed hair, I flung myself down on my bunk and lay staring up at the ceiling, dry-eyed.

What should I *do*? . . .

Blurt out the details of the whole dreadful encounter to Father? He would believe me of course – at least, I hoped so! – but would he thank me for the information? The fact that an ostensibly attractive younger woman had set her cap at him might very well be a source of smug masculine pride already. He would greatly resent being told

53

that the said woman's intent was merely predatory – and of the cheapest possible kind.

And anyhow it was absurd, ridiculous, to think that my wise and prescient sire would ever fall for such an obvious trap as Mrs Chalmers was seeking to set for him. Best leave well alone: say nothing and trust Father to know his own way. After all, he had loved my mother with an unswerving devotion which had conquered the grave; no one would ever, could ever, replace her in his heart. Least of all, surely, a creature of Natasha Chalmers' sort!

All these deliberations took far longer than the telling; the sun had fallen below the massive bulk of Fort St Angelo and the shadows were darkening through the slatted window blinds which covered my portholes when I finally roused myself from my semi-stupor at the sound of the dressing-bell for dinner. The distant tones of the orchestra had faded to silence, which meant that they had hived off a string quartet to play in the great saloon during the meal.

I got up from the bunk and regarded my crumpled, ravaged self, all hair-awry and sour-faced, in the cheval glass.

'What a mess you look, my dear,' I told myself.

There came a knock at my door. It was Annette, and never was I more glad to see her.

'Annette, I am a mess,' I confessed. 'Can you fix me up in time for dinner?'

She looked at me and at my gown, head on one side and arms akimbo.

'I reckon as how I can, ma'am,' she declared. 'Run an iron over the dress. Titivate your hair a bit. Yes, we'll have you the bell o' the ball again in no time.'

And so it was.

THREE

The great saloon of the *Gloria*, to which I descended half an hour later, was already abuzz with our guests taking their seats for dinner. I caught Father's eye and he came over to me at the foot of the stairs.

'Thought you had fallen overboard, my dear,' he said, taking my arm. 'Not like you to be absent and neglect your guests at the crucial moment.'

'I had a headache,' I lied, 'and thought it best to rest up until dinner rather than be a bore for the remainder of the evening.'

'Sensible enough,' conceded he. 'Now take your place opposite me and be more than specially charming to von Schleicher.'

The dining-table aboard the yacht comprised seven ten-foot sections which, when all were fitted together, were easily accommodated by the great saloon and would seat fifty-six people in spacious comfort. The full complement sat down to dine that night.

We sat facing, Father in the centre opposite me, with Lady Freakley on his right and the wife of the Malta Garrison Commander on his left. At my right was placed Captain von Schleicher, and Major-General Meaker the Garrison Commander was on my left. To my dismay, Charles Knight – who had made out the table plan – had put the abominable Natasha Chalmers next to General Meaker where, I told myself, she was well positioned so as to ogle my father. I cursed the natural indolence which had restrained me from checking the plan and giving it my approval. The rest of the guests were disposed down both sides of the table with regard to rank and status, ladies and gentlemen alternately. Jack Cummings, I was heartened to observe, was on the opposite side where I could see him, and not too far away. His immediate neighbour, to whom he was talking, was the meek, mousy Angela Dearing, Knight's putative fiancée; she appeared greatly to be enjoying Jack's attentions.

As I knew from experience, I should not expect much in the line of conversation from the gallant General Meaker, who was a glutton and a reputed heavy drinker. Indeed, he was already deep into his first glass of claret before the soup and fish arrived. I concentrated my interest, therefore, on the captain of the *Darmstadt*, grateful for the attentions of an attractive man to help distract my mind from the nagging problem of the appalling Natasha Chalmers and her machinations.

'The decoration and furnishings of this compartment are beyond all belief,' declared the German. 'I have dined several times aboard our own Imperial yacht the *Hohenzollern*, and stayed aboard the Tsar's *Standart*, but I have to concede that for sheer artistry of design and execution, their interiors do not bear comparison with those of *Gloria*.'

'My grandfather was greatly taken by the work of a young French artist who designed the interiors of our villa in Nice,' I explained, 'and gave him *carte blanche* with the *Gloria*. Some people, sharing the tastes of the late Queen, prefer the decor of Osborne and Sandringham; but this new twentieth-century decorative style that is the rage of Paris nowadays, I find tremendously exciting.'

The soft tread of the stewards and the chink of dishes then addressed us to the menu and we fell silent.

I myself had devised the names of the dishes and have a copy of the menu still – mute souvenir of that dreadful evening:

STEAM YACHT GLORIA

At Malta – Saturday, 17 June 1911

* * *

First Course
Consommé Kapitan Alois v. Schleicher
Vermicelli Soup HIMS *Darmstadt*
Devilled Whitebait HMS *Havoc*
Grilled Lampuki HMS *Hengist*

*

Entrées
Roast Fillet of Veal HMS *Hornet*

56

Braised Sweetbreads HMS *Horsa*

*

Second Course
Roast Ribs of Beef Commodore Myles Dangerfield
Boiled Leg of Lamb Flotilla-Leader HMS *Hecuba*

*

Third Course
Cauliflower with Cream Sauce HMS *Hasty*
Iced Pudding SY *Gloria*
Cabinet Pudding 'The Company All Assembled'

*

Dessert and Ices

* * *

The quiet buzz of conversation during the soup and fish did not
entirely mask the pleasant plashing of the fountain that poured into
a shallow alabaster basin from a conch shell held aloft by a trio of
naked naiads – a sculptured group that dominated the foot of the
elaborately carved staircase leading up to the main deck. But as the
stewards moved forward to remove the dishes, the Royal Marine
string quartet took over from the little naiads and dominated the
background with a selection from Léhar's recent opera *Gypsy Love*.

'How many crew do you employ aboard the yacht, Miss Dangerfield?' asked my right-hand neighbour, observing the stewards in
their trim white ducks and braided collars and no doubt assessing
and approving their turn-out in his punctilious Teutonic mind.

'The Captain and six officers,' I began.

'Ah, Captain Jaggers I have met,' said he, nodding stiffly to the
skipper of the *Gloria* who sat a few places away. 'And the rest?'

I delayed my reply when I saw Mrs Chalmers lean forward to
address a smiling remark to my father across the table. Thanks to
the music, I did not catch the whole of it, but the import was not lost
on me: she was reminding him that he had invited her to sea in the
Hecuba.

'The rest. . . there are about thirty seamen, engine-room staff and
stokers,' I said, still with half an eye on that woman. 'And the
purser's department comprising a chef, two cooks and ten stewards.
About fifty crew in all.'

'One cannot run a vessel of this size on less,' observed my companion. 'Now, the Russian Imperial yacht *Standart* I found to be grossly undermanned, especially in the purser's department. This greatly puzzled me, particularly since it is common knowledge that the Romanoffs are tremendously extravagant, the Tsarina most particularly – would you believe, ma'am, that she had a hamper of the little Tsarevich's favourite nectarines brought all the way from the Crimea to Kiel upon the boy's lightly expressed whim? The only explanation I could offer myself for the appalling service aboard the *Standart* was that the Tsarina, though the granddaughter of Queen Victoria, has no great love for the sea and ships. I will give you instances of what I suffered aboard the *Standart* when I was a guest. . .'

My companion having revealed himself as a person very fond of the sound of his own voice, and a gossip to boot, it was an easy matter to distance more than half my mind from what he was saying and occasionally to nod, shake my head or murmur 'Oh, yes', and 'How very odd' from time to time. This enabled me to concentrate upon the two wings of the table – to left and right – where my interests principally lay.

To my left and opposite, Jack had abandoned poor Miss Dearing for the no doubt more stimulating converse of his other neighbour, the wife of the Chief Superintendant of the Naval Dockyard, a formidable lady who had made her mark by shipping a consignment of foxes from Leicestershire with a view to hunting them on the island. Regrettably, the traditional cunning of these wily creatures had been no match for the enterprise of the Maltese peasantry who, having heard what foxes can do to chickens, had caught, killed and buried the unfortunate predators before a hunter could be tacked up or a horn blown. I was quite happy that Jack should be attending Mrs Chief Superintendant who, in addition to being a great wit, had the looks of a superannuated witch.

'. . . aboard the *Standart*, the shaving water was cold, the ice cream warm, the baths no better than tepid. As for the cuisine. . .' Captain von Schleicher was well-launched upon a peroration which he had clearly repeated often.

I addressed myself – surreptitiously – to Natasha Chalmers, who having made no attempt to converse with either von Schleicher or the gentleman on her right, was devoting her attentions to Mrs Meaker across the table. In doing so, of course, she also part-included my father in the exchange; as often as he was able – or so it seemed to me – he would abandon Lady Freakley and reply to one of that woman's remarks, or merely listen to what she was saying with a rapt attention that I found most depressing. Could it be, I asked myself, that in the end my sensible, wise and clear-headed parent would fall for her transparent blandishments?

The gallant German had changed tack. . .

'. . . as I informed the Commodore before we sat down, I have this moment received a signal from the Commander of the High Seas Fleet, ordering me to proceed to Spezia on Monday.'

'Oh, we shall miss you greatly, Captain,' I responded politely.

'Most kind, gracious lady,' responded the other. 'Unfortunately, as I told the Commodore, if it is his wish to complete the programme of manoeuvres with the *Darmstadt* it will be necessary to do so tomorrow – which means that we must bid farewell to Malta and our British friends, yourself included, immediately after the ball.'

Tomorrow?

But . . . tomorrow Jack Cummings and I were sailing to the Blue Grotto – a promised delight which I had scarcely allowed myself to dwell upon, but had taken out from time to time during the greatly fraught afternoon and evening and gloated over like a miser and his gold. Now I might be denied that delight, and it mattered little that it would almost certainly mean only a postponement: I had set my heart on going to the Blue Grotto with Jack tomorrow, and later was simply not good enough.

It was at that moment when I was feeling bereft that I caught Natasha Chalmers' eye. She had been covertly looking at me but made no attempt to turn away – as many might – at being thus caught out. Instead she met my gaze brazenly and I seemed to hear her mouthing the words again: 'That spoilt, over-indulged brat!'

Was I *really* spoilt and over-indulged? I hoped not.

*

Dinner was coming to an end; dessert and ices were being set out. In a very short while, I should be catching the ladies' eyes and leading them out to the smaller saloon, leaving the gentlemen to their brandy, port and cigars and whatever men gossip about when they are denied civilised companionship. Still nursing my deep disappointment, I smiled across at Jack Cummings and he responded in kind.

59

Captain von Schleicher was leaning sideways to address me on something when my father tapped the table to command attention.

'Ladies and gentlemen!' he said. 'Before we come to the parting of the ways, when all that is best and most beautiful in our lives departs, leaving we poor menfolk bereft and desolate. . .' This sally was greeted with titters of amusement and he continued: 'I should like to make an announcement which personally gives me the most tremendous pleasure and which, I trust, will not be lacking for interest and approval in the present company.' He glanced across at me with great fondness. 'My daughter Faith has pressed me very closely today regarding this announcement and I have been obliged to prevaricate with her, much as I love her, because of the delicate nature of the business in hand.'

(By this he meant, I told myself, that it is extremely bad form – indeed can often be fatal to his chances – for an officer prematurely to announce himself as about to become the recipient of high promotion, particularly when – as was almost certainly likely in Father's case – the honour of a knighthood is the glittering pendant to the advancement.)

'Out with it, Dangerfield!' grated Sir Jasper. ' 'Tain't civil of you to keep the whole company – myself and lady wife excepted – in a state of suspense. Give 'em your good news and leave it to me to be the first to congratulate you.'

'That I will, sir, that I will,' responded Father. 'Without further ado, ladies and gentlemen, I have the immense pleasure to announce that a great joy has entered my life at a time when I had thought myself beyond all such emotions. . .'

(What was he saying? This was no way to introduce such a solid, hard-nosed matter as promotion and a knighthood.)

'In short, ladies and gentlemen, I have tonight received a final answer to a question which I put to a certain lady here present. . .'

(Surely it was impossible?)

'Mrs Natasha Chalmers, a bereaved partner of marriage like myself, has tonight consented to become my wife and to share the rest of my days in tranquillity. Now, what do you think of that, hey? I wager a thousand guineas that no present had suspected such a thing.'

'You are forgetting my lady wife and self,' cried that crusty seadog Sir Jasper, 'who have been privy to your secret from the first.'

'And helped and advised you in the matter, Dangerfield!' interposed his spouse.

I sat there, scarcely able to comprehend what was happening about me. Everyone was on their feet, crowding to congratulate my father and that woman; she was being surrounded by my guests, all eager to plant a kiss on those damask cheeks; others were wringing my father's hand and patting his back, dubbing him 'cunning fellow', 'a dark horse', 'lucky devil', 'much to be envied, sir', 'deserving of all the very best of happiness, sir' – depending on their rank and degree of familiarity.

Lady Freakley came up to me, sailing like a triumphant line-of-battleships with all flags flying for victory.

'My dear, I am so happy for you!' she cried, embracing me. 'Just what we had hoped and prayed for, wasn't it?' She pinched my cheek mischievously. 'Little minx!' she smiled. 'After my careful prompting, I'll stake my best tiara that you played your part as matchmaker tonight – whispered the encouraging word in dear Natasha's ear, I shouldn't wonder. Hey?'

I broke from her without a word of reply, thrust my way through the throng and ran for the stairs, heedless of the glances that followed me. Nor did I slacken my pace until I was in my cabin with the door shut and locked behind me, when I threw myself upon the bunk face-downwards in a paroxysm of bitter tears.

*

A tap came upon the door.

'Who is it?' I demanded.

'It's me, darling. Are you all right?'

'Father, please go away.'

'All right. I quite understand how you must feel – not every day that a gel's papa announces he's to be wed. Natural feminine emotion to get wrought-up about it. You'll be yourself again tomorrow, and then we can chat about how we shall dispose our lives after the wedding. Natasha will be a great comfort to you. Very wise and understanding person, Natasha.'

'Please, Father – *please!*'

'All right, I'll leave you in peace to get some sleep. See you in the morning. Don't worry about the ball – the event can run itself until everyone tires out and goes home. Oh, and Faith. . .'

'Yes?'

'The *Darmstadt*'s leaving on Monday and the flotilla's accompanying her part of the way. It is my idea to carry out the last part of the

61

manoeuvres to the northward. While I'm away, you will have an excellent opportunity to seek out Natasha's company and get to know her really well. Do you follow me?'

I did not reply.

'Well, I will leave you now. Good night, my dearest girl.'

'Good night, Father.' I buried my head in my pillow and willed him to go away before I screamed out loud, just as I was soundlessly screaming inside.

Time passed. Someone – I supposed the pianist of the Royal Marine orchestra – was playing rags on the grand in the small saloon, and people were clapping hands in time to the catchy tunes. I could hear also the murmur of many voices up on the boat deck above my head. Much later, the full orchestra started to play again up there; the muffled tapping and shuffling of many feet betokened the ball's success – albeit the hostess was eating out her bitter heart within earshot.

It was quite without question that, sooner or later – preferably sooner (when he returned from sea?) – I should have to tackle Father about the awful mistake he was contemplating. But how should I go about it? To go bald-headed and recite the litany of the terrible conversation I had overheard between that woman and her inamorata would naturally, in a man of inflexible honour like Father, call for him to challenge Natasha Chalmers with this evidence. She being who she was and what she was would flatly deny it – and more, would demand to be released from their engagement. Had I not heard from her own lips the manner of her tactics?. . .

'I'll nobly offer to withdraw rather than. . .come between an honourable man and his spoilt, hysterical chit of a daughter. . .I think I can predict. . .his response.'

No way out there. I must try other means to bring him to the realisation of what he was about. I must take advice from someone better suited to the hard knocks of life than I, someone with a cool head and a clear vision.

Jack Cummings! The very person. Our trip to the Blue Grotto now having no impediment, since the flotilla would not after all be sailing until Monday, it would provide the opportunity to confide in this man who had walked into my life so short a time ago and seemingly turned it on its ear.

Tomorrow. . .

I imagined that the outing was still on, although we had made no final arrangements for the rendezvous; but I had lived my life amongst sailors – and sailors, in my experience, can be relied upon to arrange matters entirely to their satisfaction.

So it was with a quieter mind that I undressed, washed, cleaned my teeth and prepared myself for bed.

And slept like a babe, with the sound of ragtime buzzing in my ears.

*

The navy sail-boats, six of them, were moored on small buoys close inshore of a large sandy bay on the south side of the island, a cove or two away from the crossing to Gozo. Two sailors had brought one of the boats – a classic whaler – up on to the shoreline and rigged the sails. They were playing at mock wrestling in the soft sand when Jack and I arrived in the carriage we had hired from Valletta. The tars broke apart, grinning and jumping to attention as we descended to the beach.

' 'Morning, lads,' said Jack, nodding. He was in a white shirt and trousers, a boater aslant his darkly-maned head.

' 'Morning, sir!' The speaker wore the foul anchor badge of a Leading Seaman. 'All ready for you and the lady.' He looked side-long at me, doubtfully. 'Can the lady handle the mains'l and jib, sir?'

'The lady says she can.'

'I have been sailing since I was so high,' I interposed, demonstrating with the palm of my hand at knee-level. The sailors looked sceptical.

Minutes later we were afloat, Jack at the tiller and I handling the mainsheets. The slender craft took the wind, close-hauled and edged its way out of the bay, past the headland to our left, where a ruined watch-tower loomed high against the illimitable blue. I looked back to see that the sailors had resumed their mock wrestling.

We headed in an easterly direction, closing with the shore, only a stone's throw from an unscalable cliff that stretches almost the entire length of Malta's southern coastline. Away to our right was the tiny islet of Fifla, uninhabited save for a unique species of lizard, and a target for innumerable shells which the Royal Navy had fired at it – an immovable and unsinkable target – through the years; ahead were the crawling crests of the great swell that dashed itself to oblivion against the petrified sandstone bastion of Malta.

We were rolling quite heavily now, with a bare few inches on the leeward side as we crouched with shoulders bowed against the chilling spray. Skirting another headland – frighteningly close, so that the back-spray from the wall stung my cheek and I could see a shoal of small fish rising and falling against the rock – we came in sight of a cavernous cave-mouth in the centre of a shallow bay.

Jack pointed. 'The Blue Grotto!'

I nodded in reply.

He bore down on the tiller and I eased out the sheets, so that the mainsail gathered up the wind as it struck us at a fresh angle. Checking its pace, the whaler headed straight towards the gaping archway.

'We'll just about get in with the sea running the way it is!' shouted Jack.

Again I nodded, taking a tighter grip on a thwart. It looked a very low entrance to me, and the waves were driving in there at an alarming rate and fury.

Closer we went, pitching heavily now, with each succeeding sea passing under the keel of the boat. Closer still, so that the cliff-top soon overhung us and we were nosing straight for the centre of the arch, with a big roller under us, urging us in. Then this mighty roller was spent and baffled against the pillars of the arch and what was left of its power was just enough to carry us forward into the cathedral-like vault of the grotto, with a cry of triumph that rose to my lips echoing all about us, and blueness everywhere.

Blue like the lapis lazuli of a butterfly's wing: an iridescent, sight-shattering blueness beyond belief; from the dark hue of the stalactites high above us, to the deep luminosity of the great basin of water in which our craft rose and fell in the muffled ground swell; in the cerulean diamonds of sunlight flickering on the walls all about us. Nothing but the refracted blueness of sky through water – and the bass organ-pipe groaning of the sea.

I peered over the side. Mirror-clear in the blue cave bottom, one could discern each shifting grain of the sandy bed and the translucent tips of the stalagmites. A shoal of fish appeared black, shielded from the light – then they turned and flickered away, suddenly silvered.

I sat back on my thwart and sighed with a strange and profound contentment that was beyond all understanding.

Jack had clearly caught my mood and reflected it back to me.

'And now, Faith,' he said quietly, his every word magnified all about us, 'suppose you tell me what's troubling you, why you ran out on everyone last night and – most of all – why you were standing on the poop deck of the *Gloria* before dawn with your telescope trained on *Hecuba* for the first sight of me?'

*

I told him everything: of my early fears that Mrs Chalmers had set her cap at my father from the very first; about the hideous conversation on which I had been the unwilling eavesdropper; and all the rest, right up to the awful revelation that Father's after-dinner announcement was very far from what I had anticipated.

He nodded when I had finished. 'But still you haven't answered the last part of my question,' he said. 'As to why you were watching out for me since before dawn?'

I looked down at my hands, with the shifting blue bands of ghostly light playing across them.

'It seemed to me that you might not have remembered our arrangement,' I whispered, 'in view of the fact that we had never discussed a time and a place to meet.'

'You might have known I would come for you,' he said. 'As to time – you might have guessed also that I too would be up before dawn, waiting for what might be considered a respectable hour to call on a young lady.'

'Eight o'clock is not a respectable hour to call on a young lady,' I said with a false tartness. '*This* young lady seldom takes breakfast in bed before nine-thirty.'

He grinned. 'But not this morning.'

'Not this morning.'

He reached out and took my hands in his. There was no need for words; his gesture told all.

'Jack, I need your advice,' I said. 'I am quite a strong person really, but vulnerable – dreadfully vulnerable – so far as my father's concerned. Until now we have only had each other, you see.' I laughed, and was shocked to sense the note of hysteria in the sound. 'Just Father and me – and five million-odd pounds to keep us company.' And then the tears started, spilling over my lower eyelids and coursing down my cheeks. 'Now I'm being silly, and I very much wanted *not* to be silly.'

He let me have my cry; waited until I had dabbed away the tears, sniffed and composed myself again.

'So what do we have?' he mused. 'As you say, if you go to your father and tell him what you have told me, Mrs Chalmers will deny everything and use it to drive a wedge between you and the Commodore. So that's out. What is left?'

'I . . . I could simply tell him that she isn't good enough for him,' I suggested. 'And that compared with the love he had – and still bears – for my dead mother, this is just a passing fancy.'

'He won't thank you for that thought, Faith,' replied Jack. 'With some justification, he might accuse you of selfishness. He would be quite justified in pointing out that he has worshipped the memory of your mother all these years, but that a man in his position needs a woman at his side and, further, that when *you* decide to marry, you will not give a thought to leaving him alone – and so on and so forth. Do you follow me, Faith?'

I nodded miserably. 'So what do I do – what can I say?'

There were a few pebbles at the bottom of the boat. He picked one up and tossed it into the water, which instantly shed its oily surface and was crazed into a thousand myriad patterns of jagged shapes, each a subtle variant of tone and colour – and all blue.

'My advice to you at this stage, Faith,' he said, 'is to let a little time go by and for the present . . . do nothing.'

'But, Jack, they could apply for a licence and be married within the week!' I cried.

'Not this week, it would not be possible,' he said. 'We sail at dawn tomorrow and will not be back in Malta before Thursday at the earliest.'

'So what do I do in the meantime?' I snapped. 'Sit and hope that either Father comes to his senses while he is at sea, or else that woman finds a better catch before Thursday?' Ashamed, I added, 'I'm sorry, Jack, I shouldn't be short with you, having burdened you with my problem, and you are trying your best to be helpful.'

He shrugged that off. 'Tell me more about this American chap, this Hawick,' he said. 'Does he have money?'

'Not the kind of money – or influence – that would attract her,' I replied. 'And it's really influence and position that she's after.'

'But they are – or have been – lovers?'

I bowed my head. 'That was heavily implied,' I whispered.

'Is he living with her?'

66

'I shouldn't think so. Even *she* would not be so brazen – not while she is campaigning to entrap my father.'

He was silent for a while; from beyond the cave-mouth one could hear the moaning of the wind, which seemed to have increased, and the up-and-down motion within the grotto had become more marked.

'Faith, there is a course you could take during the next few days whilst we are away,' he said at length. 'You may not relish the idea, but considering the kind of people with whom you are dealing, you may feel you are well within your moral rights.'

'What are you suggesting, Jack?'

'There are fellows who call themselves "enquiry agents" or "private detectives". It is a seedy trade and mostly concerned with collecting evidence of infidelity in support of divorce proceedings.' He paused, searching my expression for a reaction. 'Malta being strongly Roman Catholic, there is no divorce, but with all the British here you may be sure that there are a few of these enterprising individuals on the island, to cater for our more . . . liberal requirements.'

'I see. You mean – pay someone to spy on Mrs Chalmers?'

'But you wouldn't want to become involved in anything so shady, Faith,' he said. 'Forget it. Disregard the idea, I should never have suggested it.'

'Oh, you greatly mistake me, Jack,' I assured him. 'To prevent that woman from marrying my father and ruining the rest of his life, I would spy on her myself! I would crawl on my hands and knees the length of Malta, from Marsaxlokk to the Gozo ferry, to find proof that would convince the whole world that she is not fit to clean his boots!'

He grinned, admiration written all over his bronzed and craggy countenance, good humour in those unbelievably deep blue eyes – now subtly enriched by the myriad blues of the grotto.

'Good for you, Faith!' he said. 'You've got style. You've got a lot of grit – and there's not an ounce of humbug in you! But now, we'd best make tracks back to the moorings; it will be a pretty hair-raising sail by the look of the sea that's risen out there!'

*

The beam sea hit us as soon as we turned parallel to the sheer wall of Malta's southern shore, and our boat's lee gunwale was momentarily driven beneath the surface, scooping up an intolerable amount of water and depositing it in my lap on its way to the bilges.

'Shorten sail, Faith!' shouted Jack above the bluster of the wind and the thrumming of tortured canvas above our heads. Accordingly I addressed myself to the task, while he brought the whaler head-on to wind and waves; slackening off the gaff and tying down the line of reef points so that we presented less sail – and therefore less hazard – to the fury of the wind.

'Lower the jib as well!' came the next order from the skipper at the tiller. This was a matter of crawling forward to the bows and gathering in the triangle of madly-flapping canvas, taming it and thrusting it under a thwart for safe keeping.

'All done!' I shouted.

'Good lass – hold tight!'

We turned back on course, pointing straight for the headland that was topped by the ruined watch-tower, beyond which lay our goal. It seemed a terribly long way. The wind did not treat us so brutally, thanks to our carrying much less canvas, but the height and power of the incoming waves beating against the side of the boat, lifting us crest-high and dropping us in their troughs, made for slow, uncomfortable and hazardous progress.

And then – to top it all – a rain squall: a veritable deluge that soaked us through on the instant, shut out all sight of the headland and reduced Malta to a grey smudge dimly visible through the shifting patterns of slanting downpour. It was as if one was in fact submerged in water: the assault upon the eyes, mouth and nostrils being such that one could neither see nor draw breath save with the greatest difficulty; every lungful of God-given air was a battle, and our range of vision so reduced as to simulate the terror of blindness.

The squall passed, as all things pass. Yet that was not the end of our troubles: next came a freak wave that, rearing high above us, broke at its towering crest before it passed under the keel, deluging the inside of the whaler with a cascade of flung spume that filled the bilges knee-high.

'Bail!' yelled Jack from the stern.

There was a tin pannikin tied to my thwart and snatching it up, I set to work: slopping the foaming sea water over the side and hideously mindful that, so low had our new burden taken us, more and more spray came surging in with every new wave.

Though I bailed with frenzy and with every ounce of energy I had

68

within me, I came to realise that the sea was gaining on me!

'Faster!' shouted a harsh voice that sounded like that of a total stranger. '*Faster!*'

'I – I can't go any faster!' I wailed and believed it.

Near to despair, I asked myself if this, then, was the way one dies at sea? With the slow, inexorable forces of merciless nature closing in for the kill; does all one's power, beliefs, love of life, instinct for survival mean nothing?

I cast an anguished glance towards the figure seated in the stern: both hands clasped upon the tiller, jockeying with each wayward shift of wind and wave; his eyes narrowed, lips firm, jaw squared and unconquered . . . unconquerable. He looked towards me and grinned – and I was filled with a great sense of peace.

Returning to my task, I saw that contrary to my fears I was palpably beginning to master the intake that surged about my calves; also that, by an adjustment of handholds on the bailer and a change in my technique, I was able almost to double my previous rate of progress.

'I'm winning – I'm winning!' I shouted a paeon to the wind, which bore it away into silence.

The moment when we rounded the headland was marked by a blessed diminishing of motion and another – rather less violent – rain squall. Jack turned to point our bows at the beach. I slackened off the mainsheet to allow the sail to spread and we were carried grandly, surfing on the crests of succeeding waves, to the shore.

I never welcomed a moment more than that when our keel grated on shingle noisily, and then slithered more quietly into soft sand. Jack was over the side in a trice and, waist-deep, dragging the whaler up on to the strand.

No one was about, there was no sign of the sailors as, reaching up, he lifted me out of the boat and carried me ashore in his arms.

I looked up into his face. Not a word passed between us. Our lips met and almost immediately the rain slackened and passed on.

I nuzzled my cheek against his. 'I was frightened for a while,' I said, 'and then, quite suddenly, it was all right.'

He pointed. Clear against the scudding clouds, a rainbow spanned like a bridge over water and land, joining the dark horizon of sea with the bare hills in the heart of the island.

*

Our hired carriage was waiting under a grove of giant prickly pears. The driver was dozing; when he saw our dripping-wet state, his typical Maltese concern and generosity was expressed by wrapping us in warm travelling rugs and assuring us of a swift journey. We were clip-clopped smartly along the rutted lanes, through tiny villages where rainwater still sluiced down from the flat-roofed cottages and ran in rivulets in which small, barefoot children splashed and squealed for joy. We quietly held hands; there was no repetition of the moment of passion which had joined us on the beach, nor did we speak until the domes and towers of Valletta came in sight and we were passing through the archways leading down to the quay and the sight of the grey warships lying in the Grand Harbour.

It was then that I found the voice to express what was nearest to my heart:

'Look after yourself during the manoeuvres, won't you? And look after my father, also, please.'

He glanced sidelong at me and his response came as a surprise: 'Why did you say that, Faith? Do you know something you should not know?'

I had no answer for that.

*

Since before dawn – when I arose, wrapped a shawl about my shoulders and went out on to the poop deck – the boats of the flotilla had sported rows of lighted portholes along their sleek sides, and arc-lights illuminated the foredecks where anchor parties were making ready to slip from their buoys. Away beyond, similar signs of a dawn departure were in evidence aboard the *Darmstadt*.

Father, from whom I had taken very brief leave the previous night, had slept aboard his command. No word of his proposed nuptials had passed between us; he had appeared absent, distracted, self-absorbed – all of which I had put down to his concentration upon the forthcoming manoeuvres. And now they were about to go to sea.

Dawn came. And from every naval ship in the harbour there arose the shrill blasts of bosuns' pipes, the blare of trumpets, rolling of drums heralding the brassy music of Royal Marine bands – as the age-old ritual of 'Colours' was carried out, as at every dawn; and scraps of red, white and blue bunting rose to flagstaffs, all save one –

that emblazoned with the sombre black cross of Imperial Germany.

Moments later, the torpedo boat destroyers slipped from their buoys as one and moved slowly forward in single line, each half a length distant from its neighbour. Gathering speed all the time, they swept close by the *Gloria* on their way to the harbour mouth.

The cluster on the leader's narrow bridge waved in passing. I identified the tall, bearded figure of my father and the dark-avised man by his side who had began to cause such havoc in my heart. I waved in return until they were obscured from my sight by those following.

On the bridge of the *Hasty*, my persistent swain Dickie Jobling waved his cap for me. Dear Dickie, another first of the month would soon be along and I had no hope to offer him. All in all, I was very near to tears; it was as if I was saying good-bye to them all for a very long time as they went off to fight – instead of their going to play elaborate war games, really no more than peacetime yachting for a few days in the now still, blue Mediterranean.

Last came the *Darmstadt*, her brass band playing selections from *Merrie England* on the quarter-deck. Captain von Schleicher was up on high, training his telescope on me. As the high-walled steel citadel swept grandly past, he stiffly saluted.

Then they were all gone and I strangely alone and bereft.

*

I searched for and discovered an advertisement in the 'Personal' column of the *Malta Courier*:

> HIGHLY CONFIDENTIAL ENQUIRIES made at the order of ladies or gentlemen. Strictest discretion assured in all circumstances. Call or write Mr Montague, 8a Strait Street, Valletta. Open 8.30 am to 12 noon, and 5.30 pm to 7 pm.

I chose to visit Mr Montague in the evening, when the blinding heat of the summer's afternoon had turned to coolness and light airs, and the commercial life of the island was resumed. Strait Street, known to generations of British sailors as 'The Gut', runs straight and narrow as a ruler through the busiest part of the city, and is lined on both sides with offices and business houses, interspersed with chophouses, cafés and bars – some of the latter being of the lowest and

71

most disreputable kind. Number 8a presented no more than a narrow doorway and a steep flight of steps, at the bottom of which was a crudely-limned notice board informing me among other matters that Mr Montague, Enquiry Agent, occupied Room 3 on the top floor.

I ascended and duly knocked on the door of Room 3, was called to enter and found myself in the company of a small, stout man of distinctly Levantine appearance, dressed in a dingy white duck suit, wing collar and a tie which I by chance recognised as that worn by alumni of Eton College.

'And how may I serve you, Miss . . . Dangerfield?' asked this worthy, eyeing my visiting card and covertly rubbing his thumb over its surface to ascertain my quality by the test of whether the text were engraved or merely printed.

'I should like you, please, to keep watch on a house in Sliema,' I said with more assurance than I would have credited possible, 'and to take note of the visitors who call there.'

'Ah, who might be the resident of said abode, dear Miss?' asked the other. 'Lady or gentleman?'

'A – a lady.'

'Aaaah!' There was a whole world of understanding – and a touch of sympathy – in the utterance and the look that went with it. 'You wish me to list this lady's visitors? I comprehend.' He made a note. 'Might one also enquire if there is one particular visitor in whom you might be interested? And if so, a brief description would be of considerable aid.' He had a habit of looking at one with his head on one side, like a quizzical dog.

'There . . . is someone particular,' I admitted, horribly aware that Mr Montague had cast me in the role of a woman wronged. And I gave him a word picture of Hawick. Also Mrs Chalmers' address.

'There will be two guineas registration fee,' he said, 'plus one guinea *per diem* and two guineas per night. You wish overnight surveillance, dear Miss?'

I nodded – and paid over my dues.

'The reports to be delivered . . . where?' he asked.

'Oh, no, not delivered!' I cried. 'I . . . will call here again and pick them up in a day or so.'

He rose when I prepared to leave and held out his hand for me to shake. Feeling that I had to say something by way of getting myself out of the room in a civilised manner, I siezed upon a commonplace: 'Do you find yourself . . . very busy, Mr Montague?'

'Oh, yes, dear Miss. With the Maltese ladies in particular. They like to know, you see, with whom their spouses spend the long hot afternoons – in order that they may make their own dispositions, you understand? Good evening, Miss Dangerfield. You may rest assured that the matter is in good hands. Strictest discretion!'

*

Arriving back aboard the *Gloria*, I found a note which had been delivered by hand awaiting me. Slitting open the crested envelope, I discovered a printed card – and my heart sank:

Miss Faith Dangerfield

Lady Freakley
At Home

Wednesday 21st June, 6pm

RSVP
Villa Giorno,
Ta'xbiex.

Your adorable stepmother-elect will be here!

There was no means, save by reason of grave illness, that I could decline the invitation; a summons to attend the Admiral's lady at her dark and overstuffed villa in a smart purlieu of the city was like a royal command which a Navy wife – or daughter – disobeyed only on pain of great demerit to herself and the career of her loved one.

But to be meeting the Chalmers woman under the vigilant eye of Lady Freakley, and to be obliged to be civil to her, to respond to her no doubt unctuous advances, her false declarations of affection! The very notion was repugnant to me and I sought about for an anodyne to assuage the bitter pill I should be obliged to swallow. I sought . . . and found it:

Mr Montague and his enquiries!

Let the egregious Levantine find but one occasion when that woman was visited by the American at a time society might deem

73

indiscreet, and Mrs Chalmers – far from marrying my father and rising in that Society – might just as well pack her bags and go to live in foreign parts – not in any territory on earth where Britain's might and the rules of decent behaviour prevailed.

Nor let it be thought that during the forthcoming 'At Home', I should make any attempt to *threaten* the wretched creature with Mr Montague's revelations – far from it; all I needed was the knowledge to nurse secretly to my side, just as children will hide lanterns under their cloaks at night, concealed sources of light private and comforting to themselves against the whole world. Given such comfort, her mockery could not touch me.

Tomorrow – I told myself – Tuesday evening, I would call upon the enquiry agent and see if he had discovered anything.

*

Tuesday, which dragged interminably through the morning and afternoon, was emotionally heightened by a strange encounter I had with Charles Knight. It happened that I chanced to go into his sanctum, the ship's office, to make some trivial enquiry of his clerk. The clerk was not present; only Knight, who sat at his desk, bowed over, his head in his hands. He looked up with a guilty start when I entered.

'Oh, dear!' I said. 'Is anything the matter, Knight? Are you not well?'

'It's . . . it's nothing, ma'am,' he said, rising. As he did so, I thought I saw him slip what seemed to be a single sheet of lilac-coloured writing-paper underneath his blotter.

With one leap, my intuition sprang to a possible explanation: 'Is anything wrong with Miss Dearing?' I asked him.

He coloured up and avoided my gaze. 'No, ma'am,' he said, but most unconvincingly. 'That is to say, she . . . Miss Dearing . . . is quite well in herself. . .'

'But?. . .' I prompted him. As so often with poor Charles Knight, he tended to bring out the domineering older sister in me. 'And do please sit down.' I took a seat myself and studied him keenly.

'The fact is. . .' he began, and could go no further.

'Out with it, man!' I urged him.

'She's broken off our . . . our understanding,' he said.

'Why is that?'

'She – gives no reason.'

74

'I see.'

Poor Knight! Though I found it difficult to comprehend why, he always struck me as being very deeply attached to that rather colourless little thing. It takes all sorts! There was nothing I could do to help or comfort him; but I determined to tackle Angela Dearing at an early opportunity and find out what it was all about.

The opportunity came sooner than I thought.

*

A battleship and two cruisers had entered harbour during the afternoon; Strait Street was a shifting pattern of white uniforms and braided blue collars when I reached there and went straight up to Mr Montague's office.

I knocked.

'Enter!'

He had drawn the blinds – against the low, late afternoon sun, I presumed. Seated behind his desk in shirt-sleeves, he looked like a stocky, balding cherub with a cigar stuck out of the corner of his mouth – which he did not venture to remove when he saw who I was.

'Oh, it's you, little Miss Trouble!' he exclaimed in what I can only describe as a protracted snarl.

'What *do* you mean, sir?' I demanded coldly, lifting my chin and giving him the benefit of my height.

'What do I mean? This is what I mean, young Miss!' So saying, he rose and darted across the room with more agility than I would have given him credit for, drew the window blinds and turned to face me, allowing the thin sunlight to play upon his by no means comely countenance which had suffered some depredation since I last encountered him.

'See that?' he snarled, pointing.

'Oh dear!' I faltered.

His right eye was closed to a slit and puffed out to the level of his cheekbone, the whole suffused with colours ranging from pale yellow, to green, to black. It was what my father – a staunch patron of the so-called 'noble art' – would have described as 'a regular shiner'.

'I would not have you think that this is all,' he said. 'There are two front teeth missing from my upper plate – see? – and because I am a highly educated English gentleman, I will not show you the

75

bruises on my chest, my back and other places, where this brute kicked me – *kicked me* – when I was down!'

'But – *who* kicked you, Mr Montague?' I demanded. 'And why are you seeming to lay your misfortune at *my* door?'

He slapped his brow with the palm of his hand. 'Who kicked me?' he echoed. 'Why, who but this party *you* described to me!' And he repeated my word picture of the American Hawick.

'Oh!' I said, comprehending all.

'I am standing in the front garden of the female party,' he said, 'hiding behind a palm tree and minding my own business. Suddenly, out of the shadows – whooosh! – he is upon me. Before he does *this* to me –' here he pointed to his black eye – 'I have a chance to recognise him as the party of the second part. After that – only pain!'

'Mr Montague,' I said, 'I am most awfully sorry to have been the unwitting agent . . . I mean – if I can make recompense for your hurts. . .'

He held up a dismissive hand. 'I want nothing from you, lady,' he declared. 'This man of yours – you must have suffered enough already at his hands and likely will suffer more. At heart I am sorry for you, little Miss Trouble! Now will you leave me? Never come back! You are bad luck!'

*

Ta'xbiex and its attendant creek is a genteel suburban backwater much favoured by the Maltese gentry, ambassadors and the like, where the cream of senior British officers and their families keep private homes. When I arrived there by cab the following evening (after a most anxious and heart-searching twenty-four hours, I might add), I was just in time to see Natasha Chalmers' well-known chocolate-coloured carriage being driven into the shade of an overhanging lilac tree, there to await its owner's departure from Lady Freakley's 'At Home'.

So – my enemy had arrived just before me. Giving me as it did the chance to make an 'entrance', that was possibly a minor strategic advantage. I certainly stood in need of such.

The Admiral's butler ushered me into the drawing-room with its high Victorian decor and furnishings. Lady Freakley advanced through a veritable plantation of potted aspidistra, circled several over-stuffed chairs and sofas and held out her hands to greet me as if

I had been a loved and loving daughter.

'My dear, divine child! How pretty you look – but as usual. Come and meet the others.' She took me by the hand. 'Lady Borg you know, of course?'

Lady Borg, a monstrous figure in lace and ribbons with the largest hat I ever saw on human head, gave me her hand and opined that the weather was getting hotter if anything, was it not? An ancient prop of one of Malta's oldest noble families, the Most Noble Marchesa Borg (to give the lady her full title) was reputed to be one of the richest women in Malta, with palaces in Mdina, Rabat, Mellieha and on Gozo, yet it was common knowledge that she sent her housekeeper to the market late on Saturday evenings to buy up speckled fruit and tired vegetables.

'And Miss Dearing, of course,' added Lady Freakley casually, indicating Angela Dearing who looked thoroughly ill, poor thing, with dark circles under her eyes and a pinched, yellowish complexion. I determined, if I should be able first to acquit myself successfully with that Chalmers woman, to have a few words with little Miss Dearing and find out why she had ditched poor Knight in such a cavalier manner.

There were other introductions, principal among them a Commander Hornchurch with his wife and daughters. Hornchurch, a newcomer, had succeeded as Sir Jasper's Chief-of-Staff and the party was by way of being in his honour. I shook hands with him and did not at all fancy the predatory way he looked me over with eyes which were much too closely set together.

'And I don't need to introduce *this* lady,' said my hostess archly. 'This lady' being none other, of course, than my so-called step-mother-elect, who was wearing a too-tight costume in brilliant green and looked for all the world like a lady snake in a green-feathered hat!

'Dear Faith,' she said and kissed my cheek. 'Have you quite recovered from the slight indisposition you suffered at your charming ball?'

'Thank you, yes,' I replied. 'It was really nothing.'

'Overwhelmed with joy at the wonderful news – that was my summation,' interposed Lady Freakley.

'Oh, undoubtedly,' drawled the other. There was not a ghost of mockery on her painted lips, but behind her regarding eyes she was sneering at me.

77

'Mrs Chalmers, my dear,' said our hostess, 'do you think I might impose upon you for the loan of your beautiful grounds one Saturday afternoon next month, to hold a garden party in aid of the Sailors' and Marines' Charitable Fund?'

'Of course, Lady Freakley,' that woman replied. She glanced sidelong at me. 'Perhaps dear Faith will come and assist me with the arrangements.'

I nodded, being determined to do no such thing even if it meant ordering Captain Jaggers to take me to sea.

'Speaking of the garden of my house in Sliema . . .' said my tormentor – and I stiffened at the words and was suddenly aware that she was eyeing me keenly, sidelong, to gauge the effect she was creating. 'I suffered a most disturbing experience the other night. On Monday night, it was, shortly after midnight. And it took place in my garden.'

'Indeed?' cried Lady Freakley. 'And what transpired, pray, my dear?'

'I had – an intruder!' Addressing our hostess, she was nevertheless still watching me.

'I saw him quite clearly from my bedroom,' she continued. 'He was hiding behind a palm tree immediately facing my window!'

'How very alarming!' declared Lady Freakley. 'And after midnight, you say? A Peeping Tom, without doubt. And what did you do, my dear? Tell me swiftly, for I am all agog!'

'I used my telephone.'

'Ah, the telephone. What a blessing it is!'

'And contacted a friend of mine – you have met him, Lady Freakley – Glendon Hawick, who is redesigning my villa. I telephoned him at the Sliema Palace Hotel where he is staying.'

'And . . . *and?* . . .'

'Hawick came round straight away – and caught the man redhanded.'

'Splendid, splendid! Is he to be charged?'

'No, no. I don't wish to take the matter further. Be assured that Mr Hawick taught him a stern lesson!'

'Ah, yes, that's the important thing. So many of these rascals get away with a small fine and are back at their evil pastime the following night.'

'Furthermore, Lady Freakley,' continued Mrs Chalmers, now giving me a very straight not to say piercing look, 'during the scrim-

mage that took place, the creature spilled a considerable amount of
the contents of his pockets – including material that indicated his
identity . . . name, trade and so forth.'

'Ah!' exclaimed our hostess.

'So I don't think I shall be bothered with him again. Would *you*
think so, Faith, my dear?' she demanded suddenly.

I started and felt – almost literally *felt* – myself grow pale.

'Um . . . I – I shouldn't think so,' I murmured. And then, near to
panic, I begged to be excused and moved quickly away.

Moments later, lost in the blessed anonymity of the crowded
drawing-room and very carefully avoiding Sir Jasper's eye when
that susceptible sea-dog looked in my direction, I almost literally
bumped into Angela Dearing, who had elbowed her way through
the press in her haste to be with me.

'Oh, Miss Dangerfield,' she whispered, 'Lady Borg has left the
room for a few moments, so may I please have a brief word with
you?' The poor creature looked so distraught that I took instant pity
on her.

'Of course, Miss Dearing. Should we go out on the balcony?' I
suggested, pointing.

Oh, no, she couldn't possibly go so far in case she missed seeing
her mistress when Lady Borg returned. 'Just a few words,' she said.
'It is about Charles – Mr Knight.'

'You have thrown him over, have you not?' I said accusingly.

'You – know about that? Oh, dear, how dreadful it is when other
people suffer the upset of being dragged into one's private troubles. I
– I expect you think I have been very cruel and inconsiderate to
Charles?' she asked with a touch of anxiety.

'Well, since you ask me, I do feel it was rather harsh of you to
break your . . . arrangement . . . without explaining why.'

'But I cannot!' she breathed. 'I *cannot* tell him why! It's much too
– too delicate!'

'Oh!' Lacking any further information – and none seemed to be
forthcoming – it was all I could comment.

'But I should like to tell you, Miss Dangerfield,' she continued,
'since you are a woman of the world and have always been so kind to
Charles and me. I simply must confide in someone wise, whom I can
trust.'

'Meet me at some time,' I suggested.

'Not on the *Gloria*!'

'Of course not. Meet me at Gauchi's tea-shop in Jubilee Street one day. When would suit you?'

'Friday, Miss Dangerfield. It has to be a Friday, when Lady Borg allows me an hour off to do my personal shopping.'

We agreed upon the coming Friday at 4 o'clock. Next instant, she espied her ladyship re-entering the drawing-room and fled.

Despite my own dreadful and immediate problem, I could still find time and place in my thoughts for Angela Dearing's troubles. Though I suppose it was only vulgar curiosity which prompted me, if I were honest.

*

By the exercising of much manoeuvring, of shifting places in the room and taking up fresh conversations whenever danger loomed, I contrived to keep out of Natasha Chalmers' way until, at seven-thirty exactly, Lady Freakley intimated to the servants – and with no more than a raising of an eyebrow – that they were to remove the tea-trolley and the salvers bearing the sherry decanters and the gentlemen's whisky and brandy; this being the signal that the 'At Home' was over.

We filed out into the late sunlight and coolness of evening.

'My carriage is waiting. I will drive you down to the jetty, Faith, dear.' Mrs Chalmers addressed the honeyed suggestion in a carrying voice that all might hear.

'Thank you, no, ma'am, I. . .'

But my polite refusal got no further as she put her face close to mine. 'You will *wish* to travel in my carriage, for I have something in the way of a bone to pick with you, you two-faced brat!' All this was said in a murmur which carried no further than the two of us; what I found particularly distasteful was that she smiled sweetly as she delivered her harsh ultimatum.

We drove along the Ta'xbiex jetty, past the rows of small yachts moored stern to the wall. And we sat in silence.

When we reached the Valletta road my companion said, without shifting her expressionless gaze from a point somewhere ahead: 'If you are so two-faced and underhand as to have me spied upon, I suggest you dispense a little more of your father's fortune in securing the services of a professional agent, instead of a grubby back-street snooper. Oh, yes, I know about your down-at-heel Mr Montague,

and not merely because he spilled his credentials all over my lawn.
When Glendon Hawick had done with him he was – in the telling
phrase of Glendon's countrymen – singing like a canary. I know
from whom it was and why it was that your Mr Montague kept
watch on my villa that night. The only thing that puzzles me is how
you came to discover about Glendon and me.'

'I overheard you – the two of you – that night on the *Gloria*,' I
replied. 'You made me feel quite sick. And to think that my
father —'

'Your father will marry me – and be happy to do so!' she declared.
'Before long they will make him an Admiral, soon after that a knight
and then a baron. He will raise me to the aristocracy and I shall be
accepted by the highest in the land. I shall enjoy it – very much.' For
the first time since we entered the carriage she met my eyes, and her
own were coldly implacable, merciless: the eyes of a creature for
whom the thought 'I want' is but a step from 'I will have – and devil
take the hindmost'.

'That's how it is and how it will be,' she stated. 'You had best
accept it, for if you get in my way again I will destroy you.'

Reaching the entrance to the Valletta quay, she gave an order to
her coachman who halted by the trot-boats, and I alighted.

To my astonishment, she was laughing quietly to herself – quite
mirthful, girlish laughter, her eyes alight with good humour.

'I must tell you,' she murmured behind the cover of her fan, so
that the coachman should not overhear, 'but I did not summon
Glendon Hawick by telephone that night. He it was who espied your
seedy little Mr Montague – from the window of my bedroom! Good-
bye, my dear. I have so enjoyed our little tête-à-tête!'

*

Charles Knight was waiting for me at the top of the gangway when I
went aboard the *Gloria*. As soon as I saw the expression on his face, I
sensed that something was terribly wrong: his whole appearance
exuded intimations of disaster.

'What is it?' I demanded. 'Has something happened to the flotilla? My father – *anyone*?. . .'

His lips were trembling as he answered: 'News just came through
on the wireless telegraph. There has been an accident. . .'

'An accident!'

He nodded. 'The signal wasn't very strong, so the operator was

81

unable to get all the message very clearly, but . . . but it appears there has been a collision between two boats of the flotilla. And one of them was *Hecuba*.'

'Oh, no – *no!* Was anyone hurt?'

'There must have been casualties. The flotilla is asking for medical assistance to be sent. I'm so sorry, Miss Dangerfield. So very sorry. . .'

FOUR

I fretted that evening; pacing back and forth across the decks, aching for further and better news from the flotilla, or from Navy House ashore in Valletta. As to the latter, I constantly anticipated the arrival of Lady Freakley, who professed to love me so dearly – or at least a message from the office of the Admiral Commanding. No such visitor or message having arrived by nine o'clock, I refused dinner and had a boat called away to take me ashore; there I presented myself at Navy House, requested to see Sir Jasper for preference or, failing that, his new Chief-of-Staff.

I was told by a supercilious duty Master-at-Arms – after he had been to 'enquire' – that neither of these two gentlemen was available, but that I might see Commander Hornchurch's aide-de-camp, Lieutenant Forsyte. The manner in which I was fobbed off on to a junior underling – I, the daughter of a senior seagoing commander – should have given me an intimation of what lay ahead. I was not to know it then, but slights and snubs in plenty awaited me from the lesser fry who were delegated to deal with my problems; it was the beginning of a doleful end.

Hornchurch's ADC kept me cooling my heels in the outer office for another ten minutes before he deigned to have me admitted to his presence. He had the grace to rise to his feet upon my entrance, but sat down after pointing me to a seat. He was about my own age: stiff-necked and arrogant as to bearing. From the painful pinkness of his fair complexion and the peeling skin on his nose, I assumed that he had just come out from England with his master – a new broom.

'I have been trying all evening to. .' I began.

'It is a most serious matter. . .' He began simultaneously.

'I'm sorry.'

'No – please continue, Miss Dangerfield.'

'I was going to say that I have instructed the wireless telegraphist aboard the *Gloria* to listen for further signals from the flotilla, but to no avail. So I came to ask you. . .'

'The first emergency signal was sent out in plain language,' interposed Lieutenant Forsyte. 'The rest have been in naval code. As *I* was about to say, this is a serious matter and certain aspects will remain secret.'

'I see. But what further can you tell me – if anything, Lieutenant Forsyte?'

He frowned. 'Simply this: the flotilla leader *Hecuba*, whilst performing a turning manoeuvre, collided with the lead ship of the other line; herself sustained certain damage and reduced her consort – *Hasty* – to a sinking condition. The latest we have is that *Hasty* sank an hour ago.'

'Oh, how terrible!' I cried. 'What about the crew – Dickie Jobling?'

'Lieutenant Jobling was unhurt, as were most of the crew. There were half-a-dozen casualties, none fatal. And that, ma'am, is all I am at liberty to tell you. That much and no more will be released to the press pending the board of enquiry – and the subsequent court-martial.'

I stared at him blankly. 'I realise there must be an enquiry into the accident,' I said. 'But to whose court-martial are you alluding?'

He eyed me sidelong. 'Possibly the officer-of-the-watch, who may have given the wrong wheel-order. But certainly Commodore Dangerfield who, as senior officer present and captain of the offending ship, will almost certainly be very seriously implicated.' He rose. 'I wish you good night, ma'am. I can tell you no more.'

*

Not from the insufferable Forsyte, but from a kindly Chief Petty Officer who had once served under Father and was now working in the shore signal station, I learned that the flotilla – now depleted by one – was returning to Malta at its best speed and was expected at first light.

It may be imagined what I made of the night that followed. My great blessing and consoler was my maid Annette, who insisted on staying up with me and brewing tea in large quantities until dawn came. We sat in the small saloon and sipped tea through the dark hours, while she diverted me with anecdotes of her life as a child in the slums of Stepney. I was put in mind of Jack's account of his childhood, but the circumstances were not comparable; his was the story of a loving, united family, but poor Annette told of a deserted mother who finally had recourse to gin for her means of surviving the appalling calls made by eight half-starving children upon her slender mental and physical faculties. The mother brought to an early grave, it was left to Annette, the eldest daughter, to bring up her siblings – which, reading between the lines of her laconic, throw-away account, she performed most satisfactorily and with good humour. In this manner did she help me to pass the long night, until the darkest hour when the soul most easily flies from the body in death, followed by the thin shaft of chilly dawn that heralds the life of a new day.

And from out of the morning, from our vantage point on the *Gloria*'s bridge, we looked through telescopes and saw the flotilla of (now only) five torpedo-boat destroyers approaching the Grand Harbour.

*

There was no *Hasty* to fumble the moorings of the group; as if in mockery of the previous occasion, the five ships came to their buoys as one. Scarcely had they made fast than a boat put out from the leader and shaped course towards the *Gloria*. I scanned those aboard and easily picked out the tall figure of my father. In vain I looked again in the hope of sighting the one man in the whole world I next most wanted to see – but my sire was accompanied in the stern-sheets only by a powerfully-built sailor whom I recognised as his personal servant, one Able Seaman Hopwell.

As the boat drew closer and swiftly moved alongside the companion ladder and Father was the first to step out, I saw with a pang of alarm and pity that his right arm was heavily bandaged and in a sling.

I met him at the top of the companionway and he enfolded me in his single arm.

'Dear Faith, how are you? I suppose you have been worried – but quite unnecessarily, I assure you.'

'Oh, Father, I've been half out of my mind. How are you? You look so tired. And your arm. . .'

'A simple fracture,' he assured me. Oh, and he did look so tired. I never saw a man so utterly beaten down by sheer weariness; it was

85

as much as he could do to keep his eyes open and the smile that never left his lips as he addressed me must have cost him an effort out of all proportion to the result – which was like the rictus grin of a corpse.

'To your bunk with you, Commodore, sir!' The stalwart Hopwell – who out of hearing of other members of the crew, frequently treated my father like a nanny or a schoolmaster – gave me a covert wink of reassurance and, taking his high-ranking charge firmly by his good elbow, led him for'ard to his cabin.

Five minutes later, Hopwell returned. Again he winked assurance at me – a constant habit of his and not one to which I could possibly take offence. A stormy petrel who had been advanced and broken more times than he could remember during his wild naval career, the ageing Hopwell had finally fallen on his feet in becoming Father's servant; the former – with the prescience that was so typical of him – having spotted something of worth in the other's character that no one – possibly not even Hopwell himself – had ever known to exist.

'The skipper hasn't slept a wink since the accident, ma'am,' he confided. 'Stayed on the bridge all that day and all the night through. Drove himself to keep his hands on the command. And he was the last to have his hurts dressed. Wouldn't let the sick bay tiffy touch him until all the rest had been tended to.'

'What about the accident, Hopwell?' I asked. 'Exactly what happened out there?'

The honest craggy face was suddenly washed of expression, the watery blue eyes looked away. 'Sorry, miss, but the flotilla's under orders not to speak of it to anyone,' he said. 'Nor is there to be any shore leave until after the board of enquiry – and that's to begin at noon today. With your permission, miss, I'll stay aboard here, wake the Commodore, tend to him, dress him in his best and escort him ashore to Navy House on time for the enquiry.'

'Of course, Hopwell,' I murmured – absently, because a notion had just come to me.

I went down to my cabin and wrote a short note to the one man whom I could not get out of my mind:

SY 'Gloria'
Malta, 22 June 1911

Dear Jack,
I was so shocked to see Father's state. I do so hope that you are well and
unhurt. Please come over at your earliest opportunity and tell me all that
has happened.
Yours very sincerely,
Faith

I then sent for the duty boat's coxswain and instructed him to take
the letter over to the *Hecuba* and deliver it personally to Lieutenant-
Commander Cummings . . . and to wait for a reply.

*

Annette brought me coffee and biscuits at 10 o'clock. I was at my
favourite place on the poop deck, nor had my eyes left the distant
lean shape of the *Hecuba* since our boat had gone over there. Half an
hour later, it still remained tantalisingly tied up at the TBD's
ladder.
I thanked my maid, while my eyes never left the object of my
entire attention.
Half-way down the coffee cup, I laid it aside and sprang to my feet
as our boat came away from the *Hecuba* and shaped course towards
us. I greeted the coxswain as he came over the side; he was carrying
an envelope.
'You've been a long time,' I said, taking it and slitting it open.
'Sorry, miss, but the officer said to wait till he'd writ the reply.
Reckon it must be quite a long 'un.'
It was by no means a long reply, though it is possible that Jack
Cummings took a long while over its composition: I could imagine
him, with his precise mind, throwing away several drafts:

HMS 'Hecuba'
Thursday, 22 June 1911

Dear Faith,
Thank you for your letter and the good wishes. I am well and unhurt.
As to visiting you at an early opportunity, I have to attend the board of
enquiry, together with the Commodore, to give evidence at noon.
In view, moreover, of possible developments, it may be prudent if we do
not meet again for the time being. Believe me, this will be for the best.
Kindest regards,
Yours very sincerely,
Jack

87

The guarded warmth of the letter did not conceal from me the certainty that something was terribly wrong.

It came to me then that I was trapped within a surrounding wall of silence, while outside the wall things were happening; lives were being bent, changed, perhaps destroyed – but I was totally shut off from all knowledge of these happenings and could rely only upon speculation . . . and vague murmurings from the recent past.

Jack Cummings:	'. . . a few snags that we discovered . . . we'll get them ironed out – in the end!'
Von Schleicher:	'. . . exercising at sea seldom goes according to plan . . . a very dangerous plaything.'
Jack again:	(When I had begged him to look after himself and Father during the manoeuvres.) 'Why did you say that, Faith? *Do you know something you should not?*'

I was still turning over these matters in my mind when, at about half-past eleven, Father came on deck with Hopwell ambling at his heels like an amiable bulldog. Dressed in his navy-blue frock coat with medals, dress epaulettes, aigulette and sword, he looked every inch the Nelson of the twentieth century as he was regarded by so many. Not for the first time, I wondered at his remarkable capacity for renewal: a short rest had quite restored him to his usual self: bright of eye, alert as to manner, quizzical, with a touch of high good humour, the tired, hurt man who had climbed aboard a few brief hours earlier was a ghost who had been laid to rest in his cabin.

He greeted me again with a fond kiss. 'Well, Faith dear, we're off to settle this unfortunate matter,' he declared. 'A few words from me will put things to rights and, smoothing out a few misunderstandings, the whole distressing business will be laid to rest, I'll wager a thousand guineas on it. I think I will have a small tincture before we depart and you, Hopwell, shall join me. Ring for the steward, will you?'

He smiled and patted my cheek. 'Cheer up, dearest,' he said. 'You look as if you are attending a funeral, instead of being present at a really positive step forward in the history of naval tactics – for that's the issue at stake this morning, I promise you.

'Ah, here comes the whisky. Help yourself, Hopwell. You won't join us, my dear? Then I pledge you. You also, Hopwell.'

'And you, sir,' responded the other. 'And Miss Dangerfield.'

The whisky drunk, Father took up his cap, kissed me and followed his servant to the gangway.

I watched them being taken ashore, and wondered at my father's splendid manner in the face of what had seemed to me to be – remembering the comments of the odious Lieutenant Forsyte – positively fraught with hazard.

Did Father carry himself with the courage of true conviction, I asked myself; or was it simply gallantry bordering on bravado?

*

It was late afternoon when he returned. I was taking a small sherry in the small saloon, having unsuccessfully tried my hand at passing away the time with a novel and then some embroidery.

The first thing that struck me was that he had been drinking. And he went straight to the drinks table and poured himself a bumper measure. Only then did he face me.

'Hello, Father,' I said. 'How did it go?'

I scarcely need have asked; it was written plainly on his face.

'It went . . . badly,' he replied. And I saw then to my relief that, though drunk by most people's standards, he was well in control of himself and articulate. Indeed, as time progressed, he proved himself to be not only articulate but also eloquent.

'How badly?' I asked him.

'This badly,' he replied. 'I am to be court-martialled. The charge being that I did "wittingly and by gross and compounded negligence hazard my ship and those ships under my command". I think I have the phraseology right. They phrase rather well, don't they – the faceless beings in their well-appointed offices who rule our lives?'

'Father, how could this have happened – to you, of all people?' I cried. 'Considering the regard in which you stand. The high promises predicted for you. It's – absurd!'

'They will try to make it stick, the faceless ones,' he said, recharging his glass. 'For they are afraid, and I am the sort who keeps 'em awake nights by feeding their fears. So I must be destroyed!'

'Destroyed – oh, surely not, Father! There is no question of your career being broken, surely?'

'They will try,' he said. 'They think they can procure evidence to support my so-called gross and compounded negligence. And they will produce witnesses to support the evidence.'

'Witnesses – who?' I demanded. 'Who would bear witness against Commodore Dangerfield?'

'My officers.'

'Oh, surely not, Father!'

'They have no choice. They will be summoned. . . put on oath. . . questioned.'

'And will tell the truth!'

He smiled sadly, self-mockingly. 'The truth, I regret, my dear Faith, will not in this case necessarily make me free.'

'Why – *why*?' I pleaded.

'Because I have transgressed against the system, dear,' he replied. 'I have taken risks where others would have been prudent. Accepting that, for all our pageantry and protocol, we of the Navy are really in the business of killing, I have had the effrontery to proceed along those lines. And now they want my skin.'

He drained his glass and went over for a refill.

'But I shall confound them!' he said. 'Yes, I shall beat them at their own game. Where would Nelson have got – what would Drake, Frobisher, Hood, Rodney and Howe have achieved – how could there have been a victory at Trafalgar followed by a hundred years of Pax Britannica – if the likes of Freakley and the rest of the drawing-room admirals had ruled the Navy in the old days?'

'When is the court martial to take place, Father?' I asked.

'As soon as possible,' he replied. 'These weighty matters – like destroying a stormy petrel – can't await the elegancies of time. A week. Less, at a guess. Perhaps a few days. Time for the members of the court to get their frock coats out of mothballs and crowd in for what they hope will be an easy kill.'

He was not to be shaken from his iron assurance, nor would he explain to me in layman's terms exactly how he had so transgressed as to be brought to his present pass.

For the details, I would have to wait for the court martial.

It was then that, for the first time, I wondered if Mrs Chalmers, his . . . fiancée, had heard of my father's predicament. And what she thought of it.

*

Father was right in his summation and the court martial was set for the following Monday morning at 10 o'clock. As the chimes of the quarter-hour rang out across the city, I presented myself at the main gate of Fort St Elmo, that star-shaped stone monolith guarding the extremity of the promontory dividing the Grand and Marsamxett harbours. There I presented to the Royal Marine captain in attendance the letter of admittance which, by a special dispensation of the Admiral Commanding, had – as I understood – been sent to various interested parties, permitting them to witness the hearing.

A marine corporal was ordered to escort me and I was led down cool stone corridors, past gun slits in the walls that looked out across wrinkled blue water far below; up innumerable stone steps worn by the feet of time, to a balcony that looked down to the floor of a spacious chamber. There was seating for perhaps fifty persons on the balcony and all save a few places were already occupied, mostly by Navy and Marine officers. There were a few women. Glancing sidelong as I took the seat indicated to me, I saw Natasha Chalmers sitting at the far end of the row behind. She must have observed my entrance, but gave no sign of having done so; dressed in a black costume and black hat decorated with ostrich feathers in the same funereal hue, she gazed expressionlessly ahead and down – down into the well of the court, where a party of neatly turned-out naval ratings were laying pens, pencils and paper before a row of six chairs set at a long, green-baize-covered table.

At ten precisely, a door at the rear of the court-room opened and six frock-coated officers entered and took their places at the table. Some of them I knew. The most senior, a four-ring captain whom I took to be the President of the Court, was a stranger to me. There were, of course, none of my father's flotilla officers among them.

Then commenced a kaleidoscope, a pattern of words and movement, much of which was totally incomprehensible to me. I only had eyes for the main protagonists: the legal and professional naval terminology drifted over my head and only touched upon reality when the to-ing and fro-ing of the arguments seemed to favour, or to disfavour, the defendant.

But I digress. . .

Next into the arena stepped my father, looking quite marvellous so that I wanted to shout out: 'How can you sit in judgement on this fine man, who is worth any ten of you?' With him was his old friend and fellow polo-player, Nicky Mattei, a Maltese aristocrat and a practising member of the Maltese bar. He it was whom Father had chosen to represent him at the hearing; indeed, the two of them had spent the entire weekend at the palatial villa belonging to Nicky's mother on the south side of the island, working on the defence.

Nicky, rising to his feet after the President of the Court had made his preamble ('. . . in accordance with the Naval Discipline Act of 1866 and the power vested in this Court . . .'), acknowledged that he was, indeed, the Most Noble Count Mattei, counsel appearing for the defendant – and very fine he looked in his black legal gown offset by the shock of flowing grey hair and Roman profile.

The prosecutor was a Lieutenant-Commander of the naval Judge-Advocate's department named Copper-Johns. He read out the charge of witting, gross and compounded negligence and summoned his first witness:

'Call Lieutenant Richard Jobling.'

Dickie came forth, faced the members of the Court and took his oath upon the Bible.

'You are Lieutenant Richard Frayne Jobling, Royal Navy, lately commanding officer of HMS *Hasty*, now sunk?'

Yes, he was, and I had never seen him look so young, so vulnerable, so totally out of place. He seemed like a small boy caught and cornered while stealing apples from a farmer's orchard, who would have wished himself anywhere else on earth.

'Describe the order which emanated from the flotilla leader immediately prior to the collision.'

'It was a simple order to break off the attack on the target . . .'

'The target, for the purposes of the exercise, was the German cruiser *Darmstadt*?'

'That is so.'

'Describe the nature of the order.'

Dickie did his best to explain exactly what one was supposed to do on receipt of the order, but only succeeded in further confusing me at any rate. A simple demonstration on a blackboard would have served better, but I suppose all the members of the Court were familiar with the manoeuvre anyhow, and Dickie's description was a mere formality.

'Is this manoeuvre much performed nowadays, Lieutenant?'

'No, sir.'

'Why?'

'Well, for one thing, it's a bit – . . .'

'Doesn't leave one much room for error, would you say?'

'Mr President . . .' Nicky Mattei rose. 'The prosecutor is leading the witness in making a conclusion.'

'I withdraw the question,' said Copper-Johns and sat down with a tight smile on his lips. He had made his point – and it had registered with the court; all six members were writing busily.

Nicky took over, cross-questioning the witness:

'In the years of your naval career, Lieutenant Jobling, lately as captain of your own ship – how many years in all?. . .'

'Six years, sir.'

'In those six years, how many times have you seen this particular manoeuvre carried out – and with success?'

'More times than I can remember,' responded Dickie with the joyful air of a boy who has been handed a big red apple on a plate.

'Thank you, Lieutenant.' Nicky sat down and smiled sweetly across at his glowering opponent.

I carefully exhaled a silent sigh of relief, for it seemed to me that Father's case had certainly been strengthened by Copper-Johns' failure to damn the particular manoeuvre as some archaic folly long since discarded – which I took to have been his intent. And Mrs Chalmers appeared to think so too; I cast a quick look in her direction, and saw the ghost of a satisfied smile on her lips.

The members of the Court were quietly conferring together, those more junior members on the wing seats having risen to stand around the President. After a short discussion, they returned to their seats and the President nodded to the prosecutor to carry on.

'I call Lieutenant-Commander Cummings.'

Jack came in, looking every inch the corsair and reminding me of the image he had conjured up in my imagination when we fought through the squall on our way back from the Blue Grotto. He radiated firm confidence and I was heartened to discern it.

Having been sworn in and identified himself, he faced the prosecutor's first question:

'Commander, what is your general opinion of the manoeuvre carried out at the close of the attack – as practised by the flotilla under Commodore Dangerfield's command?'

'It is a most useful and prudent way of disengaging after an attack.'

'You would employ it on your own initiative?'

'Unhesitatingly. It offers, in my opinion, the best means of rapid withdrawal after firing one's torpedoes and. . .'

'The Court is not interested in your speculations, sir. Just confine yourself to the facts of this case.'

Jack coloured up at this and I would not have given much for Copper-Johns' chances if he had attempted such rudeness when they were alone, out of uniform and not engaged upon the King's business. . .

The questioning continued, mostly relating to technicalities which, since I had but the haziest concept of the manoeuvre in question, were pure Greek to me. All the while, I studied the faces of the men at the long green-covered table, trying to gauge their reactions and the direction of their affiliations. It seemed to me that of the six, about four seemed to be 'pro' and two 'anti' the case for the defendant. One of the latter was quite clearly the President himself. Most of the others — all of whom I knew — appeared to regard Copper-Johns with frowning suspicion.

As for Father, I could see only the back of his head and the forthright, square set of his broad shoulders, which inspired me with complete confidence.

My attention was now drawn to a new and more comprehensible turn in the questioning:

'In short, Commander, was the manoeuvre — as performed by the flotilla under Commodore Dangerfield's orders — carried out in exactly the same terms as recommended in Fleet Instructions?'

After a moment's hesitation, Jack replied, 'Yes — with some amendments.'

'What were these — *amendments*?'

'There were adjustments of speed and distance between columns.'

Copper-Johns made a great play of exasperation, sighing deeply. 'Commander Cummings,' he said at length, 'you are not assisting this Court by prevaricating. That is no answer to the question. What precisely were these adjustments of speed and distance between columns?'

'The speed. . .'

'Yes?'

'Was to be increased from 18 to 25 knots.'

'And the distance between the two columns of three?'

'Reduced by one-third.'

'In your opinion, Commander, were these amendments prudent?'

Nicky Mattei was leaping to his feet. 'With respect, Mr President, is it permissible for this officer to criticise the orders of his superior?'

'The question is permitted,' responded the President woodenly.

'I repeat the question,' said Copper-Johns. 'I am waiting, sir.'

'In my opinion, the amendments were not prudent.'

A buzz of excited comment in the visitors' gallery was silenced by a harsh admonition from the President that would clear the Court if such a disturbance was repeated.

'Did you express this opinion at any time to Commodore Dangerfield?' demanded the prosecutor.

'Yes.'

'Many times?'

'Several times.'

'And his response?'

'He . . . made no response.'

Another sudden flurry – instantly quenched – earned the gallery a swift glance from the President.

'Commander Cummings,' said Copper-Johns, 'what were the weather conditions when the flotilla commenced the simulated torpedo attack upon the *Darmstadt*?'

'Calm sea. Light airs.'

'Visibility?'

'Variable.'

'Particularise, please!'

'There was a light, drifting sea-mist, which occasionally obscured a view of all the ships in the two columns.'

'Think very carefully before you answer this, Commander – was the ship leading the other wing, the ship steaming parallel to the *Hecuba* at a reduced distance, the *Hasty*, visible to you at all times?'

'At most times.'

'At *most* times! Was she visible to you at the moment when Commodore Dangerfield gave the order which would cause both ships to turn towards each other and lead their columns in the opposite direction?'

It was then, and only then, that I properly understood the essence of the notorious manoeuvre which had brought my father to this – and I could have screamed aloud to Jack Cummings to remain silent.

'The *Hasty* was – intermittently – not visible about that time.'

'Thank you, Commander,' said Copper-Johns. 'I have no further questions, Mr President, sir.'

All eyes were upon my father, who was scribbling a note which he then passed to his counsel. Nicky Mattei read it, nodded and rose to speak, adjusting his gown more closely about his shoulders, coolly tossing his splendid mane of hair.

'I have no questions to put to this witness, Mr President,' he said pleasantly. 'And I call the defendant, my client Commodore the Honourable Myles Dangerfield, Royal Navy.'

With steady, slow paces, Father walked to the witness' chair, swore his oath and sat down. His expression was calm, composed – as if he were sailing his racing yacht in the Solent.

'Commodore,' began Nicky, 'we have heard much about this particular manoeuvre and your amendments to the terms recommended in Fleet Instructions. Do I take it that these published instructions are precisely what they say they are – not mandatory orders, but merely guidelines?'

'That is so, sir,' replied Father. He smiled. 'You see, the tactic of a mass attack by a formation of high-speed light craft using torpedoes against a capital ship has never been employed in actual warfare. We are, so to speak, proceeding pragmatically – learning as we go.'

'And to what conclusion – or conclusions – has your own pragmatic approach led you, Commodore?'

'To the conclusion – one – that the attack must be delivered at high speed, to confuse the enemy's gunfire. Two – that the attack must be on a narrow front, with both columns close together, for full effect. Three – that the high speed must be maintained during the withdrawal, further to confuse counter-attack.'

This all seemed very reasonable and Nicky Mattei took the opportunity – or so it seemed to me – of consulting his brief for a few moments, in order to allow his client's words to sink in. Scanning the line of officers at the table, listening to the muttered comments of the people around me, I had the clear impression at that moment that Father had the sympathy and support of both Court and onlookers.

Nicky Mattei resumed, 'I see, Commodore. And you would have no hesitation in repeating the manoeuvre tomorrow – using every possible precaution, of course.'

'No hesitation whatsoever,' declared my father.

Nicky sat down and Copper-Johns rose to cross-examine. He began in honeyed tones.

'Sir, you tacitly agreed with your counsel – though you did not say as much – that you would use every possible precaution in repeating the manoeuvre, were you to do so tomorrow. Am I correct?'

'Quite correct.'

'Commodore, what is the maximum recorded speed of an H-Class torpedo-boat destroyer?'

'The maximum recorded speed carried out during trials over a measured five miles in the Solent, was 28 knots.'

'That was, no doubt, under special conditions, with the manufacturer's engineers in charge?'

'That is so.'

'It would be more accurate to say, would it not, that 25 knots under normal working conditions would be nearer the mark?'

'Yes.'

Copper-Johns stared at my father for a full half-minute in real or simulated disbelief and incomprehension; during this time the latter returned his gaze, quite unperturbed.

The prosecutor's voice, when he resumed, was strained with a note of incredulity – soft at first, but gradually increasing in impassioned crescendo as he released a tirade of denunciation at the man before him.

'I think I have it correct,' he said. 'You have pragmatically arrived at a conclusion whereby you choose to lead your ships – at their *maximum* speed, with the recommended distance between columns *reduced* by one-third – to the attack. This you do despite the repeated protests of your experienced senior subordinate officer. You give the order for the inward turn, knowing that the margin of error is only a matter of feet – and yet, on making the turn, you can only intermittently *see* the *Hasty*! This you do even at the risk of your ships, or of killing and maiming your men! And this you do in peacetime!

'*And you have the effrontery to tell this Court that you take every possible precaution?*'

Father leapt to his feet, his face working. For some time, while the hubbub filled the chamber and the President hammered in vain for silence, one could not hear the defendant's words.

And then, in the silence, 'That is not a fair comment,' said my father. 'The thinking behind my actions – what you might call my philosophy of attack. . .'

'The Court is not interested in your philosophy, sir,' responded Copper-Johns, 'but in your actions on Wednesday the twenty-first last. I have no further questions to put to the defendant.'

He sat down.

*

'I think I made my point,' said my father. 'That chap Copper-Johns is a typical trimmer, who twisted my words and motives out of all belief. Well, now it's up to the Court and we shall see what we shall see.'

'Yes, Father,' I whispered against his shoulder.

They had given us a small waiting-room where we could be alone together while the Court was debating its verdict. After the prosecutor's devastating tirade, when I had sensed, seen and heard sympathy for the defendant melt like snow before the summer sun, Nicky Mattei had risen to re-examine his client and had made a valiant attempt to mend fences all round – but to no avail, so far as I could see. The glaring discrepancies between what my father had actually done as compared with his unguarded admission of taking every precaution to safeguard ships and men, simply did not match up.

'And when I think of what Cummings told them!' I cried. 'That – that *Judas*!'

'He said what he had to say,' replied Father mildly. 'You cannot fault the chap for giving an honest answer to a straight question under oath.'

'He could have – oh, he could have been more *diplomatic*!' I persisted. 'But to stand there and blandly betray you, betray you, over and over again. . .' I began to cry and he held me more tightly.

'I'm not much good at offering comfort,' he said. 'It is a pity Natasha isn't here with us now, she would know just what to say.'

Obviously he had not seen her up in the gallery and assumed that she had not attended the hearing. I made no attempt to disabuse him; let the Chalmers woman go hang; she had only come to the Court to keep watch over what she might well consider to be her investment for her future. I was more concerned with the appalling way in which Jack Cummings – whom I had permitted to slip under my guard and lay siege to my heart – had wantonly betrayed Father in his hour of need, when all that had been required of him was to stay silent.

For Father was ruined – I knew this as certainly as if I had already heard the delivery of the verdict. No matter that he might hope, against all likelihood, that his 'philosophy of attack' had swayed the court in the end, I was inclined towards the view which he himself had expressed when he returned back aboard the *Gloria* after the findings of the board of enquiry. . .

The 'faceless beings' were out to destroy him.

*

Not twenty minutes after retirement, the Court announced that it
had reached its verdict and Father was summoned. I arrived back
on the balcony in time to see the six grave-faced judges file to their
places at the green-baize-covered table. Father was seated, but rose
upon their entrance as did we all. Glancing sidelong, I could see
nothing of Mrs Chalmers but her sable plumes; she at least was
determined to be in at the kill – or whatever.

All were seated. The President of the Court took up a single sheet
of paper, adjusted his pince-nez and, calling upon my father to
stand, read out to him as follows:

'You, the accused, are found guilty as charged and are sentenced
to be deprived of your command and severely reprimanded. This
sentence is subject to confirmation by the Judge Advocate of the
Fleet. The court is adjourned *sine die*.'

The six judges went out. Amidst a babble of voices, the people on
the balcony took their seats again, some of them craning down to see
how my father had taken the blow: he was still standing and gazing
before him, shoulders squared. Nicky Mattei reached out and,
taking his friend by the elbow, murmured what must have been a
few words of consolation. Father nodded.

I looked round to see how the Chalmers woman had taken the
deprivation of her chances to enter the aristocracy and the very
highest social circles; for she knew as well as I, or anyone present,
that the sentence was the death blow to my father's career: all that
lay ahead of him, if he did not resign his commission or opt for
premature unpaid retirement, was at best a slate-grey future as
commander of some obscure shore station.

Her seat was vacated: Natasha Chalmers had left.

*

I had ordered a carriage in advance, but there was some confusion
outside and the press of people did not permit the horses to come
through. Bereft of carriage, I gazed around for a sight of Father and
found myself looking into the impassive face of Jack Cummings.

'I am very sorry,' he said.

'Please!' I looked away.

He laid a restraining hand on my arm. 'I think you must hate me,' he said.

I blazed round at him. 'Please, sir, do not tempt me to express what I feel for you at this moment. I have quite enough on my mind without the added burden of remorse that I might feel at some date, should I tell you what I really think of your actions today. So please leave me be.'

'I imagine you regard my actions today as those of a cad and an outsider,' he said. 'Am I right?'

'You should know best what motivated your actions,' I breathed.

'But let me hear it from your own lips,' he persisted. 'I would prefer the truth.'

I drew a deep breath. 'Very well, sir, you shall have it! I regard your treacherous abandonment of my father as an act which no true officer and gentleman – as *I* understand the term – would have contemplated for one moment. Rather than betray and ruin his commander, an officer and a gentleman would have kept his silence as a matter of honour, of conscience. No matter at what cost to himself.'

He gazed at me evenly, unflinchingly, in the face of my utter contempt. 'And that is your testimony?' he asked. 'Given on oath?'

'It is.'

He smiled: it was a rueful, sad smile. 'So you see, we are both in the same boat,' he said. 'When confronted with the need to tell the truth, we mostly react in the same manner – ladies of high upbringing and outsiders both. We are constrained, sometimes against our better natures, to speak the truth, no matter how destructive it may be.

'Good-bye, Miss Dangerfield.'

He saluted, turned on his heels and was gone. His tall figure was soon swallowed up by the crowd.

MAYFAIR

London – Autumn 1911

FIVE

'There's two gentlemen called, ma'am. Asked to see the Commodore.'

'The *Captain*, Annette,' I said patiently for the umpteenth time. 'When my father took his retirement, he reverted to the rank of captain. Do please try to remember, for he gets so fussed about it. You were saying – two gentlemen? What gentlemen?'

'They didn't say, ma'am. Just asked for the master of the house.'

'And my father has already gone out?'

'Left for his club at half-past ten as usual, ma'am. You can set the clock by him.'

'Did these gentlemen leave their cards?'

'No, ma'am, for they've not gorn.'

'Not gone?'

'They asked, if the master of the house weren't in, to see the lady of the house. I said as how you wasn't up yet, but that I was just going to take up your breakfast. So they said they'd wait, and I put them in the morning-room.'

'Did you?' I said, amused. 'Well, they're in for an unconscionable long wait – whoever they are – while I have my breakfast, read my letters, bath and dress. I hope they are not terribly busy gentlemen.'

We both laughed.

It was autumn and the leaves were falling in Hyde Park across the way. We had sailed from Malta in the *Gloria* mere days after the fatal court martial; Father had not even waited for confirmation of the verdict before severing the ties with his beloved Service; it was an act in which I sensed his profound bitterness against the 'faceless ones' – though not towards the Navy which had been his whole life, his sole endeavour.

As for Mrs Chalmers, she never appeared after the court martial and I am sure that she and Father did not meet, though a certain letter which was delivered to the *Gloria* by hand may have been from her – in any event, he went around all that day with a set face and spoke only when addressed. Assuming – as was confirmed much later – that this was her way of breaking off the attachment, I discreetly did not allude to the wretched woman, nor did Father do so in my hearing.

With regard to Jack Cummings, I was suffering greatly from the shock of his betrayal and resolved to quench all thoughts of what had been – and what might have been – between us. It would not be easy, this I knew; the memory of our meetings and of what had sprung up between us would not be put aside easily. However, I had the weapons of disillusionment and contempt to strengthen my determination and to help excise certain images which were best forgotten. . .

Armed with my new resolve, I threw myself into the social life which lies open to a person of wealth and breeding.

Father and I returned to England, first to our house in Park Lane, where I made what shift I could to belatedly catch up with what was left of the London season, with Ascot, Henley, a Buckingham Palace garden party – and, of course, a visit to Cowes Week. In addition to all this, Father fleshed out the more empty days at his club, to which he departed every morning; sometimes he returned for luncheon, but more often took this either at the club or at one or other of his favourite restaurants in Mayfair or Soho.

And of course, the highlight of the social year was the Coronation, when we had a grandstand view of the procession from our upstairs drawing-room windows. There followed a round of balls and parties to mark the occasion, but since Father had retired we did not receive invitations to any official functions.

The Coronation over, I swiftly ran out of ideas for amusement. I had no close personal friends, and by then had become accustomed to the life on shipboard, or in one or other of the villas and palaces that we had rented in far-flung places.

My London summer routine involved my being called at any time between 10 o'clock and midday, depending upon the pressure of events on the previous night. The only exception to this rule was my occasional – I may add, my *very* occasional – early ride out in Rotten Row, when I had the groom bring round my favourite mare Veronica from the mews at 7 am. After dealing with my post, bathing and dressing, I might pay a few calls or do a little shopping, or go for a drive if the weather was fine. Luncheon was always a solitary affair, unless Father joined me; if he did not, as often as not I read with my novel propped up against the wine cooler.

In the afternoons, I read or embroidered. Tea was my biggest bugbear, for by this time of the day – unless I happened to be taking in a matinée – a most appalling ennui would have set in. I accepted with alacrity any and every invitation to tea, no matter how boring my hostess.

The best moment of my day was when I heard Father's key in the lock, and then he and I would take a sherry or two together in my sitting-room before the dressing-bell. Sometimes he would bring one or other of his clubland friends – mostly ex-Navy – to dine with us; on those occasions, I usually felt more alone than if I had actually eaten on my own.

That, in brief, was my life as I lived it during the summer and early autumn of 1911 after our return from Malta. It was my great ambition to persuade Father to take a house in Bermuda for the winter. We had done so several years previously when he was serving in the Caribbean station, and I had greatly enjoyed the life out there.

So much for my routine – not, one might think, greatly calculated to extend one's personal resources. It brings me to that particular Tuesday morning in the autumn whose precise date, thanks to a kindly guardian angel who sometimes watches over me, I have happily forgotten.

It was like any other rising, save that there were two unknown gentlemen waiting for me down in the morning-room. While I nibbled at my toast and marmalade, Annette ran my bath and laid out my hostess gown. And I addressed myself to my post; there was a slender pile of letters and I quickly riffled through them for signs of interest.

I first looked for the familiar crest of a foul anchor or a naval crown – betokening that it was from one of my friends and admirers in the Service. My heart lurched to see one such envelope so marked on the flap, but I suffered a slight disappointment when I discovered it was only from my faithfully unsuccessful swain Dickie Jobling. He was back in England and writing from Gosport. All was well, he told me. He was at present engaged upon an entirely new activity, details of which he would give me when we met some time in the current month – when he would also take the opportunity of proposing to me again after so long an interval.

Most boring of all, in my submission, are letters addressed by the typewriting machine. There was one such, its only promise of interest the postmark: Malta. I opened it next, to find it was from Angela Dearing. She quite understood, she told me, why I had not kept our assignation at Gauchi's tea-shop, and hoped that my father and I had now happily settled down in England. It seemed that she had left Lady Borg and secured employment in Navy House as a civilian clerk-typist. She made no mention of poor Charles Knight, who was residing aboard the *Gloria* in Bermondsey dock – no doubt eating his heart out, still, for the fickle little jade he had left behind on St Paul's gentle island. I laid her letter aside with a disapproving shake of the head.

The rest of the post comprised bills and yet more bills – and the kind of tradesmen's importunities that one sensibly consigns straight to the wastepaper basket. It always puzzles me how these people manage to obtain one's name and address. For instance, how could a trader in Dublin, desirous of selling me Irish linen and Donegal tweed, even know that I was back in England – unless it was his custom to read through the society weeklies from cover to cover?

'Bath's ready, ma'am,' said Annette from the doorway and I joined her in the bathroom.

'You're not forgetting that it's me afternoon and evening off, ma'am?' asked my excellent little maid. 'And the head housemaid'll be filling in for me as usual.'

'I had not forgotten,' I told her. Then, eyeing her fondly, I asked, 'Just what do you do with yourself on Tuesday afternoons and evenings, Annette?'

'Ah, ma'am, I has the time o' me life. First it's down to Stepney, to pick up a couple of me pals. Then we goes for a tripe and cow heel supper, or mebbe jellied eels if we're feeling a bit flush.'

'And then what?' I asked, amused and intrigued.

'Next, to the Goat and Compasses near Wapping Old Steps,' she said. 'There's an Irish band as plays Tuesdays, for singing and dancing till way past midnight. It's mostly sailors fer partners. And longshoremen, who look a bit on the rough side, but I'd sooner trust a daughter o' mine with a longshoreman than any sailor born!'

I laughed. 'Annette, it all sounds most tremendous fun,' I said. 'I'm sure you and your friends will have a better time at the Goat and Compasses tonight than I shall have at Lady Muriel's boring bridge and supper party.'

She eyed me smilingly, arms akimbo and a clean warm towel over one shoulder, all ready for me when I stepped out of the bath – every inch the lively Cockney sparrow.

'You want to come with me one Tuesday, ma'am,' she said, and I was amused and curiously touched to see that she meant it quite seriously. 'I worry about you, ma'am, I really do. Stuck here alone in this big house, with only the Commodore – beg his pardon, the Captain – to keep you company when he's home, which ain't often. Think about it, ma'am. You'd be welcomed by me and the gels.'

'Thank you, Annette, that's very, very kind of you,' I said, and had a sudden and almost irresistible compulsion to cry.

*

I was dressed and ready to go down when by chance my eye fell upon an unopened letter lying by my bedside – obviously one which had fallen out of the pile unnoticed. I picked it up. It was a brown paper envelope – my absolute bottom bench-mark for a boring letter – and addressed in typewriting. I put it in the pocket of my hostess gown and went to beard the two unknown gentlemen whom I had kept cooling their heels for the past three-quarters of an hour.

Our morning-room in Park Lane had french windows which looked out on a charming high-walled courtyard, whose ivy-covered brickwork shut out all sight and sound of the nearby houses and created a strong impression of its being the corner of an elegant country property – an effect which was heightened by a noble fountain in the centre, with a grave-faced Roman matron pouring her sparkling libation from an amphora into an oval pool where fantailed goldfish darted in and out of the shadows.

'Good morning, gentlemen. I am Miss Dangerfield. I am sorry my father was not here to see you, but is there any way in which I can help matters?'

As I saw what they appeared to be doing, I was thunderstruck. 'Good heavens!' I exclaimed. 'Will you kindly tell me what's going on here?'

They were men in their middle years, respectably rather than elegantly dressed; both with a touch of the commonplace and already wilting slightly before the hard edge of my outraged tongue.

In fact I scarcely needed to be told what they were doing – they were listing and labelling pieces of our furniture. Indeed, I now made sense of something I heard just when I was entering the door of the room, and before they discerned my presence:

'Number sixteen – one ebonised cupboard with ormolu decoration, glass-fronted. . .'

I was answered by the taller, slightly older and obvious senior of the two intruders. He fixed me with a bovine stare, part-truculent, part-defensive, but mostly self-assured.

'There's nothing you can do to help us, ma'am. But if you were so inclined, you could help yourself by discharging the commitment.'

'Who *are* you?' I demanded.

'Bailiffs, ma'am.'

Bailiffs!. . .

Bailiffs I had read about in the press and in the pages of the more sensational novels they sent me from time to time from the lending library; bailiffs were what happened to *other* people – never in a million years to the Dangerfields. The very notion was risible. Why, then, was I not laughing?

'But . . . this is ridiculous!' I cried. 'What do you mean by the commitment?'

He took out a sheaf of papers and flourished them. 'All done legally, fair and square, ma'am,' he said. 'The creditor has applied to the Court and paid his fee and the Court has levied execution. We – that is to say, my colleague Mr Griswold and me – are empowered to enter your premises with or without your permission, through an unlocked window if need be, and to break down any internal doors if necessary. We can then impound your goods to the value of the debt which, if not paid off within five days, we will cause to be sold off by auction. Hope I make it plain to you, ma'am?'

'But – this debt?' I cried, bemused. 'What debt can you possibly be speaking of? *We* don't have *debts*!'

He raised an eyebrow at that and consulted the papers in his hand. 'A matter of £1,250 owed to the agents of the ground landlord of this property,' he said.

'But this house is ours!' I cried.

'Ninety-nine-year leasehold,' he corrected me. 'Plus a ground rent of the aforementioned sum payable annually. And now ten months overdue.'

'A mistake, clearly,' I said, suddenly much relieved . . . though how I could have let this ridiculous man get under my guard was quite absurd. 'I will pay it straight away,' I added.

'Well, that will be very satisfactory,' he responded. 'Save a lot of trouble and upset all round, ma'am. Our trouble and your upset.' He uttered something half-way to a chuckle, as if he had said something amusing.

I crossed to the bureau (which, I was slightly disturbed to notice, was now embellished with a label bearing the numeral 12), and took out a cheque-book. When I had written out the cheque at his dictation, I passed it over and felt constrained, so relieved was I, to offer excuses for our small transgression.

'My father and I have only recently returned from Malta, you see? And everything has been in rather a turmoil. To some degree, we are still living out of suitcases. Quite, quite disorganised. . .'

He took the cheque and scrutinised it; then, turning to his associate, he said: 'Make a note, Mr Griswold. Cheque number D1237-dash-25, drawn on Porter and Newman's Bank, Leadenhall Street.'

'Well, that's that,' I said brightly. 'Now you can remove these labels and go. Good day, gentlemen.'

The senior of the two shook his head. 'No, ma'am,' he said. 'The numerical designations . . .' he mouthed the term again, savouring it on his palate, 'the numerical designations must remain until the cheque has been honoured. The items for disposal are already entered in Mr Grimwold's notebook under their numerical designations, you see?'

I could have laughed in his face at the very notion of one of the Dangerfield's cheques not being honoured. Dear Mr Clarence, manager of Porter and Newman's Bank in Leadenhall Street, whom I had known since I was a child, who had dandled me on his knee and given me sweets when I occasionally called there with Father – as if he would *dream* of not honouring one of the Dangerfields' cheques!

'Very well,' I said, resigned. There really seemed no purpose in arguing further, and it might make an amusing talking point to explain to one's visitors about the 'numerical designations'.

They left me, grave-faced; but I was rather amused by the whole matter now that it had been satisfactorily dispatched.

With a sigh, I crossed over to the table and, pouring myself a glass of sherry, took it out into the sunlit courtyard where, sitting on the edge of the fountain bowl, with a tiny thin spray of the Roman matron's spindrift gently cooling my cheek, I sipped the paper-thin wine and watched the goldfish darting to and fro in sudden alarm as they saw my shadow cast on the gravelled pool bottom.

Remembering the letter in my pocket, I brought it out and read it. The first few lines dried up my throat like a parching wind.

MADAME RITA
Milliner
Regal House, Bond Street, Mayfair
BRANCHES IN PARIS, NEW YORK,
ROME, BRUSSELS, ST PETERSBURG

Miss Faith Dangerfield   October 9, 1911
Grosvenor Mews Place,
Park Lane,
Mayfair.

Dear Madam,
We regret that the enclosed cheque, issued on your behalf by Mr Charles A. Knight on September 23rd last in settlement of your esteemed account with us, has been returned by Messrs Porter and Newman's Bank, Leadenhall Street, City, marked *Refer to Drawer*.

There has clearly been some error involved. While apologising in advance for any trouble you have been caused, we should deem it a favour if you would please send a replacement cheque for the sum involved (£109. 19s. 6d) at your early convenience.

Assuring you of our most careful attentions at all times.

We remain, Madam,
Yours faithfully,

George Meekings

George Meekings
Managing Director,
Madame Rita Limited

Having recovered from the first shock, I addressed myself to seeking an explanation for the appalling state of affairs, this Pelion piled on Ossa that had descended on me without warning from out of a tranquil if rather tedious sky.

My first rational thought, as soon as the initial panic had subsided, was that the fault lay with Charles Knight who, having the responsibility for dealing with minor transactions and the authority to sign and issue cheques from the family account, had made some kind of error in estimating the balance held in the bank. This theory I almost instantly dismissed; our good friend the manager at

Leadenhall Street would never have dealt with a minor error so harshly.

What then remained?. . .

I scarcely liked even to consider it, but was it not possible that Knight had been engaged in fraud? Was the discovery of this perhaps the 'delicate' matter which had led Angela Dearing to throw him over in such a cavalier manner? And had his concern for my father's gambling on the Stock Exchange been only a smoke-screen to mask his own depredations on the estate?

My first reaction was to summon Knight, but I decided after all to go and see him aboard the *Gloria*. Now. Immediately.

*

My carriage took me to Bermondsey dock by way of the City and Tower Bridge. The south bank, with its narrow, high-walled streets of eyeless warehouses, greatly depressed my spirits. The sight of the dear *Gloria*, proud in her navy blue sides and gleaming white upperworks, lying as she was in the scum-covered water of the dock, surrounded by grimy façades – a bright jewel in a pinchbeck setting – saddened me still further.

It was quiet aboard the yacht as I walked over the gangplank and out on to the main deck. No one challenged me as I went below, where I found Charles Knight was sitting alone at his desk in the ship's office. He looked up with a startled expression and rose to his feet at my entrance.

I wasted no time in preamble, merely threw down the milliners' letter and the returned cheque before him.

'This arrived with my morning's post,' I said. 'Can you explain it, Knight?'

For answer, he reached out and took a small pile of similar cheques from a wooden tray.

'I also had these returned this morning, ma'am,' he said quietly. 'As to explanations, I have none, but I have already written to Captain Dangerfield apprising him of the matter and requesting his instructions on how to deal with it.' He showed me a stamped envelope addressed to my father in Park Lane.

'Is there more to it than this?' I asked, indicating the pile of cheques to which I had added the one from Madame Rita.

There was a great deal more. . .

The previous day he had received a letter from our brokers, telling him that the Lloyds' underwriters had refused to re-insure the yacht, which meant that the *Gloria* could no longer put to sea.

'I was able to obtain temporary cover in respect of fire and damage whilst in dock,' he said. 'This was from a local Bermondsey insurance company of no great repute. The premium I paid by cheque – one of those returned here today, along with a cancellation of the policy.'

I crossed over to the porthole and stood with my back to him for quite a while, looking out along the dock, towards the entrance and the more appetising waters of the Thames. The river craft were moving to and fro and a duet of swans sailed grandly past.

Presently, when I felt that I had taken hold of myself and would not break down, I turned to face him again.

'Well then, Knight,' I said. 'Is there any more you could tell me? If there is, I beg you to do so. I have to know sooner or later, and I would rather be prepared.'

Yes, there was more he was able to tell: much more. Even then, though, during the telling, I had a premonition that what was being revealed to me was no more than the tip of an iceberg which, like that inanimate monster of the deep, lies in wait for the unwary and is able to rend and destroy from afar.

*

Past midnight. I had 'chucked' Lady Muriel's bridge and supper party, which had been no wrench. No doubt Annette and her friends were by now enjoying the last of the Irish band at the Goat and Compasses. It was still as the grave in Park Lane. The rest of the servants were in bed; I had even dismissed the butler, telling him that I would greet my father on his return with the customary night-cap of whisky and seltzer.

And I waited. . .

A far-off church clock chimed a quarter-hour and this coincided with the rattle of cab wheels in the street outside, soon followed by the somewhat fumbling sound of Father's key in the front-door lock. He came in, still wearing his silk hat tipped jauntily over one eye, the edge of his opera cloak draped negligently over one shoulder, silver-knobbed cane tucked under one arm.

'My dearest Faith,' he said, surprised. 'It was very sweet of you to wait up for me. How was Muriel Ponsonby's party?'

'I didn't go,' I replied. 'Sit down and I will pour your drink.'

'No, no, no!' he strode over to the table. 'What will you have, my dear?'

'Nothing, thank you.'

Whistling quietly under his breath, he began to pour himself a whisky and seltzer and made an unconscionable chink and clatter of it. And then – quite suddenly – the chink and clatter stopped, the whistling ceased.

'What in blazes is *this*?' he cried. And I knew that he had sighted the 'numerical designation' attached to the table.

'Don't you know – can you not guess, Father?' I responded. 'You should, surely!'

Slowly he turned. And his face was dead, as if it had been carved out of wax.

'How much do *you* know, Faith?' he asked in a surprisingly mild tone of voice.

'Quite a lot, Father. But, I suspect, not by any means all.'

Leaving his glass untended upon the table, he came over to me and, reaching out, touched my cheek so softly that if my eyes had been closed I could only have imagined it. This gesture of ineffable affection I might well have rejected right up to the moment I saw his face when he turned to regard me; but in the light of his reaction to my declaration – that of mildness and a heartrending sadness – I was quite defeated and became once again the adoring daughter whose father could do no wrong, his every action being bent towards my well-being.

'Dear Faith,' he murmured. 'In the nature of what I am, I have been very foolish and I hope you will find it in your heart to forgive me . . . when you have heard my sad tale.'

'I forgive you unheard, Father,' I whispered, laying my hand upon his that still rested against my cheek, my slow tears rolling down on both.

He knelt beside me, my proud father who once had commanded men and ships and had been marked for the highest honours. And he told me his story. . .

*

Gambling, as I had suspected during the night hours, was at the heart of it. Their mother's family had brought in the taint, with which, thank heaven, I was not infected. Grandmother had lost her husband's legacy in Monte Carlo and on the racecourses of Europe.

Father and Uncle James, his brother, while striving their level best to emulate her in their own particular milieu of the Stock Exchange, the Paris Bourse and Wall Street, had been unable to come within a mile of matching the efforts of their maternal exemplar – while nevertheless being unaware of the extent of her losses. When Grandmother died, the brothers had high hopes that her part of the inheritance would extricate *them* from certain losses – but there was no inheritance, only inherited debts.

Somehow the Press was falsely advised regarding the Dowager Lady Dangerfield's will and a scandal was averted. The two brothers paid off their mother's debts and set out to re-establish their own fortunes in the only way they knew; only to sink further and further, in the course of the years, into a descending spiral of the kind of loans and credits readily available to gentlemen of rank, influence and professed riches; until in the end they both fell completely into the hands of the moneylenders.

'It was the late King,' said my father, 'who introduced poor James to the group – themselves members of a larger syndicate – who had greatly assisted Teddy when he was Prince of Wales and Queen Victoria kept him short of the tin to support his racehorses, his yachts and his mistresses. For five years and more we were both kept afloat on the backs of these . . . gentlemen.

'Now, however, they have taken a closer look at our prospects and it is pretty certain that my recent débâcle has been a prime factor in their decisions. In short, they have pulled the rug from under us, poor Jamie and me. And the jackals – the bank included – have smelt the wounded game and are moving in for the kill.'

'And the crew of the *Gloria* along with them,' I added. 'Before long they will be pounding on our door for the three months' wages they are owed – all fifty of them! And then there will be harbour dues at £150 a day since we docked in June, together with massive bills for coaling owed in Malta, Gibraltar, Lisbon and Southampton . . . As well as foodstuffs, wine and chandlery.'

'You've been talking to Knight,' said my father.

I told him what I had been doing that day. 'Knight is a true friend and servant,' I said. 'Since he is the only one remaining aboard the *Gloria* when all the others have deserted, we simply must pay him, Father.'

He rose to his feet and looked down at me with an expression of misery beyond belief. There was also something else – the air of a man who has violated a code by which he has lived, or tried to live, all his life.

'There is not even enough in the kitty for young Knight,' he confessed. 'I went along to the club tonight, borrowed a pony from a friend – and lost it all at faro. And I swear that I set out to get the money to pay my private secretary.'

I stared at him, wide-eyed, unbelieving.

'Father – can things really be *that* bad?' I demanded. 'Do we have nothing left at all?'

He answered me, ticking the items off on his fingers as he dealt with them one by one: 'Broadly speaking, everything is either mortgaged to the last penny, or the deeds are held as security against loans. That disposes of this place, Mondisfield, the Hôtel d'Orléans, Nice and Frinton. And, of course, the *Gloria*. . .'

'Oh, not the *Gloria*!' I wailed. 'Not *her* – that's too awful!'

'So much for real estate,' continued Father implacably. 'There are then promissory notes out to the tune of three million, which are supported only by what might be called my good name.' He gave a mirthless chuckle. 'By an irony,' he added, 'if I had made a better job of sinking the *Hasty*, I could well have been dismissed the Service instead of quitting, in which case I might have been eligible for a half-pension.

'That's about the size of it, Faith dearest. There is nothing left but Carey Street for both me and poor Jamie. He is in a similar situation to myself, and we both have only ourselves to blame.'

'Oh, Father – Father!' I fled to his arms and laid his head on my shoulder, his cheek against mine. 'Things can't be all that bad! We shall win through somehow. Why . . . we're Dangerfields, aren't we? We can keep going long after everyone else has given up and gone home – that's what you always used to say to me when I fell off my pony Bimbo and the rest of the hunt had gone on without me.'

He nodded and patted my head. I think he may have been crying a little.

'It would be a kind of elegant convention to express thanks that your mother did not live to see this day,' he said at length. 'However, I cannot subscribe to that pious platitude. If she had been alive, probably this would not have happened in the first place, or if it had she would have buckled to and restored some kind of order in that miraculous way of hers. I tell you, Faith, your mother would have petitioned the Monarch if all else failed, to restore the Dangerfields' fortunes. She was quite indefatigable and had no brief for gamblers. During the five idyllic years that we were together I never so much as laid a penny wager, my hand on it.'

'Tell me about her – tell me about my mother,' I asked him, drawing him by the hand towards the sofa. 'You speak of her so rarely and I scarcely know a thing about her – save that you and she were obviously desperately attached.'

He leaned back in his seat and a reminiscent smile softened the harsh lines of strain in his face. 'We met in Venice,' he said. 'A romantic novelist could scarcely have contrived it better.

'I was on a month's leave from the Mediterranean fleet, and had decided to go off on my own instead of carousing with my shipmates as usual, in the fleshpots of the littoral. I intended to seek the quiet life of sun, scenery and a gentle dip into things cultural. The desire to pursue culture left me during my first meal in my hotel, a charming palazzo at the entrance to the Grand Canal with a view across the lagoon to S. Giorgio Maggiore on its islet. The object of my attention was a beautiful young woman sitting at a table opposite. With her was an elderly man whom by his rapt attention to this divine creature, I took to be her aged husband. You may imagine my chagrin – not to mention my indignation – at seeing such beauty and grace thrown away upon this surely lecherous old millionaire, for such was my essentially romantic nature that I had dressed them both in the trappings of characters in a cheap novelette. In the event, he turned out to be her godfather, a resident at the hotel whom she was visiting; a more delightful person I have never met. Furthermore, he quickly understood that my feelings for his god-child were returned. It is not putting it too high to say that the old fellow acted as Pandarus to our Troilus and Cressida – but I think the guilt must lie lightly on his ancient bones.

'There followed an idyllic month, during which time the two of us explored Venice, the islands of the lagoon, the churches, museums, picture galleries, palaces, restaurants and cafés . . . everything! Needless to say, by the end of this time we talked of nothing but our forthcoming marriage and the long and perfect life we should lead together – a timeless extension of our Venetian idyll.

'There were only five years separating our vows and her death, and there was never such happiness. There was you, my darling Faith, and you were the bright pendant to our perfection.

'Then one day she – she fell ill. Very, very ill. . .'

'Father!' I whispered to him, putting my hand on his lips. 'No more – please.'

He nodded. 'There is one thing more,' he said, 'and it is easy to tell. When it was all over, her godfather took me aside and said, "You must never regret or repine, my boy. You gave her five idyllic years and a beautiful child-image of herself. If she had lived for ever, she could never have known more happiness!" '

*

We talked far into the night's dark hours, my father and I – and some word or chance phrase concerning my mother was never far from his lips. He never spoke of her end, but it was clear that her illness was swift in its onset and that she was moved to a nursing home where she subsequently passed away . . . that much I gleaned from things he let fall.

Only once during that heart-to-heart was a jarring note struck, and that was when the issue of his short engagement to the Chalmers woman arose and was instantly dismissed by him as of no importance. Seizing upon the opportunity, I nevertheless pressed the point and made a wild guess:

'Father, tell me – and please don't gloss over it – did you offer marriage to Mrs Chalmers solely on account of her fortune?'

He was silent for a while and then gave a mirthless laugh that told of a mind at odds with itself, where an admission of expediency comes up against a barrier of self-contempt.

'I could answer that straight and say "Yes", my dear,' he said. 'The lure of Natasha Chalmers' millions most certainly loomed large in my mind – the more so because it was quite apparent to even the meanest intellect that she was attracted to me by my social position and that my presumed wealth scarcely came into her calculations. The thought of her millions as a cushion against bankruptcy was a certain comfort but it was even more complex than that. As recently as our last days in Malta, when the moneylenders were already rattling their sabres, I still had hopes of making a big coup on 'Change. We dyed-in-the-wool gamblers, you see my dear, we never ever quite lose faith in the miracle that we are convinced is waiting to happen just round the next corner!'

'Does Mrs Chalmers know all this?' I asked.

'When I took my early retirement,' he answered, 'I wrote to her and told her what I was doing, not mentioning my financial situation.'

'And she replied?' I framed it as a question, though I had good cause to guess the answer.

'Yes, she released me from my promise of marriage without any discernible note of regret: Natasha was only interested in being a *Lady*.'

'You were much put out, Father – by the lack of regret on her part?'

He nodded and I knew that at least we were near the truth – so far as it really mattered to him. 'Yes, I think so,' he said. 'I am of an age – a man with a grown daughter who soon must flee the nest and leave me alone – when the company of a vibrant, attractive and younger woman offers considerable temptations.'

And then came the frank admission that surely must have set him free of the past: 'It's not given to all of us, Faith – the ability to live one's entire emotional life on memories alone.'

*

By morning, I had a clear notion of what I must do in the light of our imminent, not to say omnipresent, financial collapse; it was certain now that the 'numerical designations' would *not* be removed from the furniture, and that the bailiffs would be round again in the time it took for my cheque to be returned. I would find myself some gainful employment, I decided, and with this resolution came another: until I had secured myself a position, I would not say a word about it to my father – who would certainly veto the notion.

The Times – I had seen the columns of that excellent journal in which offers of employment featured at great length; though always in the past, let it be said, one had glanced at them only as a traveller in a strange land looks upon the odd activities of the alien natives. The following morning, over breakfast in bed, I scanned the 'Positions Vacant' which, now that I addressed myself more closely to this column, I found to be much slighter than had been my previous impression; the 'Employment Required' section was five times as long.

Presently, I found what I thought I needed:

EMPLOYMENT AGENCY for LADIES OF REFINEMENT Openings available in Business and Commerce. Apply: Miss Jervis, 3rd Floor, 18–20 Oxford St. Office hours 8.30 till 7. No Gents, please.

Dismissing Annette that morning, I took some trouble over my toilette and particularly with regard to my choice of costume. Settling for a sensible grey silk suit – the skirt not too hobbled – a plain fox fur stole and a hat of modest dimensions, and wearing the very minimum of jewellery, I set out at about ten-thirty and, dismissing the idea of a carriage, walked up Park Lane and along Oxford Street to the agency – quite a distance.

The premises of Miss Jervis's establishment comprised a tiny waiting room and an office beyond. When I tapped on the outer door, a voice from beyond bade me take a seat and wait to be called. Five minutes later, the emergence from the inner sanctum of a young woman who made her hasty exit in tears did nothing to raise my spirits.

Miss Jervis was a lady of uncertain years, her hair piled up in a chignon with wisps forever falling down; she wore pince-nez and had the kind of expression that I always associate with this aid to vision. She was dressed in a skirt and blouse; no jewellery. She gazed at me from head to foot, putting a price on each item of my clothing.

'Please sit down,' she said eventually. 'Name?'

'Faith Dangerfield – Miss.'

She wrote it at the head of a form. And then, 'Address?'

'Grosvenor Mews Place, Park Lane.'

This won me a very straight look, in which I discerned something very like incredulity, if not disbelief.

'Experience?'

'I have no experience of business or commerce, but I have played an active part in the running of my father's several establishments, also of his yacht, since I came of age.'

Quite a long pause was followed by another straight look, then in a rather faint voice: 'What schooling, Miss Dangerfield?'

'I was tutored by governesses at home until I was fourteen, then spent three years at Lady Veniton's Academy near Bath. I was to have been "finished" in Lausanne, but managed to persuade my father to let me join him on his tours of duty – he was in the Royal Navy, you see, but has now retired.'

Miss Jervis, who seemed throughout this catechism to be completely at sea about me and my pretensions, suddenly appeared to comprehend my motives for appearing before her – or so she supposed. . .

'Ah, I have it now. Your father having retired from the Navy, and you being at what one might call a "loose end", you are looking for an activity to occupy your leisure hours. Correct, Miss Dangerfield?'

She seemed to have it a little wrong and I hastened to put her right on one small point: 'Yes, Miss Jervis – but for *money*.'

'Ah, yes,' she agreed, in an all-girls-together manner. 'A little pin-money never comes amiss.' She twinkled at me from behind her pince-nez and produced from a folder a sheaf of papers. 'Have you thought to invest in a small business suitable for ladies like yourself? Here are details of a flower shop in the Strand: *'Partner wanted, active or sleeping. Highest references required. £500 capital investment required.'* Now I happen to know, Miss Dangerfield, that the present owner is a titled young lady and she. . .'

'I have no capital!' I blurted out.

'Oh!' She looked disappointed with me.

'I am. . .' I sought around for the right word to cover my situation, but since I had never had use for any such this did not come easily. Then I remembered a term that my father had sometimes applied to others:

'I'm stony-broke!' I declared.

The effect was immediate; the slightly patronising, not to say ingratiating manner was switched off like an electric lamp and she glared at me as if I had been a gipsy woman at the kitchen door selling clothes-pegs.

'In that case, Miss Dangerfield,' she said, 'I would strongly advise one of two occupations which from my experience might suit your needs. The first that comes to mind is that of governess. I have here. . .' She riffled amongst her papers.

'Not a governess!' I cried. 'I've had governesses myself and I know from first-hand what it can do to dehumanise a woman. No thank you! Not for me!'

She frowned. 'I see. The other alternative is companion – usually to an elderly lady, such as. . .'

'Not for a fortune!' I exclaimed. 'Reading aloud to some poor old dear and taking her poodle for walks. That would be like death in life.'

Miss Jervis closed her folder with an air of finality. 'It follows then, Miss Dangerfield,' she said, 'that I can do nothing for you. In my experience, the labour market being what it is, a person such as yourself – all background and no foreground, if I may be allowed the definition – is nothing but a drag on the market. So I wish you good day – and the best of luck.'

My first essay into the wide world of business and commerce not having come up to my high expectations, I went to a tea-shop off Oxford Street, ordered a pot of rose congol and a Bath Oliver biscuit, and went through *The Times* advertisements again – with particular attention to those offering specific employments. I presently found one that looked quite promising:

> COUNTER ASSISTANTS reqd. in select emporium. Good wages and conditions. Apply staff entrance Goodrich's, Victoria Street. Daily before noon.

Everyone knew Goodrich's, even I knew Goodrich's, though I would never have dreamed of setting foot in the place to buy anything: a huge department store in not very smart Victoria Street. Since it was close to noon already and rather a long walk, I took a cab there and was presently directed to the staff entrance where twenty or so women were already clustered in a corridor that smelled of disinfectant. After ten minutes' tedious waiting, a sharp-featured young man in a tail-coat came and addressed us:

'Right, will you all line up, and show your hands when I come down the line. If I tap you on the shoulder, proceed on down the corridor through the door marked "Staff Only". The rest of you can go home.'

He walked down the line we had formed and made some kind of selection, though by what criteria I had no way of guessing. The state of one's hands was clearly significant. When he came to me, I held mine out; I was, of course, wearing gloves – the only woman present so attired. He looked up at me sharply, tapped me on the shoulder and moved on.

We, the chosen – six in number – gathered in the 'Staff Only' room, where we were once again addressed by the tail-coated man:

'Now, before the final selection I'll tell you the hours and the pay. It's 8.30 am to 7 pm Mondays to Fridays, except Thursdays which is half-day closing midday. Saturdays are from 9 am until 8.30 pm. Three-quarters of an hour for dinner. Wages, nineteen and sixpence a week. Anybody not satisfied with this should leave now.'

To me, the proposition sounded dreadful if not scandalous; apparently my opinion was not shared by my companions and indeed, the two nearest exchanged raised eyebrows and nods of approval.

'Right, there will be a test of your mental arithmetic,' said our interlocutor. 'Step up here one at a time. You first.' He pointed to the woman in front of me, who went forward to the desk where he was sitting. They had a mumbled dialogue, at the end of which she went and stood to one side. From her expression, one assumed that she was 'in'.

'You next!' He was pointing at me and I went forward.

'Sixteen yards of velvet at one and sixpence-three-farthings a yard,' he said. 'Quick – in your head!'

'I'm quite useless at mental arithmetic,' I confessed.

He looked disappointed, but pushed a sheet of paper and a pencil across the desk towards me. 'Try one outside your head,' he suggested. 'A bonnet at seven and sixpence-three-farthings; five yards ribbon at twopence-ha'penny a yard; spool of cotton at a ha'penny. Total?'

I was soon wading through a morass of figures. The trouble was that I had never had experience of calculating farthings! He put up with my incompetence for a quite considerable time.

'Sorry, it's beyond me,' I confessed at length.

'That's a disappointment,' he said. 'I had high hopes for you.' He really did look very sorry.

*

'What you have heard downstairs is quite true, Annette. All true. We're broke – and there is no money to pay the servants.'

She had shyly approached me on my return from the fiasco of trying to find employment.

'I thought as much, ma'am, when them fellers came yesterday – they was just like the fellers who came to our next-door neighbour when she couldn't pay her rent 'cos her old man was in chokey. What you going to *do*, ma'am?' She looked most concerned for me and near to tears.

'Well, I have been looking for work, Annette,' I told her. 'But, would you believe it? – *no one wanted me!*'

'I'd believe it, ma'am,' was her surprising declaration. 'I'm sorry, but it's got to be said. You ain't used to work. It shows in your hands, your clothes, the way you think, the way you talk. You ain't cut out for it, ma'am. No boss in his right mind would give you a look-in.'

I nodded; her views coincided with my recent experiences. 'I tried

an agency,' I told her. 'All they could offer was a post as governess
or lady's companion.'

'Pooh!'

'Quite!'

'Mind you,' she said, 'you could find yourself a billet if you didn't
aim too high, roughed your voice up a bit, kept your wits about you,
an' looked for chances to work your way up, like. It's been done
before. Kitchen skivvy to housekeeper in five years – that was Lizzie
Fairfax and she's housekeeper at a posh hotel now.'

I could have wished to emulate the meteoric rise of the egregious
Lizzie Fairfax, and said so.

'Perhaps you would help me with my accent, Annette,' I suggested, half in jest. 'Turn me into a Cockney.'

'Be glad to, ma'am,' was her response. 'After all you've done to
advance me, it's the least I can do in return.'

'But you'll be leaving me.'

'Not till you're fixed up, like.'

'Where shall you go?'

'To be another lady's maid, I expect – if I get a good reference
from you, ma'am.' She grinned cheekily.

'You will have the best reference a girl could hope for, Annette,' I
promised her. 'And I'll do better than that – I will personally recommend you to each and every lady in society who is without a maid at
this moment. How's that?'

Instead of answering, she clutched at my sleeve as if to silence me
and cocked her head to one side, listening.

'What is it?' I whispered.

'It's the newspaper lad calling out "Extra",' she said. 'And he just
shouted something else. . .'

'EXTRA! – EXTRA! ' I heard it quite clearly. And the announcement was followed by something that was quite unintelligible
to me, if not to my companion.

'*Oh my gawd!*' she cried and, turning, she fled the room.

I heard her running footfalls descending the stairs, heard her fling
open the street door and rush outside.

She returned more slowly, and I was waiting for her on the land-
ing as she came up to me with the newspaper in her hand. Her face
was a mask of grief – but the grief was all for me.

'I'll read it to you, ma'am,' she said. . .

' "Peer's Suicide. This morning, Lord Dangerfield's valet found

123

his master unconscious in his bath, having cut his wrists. Lord Dangerfield, 51, died on the way to hospital. His brother, Captain the Hon. Myles Dangerfield, succeeds to the title." '

I began to tremble, so that I was obliged to hold on to the banister for support. One thought only teemed through my mind, and I gave tongue to it:

'Father!' I breathed. 'Father – you *must* be stronger than Uncle James! For both our sakes, Father. . .'

*

Stunned by the news of Uncle James's suicide, I was sitting alone in the drawing-room awaiting Father's return when Annette announced a visitor.

'Who is it, Annette?' I asked.

'She wouldn't say, ma'am.'

'Wouldn't say? That's very odd. What is she like?'

'She's a lady, ma'am.'

'But wouldn't give her name?'

'No, ma'am.'

'Well, the last thing I wish to do at the moment is to be agreeable to strange visitors, but you must show her in.'

Annette departed.

Footsteps sounded in the hall. I caught my reflection in a pier-glass and automatically patted a stray hair back in place. The thought of my uncle's death had already nudged aside my speculations about the strange visitor, whom I dismissed as a small nuisance to be disposed of as quickly as possible.

Annette opened the door and stood aside to admit the newcomer.

She was all in red: red-plumed hat, a red silk frock and surtout, pointed red shoes peeping out from under a skirt so hobbled that it must have cost her a mighty effort to walk. And she looked divinely lovely – a Gibson girl brought to life.

'Dearest Faith!' said Natasha Chalmers. And before I could raise a hand to prevent her, or step back beyond the compass of her touch, she moved quickly towards me and planted a kiss on my cheek. 'How is my dear stepdaughter-to-be?' she asked.

The shock of her outrageous question stunned me to silence and I could only stand and stare; could only watch her as she paced across the room, paused in front of the pier-glass and touched her side-curls, adjusted her hat, stroked the line of her corsage.

She turned to me with glittering triumph in her eyes. She was holding a newspaper – *the* newspaper that carried the account of my uncle's suicide. As she tapped it with a red-gloved finger, a diamond bracelet on her supple wrist winked a million lights.

'So now you are an "Honourable", darling,' she said. 'And I shall soon be a Lady.'

I found my breath at last. 'Mrs Chalmers, you must be insane,' I said. 'Be so good as to leave.'

She shook her head, smiling, tight-lipped.

'No, my dear,' she responded. 'Your father is mine for the asking. After his disgrace in Malta I was less than happy with the arrangement, for there are plenty of fish in the sea – as the saying goes. However, things have changed for me now.'

She began to stalk up and down the room, a pantheress on the prowl – predatory, restless, with an inner fire which she was almost unable to contain.

'Malta is finished with me and I with Malta,' she said. 'I behaved with a certain indiscretion. I refer to the little *affaire* which prompted you, my dear, to set that down-at-heel snooper on my trail. Lady Freakley and company finally sniffed me out, more's the pity, and I was totally ostracised by those niminy-piminy old baggages. So I left – for fresh woods and pastures new. To tell the truth, I was at a loss.' She tapped the newspaper again. 'But this splendid and fortuitous announcement changes everything and I have come to renew my engagement to your father, my dear. I shall condescend to become Lady Dangerfield!'

SIX

The sheer effrontery of the woman's assault upon my senses had by this time dissipated the worst of its effect and my head began to reassert control over my heart. My passions cooled. I took stock of the creature before me and I knew my way ahead with her.

'Quite aside from your total disregard for the fact that this has become a house of mourning,' I said, 'and that your appalling declaration is in the most execrably bad taste, I doubt very much, Mrs Chalmers, if you would wish to marry my father – always supposing that he would have you – when you know the truth of our present state.'

If I thought that I had a stick with which to beat her, I was greatly mistaken. The words were scarcely out of my mouth before she gave a short dismissive laugh.

'You mean that the Dangerfields have run out of tin?' she said. 'All the world knows that already; it's even whispered in Valletta. So your papa is a penniless baron? There are many such around. The new, smart way out of the dilemma is to marry an American heiress. They are all at it. Many's the baronial castle that owes its new battlements, modern heating, electricity, refurbished water garden, restocked game preserves and so forth and so on, to the proceeds of some beef empire in Illinois or Texas.

'The Dangerfields are broke? I will restore their fortunes. And my price will be the title.'

'My father would never stoop so low!' I cried, my resolve ebbing away like a retreating tide from a shore.

'Little fool!' she sneered. 'I assure you that in Malta I had your noble parent eating out of my hand. Grovelling at my feet! I played him like a salmon on the end of a line. A tug here. . . a slight release of the line there. . . and all the time bringing him in to shore.'

'You're lying!' I cried. 'My father could never be won over in that disgusting and humiliating fashion!'

'What rubbish you do talk,' she sneered. 'Why, I had only to nod my head and your dear father would have ousted Glendon Hawick and shared my pillow there and then. Marriage or no marriage.'

'*Never!*' I almost screamed the word. 'My father is a man of honour! A gentleman! He would never, ever. . .'

By now she was in a paroxysm of laughter at my words and I stared at her, robbed of speech, as she rocked to and fro with her hand pressed to her side, tears of uncontrollable mirth streaming down her exquisitely painted cheeks.

Presently, when the spasm had passed and she had dabbed away the tears, she looked at me with such withering scorn as would have reduced me to nothing if my inner resolve and high indignation had not sustained me.

But her next utterance penetrated even my guard: ' "Man of honour"?' she snarled. ' "Gentleman?" What do *you* know of men? *You mincing little virgin!*'

In the silence that followed I heard my father's footfalls in the hall, then the door opened and he stood on the threshold. There was a copy of the newspaper in his hand and his expression told me that this was the cause of his untimely return from the club.

'Faith, I suppose you have heard. . .' he began.

And then he saw her.

'Why, Natasha. . .' he said.

She was upon him in the instant. It was so cleverly done – no enveloping of arms and abandonment of kisses; she simply took him by the hands and, gazing earnestly up into his eyes, spoke to him in her low and tremulous voice:

'Myles,' she breathed. 'I saw the news and came straight here. How awful for you. And for darling Faith. If there is anything I can do, my dear. *Anything*. . .'

'How very kind of you, Natasha,' he responded. And to my horror he stooped and kissed her cheek.

We remained standing. The electric tension which had been generated between the Chalmers woman and me hung about the room like the smell of asafoetida. One sensed it in her particularly, for she could not keep still, but throughout the conversation that followed felt obliged to pace up and down, sometimes moving over to the window to look out, and now and again – a recognizable compulsion in an excessively beautiful woman – pausing by the glass to satisfy herself that she still was what she believed herself to be.

'A tragic business,' said Father. 'You didn't know him well, Faith, but there was more – much more – to your Uncle Jamie than the rather unprepossessing image that he chose to present to the world.'

I made no reply.

'I think it's tragic – *tragic!*' vouchsafed Mrs Chalmers. 'My heart goes out to you, Myles.'

'I appreciate your concern, Natasha,' he replied. 'I really do.'

From behind her assumed air of gravity there then appeared the lightest trace of coquettishness; so light that it seemed to me that only another woman could have discerned it, and one would have guessed it was lost on Father.

She paused in her restless pacing and faced him, one hand on hip.

'So now we must address you as Lord Dangerfield, Myles,' she said.

Father shrugged.

'I am not entirely *au fait* with the procedure in these matters,' she said. 'Are you summoned by the King to swear fealty before your elevation to the peerage becomes official?'

'I doubt it,' said Father. 'I very much doubt if the King would wish to see me, considering the circumstances.'

'Indeed?' she said. 'How odd.' The touch of coquettishness vanished and in its place there came something else. Was it a certain anxiety, I asked myself?

'Not so very odd, Natasha,' said Father. 'It's all part of the pattern. For instance, I made my usual application for admittance to the Royal Enclosure at Ascot, but received a polite note of refusal from His Majesty's representative.'

'How shocking!' she cried. 'Why was that?'

'The reasons for vouchers of admittance being withheld are never explained,' said my father. 'Surely *you* must know that.'

'Oh,' was her only rejoinder.

'Touching also on matters social,' continued Father, 'Faith and I have noticed a distinct dearth of invitations recently. This is really very sad, for my daughter is very sociable. And although she was presented at Court, she seems to have been dropped from most hostesses' lists. The Duchess of Beauclaire, for instance, did not invite her to her daughter's coming-out ball. And Amy Beauclaire is

Faith's godmother. It is quite uncanny how the word gets around. When one is dropped, one is dropped completely. And for ever.'

It was grotesque – for me at any rate, knowing the extent of her scheming – to see the underpinnings of that woman's arrogant self-confidence falling away from her. There was a discernible physical change. For the first time, I noticed that she had the beginnings of a double chin and that there was a certain pouchiness around her eyes.

'Is this because of your . . . finances, Myles?' she asked.

'Not solely, by any means,' replied Father. 'Oh, to be an un-discharged bankrupt – as I am – is not the best credential for acceptance in high society, as you must know. But in my case there are . . . other considerations. My court-martial, for instance, will exclude me from the Palace for ever, since His Majesty – himself a former serving naval officer – is known to take a very strong line in these matters and must certainly have pricked my name in the Retired List as *persona non grata*.'

'Oh,' she murmured. And again: '*Oh*.'

'One may play ducks and drakes with one's life, my dear Natasha,' said my father, 'but one must not also expect to shine in Society. You must have noticed this in Malta, for example, which is a very closed society such as we have here. Do you follow me?'

She followed him all right! Her face turned ashen pale beneath the expensive enamelling and she bit the corner of her lip.

'I must be going,' she said at length.

'I would advise it, Natasha,' agreed my father. 'At any moment now, we may expect an invasion from the gentlemen of the press. There is nothing that excites Grub Street so much as an aristocrat down on his luck, particularly when the story is spiced with such unfortunate indiscretions as suicide, adultery and suchlike. You must have noticed the phenomenon. Yes, I would strongly advise your immediate departure. To be featured in the kind of tales which will certainly be spread all over the headlines tomorrow – even in the minor role of a dear friend and consoler in time of grief – must certainly become a stumbling block in the way of your upward progress in Society. Now, do you have a carriage, or shall I instruct my butler to call you a hansom?'

'I will arrange my own transport!' she snapped and swept towards the door. Father was there first, however, and opening it for her. The look that she flashed, first to him and then to me, had an almost physical impact of hatred.

Alone together, I met my father's eyes and saw that they were brimming with amusement.

'My poor brother, your Uncle James, would have enjoyed that little scene,' he said. 'Jamie had a quite unsuspected fount of wry humour in him; his particular pleasure was to see the mighty laid low and the arrogant put down.'

I took his hands.

'Father, I have said this before,' I told him. 'But you really are the most wonderfully perceptive person I have ever known. And to think that for one awful moment I really thought she was going to snare you!'

*

It rained on the day of Uncle James's funeral. After three solid weeks of fine weather, one would have thought that kindly fate might have looked upon the unhappy man with a little more favour.

Once, in Paris, my nursemaid had taken me for a drive on a fine afternoon to visit the grave of one of her relations at the cemetery of Père Lachaise. It was the first cemetery of my acquaintance – and I could have wished it to be my last. Intrigued by the rows of astonishing dolls' houses that scored the cypress-hung hillsides, and enchanted by the lovely wreaths of flowers and the immortelles under their neat glass domes which adorned the doorsteps of the little houses, I declared that I should like to live there. I was four at the time . . . but the memory is still quite fresh.

It was when Hélène explained to me that the houses – some of them really quite enormous, with turrets and towers, spires, stained-glass windows as in churches; some with their porches supported upon the heads of sad-faced ladies in nightgowns – were not inhabited by dolls but by dead people, that my childish enchantment was changed to the darker side of the imagination – a compulsive fascination that only children know.

'Are the dead people inside sitting in armchairs? . . . If you lifted me up, I could see inside that window – lift me up, Hélène – please! If you won't lift me up, I shall run away. . .'

And I did. While her back was turned I darted behind one of the mausoleums, down a narrow pathway that lay beyond, under a fringe of trees and out through a maze of smaller tombs to . . . a freedom of sorts.

When I heard Hélène's frantic cries they only added fuel to my firm endeavour – which was to distance myself from all interference and find a dead person's house with windows so low that I could look inside and see them sitting there, or – delicious and scarifying thought – with a door unlocked, so that I had only to knock and walk in.

Presently the sounds of Hélène's pursuit died away into silence. Presently, all too soon, it was borne in upon me that I was lost – a circumstance which did not greatly alarm me at first . . . until I saw the lady and gentleman by the door – the *open* door!

They were incredibly old and dressed all in black: black top hat and black bonnet with veiling that covered the face, black frock, black pantaloons, black gloves. And they were standing at the open door of one of the 'houses', so that I could clearly look inside and see what appeared to be some kind of bijou chapel. No armchairs. Perhaps dead people did not sit down most of the time: perhaps they were able to walk around . . . to open doors. . . .

Talk!. . .

'What are you doing all alone, little girl?' – this from behind the heavy veiling of the 'dead' lady's hat.

I ran. I was still running when my footfalls led me out on to a wide carriage drive, where I narrowly avoided going under the hooves of a pair of beplumed black horses pulling a glass coach. People crowded round me; soon I was sobbing my heart out on Hélène's shoulder and pleading with the distraught nursemaid to take me home.

I have never willingly entered a cemetery again, and since it was unheard of amongst females of my class to attend even the funerals of relations save in the most exceptional circumstances, it is a resolve that I am unlikely to break very often. For it has to be said that although I now know about the configuration of mausoleums in general (and French ones in particular) and am aware that the elderly couple in mourning had entered the 'house' to pay their respects to the dead loved ones lying beneath the little chapel, I am sometimes able to persuade myself – on a dark night when I am alone in an empty house, or perhaps when my footsteps lead me too far on a country walk and I am reduced to a long traipse back in the gathering gloom – *that they were inmates coming out!*

*

Father and I were in the carriage immediately behind the hearse as it went up Highgate Hill in the rain.

'You should not have come, my dear,' murmured Father. ' 'Tisn't proper – and there'll be gawping crowds, I wager a thousand, after the damned newspaper Johnnies have been at us.'

I looked behind; there was only one other carriage following, and that contained the solitary figure of Uncle James's faithful valet Symonds, who had discovered his dying master. My father's brother had long lived as a recluse, without lovers or friends – and now we had no living relations.

'I had to come with you, Father,' I responded, squeezing his arm. 'The idea of you facing this ordeal with just old Symonds. . .'

'It looks quiet enough,' he said, glancing at the empty streets about us, all in the teeming rain. 'The weather will keep away the more determined of the ghouls, I shouldn't wonder. In any event, they will surely respect our feelings.'

'Respect our feelings?'

I could have laughed aloud. We could anticipate no respect from the great public – not if the response of the local and national press was any indication.

The morning following the news of Uncle's death – and only shortly after Natasha Chalmers' departure – the reporters began to hold Grosvenor Mews Place under siege. The very lightest refusal to admit them, or even to answer the door to them, seemed only to add fuel to their apparently righteous fury: they climbed railings, camped out in the front area, pressed faces to shuttered windows; moreover, they attempted to suborn the staff by offering large sums of money for what they described as 'hot stories', or even photographs of Father and me. On the eve of the funeral, after Annette had laundered some of my small-clothes and hung them out to dry in the little kitchen yard, she returned later to find them gone – presumably stolen by a 'souvenir hunter'.

As to the matter contained within the newspaper reports, I need only mention a few to indicate the tone of calumny lightly wrapped in hypocrisy.

By some means, within hours of my uncle's death they had found out about poor Grandmama's financial peccadillos and the two brothers' long slide down into penury – as exemplified by the head-lines:

DEAD PEERESS GAMBLED AWAY MILLIONS . . . THE SECRET LIVES OF PEER AND NAVAL LEADER . . . £17,000,000 TO NOTHING – IN 20 YEARS!

There were pictures of all of us, gleaned from heaven knows where, even a Kodak of me taken in Frinton when I was about sixteen, wearing a sailor dress and hat. The legend underneath read 'The Hon. Miss Faith Dangerfield. After an upbringing in the lap of luxury, she faces a future of dire poverty.' This was notable not only because it was the first time I was referred to as an 'Hon.' in print, but also because it was my first acceptance that Father's elevation had raised me to that dizzy height!

To add to this rubbish, they had scoured more grimy depths to show my father's court-martial in a false and most unsavoury light:

WHAT REALLY HAPPENED TO HMS *HASTY?* . . . QUESTIONS TO BE ASKED IN PARLIAMENT . . . DID THE NAVAL ESTABLISHMENT CONCEAL TRUTH BEHIND MALTA COURT-MARTIAL? . . . INDEPENDENT MP DEMANDS ENQUIRY. . .

All that was bad enough; but worse – far worse – were wicked lies and half-truths dressed up as indisputable fact and put out by the notorious and sensation-seeking weekly scandal sheet called the *Thames Examiner*, owned by the muck-raking newspaper tycoon Lord Bathchurch. A few samples from this paper will suffice to justify the unease I felt as we mounted Highgate Hill that rainswept afternoon:

Under the heading THE TRUE PRICE OF PROFLIGACY, was an article illustrated by a photo of the ship's company of the *Gloria* taken in Malta, and almost certainly obtained – presumably for cash – from a member of the crew:

'. . . a hidden tragedy appended to this story of mindless waste and dissolution may be found amongst those whose livelihood formerly depended upon these titled spendthrifts. The fifty-two members of Dangerfield's luxury yacht crew, photographed above, have not been paid for twelve months. Without warning, without so much as an apology, all fifty-two were thrown out upon the over-crowded seafaring service, where they have been unable to find new employment and have been reduced to penury. Worse – to beggary!'

The staff of Grosvenor Mews Place were similarly picked out for Bathchurch's attention:

'. . . an angry and embittered butler, housekeeper and staff to the number of sixteen are the latest victims of the Dangerfield collapse. Our reporter, interviewing a 15-year-old kitchen-maid who prefers to remain anonymous, was told that Lord Dangerfield and his daughter the Honourable Faith still breakfast in bed, take wine with luncheon and dinner, entertain regally, continue to keep a string of racehorses in training at Newmarket. . .'

And worst of all was a naked appeal to the envy, malice and uncharitableness that lies buried in the hearts of all of us, rich and poor, meek and mighty alike:

'. . . the bitterness of workless men, the anguish of their women-folk as they try in vain to shut their ears to the cries of their hungry bairns, all these call out for retribution upon the idle, the shame-lessly profligate, heedlessly wasteful, overweeningly self-exalting. . .'

And this, to me, spelled trouble.

*

As our carriage rattled through the wrought-iron gates of the ceme-tery, the only sign of spectators was a small group of people gathered close by: silent, forlorn, dripping wet and seemingly content only to stare at the hearse with its coffin, followed by two carriages.

No sooner were we in the graveyard than it seemed to me that I was back in Père Lachaise cemetery all those years before – save that the rain was tumbling down, I was no longer a frightened child and not alone. There were the same 'dolls' houses – not so large, for the most part, but many of them frantically demonstrating the solid material and spiritual worth of their inmates. We traversed by twist-ing paths to the heart of this silent place of the dead, where two workmen bearing shovels stood by the lip of an open grave but moved discreetly aside at our approach.

We alighted and the undertakers' men drew forth the coffin. Poor old Symonds, tearful, took his place beside Father and me before the open maw of raw earth.

No sooner were we in place than from out of the dripping trees about us, and in and out of the mildewed monoliths of granite and marble – between the forlorn carved angels, the broken columns – there appeared a host of people, men and women, who formed a semi-circle before us.

Rain-soaked, silent, smouldering, they watched us . . . their mind-less hatred as tangible as if one had only to reach out one's hand and feel its intractable structure. Nothing that could be done, I thought, nothing one could possibly say, would bend these people towards the understanding that we, like they, were human beings who were born, became ill, laughed, grieved, suffered and died. Amongst this crowd a couple of ill-limned, crude banners were raised:

I closed my eyes against it all.

*

There was no parson.

Only my father, hatless, advancing to the grave-mouth and looking down on the coffin below, its brass plate spelling out the bald history of the living and dying of James Arthur Joscelyn, 2nd Baron Dangerfield of Heathfield and Channock.

Tall and gaunt in the shapeless black greatcoat which reached his ankles, his fine hair plastered wetly across his broad brow, the beard not so crisply trimmed as during his naval days, but splayed out and wild-looking, he appeared for all the world like some prophet of old.

He remained in silent contemplation for what seemed an immeasurable time, while the rain came down and there was not a stir, or a murmur, from the watchers.

Presently the man by the graveside straightened up, cleared his throat and looked about him. And in that instant, I guessed his intention.

My father was going to speak: he was about to deliver a funeral oration, a panegyric upon his dead brother, in an attempt to offset the vile scandals of the press – in order, perhaps, to quench the sullen fury of our onlookers with their scrawled banners of hatred, to save his brother's grave from desecration – and us from heaven-knows-what.

And I was afraid. . .

What use could it be? Poor Uncle James was not of the mettle of which great men are made. Not even Mark Anthony, speaking through the voice of Shakespeare, could have added one inch to the stature of that rather grey man, whom I had scarcely known in my childhood save as a relation who was notoriously mean with his Christmas presents and who sulked when he lost at croquet; who wore a carnation in a metal tube tucked into his buttonhole – and who had glowered at me – a child – when I asked him did the water not spill out of the tube when he did cartwheels?

Not even Captain (late Commodore) Lord Dangerfield could perform the miracle of turning his poor, self-destroyed brother into a figure of veneration.

I closed my eyes, clasped my hands together and waited.

'There will be no prayers today,' announced my father. 'My brother was not a religious man as the world measures religious men. All his life he sought blindly for a sort of truth, but in his latter years he confessed to me – and with some sorrow – that he had abandoned all hope of finding it.

'It remains for me to speak at his end.

'My brother differed from me in every respect save one – he was a compulsive gambler. This flaw in the pair of us is an illness of the mind, often inherited. It is of the kind that, under different guises, may drive a man to drink and the ruination of his family life; or to idleness and ruin; or to the mad pursuit of power for its own sake and to the misery of millions of his fellows. *Or* – as in our case – to the irresistible compulsion to pit our wits against the great goddess Chance.

'The immutable law under which we gamblers suffer, and perish, is that we lose as much as we win in the short run – and in the long run we lose all. Our tragedy is that we refuse to face up to this immutable law, perhaps because deep in our hearts we know that the true thrill of gambling lies in the perverted thrill that comes from *losing*! There is no other explanation for the hold it maintaines over us.

'So much for what the world would call the vice that my dead brother shared with me. Now I will speak of the man who lies here, who was the companion of my young boyhood until our roads parted.

'This was a simple man. You have read of profligacy and waste, of self-exaltation. But this man was no profligate; he, who would stake all on the throw of the dice, lived simply, fed and clothed himself with frugality. Nothing was ever wasted in his house. The clothes in which he lies buried here are those he bought years ago; the cuffs of the coat carefully mended, the boots cobbled and cobbled again, the collar of the shirt twice-turned.

'He lived like a miser. But if he is to be condemned as a miser, he cannot also be condemned as a profligate. The world cannot lay *both* charges at his door.

'You have read of the armies of servants who waited upon the every whim of the Dangerfields. My brother employed but one servant in his life, and this good and faithful man stands at my back at this moment. He grieves for someone who was not only his employer, but his friend. And his old age is provided for by that friend and employer.

'My brother, you see, for all that he played pitch-and-toss with the goddess Chance – and lost – died owing not a penny. His last penny went to the goddess . . . and when that was lost, life had nothing left for him. So he arranged for his own ending – which was strictly in accord with his convictions and his conscience.

'I will speed my farewells to him with some lines by Tennyson, which are not inapposite. They come from the epic poem *Ulysses*, where the aged Ulysses is addressing his old crewmen:

> We are not now that strength which in old days
> Moved earth and heaven; that which we are, we are;
> One equal temper of heroic hearts,
> Made weak by time and fate, but strong in will
> To strive, to seek, to find, and not to yield.

My father closed his book of verse. 'Fill in the grave,' he said, 'and may the earth not lie heavy on the bones of this good man.'

*

I clung to my father, too far gone in proud tears to speak.

The crowd had departed: silently, not looking back, leaving the three of us alone by the newly-filled grave. Even the gravediggers had gone; all that remained were the tattered banners that the people had left behind.

'Only you could have done it, Father,' I whispered at last. 'Only you would have had the courage. The utter conviction.'

'Not courage, my dear. Conviction . . . yes, perhaps. It is the gambler in me, you see? I was always a better gambler than James. When James had lost all, he gave up and died – not through lack of courage but lack of conviction. I, the better gambler, still believe that the great goddess Chance – Lady Luck – has something in store for me. So I still live.

'Just as I believe that, like Tennyson's Ulysses, Jamie will find his newer world . . . touch the Happy Isles . . . see the great Achilles.'

We parted company with Symonds. The poor fellow's spirits had been greatly raised by the outcome of the funeral which he, a timid and self-effacing little man, had nevertheless steeled himself to attend despite his fears following the newspaper attacks. Now he went on his way and we set out to Grosvenor Mews Place – and whatever fate had next to offer.

We might have guessed that something odd was afoot when we

reached Park Lane and saw that, against all custom and protocol, Father's wind- and weather-bedraggled White Ensign – the same that he had flown aboard his first seagoing command to his last – was fluttering bravely from the flagstaff over the front porch. At half-mast.

'What the dickens? . . .' ejaculated my parent. 'Who put *that* up there?'

'We shall soon find out,' I replied.

Upon entering the front door (which was ajar – and that was unusual in itself), we found ourselves facing the entire domestic staff of the establishment – all fifteen, though many of them had already secured themselves new positions. They were lined up to greet us, Fox the butler to the fore.

'Welcome home, ma'am,' he said gravely. 'And you, m'lord.'

'Thank you, Fox,' responded my father in like manner.

'On behalf of the staff, m'lord, I would like to offer sincere condolences on your sad loss,' continued the butler.

'Thank you all,' we both replied.

'Tea is served in the drawing-room, m'lord.'

And such a tea! They had provided from out of their own pockets (for I knew as well as any that our larders had run short of such fare a week and more since), a most sumptuous tea for two, of the classic kind that the English of all classes regard as an essential accompaniment to a family funeral.

Nodding and smiling, they stood and watched as we took our seats by the tea trolley and I poured our favourite orange congol; they then filed out. My last view of them through the tears that were beginning to haze my sight was of their smiling faces as Fox the butler, bowing, closed the double doors of the drawing-room and left we two mourners alone in the room sadly denuded of furniture which the bailiffs had removed for sale.

In such a manner, and without any reference to it on their part, did our faithful domestic staff nail a newspaper lie.

*

It was a Wednesday morning, the day following Annette's afternoon and evening off – a convention that she continued to observe although strictly she was no longer in my employ. I had been instrumental in securing for her the post of lady's maid to an old school-friend of mine. Deirdre Vallence. This friend being still on holiday in Deauville, Annette was remaining with me until the end of the week as part maid, part companion-guest.

I was out of bed and arranging my own hair when she came in with our tray of coffee and toast which she laid down on my dressing-table. We partook of breakfast together, as had become our custom.

'How did you get on last night?' I asked.

'Splendid, ma'am,' she replied, stirring her coffee and looking at me with the arch, gamine expression she always employed when she was 'up to something'.

'Well, what is it now?' I asked, amused.

'I reckon I've found a job for you,' she declared.

'Yes?' I replied, intrigued.

'Saw the notice last night when I was on the way to meet the gels,' she said. 'Now, the way I look at it, ma'am, 'tis no use your going to some posh hotel and asking for the job of housekeeper, assistant manageress or the like, for they'd say: "We likes the look of you, Miss Dangerfield, but you've had no hexperience." That's what beats you all along the line, ma'am – you're lacking in hexperience.'

'I'm afraid you are right, Annette,' I confessed, ruefully recalling my previous encounters in the labour market. 'But as you often say, on the other hand employers won't take me on at the bottom of the ladder, to gain experience, because I'm too . . . too . . .'

'Ladylike!' She said it for me. 'Now, this job I was telling you of, they ain't looking for ladies, but if you was able to talk your way into it and start from the bottom, you'd get-experience a-plenty.'

'And rise to the top – like your friend Lizzie Fairfax,' I added, remembering the story of that notable exemplar.

'Kitchen skivvy to housekeeper in five years, that was Lizzie,' she declared. 'And if Lizzie could do it – and in my opinion she has a most unfortunate manner with dogs and young children, not to mention her squint – *you* could do it on your head, ma'am.'

I thought about it for a while. 'It would have been very much simpler if I had offered myself as lady's maid to someone like Deirdre Vallence,' I said, and heard the wistful note in my voice.

'You wouldn't have liked it – neither would Mrs Vallence!' declared my mentor. 'Ma'am, you'll have to strike out on your own as a new person, really you will. When you've climbed the ladder, when you've got to the top, like what Lizzie Fairfax did, then you can be yourself again – in Lizzie's case, a right Tartar!'

139

This sounded all very true, if somewhat depressing. 'Then tell me about this job you saw advertised, Annette,' I asked her.

'It's at the Cawnpore Hotel in South Audley Street,' she replied.

'I know it,' I said, 'though I have never set foot in the place. It's quite smart, I believe, but mainly frequented by prominent businessmen from the provinces, so I once heard. Thank heavens you didn't say the Ritz, Annette! I couldn't possibly set foot in the Ritz and ask for a position – the very doorman would fall down in a dead faint, for he has known me since I was in short frocks.'

'Well,' she said, 'the notice is outside the kitchen area at the back and I saw it on my way past. It says: "Wanted – Housekeeper's Assistant. Good Wages. Live in." There – what do you think?'

'Living in? I don't know about that,' I hesitated.

'Well, ma'am, you're going to have to find somewhere to live pretty soon, you are really. This place is going under the hammer, isn't it? Then where will you be?'

'I was thinking about my father,' I said. 'If I desert him by taking a place that offers accommodation, what will happen to *him*?'

She started to speak. . .

'What was that you said, Annette?'

'Nothing, ma'am,' she responded flatly. 'Nothing at all.'

'Well then, dear Annette – tell me what you think about this job. You know the ropes so speak to me plainly, I beg you.'

'Well, ma'am,' she said, 'to start with you'll be worked stiff, but you'll learn a lot. My best advice would be to keep yourself to yourself, like. Don't put on superior airs (not that you ever do), but don't pal up with the women you're working with. Remember, when you get on you'll be giving them orders – and it don't pay to boss folks around what knew you when you was a nobody!'

That seemed good advice to me, and I resolved to go along to the Cawnpore Hotel and apply for the position – if it was still vacant. The two of us cleared away the breakfast things and washed them up in the bijou kitchen adjoining my suite; this done, we retired to the bedroom again, where Annette folded her hands in her lap primly, assumed a schoolmarmish expression and addressed me with mock severity:

'Right! Next lesson in how to talk proper,' she announced in the manner she had come to adopt for these occasions.

'First – apples and pairs?'

'That's Cockney rhyming slang for "stairs", Annette.'

'Very good! Try – Rory O'More.'

'Door.'

'Good. How about – daisies?'

'That means boots.'

'Why?'

'Daisy roots – boots.'

And so it went on for five minutes or more, as was now usual every morning after our breakfast. Presently my instructor, seemingly pleased with my progress, proceeded to the next and more demanding part of the lesson, which was what one might have called *viva voce* composition.

'Tell me,' demanded my teacher, 'what happened to you when you got up this morning. What you did, like?'

'Well,' I began, tuning my mind and ear to the wilder strains of the Cockney accent (and I am not a bad mimic), 'oi 'ad me barf. Cleaned me teef an' washed me fice. Then oi wighted fer you to bring in me breakfuss. . .'

She broke in on my discourse, her expression affronted.

'You don't 'ave to overdo it!' she declared. 'You don't 'ave to make *mock* on us – ma'am!'

*

The lesson over, I dressed. For the occasion, Annette lent me her 'walking-out clothes', the garb of a typical London working girl on her day out. In her case, this comprised a grey cotton skirt and short leg-o'-mutton-sleeved jacket to match, a neat white blouse lightly starched at collar and cuffs, buttoned boots and a jaunty straw boater worn straight on top of one's piled-up hair and well forward. We toyed with the notion of gloves, but after some thought Annette determined that they were 'a bit too lah-di-dah'.

On the way out of the house, with my mentor's good wishes following me down the stair-well, I paused to riffle through the newly-delivered post lying on the hall table. At first glance, there was nothing of interest; only boring looking stuff in buff-coloured envelopes, all addressed to my father and most of them typewritten. And then, right at the bottom of the pile I perceived a pristine white one, reverse side uppermost with the blazon of the naval crown on its flap. I turned it over, experiencing – I must own – a distinct feeling of disappointment that it was addressed to me in Dickie Jobling's slashing hand. Slitting open the envelope, I found a thick wad of writing paper tightly scribbed upon both sides. A veritable epistle! I slipped it into my reticule, there to await an odd half-hour of the day when I could relax and discover what my old swain had been about in the months between. No hurry, no hurry at all.

There was no other communication for me. . .

*

Now the Cawnpore Hotel had had an interesting history. Built during the late Regency period, it had been the headquarters of the Prince Regent's set during the most dissolute part of His Highness's rule as leader of fashion and Society. Beau Brummell, Prinny's favourite and arbiter of dress, had fought a duel for his honour in the mews of the house and had pinked his man; the main ballroom's ceiling was pockmarked with pistol balls which had been discharged up there during one of the gentlemanly routs that marked the Regency's decadence; the later managements had taken pains not to have the holes plastered over: style is all.

The later history of the establishment was even more rackety. Around the middle of the nineteenth century, the Cawnpore had achieved a certain notoriety as a centre of gambling much frequented by the St James's and Pall Mall clubmen; it is certain that, had Father been of an age at that time, he would surely have figured largely in the hotel's history! But it was during the 1880s and 1890s that the place really achieved a reputation of solid worth, coupled with an excellent cuisine, total respectability and a touch of provincial fubsiness which characterised it at the present time – and incidentally ensured that none of the staff would know me by sight: Father, a confirmed metropolitan and cosmopolitan, despised all things provincial and would not have set foot in the Cawnpore for a gift during his heyday, nor taken any of his family or friends there.

It was before this highly worthy hotel, therefore, that I stood that morning, contemplating my enterprise. I was not known there by sight; the solitary photograph published in the press (the picture of me posed on the beach at Frinton) gave no hint of my current appearance; I had a certain expertise with the Cockney accent and dialect wherewith to disguise my customary ladylike tones. And I had decided to change my name!

*

Presenting myself to the hall porter and making known my errand, I was directed to follow a pageboy to the housekeeper's department;

this was situated on the top floor of the huge building, high in the eaves. Nor was this the end of my climb: yet another steep flight of rickety stairs presently brought my guide and me to a door adjacent to a brick chimney-stack. When the lad knocked upon the door, a deeply resonant female voice bade us enter.

It is here that I must digress and, anticipating much that followed, dwell a little upon the woman I was about to meet. . .

At first sight she was impressive, being of darkly dramatic appearance, with greying hair swept back in two scoops on either side of the head and parted in the middle – more after the fashion of the mid-Victorians than our own. She sat at a plain wooden-topped desk, with a thick ledger of sorts open before her. Upon my entrance, she looked up and regarded me from head to foot with large and surprisingly lustrous dark eyes. Her hands were long, pale and strong-looking; her face – so entirely dominated by the wonderful eyes that one took in its general appearance only at second glance – was thin and pale, strongly-boned, more striking than beautiful.

After briefly enquiring my business, she invited me to sit down, meanwhile laying aside a cigarette which she had taken from her lips. I was surprised to see this, having always associated the habit with 'fast' women; anyone less obviously 'fast' would have been hard to find. It was then I determined that – the eyes apart – the most arresting thing about her was her voice: deep, tremulous, beautifully articulated and modulated, but largely confined to the darker tones – the voice of a consumptive.

'I am Mrs Carradine,' she declared. 'And your name, you say, is Faith Fields. Have you any experience in hotel work?'

'No, ma'am,' I answered her, allowing only the slightest Cockney inflection to mask my customary manner of speech. 'But I'm very willing to learn.'

'And what employment have you had?'

'I looked after my widowed father,' was my reply which, allowing for much I could have added, was substantially the truth.

Mrs Carradine appeared to take this statement on its face value, for she nodded, tapped her cheek with one forefinger and looked absent for some moments; but the arresting eyes were soon fixed on me again.

'Do you want this position very much, Miss Fields?' she asked next.

'Why yes, I do, ma'am,' I replied, emboldened to add ,'Please, why do you ask?'

'Because it is hard work,' she answered. 'The hours are long, the pay low and some of the tasks you will be given are menial.'

(She has seen through my pretence, I told myself. I should have laid on the Cockney accent more heavily . . . and not dressed half so neatly.)

'I – I'm not frightened of hard work, ma'am,' I said. 'And I really do need the job.'

She nodded. 'Very well, Fields,' she said in a businesslike tone. 'I will take you on trial. The wages are fifteen shillings a week and all found – that is to say, breakfast, dinner and tea. You will sleep in the accommodation provided. The hours are from 5 am until 3 pm, alternating weekly with 10 am to 8 pm. Alternate Saturdays free. Do you accept?'

I nodded.

The pale mask seemed to soften and she almost smiled.

'I will show you your accommodation,' she said. 'If you can move in your traps tomorrow, you may start work on Friday.'

*

'Did you get the job, ma'am? Tell me, quick!'

Annette must have been watching for me at the window all morning; she was at the door when I mounted the steps, her eyes dancing with excitement.

'Yes, I got it,' was my reply. 'And I hope I've done the right thing. Oh, Annette, some of it sounds – and looks – pretty awful.'

'Come and have a sit-down and put your feet up, dearie,' she said, 'and then tell me all about it.'

We sat together in the morning-room, where the bailiffs had left us nothing but a chaise-longue and a couple of armchairs. As we sipped tea I gave my friend-cum-lady's maid an account of my morning's adventure, commencing with my interview with Mrs Carradine. My description of the latter greatly puzzled Annette.

'Don't sound like a *working* woman to me,' was her comment. 'More like someone what's come down in the world.'

'I think you're right,' I concurred. 'From something she let slip, I gathered that she once worked at something entirely different but had to give it up because of her health. And she's not the housekeeper, only the assistant. The housekeeper proper lives in rather grand style, so she implied, and was not likely to come into contact with the likes of me. Anyhow, Mrs Carradine showed me what she called my "accommodation". . .'

Annette looked concerned. 'Oh, dear, ma'am,' she said, 'was it?. . .'

'Pretty awful,' I replied. 'Most of the domestic staff in the house-keeper's department appear to inhabit the roof. My room – it's more like a large boot-box – is one of several in a dark corridor under the eaves. It's about a quarter the size of yours, Annette, and there's no window, only one electric lamp. The bed's quite reasonable and there's a table, chair, chest of drawers, washstand and so forth.'

'Oh, Miss Dangerfield, ma'am!' Annette's eyes were tragic for me and misted with tears. 'To think you've had to come to this!'

'But it's clean,' I said briskly. 'Clean sheets, scrubbed floor, every-thing spick and span. But, of course, I suppose. . .' an idea struck me.

She nodded. 'It's you what'll have to keep it spick and span, ma'am,' she said, confirming my thought.

'Oh, dear, I have an awful lot to learn before I reach the top of the ladder like Lizzie Fairfax . . . I, who never made a bed or scrubbed a floor in my life!'

*

Father joined me for luncheon, though lately he had been in the habit of eating at his club. I had been puzzled as to how he found the means to continue to patronise the exclusive 'Naval & Yachting' in St James's, till he let drop on another occasion that certain fellow-members had clubbed together anonymously to pay his annual sub-scription, and that he was also granted a very tolerable credit limit there. This greatly surprised me, both as to the generosity of his friends and his bland readiness to accept what many would have regarded as charity – until he gently pointed out that, in the past, he had himself lavishly subscribed to the support of fellow-members of the 'Naval & Yachting' who had fallen on lean times by reason of old age, change of fortune or sheer bad luck. There was, he said, a freemasonry amongst men of the seagoing fraternity which trans-cended the barriers of charity on the one hand and false pride on the other. And anyhow, said Father by way of settling the issue, he was confident that Lady Luck would once again smile upon him; it was only a matter of time, and then he would settle up with the dear old 'Naval & Yachting' for sustaining him during the lean times.

This particular day, the day when I obtained the position at the Cawnpore, I was more than dismayed to see my parent at a moment's notice, since I had not yet decided how I should broach the subject of

145

my job – or, indeed, whether I should ever find the courage to do so.

Luncheon presented no problems that Wednesday: the remainder of the kitchen staff (and they were all more or less packed ready for departure) had raided the stockpot and produced a rich and nourishing ragout – not a dish particularly suited to a hot midday in the late summer, but beggars cannot be choosers.

Instead of his formerly habitual carafe of lunchtime claret, Father indulged in a cheap half-bottle of stout and addressed himself to the meal. We ate in silence and it was not until the cheese and biscuits that he dropped his bombshell:

'Faith, my dearest,' he said, 'you must steel yourself for some bad news. I have to tell you that we are to be evicted from this house next Wednesday . . . and I don't know what to say to you, I really don't. . .'
He bowed his head.

Upsetting my chair in the act of leaping to my feet, I flew to him, fell to my knees and threw my arms about his waist, staring up at that fine grief-stricken countenance which I loved and honoured so dearly. It was the first and only time throughout all the tribulations which had begun on that never-to-be-forgotten day in Malta, when he had come even near to breaking down. But now there were lines of defeat on his brow and scoring his cheeks.

'Father . . .' I began.

'No, let me speak first,' he said gently. 'There is nowhere I can take you, my dear. Everything's gone – Mondisfield, Frinton, all the rest. The vultures have left this place to the last, and I suppose we should be grateful to have been allowed a brief stay of execution. But – after Wednesday. . .'

'Father, please don't worry about me,' I urged him, the beginnings of a stratagem forming in my mind. 'I have friends – plenty of friends – who will give me a temporary home. But what about you?'

Something like an expression of guarded relief crossed his countenance. 'Are you sure of that, Faith?' he asked. 'For, if you are, we are at least settled for the time being. You see, the house committee have offered me gratis accommodation at the club until we're on our feet again, but, of course – no ladies being allowed on the premises – I had to turn it down. But, Faith, if you can make arrangements. . .'

'Oh, I can – I can!' I promised him truthfully.

'Are you *quite* sure, my dear?'

'Yes! I can go to . . . to Deirdre Vallence. Annette's starting there too so I shall even have half-share of a lady's maid. I shall be in clover.'

'Well, that's settled then,' said Father. 'For the time being, at any rate, we can put our minds at ease.'

*

I spent that afternoon sorting through my belongings, beginning with my considerable wardrobe of clothes. I had resolved to take with me to the Cawnpore only one trunk (there was scarcely room for more in my little cubby-hole!), and in this I laid the clothes which would be most useful in my greatly reduced state. Some of the useless, pretty things I gave to Annette. All the rest I consigned – along with the other belongings I was not taking with me to my new life – to two other trunks which, together with Father's unwanted gear, we had decided to put into store for the time being.

As to jewellery, of which I had had a fair amount, all had been sold to help pay off the arrears of wages owed to our domestic staffs and the crew of the *Gloria*. By the end of that afternoon, I – the Honourable Faith Dangerfield – stood bereft of all save what I stood up in, plus one medium-sized trunk. Yet I felt no way diminished on that account; to have secured a place for myself, to have been assured that Father was settled – that was everything. Furthermore, my 'white lie' about staying with Deirdre would work to my advantage in the short run (and now that I could no longer depend on the *certainty* of everything as I had throughout my life so far, I was getting into the habit of measuring out time in small packets), because I should be able to communicate with Father by letter through Annette, and she could forward any letters to me from him – not that my darling parent was much of a correspondent!

That night I retired early, so as to be ready for the ordeal of moving into the Cawnpore. I was in bed, reading a few pages of a novel and just on the point of turning out my bedside lamp – when I remembered Dickie Jobling's letter which had arrived that morning.

Struck with the pang of conscience that always assaulted me in my off-hand dealings with my faithful swain, I leapt out of bed and retrived the missive from my reticule.

The letter was longer than usual, but the convoluted grammar and syntax, schoolboyish spelling and general boring account of his life and times were typical of all the other letters I had ever received from him . . . and they were many.

The mystery of his translation to Gosport in Hampshire was soon explained: he was learning to fly aeroplanes! 'I've been seconded to a very odd group of chaps who call themselves the Army Air Battalion,' he wrote. 'Still in the Navy though and still keaping (*sic*) my own uniform.'

Of more interest to me was the fate of Father's old flotilla. Apparently the result of the manoeuvres and sinking of the *Hasty* had given the Admiralty some second thoughts about the uses of torpedo-boat destroyers (in Dickie's artless phrase, 'the whole concept is being re-thunk.'). The flotilla had been paid off, the officers and men assigned to other ships and the five vessels brought home for extensive refitting. It was here that Dickie went off into boring technicalities which – my jaded mind being quite incapable of assimilating – I skip-read through two more interminable pages. Then he remembered his manners and addressed himself to the issue of the Dangerfields' present predicament. Yes, he had read about us in all the papers and thought the whole affair had been handled most 'scandelously'. Lord Bathcurch of the *Thames Examiner* was no better than those anarchist Johnnies in Russia who went around chucking bombs, and should be taken out and shot.

His warm heart prevailing, and his great kindness showing through the rambling phrases like a good deed in a naughty world, Dickie then open-handedly offered any help which lay within his power to both Father and me. Nor did he dangle before me the inducement of a rich marriage – which lay well within his power, but which his sense of rightness restrained him from flaunting. It was on this note, four or five sides of paper later, that he closed the main body of the letter, ending with his renewed protestations of his undying affection, *et cetera, et cetera*.

Then followed extensive postscripts . . .

A name leapt out at me from the first of these, causing my hackles to rise like one gamecock in confrontation with another. Mrs Chalmers, wrote my correspondent, had left Malta under a social cloud and was back in England. On the grapevine, he had heard she had been found to be 'carrying-on' with the American chap whom she always had in tow, and ostracised on that account. In his felicitous phrases: 'She tried to brasen it out, but old Lady Freakley and the rest of the old biddies were having none of it. I think if she hadn't taken the hint and left, they'd have clubbed together and bought them both a one-way steamship ticket to England!' He closed the paragraph by adding that my father was jolly lucky to have escaped from the woman – a sentiment which I heartily endorsed.

And then – another name, to close the letter. . .

'P.P.S. Jack Cummings is also back in England. The lucky blighter has been picked for a staff course at Greenwich, which means our lords and masters have got him spotted for advancement. I expect we shall soon see him in his brass hat. An Admiral in no time, I shouldn't wonder! Still, I have to admit I can't help but admire the chap, even if he is a bit too pushy for my taste. I suppose this is because he's had to come a long way the hard way, but it's to be hoped that now he's getting somewhere he'll ease off a bit and stop trying to prove himself to all and sundrey.'

Not entirely to my surprise, when I finally turned out my light, my thoughts sped instantly to the man who was the subject of Dickie's final paragraph. Lying back against the pillows, staring up at the ceiling, with the lights of the traffic passing from one end of the room to the other in counterfeit of their movement up and down Park Lane outside, I found myself balancing my resentment against Jack Cummings for betraying my father against the undoubted fact (which I was really facing for the first time) of my continued attachment to his memory. Why else, I asked myself, had my heart lifted whenever an envelope bearing the naval symbol appeared on the hall table?

No, I had not forgotten Jack Cummings: there was still the pull between resentment and memories.

Memories of our first meeting . . .

The 'corsair', all unexpected, out of a summer's morning. How he then became in turn the martinet and the gamin; his quite merciless summation of my character, when a lesser man might have glossed over the situation with a few well-turned compliments. How many times had played through that day in my mind, like a toy theatre show of my childhood?

And then, most memorably, our sailing outing to the Blue Grotto, culminating in the nightmarish sail back to the safety of the bay, when my near-fatal despair had been quenched by his inspiring calm.

Lastly – most unforgettably – how he had carried me up the beach in his arms, with the last of the rain drifting against his cheek and mine . . . how we had briefly kissed in an instant of transient passion which was most memorably and eternally protracted in my waking and sleeping hours, so that one part of me remained forever on that lonely beach in far-off Malta, in the arms of the man I could not bring myself to forget, with the great arch of a rainbow above us.

SEVEN

'Wake up – Wake up!'

I rolled over in bed, sat up and was met by the unaccustomed chill of an entirely unheated room: no warm glow of dying ashes from the grate pinkly reflected from my ceiling.

'Who – who is it?' I faltered.

'It's the waker,' came the response. 'Five o'clock and time to be up! Are you out of bed?'

'Not – not yet,' I replied.

'Well, if you're late it's your own look-out. I ain't coming back.' The speaker's footfalls went on down the corridor outside; there came a hammering upon an adjacent door, another dawn challenge.

I set one foot out of bed and touched cold linoleum.

So began my first day as a residential employee at the Cawnpore Hotel, South Audley Street, which was further informed by the chill kiss of unheated water in the hand-basin and the sight of myself looking curiously pale and pinch-cheeked in a wall mirror under a single, unshaded electric lamp . . . plus the sore realisation of all I had lost only half-overlaid as yet by my firm determination to succeed in this, the first real personal enterprise of my life.

*

The evening before, after taking leave of my father and my home (and he wishing me every happiness at Deirdre's, coupled with assurances that Lady Luck would soon reunite us), I had established myself in my quarters at the hotel and been instructed by one of Mrs Carradine's assistants to next morning make my way down to a large room in the basement called the 'muster room' where, said my informant, I should be instructed in my day's work. Two items of equipment only were provided by the hotel for the likes of myself: an ankle-length, short-sleeved overall of fawn calico which was so stiff that it could quite easily be stood up by itself against a wall, and a mob-cap of similar material. This unbecoming 'uniform' gave the wearer the general appearance of how I have always imagined a female convict might look.

So I washed in cold water, dressed myself, covered my skirt and blouse with the overall, tucked my hair under the cap and regarded myself in the tiny fly-blown mirror above the wash-basin.

'How Lady Freakley and the old biddies in Valletta would throw up their hands to see you now, my dear,' I told myself.

I ventured out into the corridor, in time to see my next-door neighbour emerge from her room also.

'Hello,' she said. 'You the new girl, I s'pose? My name's Suzie Biggs.' She was small and pretty, with a cheeky turned-up nose and a wide mouth that forever puckered with good humour at the corners. I liked her on sight.

I introduced myself. 'Have you been here long?' I asked.

'Only a week,' she said. 'Just long enough to know my way around. Get to know a few of the dodges. Learn the folks to keep clear of. Make up my mind what to aim for.'

Amused at her forthrightness, I asked, 'Well, for a start, what do you aim for, Suzie? May I call you Suzie?'

She nodded. 'I aim to get myself out of this cleaning woman lark. "Housekeeper's assistant" – pah!' She gave the term the best of her Cockney scorn. 'We're nothing but slaveys, that's all we are, Faith – as you'll soon find out. Why, even the chambermaids look down their noses at us – them with their clean hands – and you can't get much lower than a chambermaid.'

We were now progressing down innumerable flights of dingy stairs at the back of the hotel. Uncarpeted and badly lit, they put one in mind of some dreadful institution for the destitute as described by Dickens.

'Then what do you want to do?' I asked.

'Get myself promoted to a job in the reception hall, the front hall,' replied my informant. 'Nice and warm in winter. Wear your nicest clothes. Clean hands. Meet nice people.'

'Ah, you mean a kind of clerk behind the reception desk?' I ventured.

She shook her head. 'Not that. Couldn't do that, Faith. Can't read, nor yet write more'n my name. No – it's the job behind the flower kiosk that I'm after. Mrs Sennett, what's there now, she's just about on her last legs. When she drops off the hook, little Suzie's moving in behind that kiosk if it's the last thing she does.' She smiled brilliantly and made delicate movements with her arms and hands, as if presenting a flower. '*Naice carnation buttonhole, sir? Let me put it in for you. Oh, keep the change? Thenks awfully!* That's the life for me, Faith.'

I laughed with her.

The stairs ended and we were in the basement.

'A quick word, in case we don't meet up again till breakfast, Faith. Folks to look out for. Look out for Mrs Ivor, our supervisor. She's fair, but she's a right tyrant and very harsh. If she got it into her mind that you was swinging the lead, she'd have you out in the street with your half-day's wages and nothing more. And Faith. . .'

'Yes?'

'Don't trust any of the gels. Some – most of them – are all right at heart. But even the best of 'em will take the mickey out of a new gel. So watch out for tricks.'

'I'll remember that. Thanks, Suzie.'

The 'muster room' proved to be a huge apartment almost entirely surrounded on all four walls and ceiling by central heating pipes which popped and gurgled continuously, notwithstanding which the chamber was as cold as a mortuary. About twenty women were assembled there and perhaps half as many men – and more were filing in, all in fawn overalls.

Presently, when everyone was gathered and the coughing ceased, two figures got up on to a small platform at the far end. I recognised Mrs Carradine immediately; she looked as pale as death, yet completely master of herself as she gazed evenly over the serried row of faces before her. Her companion was a large woman dressed in black; she had a watch and chain hanging from a thick waist-belt that spanned her broad middle; iron-grey hair and a severe expression.

'Mrs Ivor,' whispered Suzie at my side. 'So now you know who to look out for.'

I nodded.

'She's giving out the tasks now,' said Suzie under her breath. 'Listen for your name, for she gets real nasty if she has to repeat anything.'

In a stentorian voice, the supervisor began to read out from a list:

'Nagel, Fairworthy, Smith J., Druce. . .'

Four women went swiftly to the front of the gathering, facing the platform.

'You four in the hall and main staircase,' boomed Mrs Ivor. 'And I don't want to see any unemptied spittoons or ash-trays. Yesterday the picture frames weren't dusted. I had to sack one woman. Don't let me find you scrimshanking. Away with you!'

They went – in a hurry. Horrified, I watched the woman at her work and was put in mind of the worst excesses I had read of in the evil days of old Rome, or the plantations of southern America. As my new friend had said, this was indeed a manifestation of sheer slavery, with people treated like beasts of burden.

More groups of women – men too, for they did the heavier work outside – were called out and given their tasks. And then:

'Meecham, Shelley, Davis, Fields. . .'

Suzie nudged me. 'Off you go. Good luck, kid.'

I hurried to the front with my three workmates as Mrs Ivor looked at us over her list.

'Smoking-room and gentlemen's bar!' she barked. 'I had to move the women who have been doing it for the last three weeks; they'd learned all the short cuts and dodges. Don't you do the same. Off with you.'

As I left, I caught Mrs Carradine's eye. If she recognised me, she gave no sign of having done so.

Following my three companions, who bunched together chattering amongst themselves and ignoring me completely, I came with them to the smoking-room, a large public room on the ground floor whose windows looked out on to South Audley Street – where I found to my surprise that not only was I up, about and ready to start work, but half Mayfair seemed to be on the move. Delivery men, hawkers, street-sweepers, policemen, shopgirls – all were hurrying, even young children, the whole bustling army of the metropolis that such lie-abeds as my former self slept through in ignorance.

'Wassay your name was?' It was the oldest of my three workmates who addressed me. She had a hard expression and sly eyes. The other two were much younger, scarcely twenty, they gave me flat stares. 'Shields, or summat?'

'Fields,' I supplied. 'Faith Fields. Very pleased to meet you.'

I held out my hand.

All three burst into mocking laughter.

'Oh, la-di-dah! Ay'm the Duchess of Dustbin. Ain't we met at

Ascot?' This from the older woman. She ignored my proffered hand and, the laughter having subsided, assumed a cunning look.

'Fields can do a sweep-out,' she said. 'Nancy and Jessie, get on with the dusting. Me the brass and copper. All right?'

As she had taken charge, whether 'officially' or otherwise, there seemed no point in a mere beginner doing other than to accept instructions. I took a broom that she thrust into my hand and started to sweep the floor, while the girls produced dusters. Our 'leader', whom the others addressed as Madge, gathered together an armful of brass candlesticks and salvers, settled herself down in a comfortable chair at a table and began polishing; if not the easiest, this was obviously the most reposeful task.

It came to me then that I had never wielded a broom in my life. I essayed a few awkward strokes along the parquet flooring that bordered the rugs and carpets . . . and was immediately the victim of loud verbal assault from my companions.

'Hey! What you up to?'

'Poooh! What you think you're doing?'

A certain amount – indeed a great deal – of dust had risen from my efforts. I myself was choking.

'Ain't you ever swept before!' The challenge came from Madge.

There seemed little point in hedging. 'No, as a matter of fact, I haven't,' I confessed.

'You been livin' in a field all your life?'

'But I'm willing to learn,' I declared. 'It can't be all that hard.'

'Well, you look here, Duchess,' said Madge. 'First off, you fetch a pannikin of water and you sprinkles it on the floor to lay the dust – *afore* you start sweeping. Any child in arms knows that!'

I went into the adjoining gentlemen's bar, where I found a suitable vessel which I filled with water from the sink behind the counter. As I was doing this, I heard my companions muttering together in the next room. Their discourse was punctuated by occasional sniggers and I had the impression that I was the subject of their confabulations and felt uneasy. However, they were all about their tasks, straight-faced, when I re-entered the smoking-room, and took no notice of me until I had begun wetting the floor.

'Hey! What you think you're doin' – havin' a bath?'

'You're soakin' me through!'

'Oh, dear,' I said. 'Am I using too much water?'

One of the younger girls – Nancy, who struck me as being the nicest of the trio and at least didn't join in most of the ridicule directed at me – took the pannikin from my hand and began to sprinkle water on that part of the floor that was not already swimming with it: gently, like light summer rain.

'See how to do it?' she said.

'Yes, thank you, Nancy,' I replied. 'I've got the idea now.'

As I had supposed, there was really nothing to sweeping floors when you know how. In no time, I had gathered the moist dust into neat piles along the edge of the carpets and even managed to disperse the excess water somehow.

'Where does the dust go?' I asked.

'Under the carpet,' responded Madge, spitting on a piece of brass-work and rubbing hard. She did not look up, but concentrated on her task, serious-faced.

'Is . . . is that a good idea?' I asked.

'It's the way we do it at the Cawnpore,' she responded. 'The men come round every week, lift up all the carpets and clean under 'em. Mrs Ivor, she won't thank you for wasting your time by dumping bits of dust here and there. Once a week's her style.'

I made no demur, but did as I was advised.

The task of furbishing the smoking-room was quite Augean in scale. The dusting, sweeping and polishing of bright-work having been done, there remained the oak panelling to be wiped down and polished, a fire to be laid in the huge open grate, ash-trays and spittoons to be emptied into the fire (the latter – a most distasteful task – being given to me). We had begun at half-past five. By half-past six, the room was more or less spotless and a merry fire burning in the grate.

We next moved into the adjacent gentlemen's saloon bar, which we dealt with in like manner, each doing similar tasks. I had by now achieved a certain expertise in wiping-down and polishing; not to mention floor-sprinkling, brushing and depositing the dust under the big oriental carpet.

That brought us to 7.15 – and the promise of breakfast. I was famished: I who until recently had never sat up in bed for my breakfast tray before nine!

'Watch yourselves, gels!' hissed Madge from the door, where she had stationed herself. " 'Ere comes 'er Nibs!'

Mrs Ivor swept in like a heavy cruiser entering harbour. Following in her wake was a young and anxious-looking gentleman in a frock-coat.

'Finished?' boomed the supervisor.

'Yes'm,' said Madge, our spokesman.

'We'll see about that!' declared Mrs Ivor. 'Mr Waterford, pray be so kind as to inspect the smoking-room, will you?'

'With the greatest of pleasure, Mrs Ivor,' responded the young man. He turned to obey, but found me standing in his path. Confused by this sudden confrontation at close quarters, I was slow to move.

He flushed to his ears. 'Pardon me . . . Miss,' he stammered. 'Do you mind, please?'

I moved aside and he smiled nervous thanks. What a pleasant young man, I thought.

Mrs Ivor was by then inspecting the bright-work. This she did by rubbing a thumb across the surface of candlestick, salver, ash-tray or what-have-you, and closely inspecting it – presumably – for the slightest sign of discolouration. She grudgingly passed all of Madge's polishing. Next came the panelling, the state behind the bar counter: its sinks, glasses (which we had all washed and polished).

And then . . . my floor.

'Who did this?' she demanded.

Heart beating faster, I owned that I had.

'You're the new woman?' she demanded. 'Name?'

I told her.

'I've seen better sweeping,' she said. And turned up the edge of the carpet with the toe of her buttoned boot – to reveal the long line of damp dust which I had carefully swept under there for collection.

In the silence that followed – and I knew at once from her expression that I had allowed myself to fall into a trap – young Mr Waterford re-entered from the smoking-room. He was witness to all that followed.

'This is your work?' demanded the Supervisor.

I nodded.

One of the girls spoke up – the one named Jessie, a minx if I ever saw one of that breed, with slanting eyes like a cat and a syrupy smile, though superficially as pretty as a girl on a chocolate box.

'Mrs Ivor, ma'am, Madge told her not to sweep under carpets,' said this she-Judas, 'only she wouldn't listen, but said she knew the proper way to do it.'

I opened my mouth to deny the imputation – but some imp of prudence whispered to me to keep silent.

'Did she now, did she now?' growled the supervisor. She turned to

156

Mr Waterford. 'How did you find the smoking-room, Mr Waterford?' she asked.

He glanced swiftly at me and then looked back at her. 'Parts of it were . . . very fine,' he replied.

'Did you look under the carpets, pray?'

He nodded.

'Same as in here?'

'I – I'm afraid so, Mrs Ivor,' he said. 'But I think we must overlook this offence on the young woman's first day here, she . . . not being used to our ways.'

Mrs Ivor shrugged, as if accepting the justice of an essentially unpalatable judgement; I remembered Suzie's summation of her as a harsh task-master, though fair.

'As you say, Mr Waterford,' she conceded. 'You are an under-manager and I am just here to make these women work.' So saying, she turned and swept out of the room; but paused in the doorway, pointed at me and barked, 'Sweep it up, your muck! Put it in the fire! *Now!*'

'Yes, ma'am!' I cried.

When they had gone, that dreadful little creature Jessie and her mentor Madge fell around laughing.

I blazed at them. 'That was a perfectly rotten trick to play on me. Why, you might have got me the sack!'

They both sneered.

'Nah!' said Madge. 'Old Ma Ivor would never give a new gel the sack on her first day. Bet it scared you though, eh?'

They both laughed again: young witch and old witch.

'I don't think it's very funny!' I cried.

The young minx's grin faded. She didn't think it was very funny either, and I knew in one revealing flash of insight that there had been more than a mere prank behind her betrayal.

'You want to learn to take a joke, Duchess,' she said, 'or you won't last long at the Cawnpore.'

'Best you go back to the Duke, if you can't take a joke from the gels,' said Madge, unsmiling.

We left the rooms, having tidied up; I had put the sweepings on the fire, as ordered. On our way out the girl Nancy took my arm and, holding me back, whispered in my ear:

'Faith, you've got to learn to put up with that kind of thing. If they know they're getting at you and cutting you down, they'll only make

157

things worse for you. Be like me – let it wash off you, like water off a duck's back.'

*

The chamber designated as the staff dining-room was in the basement and adjacent to the muster room. All who might be termed the rank and file of the hotel staff took their meals there, but even then a certain hierarchy was maintained: the chambermaids, waitresses, barmaids and clerical staff ate apart from we cleaning women, who had a special section of the room well away from our 'betters'.

'Yoo-hoo – Faith!'

My new friend Suzie waved to me and indicated that she had saved me a seat. I joined her.

'How did you get on?' she asked.

I told her the sorry tale of my adventures and she shook her head. 'I know that Madge,' she said. 'A real hard nut. If she gets it into her mind that a gel's putting on airs, she makes her life a misery. As for that Jessie creature – she's Madge's little pet and I wouldn't trust her further than I could throw a half-brick. The only consolation is that sooner or later, Mrs Ivor will rumble what a bad lot she is and sack her. Are you hungry?'

I nodded.

Breakfast began with porridge, which was served in huge vessels like soup tureens, two to each table; one helped oneself. It was ample and good, though rather on the stodgy side and lacking in sugar. I was so hungry that I cleaned my plate mirror-bright. This was followed by a comestible that was strange to me, called black pudding. I tackled it tentatively, but found it quite satisfying. Bread and butter was available ad lib. And all washed down with cocoa.

As we ate, we talked. Indeed, the whole room was so a-buzz with general conversation that Suzie and I carried on our duologue in a near-shout.

'Who's Mr Waterford?' I asked.

'He's one of the under-managers,' replied Suzie. 'I don't know much about him, but they say he's rather nice. A bit wet behind the ears, but his heart's in the right place.'

Remembering his courtesy towards me, and the timely word he had spoken to Mrs Ivor on my behalf, I resolved to keep on good terms with the shy young Mr Waterford. In the ménage in which I had found myself, it would clearly be of advantage to possess allies.

158

'So what happens next?' I quizzed her.

'The rest of the morning's our own – till 8 o'clock,' said Suzie. 'Then we all go to the muster room again. After that, it's all hell let loose until we pack up – with midday dinner in half-hour shifts from 12 to 2 o'clock.

'It works this way. After 8 o'clock, when they start serving the guests' breakfasts in the dining-room and their bedrooms and suites are unoccupied, we move in and clean out – just the same as we did in the public rooms earlier on. By the time breakfast's over and guests are beginning to move out of the hotel, the cleaning women do out the empty rooms ready for the new lot who'll be coming in. This usually keeps us busy until about 6 o'clock.'

'And then what, Suzie?'

'We round off the day by refurbishing the rooms that haven't been occupied for a day or so. And just to make sure that we don't have a minute to call our own, we then fill in time by cleaning the staff staircases and corridors. There's never a dull moment!'

'Only of course, because we've got the early shift today, we shall be finished by three,' I added.

'By 3 o'clock you'll be done for, Faith,' she told me. 'Speaking personally, I'd rather have the 10 to 8 shift – which we'll be doing next week. A nice lie-in in the mornings! But whichever way you look at it, a ten-hour day being a slavey's no fun, no fun at all. Roll on that flower kiosk in the front hall!'

And roll on whatever advancement *I* might secure for myself, I could have added.

*

Next on the list of people to look out for – supplied by my helpful friend – was the head floor maid, Bullington by name, who was responsible for the bedrooms and suites – 150 in all – in the Cawn-pore. According to Suzie, she had all the vices of Mrs Ivor without the leavening of fairness. Watch out for Bullington. I resolved so to do.

We went to the muster room, where the assignment of tasks was carried out at the rush. As I was later to learn, some manipulation of a grapevine passed the information – via headquarters in Mrs Car-radine's office – with regard to those guest bedrooms which had been vacated. Then it was a matter of: 'You, you and you – clean out room 15!' And away we went.

We were not allowed to touch beds; that was for the chamber-maids with their clean hands; to us fell the tasks of taking out the rugs and beating them in the open air on the fire escapes; wiping down paintwork, emptying slops and the eternity of dusting and sweeping, dusting and sweeping.

Somewhat to my dismay, I continued to be grouped in with Madge and the two girls – though I had no quarrel with young Nancy. As before, the older woman took command of our party and I was relegated to the dirtiest and most tedious tasks. This I bore with meek resignation while seething inside; and with a resolve that, let me but learn the tricks of my new trade and I would strike a blow for my freedom.

It so happened that, on that very first morning, I had a chance opportunity – all unwittingly – to pay Madge out for getting me into trouble with Mrs Ivor.

It happened this way . . .

Shortly before noon, after having cleaned out so many rooms that I had lost count, we were directed to one on the second floor – a double room where, by the appearance of things, the inmates had held an all-night stag party. There were empty bottles and glasses galore, spilled snacks trampled into the carpets, dirty plates and crumpled napkins – and someone had been sick in a corner.

'All this just before dinner, and I'm fair worn out,' declared Madge. 'All right, Fields, go and fetch a bucket of water and clean up that mess over there. You others can start beating the carpets. I'll rest my feet for a minute.'

I went to do her bidding, filled a bucket in one of the bathrooms in the corridor and was on my way back when I beheld what I can only describe as a procession of functionaries: half a dozen women led by a tall apparition in the long black frock affected by the senior members of the hotel staff. Thin as a crane and hard of countenance, her grey hair was scraped back and knotted at the nape. Berry-black eyes gleamed from behind a pince-nez, and she loped in long, swing-ing strides, like a tigress on the prowl. Behind her came acolytes, all bearing sheaves of paper and pencils held ready.

The leader of this procession halted before me and pointed.

'Who are *you*?' she demanded. 'I don't know *you*!'

One of her followers intervened. 'Mrs Bullington, this may be one of the new cleaning women – Walker, or Fields.'

'Fields,' I supplied. 'Ma'am,' I added.

'Where are you working?' demanded the terrifying Bullington, who was everything that Suzie had made her out to be – a regular Gorgon.

'Two-one-three, ma'am,' I replied.

'Ah, the room that was occupied by those Yorkshire business-men,' she countered. She turned to her acolytes. 'Didn't we have complaints about noise, and did the chambermaids not refuse to make the beds?'

'Yes, Mrs Bullington. Not until the mess has been cleaned up.'

She glared at me. 'And have you begun to clean up in there?'

'Just beginning, ma'am,' I replied.

'Let us take a look,' she said.

I opened the door for her and she swept in, followed by her entourage. Nancy and Jessie were taking up the carpets; they stared at the newcomers in slack-mouthed, wide-eyed awe and dismay.

Madge was fast asleep and snoring on one of the unmade beds!

*

As I told Suzie at midday dinner, I have never in my life seen such a delivery of wrath, such a downfall of a petty tyrant – nor felt myself so vulnerable to accusation as after that noon confrontation in room 213.

'*Asleep*, you say, Faith?' repeated Suzie after me. 'Asleep on the job – and in comes Bullington and catches her at it? Cor!'

'I've heard naval Chief Petty Officers – when they have not been aware that I was within earshot – delivering what you might call a reprimand,' I told her. 'They have nothing on Bullington; she is in a class of her own! She reduced Madge to a quavering jelly. And all without a single swear-word. Nor did she even raise her voice unduly.'

'What happened then?' asked my friend.

'Well, after she had given Madge a dressing-down and brought her to tears, she then informed her that it was her last chance at the Cawnpore. Next time it would be the sack without a reference, she said. As for today, Madge is to lose a whole day's pay.'

'A whole day? She isn't going to like that, Faith!'

'Nor does she,' I responded. 'And who do you think she blames for it?'

'Not you, Faith – surely she doesn't blame you!'

'That she does, Suzie!' I replied. 'No sooner was Bullington's back turned than she was at me: accused me of deliberately enticing – that was the word she used – 'enticing' Bullington into the room so that she would find her asleep on the job. She said I had done it to pay her back for what she called the little joke she and Jessie had played on me with Mrs Ivor.'

'And what did you say to that, Faith?' asked Suzie.

'I answered her with a very rude word which I once overheard my father use in not dissimilar circumstances,' I replied. 'But all in all, I don't think the whole episode has done me a lot of good.'

Indeed, glancing along to the next table where Madge sat with her little friend and supporter Jessie, I could not but repeat this observation in my mind. They were both looking sidelong at me, and with unconcealed malevolence. Madge was muttering something to her companion out of the corner of her mouth – and Jessie was giving her feline, slant-eyed grin.

I had made bad enemies at the Cawnpore Hotel . . . and on my first morning, too!

*

Our half-hour midday dinner-time over, we returned to the fray, where we worked through solidly until 3 pm, when we were relieved by the late shift who had started at 10 am. Blessedly, I did not have to spend the rest of the time with my morning companions, but was hived off to do a particularly filthy job of cleaning ovens in the restaurant kitchens, a task that had me in such a state that it took half an hour of scrubbing in cold water to get my hands free of the greasy swarf. After that I fell on to my narrow bed, fully clothed, and slept the clock round from utter exhaustion.

So ended my first day at the Cawnpore Hotel.

*

Two weeks later, I was mistress of my trade. . .

Show me a dusty floor and I would have it sprinkled, swept, the dust scooped up and disposed of as neatly as you please. Is there a fire to be laid and lit? I was adept as any Baden-Powell Boy Scout at making a blaze in the most intractable chimney with a pile of chippings and one match. It was generally accepted that there was no one to touch my bright-work polishing. But I never did conquer my distaste at emptying spittoons or clearing up messes.

Suzie became and remained my staunch friend; likewise little

Nancy Davis who, like myself, had had the misfortune to be teamed up on that disastrous day with Madge and her friend Jessie. As luck would have it, I did not have to work with this pair again during those first two weeks; but I had not seen, heard nor experienced the end of their machinations.

Mr Stanley Waterford, the young under-manager, seldom moved into my orbit, but he was always punctilious in wishing me good-day when our paths crossed. I had a very clear notion that he was rather taken with me; one always senses these things.

Mrs Carradine I saw only twice in all that time and she never so much as acknowledged my presence. As for the semi-mythological 'Queen Bee of the Cawnpore' who was reputed to dwell in sybaritic glory on the sixth floor, she remained a myth so far as I was concerned.

I worked hard and, as I have said, learned my trade – which after all was only a matter of precept and practice, plus application – but saw no way clear to advancement. Not until a chance alignment of circumstances brought me in touch with a tragedy was I given the opportunity to make that first and most difficult step upwards from the bottom rung of the ladder.

It happened one mid-morning. A summons went out to attend at suite 17 to clean up. ('Binks, Smith and Fields to suite 17!')

We three, so ordered, raced up the service stairs with buckets, brushes, mops and dusters in our hands. Suites were few and far between; this meant a long job, with a bathroom and sitting-room to do in addition to the bedroom; it might take us until dinner-time to finish.

To our astonishment and dismay, the formidable figure of the head floor maid, the redoubtable Bullington, was standing outside the door of suite 17 rattling her chatelaine of bright keys.

'Can't you get in, ma'am?' asked Binks – a North Country girl who was not easily overawed, not even by the Gorgon of the Cawnpore.

'No!' responded Mrs Bullington. 'It's bolted on the inside. Same as when the chambermaid tried to get in last evening to turn back the bedclothes. I don't like it.' She glowered at the three of us through her pince-nez as if, in some arcane manner, we were responsible. 'The woman may have taken ill,' she added.

'Maybe she fell asleep in the bath and got drowned,' essayed Binks with a certain relish.

163

'Why don't you have the door broken down?' I suggested. 'That would seem to be the sensible thing to do.'

Bullington stared at me through her pince-nez with stunned affront, while my companions gave me the kind of looks usually reserved for someone who has just become the victim of a particularly horrible accident. I realised that I must have unwittingly reverted to my former manner of addressing servants ('Annette, my bath is cold. Please see to it, will you?').

Astoundingly, I was not instantly turned to stone by her Gorgon stare, nor did her response go further along those lines; instead she appeared to subside within herself, answering me quite calmly and with a nod of grudging approval.

'Only the manager or the duty under-manager can order a door to be forced. I'll send for him.' Binks and Smith stared at me in awe.

In fact it was young Mr Waterford who came. Having listened to Bullington's views on the locked door, he showed more forthrightness than one would have given him credit for on early acquaintance and, turning to the hotel fireman who had accompanied him, he ordered the man to break down the door.

Three strokes of the latter's axe sufficed and we entered the suite in the order: the under-manager, the fireman, myself and the other females.

The bedroom was empty, the bedclothes tousled.

'We'll try the bathroom' said the under-manager. 'One of you' – pointing – 'take a look in the sitting-room.'

I was at his elbow when he pushed open the bathroom door. What he saw there brought an exclamation to his lips, while my colleague Binks gave a low moan and fainted backwards into the arms of the fireman.

I knew in the instant what had to be done; seizing Mrs Bullington by the elbow, I pulled her inside the room; the under-manager I pushed out of the door with no ceremony at all.

'But . . . but. . .' he began.

'This is no place for a man,' I snapped. 'Fetch a doctor. If there isn't a resident doctor in the hotel, I suggest you have all the public rooms paged for one. Also telephone around.'

'A doctor – yes, yes!' he said. And went.

I shut the door and fell on my knees beside the figure of the woman who lay in a crumpled heap close by the bath, face-uppermost, eyes closed. She looked to be in her late thirties and her hair and skin were covered with dried soap, the more clearly seen because she was entirely nude. A thick stream of bright blood, already congealing, had issued from the back of her head and covered nearly half the bathroom floor.

'She must have slipped and hit her head on falling,' I said.

'What do we do until the doctor comes?' asked Bullington.

'Best to do nothing,' I replied. 'Get all those bath towels down from the rack and we can cover her over.' Then, remembering something I had learned on the hunting field, I reached up, took a hand mirror from the dressing-table and placed it in front of the woman's slightly-parted lips. After a few moments, a faint misting appeared on the glass.

'She's still breathing,' I said with relief.

'Shouldn't we give her something to rest her head on – a cushion?' asked my companion, who had clearly decided to let me take the initiative in the matter of first aid.

'She won't die of discomfort,' I retorted. 'But . . . yes, we'll take a chance on it. Go and fetch one, will you?'

When my distinctly overawed and frightened companion returned with a cushion, I gently slipped it under the head of the unconscious woman, in the process of which careful enterprise I was horrified to see a fresh effusion of blood emerge from the hidden wound. The head floor maid whimpered with horror and our patient gave a low moan.

'Don't worry, you're going to be all right,' I whispered, in no real hope that she would hear and understand me.

Then followed an interval which could not possibly have been more than five minutes at the most, during which time I knelt beside the stricken guest of suite 17, holding one of her limp hands and gently chafing it. In such a manner had I once knelt beside the unconscious form of a young whipper-in of the Quorn, and he lying with both legs broken, with the music of the hounds in the far distance and my hope of help fast fading.

In this instance, help came in the form of a burly physician who had been surprised at his breakfast and brought up in haste. He approved of my not having moved the patient unduly, and having covered her over to reduce the chilling effect of shock. She had a fractured skull, he opined, but stood a fair chance if she was rushed to hospital.

I was standing by the door of the suite when the ambulance men carried her out to the lift. She looked very small and vulnerable, and I wondered who she was and who might be worrying about her before long.

'You handled that very well ... Miss Fields,' said the under-manager at my elbow. At close quarters, he revealed himself as having dark hazel eyes which nicely matched the chestnut hair that tended to curl round the back of his ears. Behind the gentle manner I nevertheless detected a certain assurance.

'Thank you, Mr Waterford,' I said.

'I've watched you around the hotel,' he said. 'Do you like the work here?'

'Well enough,' I replied.

'I would guess that it's not the kind of work you are used to,' he essayed.

'Not really,' I conceded (and it was *all* I was going to concede). 'But I'm picking it up quite quickly, I think.'

'Yes, I'm sure you are. You seem ... very capable.'

'Very kind of you to say so, Mr Waterford.'

'I'll see you are commended for your prompt and efficient action this morning,' he said.

'Thank you, sir,' I replied.

He left me alone with Mrs Bullington. The Gorgon of the Cawnpore looked at me through her pince-nez with something more than approval; there was almost affection in her glance. It came to me then that people are invariably better than reputation would have them, and often nicer than they would believe themselves to be.

'Thank you for your help, Fields,' she said now with a gruffness of a person not much given to handing out either praise or thanks. 'Don't know what I'd have done without you. Can't stand the sight of blood and suffering myself.'

Gratefully accepting her implied compliment, I went into the suite to help Binks and Smith clear up.

*

After our midday dinner, I had a message to go upstairs and see Mrs Carradine. It occurred to me that the summons might not be un-connected with the events of the morning, nor was I mistaken. When I reached her room by the chimney stack, she was seated at her desk with the receiving end of the telephone instrument against her ear. Her pale countenance wore an expression of dramatic gravity in the diffused light of her desk-lamp.

'Thank you,' she said at length and replaced the earpiece. She eyed me unwaveringly. 'That was the hospital,' she said, 'with news of Miss Langsdorff – the lady from suite seventeen.'

'How is she?'

'She died at midday without recovering consciousness,' was the answer.

'Oh, how awful!'

'All that could be done, was done,' said Mrs Carradine, taking a cigarette from a gunmetal case and proceeding to light it with a lucifer match. 'But it was too late. She must have fallen and hit her head last night. The doctor said it was surprising that she lasted as long as she did.' She drew deeply on the aromatic smoke. 'In any event, you acquitted yourself with commendable self-possession.'

'Thank you.'

'Not to say . . . authority.'

I did not reply.

She blew a smoke ring and dispassionately watched it rise to the low ceiling and disperse.

'The self-possession that comes with having exercised authority over others is neither easily lost, nor concealed,' she said.

Still I said nothing.

'I would hardly have thought that merely looking after a widowed father could have developed your talent to such a degree.'

I remained silent.

She shrugged. 'Well, if you have nothing to add to what you have already told me, Miss Fields, I have some news for you. And I hope you'll think it is good news. Thanks to the recommendation of the under-manager, Mr Waterford, and also on account of my own observations, you are to be promoted.'

She must have seen the sudden delight and triumph in my eyes, for a slight and cynical smile disturbed the corners of her lips and she looked at me with an expression which – the slight cynicism aside – was all enigma.

'You should indeed rejoice in your rapid advancement, Miss Fields,' she observed in that deep, sonorous voice of hers, 'and give thanks that looking after the widowed father has paid a quite handsome dividend.'

*

167

The 'promotion' was of a sort that would have occasioned me the most profound dismay a few weeks previously; but compared with the rigours of dawn rising, dusting, cleaning, polishing and emptying slops and spittoons, it was like a translation to a life of easeful privilege. Apparently the woman who supervised the service in the gentlemen's smoking-room and saloon bar with the assistance of three waitresses had been caught – in Mrs Carradine's telling phrase – 'with her fingers in the till' the previous day and had been summarily dismissed, her assistants along with her. Three replacement waitresses had been found from amongst the hotel staff, but they lacked a dominant, resourceful and – above all – honest leader. I had been chosen to fill the role, partly on account of my showing in that morning's tragic crisis but also, in my view, because of certain suspicions which Mrs Carradine entertained about my true background. Naturally, in view of my ambition, I was delighted.

Mrs Carradine herself schooled me for the task and instructed me about my duties.

The nominal hours for supervisor were from 10 am until midnight, but one need not be in close attendance all that time – one was merely *responsible* for the good working of bar and smoking room, along with procuring stock from the hotel cellarer, reckoning up the contents of the till twice daily, and attending to such tasks as contribute to the smooth running of part of a first-class establishment like the Cawnpore. Best of all, I could move immediately into the room vacated by my predecessor – vastly superior to my original cubbyhole – and was permitted to wear my own clothing, provided it comprised a plain black dress with no jewellery.

The following morning I had a late lie-in, luxuriated in a hot bath (the use of which was available to me in my new quarters), put on a nice black frock which I had with me in my luggage and sallied forth to my first day in the new job.

The three new assistants were already there; two of them were augmenting the rough work (now so familiar to me!) which had already been done by the cleaning woman in the early hours, doing a little light dusting, making up the fire and arranging the chairs. They greeted me affably; both strangers to me, they seemed decent-looking and amiable young women. I left them to their tasks in the smoking-room and went into the saloon bar.

My third assistant was behind the counter, arranging bottles and glasses on the shelves, her back to me. She turned at the sound of my footfalls and I found myself looking at the ingratiating, feline smile and tip-turned, mincingly malevolent eyes of Jessie.

'Good morning, Miss Fields,' she purred.

EIGHT

Stuck with Jessie Davis – it was grotesque! My first advancement up the ladder at the Cawnpore – and I was to be saddled with a creature whom I knew instinctively – who had proved herself – to be a natural enemy.

I had half a mind to go straight to Mrs Carradine and ask for the girl's removal from my charge, but after a while dismissed the idea as sounding mean and petty to the ear. The notion *was* mean and petty. Like myself, the girl had improved her position and was in all probability as anxious to make an honest effort and justify her promotion as I. Who was I to put her down? She could not help looking sly. She *was* sly.

And, I told myself, she would stand watching. . .

A week passed and I had no cause for complaint about Jessie; she did her work well and uncomplainingly. However, there was an awkwardness between us; when by chance we were left together alone – in the saloon bar, for instance, when all the customers had drifted away for luncheon – the very act of making even casual conversation imposed a constraint on me and, I suppose, on her. Therefore I would make some pretext to busy myself somewhere else, or else dispatch her on some errand or other.

Also, on her first Sunday half-day with me, I chanced to see her walking out of the staff entrance and across the street in the company of her mentor Madge Meecham; both were in their Sunday best and chattering together in the intimate, nudging and winking way they had. This gave me food for further thought.

Though I say it myself, the running of the gentlemen's bar and smoking-room made no more demands upon my abilities than, for instance, acting as chatelaine aboard the dear old *Gloria*; calling only for an extended form of the kind of hospitality which Father and I had certainly dispensed, afloat and ashore, during our golden days. The regular clientele, in particular, were a source of considerable satisfaction, for they readily showed their appreciation of my work and treated me in a kindly, avuncular manner – with total respect. Having had slight misgivings that the job was really no more than that of glorified barmaid (a class of person of whom I had previously heard only at second and third hand), I was much relieved.

Plain sailing, then. . .

But not for long.

*

The sudden departure of my predecessor had called for an *ad hoc* stocktaking, carried out by members of the junior management (such as Mr Waterford), to ensure that – as well as 'having her fingers in the till' – the woman had not been indulging in another of the classic swindles of the licenced victuallers' trade: that of 'milking' the stock. Fortunately for her, the stock of the saloon bar – kept in a locked compartment called the still-room, with the master key held by the supervisor – was found to be intact to the last bottle, the last barrel.

Formal stocktaking in the hotel was carried out half-yearly by an outside agency; this chanced to fall just under a month after my assuming supervision of the smoking-room and saloon bar. The personages who carried out the task were blank-faced, uncommunicative, almost morose; one had the impression that they had seen a lot of chicanery and duplicity in their time and were trusting no one – not even honest-looking lady supervisors – until they had done their sums. I left them to it, serenely assured in myself that their sums would turn out right.

Alas for serenity. . .

I had a call from Mrs Carradine: would I go up and see her immediately? With no thought of anything untoward, I straightened my hair and went to her office. She was sitting behind her desk with a thick pile of papers before her; nor did she look up when I entered, but maintained a frowning attention upon the papers, dragging heavily upon a cigarette from time to time.

She did not ask me to sit down – which was odd for her.

Presently she looked up. Those wonderful, luminous eyes were ever so slightly narrowed and there was a pinched look about her mouth. Two bright spots which habitually marked her prominent cheekbones seemed more intensely carmine.

'Your stock is badly down, Fields,' she said without preamble. 'Do you have any explanation?'

'I — I don't understand, Mrs Carradine,' I faltered. 'It was all intact when I took over and I've been most careful to record every item brought out of the still-room. My stock book shows. . .'

'I have your stock book here, Fields,' she interposed. 'It indeed purports to show the consumption in the saloon bar and smoking-room, and this matches the till receipts. Unfortunately . . .' here she drew deeply upon her cigarette, exhaled, coughed and fixed her gaze upon me. 'Unfortunately, the residual stock in the still-room does not marry up with what should be remaining there.'

'Possibly I haven't allowed for spillage,' I suggested, bemused.

'I have allowed you a generous margin for spillage, Fields,' she retorted. 'Three times the norm, in fact. There still remains much that is unaccounted for.'

'But — *how* much, Mrs Carradine?' I cried.

She referred to a paper before her. 'In total, three cases of whisky, three of gin, four of brandy and two each of port and sherry, together with various single bottles of liqueurs totalling two dozen in all. The auditors assess the retail value of the missing stock at . . .' and she mentioned a figure that was astronomically beyond several years of my wages.

'Well, what do you say, Fields? As supervisor, you are ultimately responsible for the stock in your charge.'

I spread my hands in puzzlement. 'Mrs Carradine, I just don't know what to say,' I expostulated. 'What you tell me is a complete mystery to me. A nightmare. Why, I have been most careful. I —'

'Do you trust your staff?' she interposed.

(Did I trust my staff? Did I trust Jessie Davis? She might well ask.)

She may have seen me hesitate. 'I have no reason to suppose that any of the three girls could have anything to do with the missing stock,' I responded in more than scrupulous honesty. For what else could I say? Should I have said: 'Jessie Davis once conspired to play a mean trick on me; she doesn't like me because she thinks I turned the tables on her friend and in my opinion she is two-faced and sly.'

'Well, we shall be obliged to call in the police,' said Mrs Carradine. 'I'm very sorry, Fields, but for the present I shall have to ask you to pass over the still-room key into my possession.'

She held out her hand. I detached the key from its ring and gave it to her.

'That will be all, Fields,' she said. 'For the present.'

*

I said nothing to anyone about my dilemma: neither to Suzie nor to Nancy, the nearest to confidants I had in the hotel. Nor did I think of tackling Jessie Davis about the matter; if guilty (as I supposed she might be – and who else?), she must have realised that the auditors had uncovered the depredation during their searchings and must be awaiting signs of trouble.

I gave her no reason to suppose that I, for one, was troubled, but went about my normal duties in my habitual manner.

Once only, that day, I may have lowered my guard when she came up to me shortly after luncheon.

'We're nearly out of whisky, Miss Fields,' she said. 'Can I have the still-room key and get a couple of bottles?'

Confused for a moment, I replied, 'I don't have it with me at the moment, Jessie. You will have to make do until later.'

'Yes, miss.' Her feline eyes told me nothing.

Staff dinner-time came, but I had no appetite and spent an hour in my room, pacing up and down, up and down in an agony of suspense. The police had been sent for. It was inevitable that I should be questioned. Then what should I say? Should I speak of my suspicions regarding Jessie Davis? Even in the face of an accusation against myself, it was hardly fair. Perhaps – and the thought gave me a small glow of hope – the police would discover that the still-room had been broken into from the outside, by a gang of total strangers. That would exculpate us all.

There came a knock on my door; I went to open it.

Jessie Davis stood there. 'Been looking for you everywhere, Miss Fields,' she said. 'Mrs Carradine sent for to say would you go up and see her right away.'

Did I detect a glance of unholy triumph only half-concealed in those slanting eyes?

*

There was a man with Mrs Carradine, a large man in a dark suit and a very tall collar; his big moustache was in the military style, his hair neatly parted in the middle and cropped close about the ears

173

and in the neck. I immediately marked him as a police officer before Mrs Carradine introduced him.

'This is Inspector Craddock, Fields,' she said, 'who by chance happens to be an old acquaintance – I may say, friend – of mine.'

'You may indeed, Beatrice. Indeed you may,' responded the Inspector in a deep, booming voice not unlike my father's.

'Sit down, Fields. The Inspector would like to ask you a few questions.'

I sat, folded my hands on my lap; willed them to remain steady, fought to keep my nether lip from trembling. Waited.

'Now, Miss Fields,' said Craddock, 'this is a bad business, and since you hold the position of responsibility it is inevitable that you should come in for your fair share of suspicion. Let us lay that card on the table for a start. There is no question of pre-judgement. It's simply that I wish to clear matters up so far as you're concerned. Do you take my point?'

That sounded very reasonable and I relaxed. 'Yes, Inspector,' I replied.

'Did you have any part in the theft?'

I gasped. 'No!' I cried, caught unawares. '*No!*'

'You have the key of the still-room, also keys of the saloon bar – which includes a key for the door out on to the back area. . .'

'Yes.'

'The back area . . . where an accomplice might come under cover of night and load up the stolen spirits on a vehicle.'

'I don't know any such person,' I said.

'A man friend, perhaps?'

'No!'

'Although blameless yourself, possibly you fell under his influence – as so often happens with perfectly respectable women – and, much against your better judgement you acceded to his plan.'

'*No!*' I almost screamed the word. 'You're trying to trap me!'

'What is this man's name, Miss Fields?'

'There is no such man!'

'He's no use to you, Miss Fields – how can he be?'

'I know – *no – such – man!*'

'His name – and you will get away practically scot-free.'

'I've told you. . . '

'A nominal sentence, this being your first offence. It *is* your first offence, isn't it, Miss Fields?'

'Leave me alone!' I cried.

There was a long silence while I sat with my head bowed, making no attempt to stop my trembling.

Presently the relentless voice started up again:

'He is blackmailing you, isn't he?'

'Noooo. . .' I breathed.

'Got a hold over you, has he? That's what made you do it?'

I shook my head, too choked with tears to reply to the hideous speculations that he was throwing at me.

'The law doesn't protect a blackmailer, Miss Fields. No matter what sort of hold he has over you, it will be disregarded. You will be protected.'

'It's not true!' I cried. 'Everything you say is pure fantasy. Will you please leave me alone? *Please!* I know nothing of the theft!'

Silence.

The Inspector coughed. 'Well, Mrs Carradine, what do you think?' he asked.

I lifted my head. She was looking straight at me . . . they were both looking straight at me.

'Quite clearly she is innocent,' replied she – and smiled.

'I've known you quite a long time, Beatrice,' said the Inspector, 'and have never once doubted your judgement. That's my opinion, also.'

He got to his feet. 'Sorry to have given you such a rough time, Miss Fields,' he said, 'but for your own sake it had to be done. It was worse for you because you're innocent, you see? Had you been guilty, you would have jumped at the easy options I offered to you.'

'Is that all?' I asked, bemused.

'Yes, you can go now, Miss Fields,' he said. 'But please hold yourself near at hand, in readiness.'

I went out without a word or a backward glance. Outside, at the top of the stairs, I succumbed to a paroxysm of trembling which lasted longer than I liked. When it was over, I squared my shoulders and went down.

*

I knew then, for the first time, how my father must have felt at his court martial: the notion of one's innocence – one's innocent intent – being impugned by clever words. But at least I had the consolation of being acquitted.

What would follow?

I noticed that Jessie Davis scrupulously avoided my eye and I took good care to keep well clear of her. After my brief but merciless interrogation, it seemed to me that the big, bluff police Inspector, who had the stolid, comfortable look of a typical bourgeois, possessed a mind of quicksilver and a ruthlessness that brooked of no delay, no scruples. There would be further action . .'. and soon.

'*Hold yourself near at hand, in readiness.*' Those had been his words.

I had not long to wait. Another summons to Mrs Carradine's office reached me as I was greeting the first of my evening regulars: a pair of retired gentlemen formerly of the Colonial Service, widowers both, who sat and talked over old times in the Sudan, Rhodesia and other far-flung corners of Empire and Protectorate until the bar closed at midnight. Wishing them a pleasant evening, I went up for my second encounter of the day with the long arm of the law.

*

On this occasion the gathering in Mrs Carradine's office had been augmented by the addition of two others: a uniformed policeman who stood with arms folded by the wall, and a man in rough work-man's clothes with a shifty eye and thick stubble around his jowls; he was seated, and looked sharply at me with narrowed eyes as I entered.

'You wanted me?' I essayed.

'Yes, Miss Fields,' said the Inspector. He pointed to the seated figure. 'Do you know this man?'

'I never saw him before in my life,' I replied with total conviction.

'She's lying!' shouted the creature in the rough clothes. 'We fixed it together. Don't try to lie your way out o' this, F. thie!' The last astonishing injunction he aimed at me directly.

'Be quiet, Skerritt,' growled Inspector Craddock, and then to me: 'This is Edward Skerritt, by trade a rag-and-bone man. This after-noon he was arrested on suspicion of theft, following a report that he was selling bottles and cases of spirits believed to have been stolen from this hotel – for the items match up with the missing goods.

'He claims, Miss Fields, that you were his accomplice in this enterprise, that you approached him while he was going about his lawful business as rag-and-bone man in Hackney. . .'

'That's right – she did, she did!' interposed the wretch.

'Be silent!' barked the Inspector. 'He claims that you proposed a conspiracy to rob the hotel,' he continued. 'That you arranged a meeting in the back area of the hotel one night last week; that you admitted him into the saloon bar, opened up the still-room and supervised the theft of the goods in question. That, Miss Fields, is what he claims.'

'True, every word!' declared Skerritt, staring at me as bold as brass.

'I would add,' said Craddock, 'that in implicating you – his alleged accomplice – Skerritt hopes to get a reduced sentence by turning King's Evidence. You may think this is the motive of his accusation; it is not for me to say.'

'There is not a word of truth in his accusation,' I said quite calmly, for I felt calm. 'As I said, I have never set eyes on him before.'

'Oh, come on, Faithie,' said the man Skerritt, leering. 'After all our careful schemes, you'd ditch old Ted? Come, now. . .'

'Furthermore,' I added, 'I have *never* been addressed as 'Faithie' by anyone in all my life!'

Oddly, this last declaration seemed to strike home to Skerritt, for he made no response but looked uneasily about him: at the door, at the sizable police constable who leaned against the wall just behind him with arms folded.

Presently Inspector Craddock said, in a disarmingly conciliatory tone, 'Now see here, Skerritt, isn't there a chance that you may be mistaken? I put it to you – is there not someone else in the hotel whom you know better than Miss Fields? A friend – a real old friend? Think about it.'

The man shook his head firmly. 'Till I was directed here by that lady there, I didn't never set eyes on the Cawnpore 'otel!' he declared.

'You have no friends here amongst the staff?' persisted Craddock.

I glanced across at Mrs Carradine; she was making notes on a pad of paper before her.

'No,' declared Skerritt.

'No friend – no relation – wife or sister, perhaps?'

'No.'

'Would you go into the witness box and swear that on oath, Skerritt?'

'As God is my judge, sir.'

Inspector Craddock gave a sigh – whether in weariness or in

triumph, it would have been difficult to determine.

'Constable, bring in the other woman,' said he.

The uniformed man obeyed and I looked round to see Madge Meecham being ushered in. She looked quite composed. Her gaze glissaded over me, over Craddock and Mrs Carradine, briefly over the wretch Skerritt, touched upon me – and then settled hard upon the uniformed constable.

'What's this then?' she demanded. 'What I been brought up 'ere by the rozzers for, then?'

Inspector Craddock pointed to Skerritt.

'Mrs Meecham, do you know this man?' he asked.

She gazed at Ned Skerritt impassively. 'Never seen 'im before,' she declared.

'And you, Skerritt – do you know this woman?' demanded Craddock.

'Naw!' The rag-and-bone man shook his head in contempt.

Silence.

'Well, that brings us to a slight impasse,' said Inspector Craddock. 'No one appears to know anybody, so we might as well close down the enquiry and all go home.' He smiled across at me.

'I'd like to know what this is all about!' declared Madge Meecham. It was quite clear that she felt the Inspector had put himself at something of a disadvantage. The same applied to Skerritt, who was grinning quite openly.

For answer, Craddock sat back in his chair. His normally impassive countenance broke into a slight smile that was like the dawn rising after a long, dark night.

'Constable, bring in the other woman,' he said. Very quietly.

'Yessir.'

The door was opened and in walked Jessie Davis. I had the impression – the very clear impression – that her reaction to the scene in which she found herself was quite different from that which Madge Meecham had experienced. To her, the gathering was a complete surprise. And shock.

When she saw her friend and mentor, she drew a shocked intake of breath. When she saw Skerritt, she cried out loud: 'Oh my gawd! They caught you, then!'

'Shut yer mouth, little fool!' cried Madge Meecham.

The girl backed away from her friend's fury. 'Not for you I won't!' she cried. 'You ain't getting me in on this. All I done was to get a wax impression of the still-room key. That's all I done!'

'Gawd, I could kill you!' screeched Meecham.

Skerritt adopted a more philosophical attitude to the situation. He merely passed a grimy hand across his brow and muttered, 'Brahmas! Whyfor did I ever get mixed up wi' brahmas in the line o' business?'

*

It was all over and the three had been taken away. Mrs Carradine produced tea and we sat around her desk and sipped while Inspector Craddock talked.

'Those people – semi-professionals only,' he said. 'A brief enquiry around Hackney, and by midday we elicited that Skerritt and Meecham used to live together in the district as common-law man and wife. The girl Jessie was just a tool. Meecham was half-aware that she would probably be confronted with Skerritt, and both were hard-faced enough to brazen it out. As you saw, the girl Jessie just collapsed in a heap.' He stirred his tea thoughtfully. 'It's a hard business we serve, Beatrice,' he said. 'I sometimes wonder that a person of your sensibility can still bring herself to speak to me.'

'You serve the law very well, Bernard,' she responded. 'I never saw you shift from the path of right by so much as a smidgen.'

'I'm very impressed,' I said, putting in my half-pennyworth. 'And I have felt the weight of Inspector Craddock's method this day!'

We drank up our tea and smiled at each other over the rims of our cups.

My relief was tremendous – beyond all reckoning. . .

*

The following day I was informed by Mr Waterford that the great panjandrum herself, the legendary housekeeper of the Cawnpore Hotel in person, commanded my presence in her palatial suite on the sixth floor. It was with considerable trepidation that I steeled myself to mount in the lift and present myself at her door.

'Enter!'

I went in and was immediately assaulted by the scent of patchouli and the strident yapping of a small dog. The latter turned out to be a Pekingese of discernibly advanced years and savage mien, who was seated on the lap of the tiniest lady I ever beheld. She in turn was sitting in an old-fashioned Regency sofa, with a gramophone set upon a low table at her side, its enormous horn dominating that end of the over-furnished, overstuffed room like the open maw of some flesh-eating tropical plant.

The housekeeper held out a small hand to me. 'Come and sit down, my dear,' she said. 'My nephew has spoken of you most warmly. Sit down and tell me about yourself. Be quiet, Wink-Wink, or there will be no chocolate for you.' The latter remark was addressed to the small dog.

Her hand was soft and warm, its tiny bones fragile to the touch like those of a cage-bird. Her face, which was densely covered with rice powder, was a smooth mask of beatitude; had I not learned, during my short spell at the hotel, that this same Mrs Cornwall ruled the establishment like an eastern potentate of the most auto-cratic kind, I would have put her down as one of those sweet old ladies whom nurse-companions wheel up and down the promenades of Brighton, Weston-super-Mare, Felixstowe and Frinton.

It occurred to me to wonder who was her nephew. . .

'There is very little to tell, ma'am,' I said, extempore. 'Save that I'm very happy here.'

'Do you like music?' she asked.

Confused by the unexpectedness of the question, I could only stammer that yes, indeed, I did.

'Then who is this?' she replied, reaching out to set the gramo-phone in motion.

There followed a crackle, a chord played upon a pianoforte and a voice – clear as crystal and true as a bell – came from out of the great horn. It was a woman's voice, a young woman's voice. The song, of which the burden was lost love and regrets, was brief – a matter of two or three verses and a chorus, and then the machine fell silent.

'Now, who do you think that was?' repeated Mrs Cornwall.

'Why, surely it was you, ma'am,' I replied, drawing a bow at a venture.

The smooth countenance broke into a broad and seraphic smile, in the course of which some rice powder fell in a light white shower upon her corsage. 'Clever gel, you are quite right,' she declared. 'I sang *Only a dead rose to remember* when I was first at the Alham-bra, and the Prince of Wales, as he then was, called round at my dressing-room with his entourage. I was . . . a great friend of the Prince's when I was young. . .' Her voice tailed away into sadness and it was some time before she resumed her monologue:

'Mrs Carradine also was of the theatrical profession, did you know? Yes, she was on the legitimate stage, as the term is. Played Portia, Lady Macbeth – most of the strong dramatic roles. But grief at her husband's death intervened in her career, that and her health, which broke and finally drove her from the stage. She speaks very highly of you.

'Do you visit the Music Hall often?'

'No, ma'am,' I replied. 'I have never been to a Music Hall.'

'Never?' she echoed. 'I find that very hard to believe, miss.' And there was marked disapproval in her tone.

I explained as best as I was able – and with some truth – that I had spent much of my life in the country, and most of it away from London. This appeared to mollify the old lady to some degree.

'That must be rectified,' she said. 'I will instruct my nephew to escort you to the Oxford this very week. Appearing there currently are Miss Marie Lloyd and Mr George Robey. The latter's talents I consider to be largely wasted. He needs the vehicle of a major West End musical play to bring out his potential. Miss Lloyd is very fine, and would be magnificent if only she had studied *bel canto*. I studied *bel canto*.' She held out her small hand for me to take. 'Good-bye, my dear. I'm sure there was something else I had to say to you – the reason why I asked you to come and see me. Ah! I remember – Mrs Carradine says you acquitted yourself very well during that most unfortunate business of the theft. Very pleased with you, my dear . . . very pleased!'

I took the old lady's hand and thanked her.

That same evening, Mr Stanley Waterford sought me out in the gentlemen's bar – where I sat at my tall desk writing out my next day's requisitions for wines, beers and spirits – and asked me if I would care to accompany him to the Oxford Music Hall the following night.

It was then that I knew he must be the nephew of the doyenne of the Cawnpore Hotel. And that this was an invitation that brooked of no refusal.

*

Punctually at 7.30, as arranged, I met Mr Waterford in the faience-walled and marble-floored hallway of the hotel. He was there first, awaiting me, and offered me his arm, saying that there was no need of a cab since it was only a stone's-throw to the Oxford.

In truth it was a pretty long stone's throw, being at St Giles' Circus. The building itself (which no longer stands) was a confection of mingled styles – all of them vulgar in a jolly, unbuttoned sort of way, with lavish employment of engraved glass, fat putti of gilded plaster work, plaster swags of outrageous fruit embellishing the fronts of boxes and galleries, popping gas-lamps and red plush everywhere.

I had not been to the theatre often, my father not being a great supporter of the thespian art, but on the odd occasions when I had been to pantomimes and the like at the invitation of school friends, I had always imagined that the only place to sit was in one of the neat little boxes almost overhanging the stage. Mr Waterford had other standards; he bought two tickets for the upper circle at 1/3d each, which put us midway between the bourgeoisie of the dress circle and the proletariat of the gallery – a precise social distinction whose nicety of balance was only apparent to me later.

He bought programmes and a bar of chocolate and opined that it was going to be 'a ripping good show'. It was. I can't remember an evening of entertainment I enjoyed better. Marie Lloyd sang *A Little Of What You Fancy Does You Good* and other ballads in hilarious but questionable taste, and George Robey, dark eyebrows and all, had the audience in stitches, so that one's sides still ached from laughing right through *God Save the King*.

We went out into the night to the clip-clop of assembled cabs. I was grateful when Mr Waterford hailed one and we returned to South Audley Street in better style than we had left. I was less grateful, yet not wholly displeased, when my escort proposed marriage to me just north of Oxford Street – an offer which I gracefully declined, while agreeing with him that we could still remain friends.

*

Autumn came, and in the weeks between no more than a couple of brief notes from Father, by way of Annette, informing me that all was well and that he expected news of an improvement in our mutual fortunes at any time. This information I parried with similar brief generalities about my own doings, my main concern being that Father was well and seemingly happy with his friends at the 'Naval & Yachting'. Annette also had settled down well with Deirdre Vallence, which did not surprise me because Deirdre – who had been a rather nervy little girl at boarding school – had married and become a large, gentle and contented mother of three, which spoke well for the manifest benefits of marriage and motherhood.

This brings me to a date fixed firmly in my memory – October 21st. It was a Saturday, normally the busiest day of the week, with heavy bookings for luncheon and dinner and hardly a bed to be had. The date itself should have alerted me – of all people– to the significance of the unusually heavy demands upon the restaurant and private dining-rooms (all of which reflected on the increased patronage of my own department); but I passed the day busy as a bee and never thought to question why.

Evening came. The pressure of work in the smoking-room and bar was such that I had had to appeal to Mrs Carradine for two extra waitresses to serve at tables and was indeed obliged to give a hand there myself.

It was while I was serving two of my regular customers (a pair of retired stockbrokers who played chess together at a corner table every night of the week) that the door opened and I noticed, out of the corner of my eye, a party of gentlemen in evening dress looking about them for somewhere to sit. I was about to turn and guide them to a table when, to my sudden and shocked alarm, I found myself looking straight at the arresting profile, the naval beard – simulacrum of the King and the Tsar – the tall and ramrod-backed figure of . . . *my father!*

He had a cigarette stuck jauntily in the corner of his mouth, he was shooting his cuffs and adjusting his white tie, looking about him with the amiably proprietorial air that I knew so well. Meanwhile, I was gaping at him, wide-eyed and open-mouthed I shouldn't wonder. In less time than it takes to tell, I should have been confronted and all my subterfuges publicly revealed – this to my parent's distress and mortification, as well as my own. Before that instant came to pass, however, I propelled myself into action. Turning on my heel, I walked swiftly away into the bar and, hiding myself behind a screen, closed my eyes and wished I were anywhere else on earth.

*

This was a crisis – an impasse – from which I could not possibly extricate myself without Mrs Carradine's help.

Leaving the bar by the staff door at the rear, I went up the service stairs to her room in the eaves, knocked and waited until she asked me to come in.

'Why, Fields, I'm surprised you managed to get away to come and see me tonight. What is the matter, child? You look as if you've seen a ghost. I think you should sit down.'

'Thank you, no, Mrs Carradine,' I breathed.

'And why not?' Her eyes, though rimmed with dark circles of sleeplessness were burning with a strange brilliance, and her pale face was touched at both prominent cheekbones with livid spots of carmine. It seemed to me, from the surging restlessness conveyed by her attitude, that her very spirit was struggling to escape from out of that gaunt frail frame.

'I won't waste your time, Miss Carradine,' I said. 'You can discharge me if you like – you would be well within your rights – but, busy or not, I cannot carry out my duties down there tonight.'

There was a moment's silence before she spoke.

'I think you should sit down after all,' she said evenly, taking from her pocket her gunmetal cigarette case, 'and explain yourself. I am not to be persuaded that tonight's pressure of work has got you down. Not *you*! Not after your experience with the widowed father.' She smiled, half-mocking, through a cloud of cigarette smoke.

'It's not the work,' I said. 'You must know that.'

'I do indeed,' she said. 'And there will be plenty of activity tonight. Saturday's bad enough in all conscience – but with the usual parties of naval gentlemen celebrating Trafalgar, it will be Bedlam down there until midnight and beyond.'

'Trafalgar!' I exclaimed as the scales fell from my eyes. That explained my father's presence in all the finery of his evening dress. From early childhood, I could recall the enthusiasm with which my parent had always insisted upon celebrating Nelson's climacteric victory; how in harbour the *Gloria* was always dressed overall and illuminated fore to aft on Trafalgar night.

'So why must you absent yourself?' asked Mrs Carradine, breaking in on my thoughts. 'Why talk about being discharged, when all that is necessary is to perform your duties in your usual efficient manner?' Again that gently cynical smile. 'I would have thought that, with your cast-iron principles, you would have been particularly susceptible to the call of duty.'

'I haven't expressed myself very well, Mrs Carradine,' I said. 'The point is, there is someone. . .'

184

'Someone?'

'Someone down in the public rooms tonight whom I do not want to meet.'

'I see. Just that?'

'Yes.'

'And it is that important to you?'

'Yes, it is. I'm sorry.'

She rose with an unbelievable elegance of movement, her tall figure moving in what I had come to recognise as her idiosyncratic swaying walk towards the window. Pulling aside the curtain, she looked out across the dark roofs of Mayfair.

'Then we must accommodate you, Faith Fields,' she said at length. 'Don't worry, I will make special provision for someone else to supervise in the smoking-room and gentlemen's bar.' She turned to face me, the cynicism washed clean away from her smile. 'Knowing you, your conscience will keep you hard at work of some sort tonight.'

'I'll do my monthly bar accounts!' I cried, rejoicing that this strange and compelling woman had resolved my dilemma. 'Mrs Carradine, how can I possibly thank you enough?'

She shook her head. 'I don't ask for your thanks,' she said. 'This is not a favour. Your work alone entitles you to a certain consideration.'

No more passed between us. I left her. On my way to my own room, I heard her racking cough up there in the rafters.

*

How well Mrs Carradine knew the essential me! Conscience-driven, I slaved away on my accounts – and it was a hard penance, for I am a poor hand at figures in the best of circumstances. As the night drew on, I could hear the sound of male voices raised in chorus coming from below and could well imagine my father joining in with the rest. This did little to aid my arithmetic.

It was well past midnight when the last of the merrymakers went on their way, to the rattle of cab-wheels, the sound of a motor car's machinery coughing itself reluctantly to life, the loud exchanges of farewell echoing up and down high-fronted South Audley Street. Then . . . silence.

I went down to the smoking-room, where my girls were making some inroads at clearing up the worst of the evening's depredations.

The rest would be left for the early shift of cleaning women, in whose ranks I had first joined the Cawnpore.

'He's gone. They've all gone.'

I turned to see Mrs Carradine watching me from the doorway leading into the bar. One long, emaciated but incredibly elegant arm was raised to support herself against the jamb. Poised, vibrant in her sombre black dress, she looked like a dancer in some macabre ballet.

'Yes, he's gone,' she repeated. 'The widowed father, from whom you learned all your assurance and authority, has gone – *Miss Dangerfield.*'

I drew a deep and shuddering breath. Above all, it seemed important to remain calm.

'When do you want me to leave?' I asked. 'If you don't mind, I should prefer to wait until tomorrow morning. I have to pack and. . .'

'And you have nowhere to go, either,' she supplied. 'Don't be so melodramatic, my dear. Come and sit down.' She indicated a table at one corner of the empty bar.

Numb, puzzled, stricken to silence, I obeyed her. She fetched two glasses and a bottle of brandy from which she poured us both a measure.

Raising her glass, she said: 'To "The Immortal Memory" – this being the naval toast for the occasion, as I have learned tonight.' She smiled, and I felt an onrush of warmth from the sheer brilliance of that smile. 'To which I think we should add the name of your gallant father, Faith – Captain Lord Dangerfield – as grand a fellow as I ever met of an evening . . . and I have met a few!'

Bemused, I pledged her astonishing toast. Our glasses clinked together.

'You were here all night!' I exclaimed. '*You* took my place here and met my father?'

'Drank with him and his comrades too,' she responded cheerfully, draining her glass and refilling it. 'I have to confess, my dear, that it was my curiosity – as much as my concern for you – which prompted me to find out exactly who it was you didn't want to meet and why. So I came, I saw and I listened.'

In a very small voice, I heard myself ask, 'Did my father enjoy his Trafalgar evening? He usually does.'

'If the amount of drink and victuals that he and his equally distinguished naval friends consumed in the private dining-room is any yardstick,' she responded, 'I would say yes. Likewise, by their spirited renditions of *Heart of Oak*, *Tom Bowling*, and other nautical airs, I would say that they derived much pleasure from honouring the memory of Lord Nelson.'

'They – my father particularly – behaved themselves?' I ventured.

'Officers and gentlemen to the end,' she assured me. 'Faith, I can understand why you began this charade in the first place,' she added, replenishing my glass, 'but do you *really* have to continue it?'

I had no immediate answer for her.

*

Trusting her entirely, I told Mrs Carradine my whole story right from the first – right from the moment when, having resigned myself to the life of a social butterfly without the exciting naval connections, I had been confronted – all unprepared and unexpectedly – with the bailiffs and their 'numerical designations'.

I went on to tell how, with Annette's connivance, I had tried to fight my way into paid employment by any means that lay to hand – but all without telling my parent, for fear of injuring his masculine pride; he whose notion of weathering ill-fortune was to retain membership of his beloved club, keep in with his old comrades and – in the immortal philosophy of Mr Micawber – wait for something to turn up.

She laughed aloud when I told her how Annette had instructed me in Cockney speech.

'It was that which told me you were not who you made yourself out to be, my dear,' she informed me. 'That pathetic attempt at the Cockney accent – really! Remember, I'm a professional and a pro can spot an amateur actress a mile off. Straight away, I knew you were right out of the top drawer and acting down.'

'I always had a notion you did,' I confessed ruefully. 'But now, Mrs Carradine – advise me, please! What am I going to do about Father? As you said, I'm playing a charade and tonight is proof that I can't keep it up for much longer before he finds out.'

She reached across the table and took my hands. In hers, mine were enclosed in a dry heat of almost frightening energy. It was as if all the pent-in passion for life that her illness imposed upon her was being forced through her feverish body into my own, to strengthen and sustain me.

'Listen to me,' she said. 'You have fallen a long way, Faith. It takes a person like I am – someone who has fallen too, and lost everything that makes life worth living – love, a beloved profession, one's health. . .' She bowed her head for a few moments, then recovered herself. 'Faith, the way you have pulled yourself up and made something of yourself, why, it's truly splendid. Something to be proud of. If you were my daughter, I would wrap my arms about you and kiss you from sheer pride.

'Then there's your father. He has lost a lot too, Faith. Being women as we are, and more sensible, more practical than they, we shall never know what it costs a man like your father to accept the charity of his old friends. Yes – charity. At the end of tonight's celebrations, it wasn't your father who put his hand in his wallet and paid for the evening's entertainment. And I could see that it hurt him badly.'

I nodded. 'He's terribly proud,' I said. 'But he takes consolation from the fact that he himself helped out some of his old comrades during their hard times and that, when his ship comes in again, he can repay. That's how it is with him. That's his consolation, Mrs Carradine.'

The feverish hands pressed mine harder, increasing the strange bond that she had established between us. 'Go to him, Faith,' she whispered. 'Go to see him soon. Tomorrow. He's a lonely man, and needs you, needs the truth that you can bring him. Tell him everything, before he finds out as he might so easily have done tonight – right here in front of his comrades – and misunderstood. It's not just that his beloved daughter is working in a hotel bar, but that she has squared her shoulders against adversity and gone out and made something of herself.

'Let him hear, and judge you, Faith. Pay him that compliment of love and trust!'

*

As I walked across Mayfair that Sunday morning the bells were ringing for matins, the autumnal sun turned the weathered brickwork to a golden haze, the trees in the quiet squares shed their leaves with every passing zephyr and all was peace.

Down into St James's, my footfalls dawdled, not because I feared the ordeal which lay ahead of me: far from it, I regarded my coming encounter as a release from the life of lies that I had been living since

188

Father and I were parted; but I knew that, whichever way the meeting went, things would never be the same between us again. And my fear was for the change.

I came to the 'Naval & Yachting', that citadel of male privilege; there were many such in the aristocratic enclave, but this one added to its exclusivity by closing the doors to landsmen. Nor was the exclusion operated solely in favour of the privileged male seafarer; like the Royal Yacht Squadron, the 'N.&Y.' had blackballed Sir Thomas Lipton because that great yachtsman was also a grocer; moreover it was rumoured (and had never been denied) that an application from the German Kaiser had been similarly rejected.

Braving those frowning portals, I was immediately barred from further progress by an indignant hall porter whom from his manner and address I recognised as that familiar figure – a retired Chief Petty Officer, RN.

'Madam!' he cried, outraged. 'You can't come in 'ere, this is gentlemen only. What was it you wanted?'

I made my needs known. Ah, then, if it was Lord Dangerfield madam was after, perhaps madam would take a seat and his lordship would be enquired after. What name, please? *Miss* Dangerfield? Ah!

From then on, the functionary's manner unbent slightly; not enough to make any real difference, but just within the bounds of perception. I was brought a chair to sit upon, but was kept strictly within the porter's gaze (in case I should stray, perhaps?) while a page-boy was sent to find my father.

I sat in patience, regarding the portraits of long-dead admirals and yacht masters which lined the walls of the entrance lobby.

Presently came the sound of footsteps that I knew well. And: 'Why, Faith, my dearest – what a wonderful surprise! Did you just come up from Dorset? How are you, my love?'

Father embraced me, looked me up and down and declared that the country air was doing me good. He himself was dressed in weekend tweeds and appeared none the worse for his late-night celebrations at the Cawnpore.

'Father, I must speak with you on a very important matter,' I told him. 'Now . . . right away. Is there anywhere we can be alone?'

'Certainly not in the "N.&Y."! But it just so happens that I was getting ready to go out and feed the ducks,' said Father. And to the hall porter: 'Do you have my crusts and crumbs, Micklewright?'

'Yes, me lord! Bagley – 'is lordship's usual duck food!'

The page-boy produced a brown paper bag and gravely handed it to my father. Arm-in-arm, we walked out into the sunshine of St James's and bent our footsteps towards the Park and the lake of ducks.

Presently we were sitting on a park bench, with the greedy birds facing us, advancing and retreating to snap up the proffered scraps; stabbing at each other with irritable beaks if one or another of the congregation was so bold as to move out of the pecking order.

'That one, I call Fortescue,' said Father, pointing. 'Do you remember the Flag Captain at the Nore? He had just such a way of slipping out of line when no one was watching him and grabbing the best favours going. You really do look very well, my dear. How is little Deirdre Vallence? Has she filled out yet?'

The moment had come when all the lying must stop...

'Father,' I began, 'did you enjoy your Trafalgar evening at the Cawnpore?'

He looked puzzled for a moment, then grinned. 'Ah, you've been talking to Chief Micklewright while you were waiting,' he said. 'And he's been telling tales out of school.'

'No, Father,' I replied. 'I didn't hear about it from anyone. You see ... I saw you there.'

His rich blue gaze was fixed upon me in astonishment. 'You *saw* me there?' he repeated.

'Yes, Father. You see, I work there – living in.'

'You *work* there – living in?'

'Yes, Father. I began there as a cleaner.' Fearing his reaction, I rushed on: 'And I worked my way up – rather quickly – to supervisor of the smoking-room and gentlemen's bar. A kind of ... glorfied barmaid, really.'

'I see.'

His expression betrayed nothing of what he thought and I sought to justify myself. 'It was impossible to get what one might call a ladylike job, you see? For a start, there aren't any; only governesses and companions, and I really couldn't bear that. And for attractive positions – running flower shops and the like – one needs capital. Employers simply don't want to know about gentlefolk, or so it seems to me. I ... I expect you would have found it the same, Father.'

'Worse, I expect,' he replied. 'As a retired officer, I could have joined the board of several companies. As a retired officer who is also an undischarged bankrupt, I would be shown the door. Peer or no peer.'

I reached out my hand and touched his tentatively.

'Are you . . . angry with me, Father?' I asked. 'For lying to you – and all the rest?'

For answer, he took hold of my hand and, drawing me to my feet, tucked my arm in his.

'Let's go for a walk,' he said mildly.

The morning was bright and fresh down by the river. We walked quickly, not saying very much; avoiding the topic of my shameful behaviour, falling back upon the commonplace. Father observed that the unusual height of the river could be accounted for by the equi-noctial gales; this naturally led us to matters nautical and he told me that the *Gloria* had come up for sale in Deptford and had been knocked down for a pittance. We walked sadly and in silence for quite a while after that.

Our footsteps seemed to lead us over Lambeth Bridge, where we paused in the middle to watch a string of barges chugging past below; a little boy in the stern waved up at us, shielding his eyes from the sun, and we waved back.

Father took my hand again. 'We'll go a little further,' he said.

We came to a mean street off Lambeth Road – a place of small shops tucked in between ale-houses and dwelling-houses, where people sat out on holystoned steps, their inquisitive eyes following us. At the end of this street, tucked away around a corner, was a shop with a gaily-painted front and the legend picked out in red and gold lettering:

A. FROST — PURVEYOR OF TRIPE & COWHEEL

Father turned to enter the shop: wonderingly, I followed him. It was cool inside and smelled of sawdust and vinegar. Upon our entry a short, stout man bustled out from a back area, wiping his hands on a cloth.

' 'Morning, guv'nor and lady. What'll it be then?"

'Good morning, Arthur,' replied my father.

The effect upon the other was quite remarkable. He peered more closely at my parent (it was dim and shadowy in the shop), and exclaimed: ' 'Swelp me, if it ain't the Toff! Blimey, I didn't recognise you in your Sunday best, Toff old shiner!'

'No use being poor and looking poor,' responded Father. 'How's trade today, Arthur?'

' 'Bout the same. What you doin' here on your Sunday off, anyhow?'

'Brought my daughter to meet you,' said my father, taking my hand. 'Faith, I'd like you to meet Arthur Frost – my employer.'

' 'Ow d'you do, Faith?' Mr Frost pumped my proffered hand with vigour, meantime calling out, 'Hey, Alice! Toff's 'ere with his little jug o' water. Come and say hello!'

Wonderingly, speechless, I accepted the good wishes of a lady who emerged from the back of the shop. If she was not Mr Frost's wife, she could well have been his twin sister.

'You in work, duckie?' she asked.

I found my voice. 'Yes. I . . . I'm a barmaid,' I said.

'It's lovely clean work,' she commented. 'Are you goin' to stop for a bit o' dinner, Toff?' she asked Father.

'Not today Alice, thanks,' said he. 'Got to be on our way. See you tomorrow. Come, Faith.'

The woman winked at me. 'No one can sell tripe 'n' cowheel like your old man,' she declared. 'It's the way he 'as, you know. Talk the hind leg off a donkey, can your old man. Bye, love – call again some time.'

Outside, I let my father walk me just clear of the shop and then, my eyes brimming and a lump rising in my throat, I threw my arms about him, oblivious of the onlookers.

'Well, that's it, old girl,' he said. 'Like father, like daughter – they can't keep a Dangerfield down. And we're terrible liars – we even lie to each other!'

Somewhere up on high, I think I heard a lark sing.

'Daddy darling, you're wonderful,' I told him. 'Oh, how I do love you so!'

ST GEORGE'S SQUARE, PIMLICO

NINE

'So Father and I decided that, now we're both in work and earning, we would set up house together somewhere. Would that be all right with the hotel, Mrs Carradine? About living out, I mean?'

'There won't be any objection,' she replied, 'provided you're here when you're needed, Faith. However, I will arrange matters with Mrs Cornwall, just to make it official. You'll take furnished rooms, I expect?'

'Yes, somewhere fairly cheap of course.'

'I can recommend a Mrs Slyte who lets furnished rooms in St George's Square. That would be midway to work for you and your father.'

I shook my head, bemused.

'Why do you smile, Faith?' she asked.

'I just can't get used to the idea of my father serving behind the counter of a tripe and cowheel shop,' I said. 'Why, he's gone through his entire life so far without even knowing what tripe and cowheel are, I shouldn't wonder.'

'And he makes a good job of it?'

'They think the world of him. They call him "Toff" and treat him as one of themselves. It's wonderful.'

'It's character, Faith,' she said. 'Just character. You have it too. And now, before you get too swollen-headed from my compliments, you did volunteer to help me with the inventory of the bedding and crockery. . .'

*

I followed up Mrs Carradine's recommendation and called to see Mrs Slyte, who offered a first floor suite comprising living-room, two bedrooms, a kitchen and bathroom, all furnished, for 27/6d a week. This was marginally more than we wanted to pay – indeed, rather more than we could afford on our combined wages, particularly since we would have to find omnibus fares and extra meals. In the event, I brought Father to see the place; he looked around, approved of quiet and secluded St George's Square, thought the furnishings were quite adequate, the rooms clean and neat, and – most importantly – he 'liked the cut of Mrs Slyte's jib'. By skimping and scraping we reckoned we could just about manage the rent. So we took it.

The day of our great decision coincided with an echo from the past which affected me more than I would have believed – indeed, more than I cared for. It happened during my periodical checking of the bar and smoking-room, before we opened for business after breakfast was finished in the hotel. As I walked around, plumping cushions, emptying the odd ash-tray that the cleaning women had overlooked, flicking away a spot of dust here and there and squaring up the piles of magazines on the occasional tables, I happened to drop one of the popular society papers – and it fell open at the page of photographs of a naval wedding: Miss So-and-So, daughter of Admiral and Mrs So-and-So married to Lieutenant Whatsisname, RN. And there in the middle of it all was Jack Cummings, standing in double line with a dozen or so others and making an archway of swords for the happy couple to pass under. He looked every inch the corsair, and I am ashamed to admit that I tore out the picture and kept it. Nor did the matter end there, for I raised it with Father the next time we met.

'I see the appalling Cummings has been promoted to full Commander,' I said, with false malevolence.

'Didn't know you were *au fait* with the *Gazette* and the Navy List,' responded my father, amused.

'I saw a picture of him taken at a wedding,' I explained.

'Yes, he got his brass hat last month,' said Father. 'Pushy sort of chap, but he'll obviously go far. Damnably capable.'

'Capable of anything, I would think,' I commented, watchful of the effect my words were having upon my parent. 'He certainly went out of his way to queer your pitch, Father.'

But he was not to be drawn; he could not give me any indication of his feelings about Jack Cummings, save the usual male jargon about the other having done his duty and answered as he saw fit under oath . . . when all the time I knew I had been desperately hoping he would say something like: 'I've got an open mind about Cummings and I've decided to take the opportunity of his promotion to write and congratulate him. Perhaps invite him round to the 'Naval and Yachting,' for a drink'.

But he said nothing of the kind, so I decided that notwithstanding the male code of duty and all that rubbish, he felt about Jack the way the vengeful, aggressive half of me felt. Which was that the other had behaved in a thoroughly ungentlemanly manner at the court-martial.

So why, I asked myself – and could find no answer – did I nevertheless continue to keep the torn-out photograph of Jack Cummings, and take it out from time to time and look at it? And relive a seductive moment on a beach in Malta?

*

The brilliant summer of that Coronation year (one Wednesday in August, the temperature in London reached the record height of 100°F) mellowed through a mild autumn into a wet winter, and Father and I settled down to our new life in St George's Square. The quite adequate furnishings we augmented by a few nice pieces which we had been able to salvage from the wrecks of our lost homes; what was left – bits and pieces and a large tea chest stuffed with unresolvable junk – we stowed away in the basement, to await a quiet weekend when we could sort it out.

Our weekday routine was now established. We took turns to rise on alternate mornings to make coffee and toast; then Father left for Lambeth, where the shop opened at 8.30, leaving me to wash up and tidy around before travelling by tramcar to Hyde Park Corner in time to open the smoking-room and bar at the civilised hour of 10 am. As a *quid pro quo* for our excellent accommodation, I was able to attain our landlady's fourteen-year-old son a job as living-in boot boy at the Cawnpore; and as a further advantage, Mrs Slyte was so grateful that she undertook to do my cleaning and laundry at a very cheap rate, which left me virtually free of household commitments and able to devote myself very largely to what I had begun to look upon as my 'career'.

It pleased me greatly to be able to acknowledge to myself that, under my supervision, the bar and smoking-room prospered – and profited – very handsomely. The takings were increased by twelve per cent over the equivalent period of the previous year, and this did not include Coronation week.

Both Father and I worked Saturdays and alternate Sundays. We usually managed to arrange the same free Sundays, and would spend them taking an omnibus ride to Kew or Wimbledon Common, or attend a concert at the Albert Hall; my first introduction to 'The Messiah' was a performance by the Huddersfield Choral Society conducted by Sir Henry Wood.

For lighter entertainment, on my occasional evenings off (poor Father worked most nights until the tripe and cowheel shop closed at 8.30), I visited a music hall with that inveterate habitué Stanley Waterford. Stanley, to whom I became quite attached in the manner of an older sister or cousin, refrained from touching upon the issue of matrimony, but – a great gossip – was a mine of information concerning the hotel, its management and its clientele. On some evenings when we came out of the Oxford or the Strand, the Canterbury or Collins's – temples of pleasure made famous by the talents of the Great Vance, Albert Chevalier, Vesta Tilley, Little Titch and the other darlings of public taste – he would invite me to supper at a chop-house and there divert me with apocryphal tales of long-dead patrons of the Cawnpore: of the retired Indian Army colonel who kept a python in his bathroom; the famous American diva whose habit of doing her voice exercises on the balcony of her room while still in night attire frequently stopped the early morning traffic in South Audley Street; the murderer from Hamburg who was cornered and captured in Room 47 on the fourth floor, after having attempted to kill himself by leaping out of the window when the police burst in . . . and whose tortured spirit, according to the older members of the hotel staff, still haunted that room, so that impressionable young chambermaids will not enter to turn back the bed save in pairs.

But it was Stanley's fleshing out of the hotel's history, some of which I already knew, that most intrigued me. It seems that the establishment's transition in the 1880s from a raffish gambling den to a shrine of upper middle-class respectability was by no means achieved without certain social difficulties. The gentleman who inherited the residue of the 99-year lease on the property scandalised his family by falling in love with and threatening to marry a young woman of the music halls. A man of title, he might well have achieved his ambition and wedded the girl, for the 'naughty eighties'

and the even more 'naughty nineties' were an open season for peers
marrying actresses and the like. However, there was a surprising
impediment to the young nobleman's desires for the lady in question, far from wanting to marry her lord, insisted upon remaining
single. She had taken account of no fewer than six women with
whom her swain had formed attachments in the past, and did not
much relish the notion of spending her declining years as chatelaine
of some miasma-ridden stately home in the shires, while his lordship
cavorted with newer, younger actresses and others in Cannes and
Deauville. Their relationship could continue as it was, she said. And
for an insurance policy, she demanded and got the Cawnpore Hotel
– lock, stock and barrel.

The lady in question, said Stanley shyly (after having sworn me to
secrecy) was none other than his aunt, the so-called Mrs Cornwall,
who was no 'Mrs' and had taken the appellation Cornwall because
the major part of her lover's properties lay within the duchy.

And that, he added, was why his aunt ruled the affairs of the
Cawnpore with a rod of iron. The only impediment to her unchall-
enged control was the existence of a board of directors appointed by
the trustees of her dead lover's estate; by the operation of a few lines
of small print inserted by the trustees' lawyers and overlooked by
Mrs Cornwall's legal advisers, they were able in certain circumstances (which they could dictate), to override her wishes – a right
they had exercised on several occasions, much to the old lady's fury.
The last time, said Stanley, was when the board had forbidden his
aunt to negotiate with the Home Secretary for the provision of a
gambling licence for the hotel; the staff went in fear and trembling
for a week after that, he recalled, and Wink-Wink the Peke had not
been heard to yap in all that time.

I call to mind this particular anecdote because it had some bearing on a particularly unpleasant incident which took place some
weeks later, when a ghost from my past rose up and made to destroy
my treasured career.

*

My relationship with Mrs Carradine developed along the lines of the
kind of friendship which can often exist between an older and a
younger woman – a little more than a sisterly connection and not
quite that of mother and daughter. She encouraged me to address

199

her as Beatrice, though I found it easier to slip back into the more formal style.

And she was ill; terribly, terribly ill. Only I, who visited her daily in her room under the eaves and saw her struggle against the dread disease that was almost literally eating her alive, could begin to know the strength of that gallant heart which fought against her disability; the restless energy, the wild enthusiasms and the bright optimism – itself a significant symptom of the malady – which coloured her existence. One morning I entered to find her lying on a couch in the corner of her office, her face ashen, a handkerchief pressed to her lips (which she quickly screwed up and thrust into her pocket), and realised that she had had another of the agonised coughing fits which were becoming ever more frequent. I managed to persuade her to accept her doctor's advice (which she had once let slip to me and dismissed with typical scorn), to be admitted into a sanatorium for treatment. This time, even she had come to realise that she could no longer continue working as she had been doing.

'And I can only take the opportunity because of you, Faith,' she told me. 'Thanks to you, I know I can leave the place in capable hands.'

I would add that it had been obvious from the first that the 'assistant housekeeper' was truly the manager of the hotel in all but name. The male functionary who actually bore this title, along with his two assistants (of whom Stanley Waterford was possibly the least effective of the pair) were no more than sops to the hotel tradition of masculine dominance – whereas the Cawnpore was truly a matriarchal institution. From Mrs Cornwall at the top, through Beatrice Carradine to the likes of myself, women really ruled the roost there.

I saw Beatrice off from King's Cross Station on her way to a prolonged stay at a sanatorium in the Peak District of Derbyshire, and returned to work as the temporary acting assistant housekeeper of the prestigious Cawnpore Hotel. That night, by way of a gesture towards my modest achievement, Father took me out to a late supper at a pleasant establishment in Pimlico, where we had lamb cutlets and toasted each other in stout.

*

The trouble came from out of the blue: quietly at first, so that one was taken all unawares when it blazed alive in its full fury.

It all began with a call from the reception desk in the main hall.

The Cawnpore, though equipped with an excellent telephone system with an exchange that could handle six outside lines, relied upon the old and trusted method of voice pipes for internal communication.

The whistle at the cap of the voice-pipe in Beatrice Carradine's office shrilled out; it was Stanley Waterford:

'Is that Miss Fields?' (To prevent confusion amongst the staff, I still retained my nom de plume.)

'Yes, Stanley. What is it?' He sounded very worried.

'Faith, would you please come down? One of the guests insists that a diamond bracelet has been stolen from her room.' He lowered his voice. 'She is threatening all kinds of action. Perhaps you can calm her down – and her gentleman friend – while we make a search?'

'All right, Stanley,' I replied, perhaps a trifle patronisingly. 'Keep calm – I will come down straight away to calm your irate lady.'

A touch to my hair in the mirror and then I went downstairs – unknowingly for a very significant encounter with the probing finger of idle fate.

There was a group of people at the reception desk, behind which stood poor Stanley looking like a well-meaning sheepdog who has quite lost control of his charges and just seen them disappear over the hillside.

A man and a woman – obviously the guests in question – were standing with their backs to me. Alongside was one of the chamber-maids; the poor creature was in tears. And also a pile of expensive-looking luggage: cabin trunks, hat-boxes, suitcases.

Stanley caught my eye and breathed an obvious sigh of relief; I smiled reassurance at him.

'Mr Waterford, can I be of any assistance in your problem?' I asked in the calm, clear voice which I had found by experience was effective in cutting through most of the minor hysteria which existed in a busy hotel full of all kinds of folk – easy-going and difficult, both.

'Miss Fields,' he explained, 'this lady complains that her diamond bracelet, which she wore to dinner in the restaurant last night, was missing when she came to pack away her jewel case prior to leaving this morning.'

'I see,' was my response. 'Madam, I am extremely sorry to hear of your . . .'

And my voice died away as I found myself looking into the countenance of wild-rose beauty and the suddenly hate-filled eyes of

Natasha Chalmers, formerly my father's fiancée!

'Are you the person in charge here?' she demanded with a sang-froid for which I will always give her credit – a sangfroid which, let it be added, I had only once seen demolished, and that by my father at our last encounter.

'I am, madam,' I replied, not to be outdone in coolness.

'Then you will see to it that the bracelet and or the culprit, are found, or it will be the worse for you!' The speaker was her 'gentle-man friend', a man of about my father's age, perhaps slightly older. He was short and thick-set, with a ruddy complexion and angry slightly protruding eyes. A choleric man. A violent man. He stood regarding me from under grizzled, gingerish eyebrows, a savage mouth framed by a soup-strainer moustache of the same hue. One word to describe him came to my mind: 'loathsome'.

'Who am I addressing, sir?' I asked.

'This is Lord Bathchurch,' supplied Stanley.

Lord Bathchurch of the *Thames Examiner*! The scandal sheet which had pilloried my father and my poor dead uncle right to his grave! I had thought the face vaguely familiar from newspaper photographs, though Bathchurch was known to be as reticent about his own private life as he was forthcoming about the vagaries of other folks. And *he* was Natasha Chalmers' new gentleman friend! I wondered if she had expectations of a title at last . . .

'Be assured, my lord,' I said, 'that every effort will be made to find the bracelet.'

'And damn quickly too!' he blared. 'Mrs Chalmers and I are catching the Liverpool boat train at eleven. If by then that bracelet has not been found and the miscreant brought to book . . .' here he threw a savage glance at the little chambermaid, who burst into another flood of tears, '. . . there'll be trouble. Big trouble. I know how to wield a thick stick, young woman. Now – what are you going to do about it, hey?'

I could have screamed my hatred and detestation in his face; instead I managed to retain my dignity and even continued to address him in the customary form of servant to master.

'What I propose, my lord,' I replied, 'is to instigate a thorough search of madam's room, taking up the carpets, moving away all the furniture and so on.'

'That has already been done!' interposed Natasha Chalmers. 'Why do we shilly-shally? This creature . . .' she pointed to the chambermaid, 'has obviously taken the bracelet. Send for the police. Send for them at once!'

I drew a deep breath. 'With respect, no, madam,' I said. 'First a really thorough search – and then the police.'

'I didn't do it, Miss Fields!' wailed the wretched little chambermaid, by name Nancy Vickers. 'I didn't, honest!'

'Lying wretch!' cried that woman. 'Hubert,' she addressed Bathchurch, 'will you demand that this *person* summons the police? Then we must go, or we shall miss our train.'

I folded my arms and stood very straight; I knew what was coming.

The angry, choleric eyes bore into me, the savage mouth a brutal slash beneath the bristling moustache. His breath smelled of stale tobacco and spirits.

'The police!' he grated. '*Now* – if you value your job!'

The good name of the hotel might have been sufficient to direct my actions; but there was more to it than that. There was the memory of the vicious attack upon the Dangerfields in that loathsome man's horrible paper. There was the memory of that woman and her repeated machinations. There was the fact that little Nancy Vickers to my certain knowledge was quite incapable of theft, and might well be arrested, thrown into a cell and driven half out of her mind with terror.

Bathchurch thrust his vile face closer to mine.

'Are you defying me, young woman?' he snarled.

'Defiance scarcely comes into it, my lord,' I replied. 'There are certain ways of dealing with such matters and I intend to follow the procedure that is the normal practice in this hotel. We do not immediately assume that the loss or misplacement of a guest's property is a matter for the police.'

'I didn't *do* it, Miss Fields!' cried Nancy Vickers yet again.

Lord Bathchurch pointed his stubby finger straight into my face.

'You are *insolent!*' he shouted.

'She has always been that way,' interposed Natasha Chalmers. 'A spoilt brat . . . but now, happily, she has got her deserts and come down in the world.'

He looked surprised. 'You know this woman, Natasha?' he asked.

'I know her,' she replied, glancing at me with gleeful malevolence. 'I can tell you all about her later. Settle the matter and let's be gone, or else we shall miss the train.'

'I'll settle her hash, right enough!' said Bathchurch, turning back to me. 'You're *finished*, young woman,' he declared. 'Your chairman, Lord Barnworthy, is a personal friend of mine. Whether or not the bracelet turns up, I shall see to it that you're sent packing. Packing! And without a reference! Come, Natasha. The taxi's outside.'

'One thing, your lordship,' I said as they turned to go. 'When the bracelet is found – as I hope and believe it will be – the hotel can dispatch it to Liverpool immediately. I presume you have left a forwarding address.'

'Yes, yes, we have the shipping company and the name of the liner,' interposed Stanley Waterford, who had been watching and listening throughout the exchange with wide eyes and mouth agape.

Lord Bathchurch did not deign to reply, but Natasha Chalmers saw fit to cast me a triumphant hate-filled glance as she went out of the door.

Possessing – as she almost certainly did, as I once had – a valuable bracelet for every day of the week, she must certainly have reckoned its loss well worth while for having almost certainly ruined my career at the Cawnpore.

'Faith, I'm sorry,' said Stanley. 'I only asked you to come down to pour oil on troubled waters in the way you have. But this. . .' he spread his hands helplessly.

'Will that man . . . is he really able to make real trouble for me, Stanley?' I asked.

'I'm very much afraid so,' he said, lowering his voice and looking about him, though there was no one within hearing distance. 'I'm quite sure that my aunt would support you through thick and thin, but her backing could do you more harm than good if Barnworthy were to order you to be sacked at that fellow's instigation. Let us only hope that the bracelet turns up and he doesn't carry out his threat.'

'There's not much hope there,' I replied. 'After what's happened between us in the past, Mrs Chalmers couldn't resist doing me a bad turn. She'll make him carry out his threat.'

And I knew this was so.

*

When I went home that evening, the bracelet had not been found although the room had been ransacked. The police had been sent for and little Nancy Vickers had been interrogated, but fortunately they were satisfied that no charge could be laid against her – though she had had access to the room during the time when Natasha Chalmers and her paramour were at breakfast.

I felt utterly wretched about my prospects. That unholy pair might well get me the sack, though I supposed that if she was not able to save me, Mrs Cornwall would at least give me a good reference, with the aid of which I might get myself fixed up in another first-class West End hotel; at least I would not be entering the labour market at the bottom again, with the added burden of being a 'lady'. But – and this was what rankled – I had made something of myself at the Cawnpore and I was frankly proud of my effort. Furthermore I loved my job. I liked the people. And I was bitterly – tearfully – angry that those creatures should have threatened all I had worked and striven for.

Father arrived home at around ten-thirty; the folks of Lambeth supped late after their work and the shop was open and thriving at all hours.

He found me in tears.

'Out with it, darling girl,' he said, putting an arm round my shoulders and drawing me to him.

I told him about the re-emergence of the Chalmers woman, about Bathchurch and his threat.

'It hasn't happened yet,' was his typical comment. 'Tomorrow's another day, my love. Sufficient unto the day! Why, before the appalling Bathchurch makes his complaint to Barnworthy, something else might have come into his life to distract him. Or you might have been offered another and much more splendid job in another hotel. The bracelet will undoubtedly turn up. Yes, this whole business has the unmistakable tang of an affair that will be forgotten in no time. I promise you. Why, I'd wager a thousand guineas on it, so I would.'

I smiled through my tears and laid a gentle finger on his lips. 'You promised me, Father,' I said, 'when we left Grosvenor Mews Place, that you would never, ever swear that oath again.'

Father grinned. 'So I did, so I did,' he admitted. 'Nor have I sworn it often – nor gambled a penny piece since that day. Furthermore, if I had certain knowledge of this year's Derby winner, I would write the nag's name on a piece of paper and consign it to the fire. My word on it. A thousand guineas on my word!'

We laughed together and I hugged him close. In such a manner had my father the knack of driving away my dark thoughts; he had always possessed it.

'What are you doing for luncheon tomorrow?' he asked.

'Well . . . taking it at the hotel, as usual,' I replied, 'no kindly handsome gentleman having offered me any alternative.'

'This kindly handsome gentleman is offering you an alternative,' he replied.

'That sounds nice.'

'Shall you be free to meet me at twelve-thirty?'.

'Yes.'

'Might I suggest St James's Park – third bench on the right from Horse Guards Parade – facing the duck-pond?'

'I shall bring crusts and crumbs for Fortescue and friends,' I promised. 'What will you bring?'

'Wait and see!'

*

I had a retrospective dream that night. First of all I dreamed of Dickie Jobling. Now, it must not be thought that my most constant suitor (poor Stanley Waterford could scarcely be counted) had entirely given me up, nor had I seen the end of him after his letter from Gosport in Hampshire. Soon after Christmas, he had descended on me unannounced at the hotel to take me out to supper after I had finished work.

There followed the traditional ritual of proposal, with the set-piece words (prompted by me, when he forgot them) and the standard refusal. Dickie, not one whit abashed, then treated me to a most marvellous repast, fleshed out with his account of learning to fly with the Army Air Battalion – soon, he told me, to be retitled the Royal Flying Corps. Dear Dickie's native exuberance was severely restricted that night by reason of a plaster cast that contained his right leg from hip to ankle, or he would have had me on the dance floor and joining him in *Alexander's Ragtime Band* and other popular rags rendered by the restaurant orchestra. The unfortunately broken limb, so he informed me, was a memento of his previous week's flying instruction. As he explained, it is relatively easy to get an aeroplane into the air; bringing pilot and machine back on to terra firma in two separate but fully working elements posed certain difficulties.

I dreamed of Dickie in his flying machine. . .

I dreamed of Jack Cummings. Ever since coming across the picture of him at the naval wedding, I had kept a secret scrapbook of his doings; not, I told myself, out of any romantic interest, past or present, but simply because this was a man whom I had known as a nobody, but who might very well achieve some considerable distinction in his career.

There was, for instance, the paragraph in the *London Gazette* informing all who cared to know that Cdr J. Cummings, DSO had passed out top of his Staff Course at Greenwich and was appointed to HMS *Juncta* as Commanding Officer. This I had stuck in the scrapbook. What I had not also included was the following item from the 'Court and Social' in the *Morning Post*:

> . . . The engagement is announced between Cdr. Jack Cummings, DSO, RN, son of the late Mr and Mrs T. Cummings of Plymouth, Devon and Stephanie, younger daughter of the late Major P.B. Trafford and Mrs Trafford, of Brookshire Hall, Brookshire, Leicestershire.

This cutting I had consigned to the wastepaper basket, and the scrapbook to the back of the drawer. But there was yet another announcement a mere week or so later:

> Cdr. J. Cummings, RN and Miss S. Trafford. The engagement between the above has been terminated and the marriage will not now take place. . .

This sent me scurrying for the scrapbook in the back of the drawer, to be reinstated in my small collection of commonplace books.

*

Next morning a glum-faced Stanley greeted me with the news that the bracelet had not turned up. This put a considerable damper on my new optimism; but I squared my shoulders, went out to the Park quite early and took my place at the bench where Father and I had once fed the ducks and begun a string of confidences which had brought us to our present, mutually happy state.

For a duck fancier, I had learned, the kitchen of the Cawnpore was a veritable Aladdin's cave of comestible goodies; the pastry chef had provided me with a sizable brown paper bag of duck food of the most luxurious sort: Captain Fortescue and his less adventurous companions fed richly and extravagantly that noon.

Big Ben struck the half hour and still there was no sign of Father. I was not in any way perturbed, for he had a long walk from Lambeth and both on the score of thrift and in pursuit of physical fitness, he eschewed public transport and relied upon shank's pony for getting around in the metropolis. My brown paper bag empty, Captain Fortescue and his fellows having retired in search of other purveyors, I sat back and let the gentle beauty of the early spring day well over me and warm my spirit.

I think the unseasonable warmth and my curious sense of well-being may almost have sent me into a doze. Certainly I recall hearing the footsteps approaching me along the path from my right, coming from the direction of the Palace; they were a man's footsteps, but my mind also registered that they were not those of my father who, though fast-walking and vigorous, nevertheless walked with the heavy, measured tread of a man in his prime; these were the light and swinging footsteps of a younger man and I did not open my eyes.

And then it seemed to me that a great stillness had descended, all unbidden, upon my contained world, and I was unaccountably poised of a sudden on the brink of a certain splendour that was just beyond the reach of my questing fingers. Time moved with the slow deliberation of a fugue swelling from the organ notes that fill the vastness of some mighty cathedral, or a sublime violinist sketching out the air of one of the slow, stately pavanes of old Spain.

I opened my eyes . . . and we were looking at each other across a vast distance of space. He had not changed; I had not changed since that rain-kissed day on the lonely beach in Malta; only my heart had awakened.

'Faith,' murmured Jack Cummings.

Just my name; that was all.

*

The doorman at the Ritz recognised me at once; the old fellow as good as picked me up and kissed me like he used to do when Father brought me as a little girl.

We lingered over the menu and I think we may have held hands. So much about that oddly memorable day has faded into a pink mist of memories that I occasionally take out, refurbish, dust down and then put back ready to warm another grey day – so that the details of what really took place between us have blurred and shifted. But we were certainly an unconscionable time over our luncheon, and in any other restaurant save the Ritz the waiters would have been pointedly putting chairs on to tables to signify their disapproval.

This was the burden of our conversation, stripped of most of the pink mist with which I have glamorised the occasion in the years since:

'I don't think my father ever intended to meet me today.'

He replied, 'Take your choice. Here's the evidence. He telephoned me at Greenwich on Tuesday. Invited me to lunch, and was most particular about where we should meet. . .'

'In St James's Park,' I supplied. 'Third bench on the right from Horse Guards Parade. . .'

'Facing the duck-pond. He's a rum cove, your father.'

'Full of surprises – as I've often guessed in the past, but of which he has thoroughly convinced me lately.'

Jack looked thoughtfully into the lees of his wine glass. 'He's never ceased to surprise *me*,' he said, with a touch of something that sounded like wistfulness.

Now, if there was anything I had resolved from the moment it became clear that our 'accidental' meeting had been no accident at all, it was to shut my mind and seal my lips with respect to any thought of Father's court martial and Jack Cummings's part in it. And his last remark, and the manner in which it had been delivered, seemed to me to veer perilously close to the kind of questions and answers I intended to avoid – on that particular day, at least.

So, searching around for and finding a topic that would sweep the forbidden subject under the carpet, I said, 'I saw the announcement of your engagement in the *Post*.'

His eyes – those unfathomable blue eyes – swept to meet my gaze. 'Did you not also see the retraction?' he asked.

'Of course.'

'Well, there you have it,' he stated and seemed inclined to let it rest there.

I, however, was not so inclined. 'It struck me as being rather precipitate, for you,' I said. 'I have always thought of you as being the kind of person who would be slow to come to that sort of decision, and even slower to change his mind when once made up. Am I wrong? Not that it is really any business of mine.'

'It was an . . . aberration.'

'I see.' On that note I was perfectly willing to let the topic die.

It was then, after I had slightly muddied the waters of our discourse and — for my part, at least — a certain constraint had sprung up as a barrier between us, that Jack Cummings performed a feat of entirely unselfconscious magic which I had first seen him demonstrate on the foreshore in Malta: the trick of turning from gravity to gaiety, from shadow to sunlight, corsair to gamin.

'Did you hear about Lady Freakley's dreadful social blunder?' he asked, treating me to that wide lop-sided grin that informed his change of character.

'Why, no,' I replied, responding to his mood. 'Since the flotilla paid off, I've heard no news from Malta worth a mention. Whatever did she do? And she so careful about the proprieties!'

'I had the story from a friend of mine in *Iron Duke*, who was there in Malta for the Coronation celebrations,' said Jack. 'The gaffe occurred during a reception given at the Governor's palace. Present, of course, was everyone who *was* everyone, visiting foreign dignitaries and all. Now Lady F., mindful of the fact that her two unmarried nieces were due to pay her a protracted visit (and she had been trailing her cloak amongst most of the eligible young bachelors on the island), had great hopes of meeting one or two likely marriage prospects at the reception. And you know her propensity for matchmaking, Faith?'

'Do I not?' was my heartfelt response to that.

'Picture the scene,' continued my informant (and he did really tell a tale most entertainingly, even making a pretty good attempt at Lady Freakley's manner and speech). 'There is Lady F., all poised to pounce upon a likely and eligible bachelor or two. Enter stage left the Italian Minister of Trade and Fisheries who, as she happens to have heard, is negotiating for the purchase of a villa on Gozo — and by all accounts he is a millionaire as well as a prince of the Italian aristocracy. More about him than that is not known in Malta. As far as her ladyship is concerned, he is young, rich and eligible and he enters the room with an elderly lady — clearly his mother — upon his arm.

'At an early opportunity, Lady F. gets the poor young prince to herself. Within minutes, she has secured from him a promise to come to dinner to meet her nieces, to go to sea with the Navy, to play polo and all that. Triumph for the matchmaker!

'And then Sir Jasper, fresh from the buffet table, sails into view, a little unsteady from having overdone the liquid ballast.

' "My dear Prince," trills Lady F., "may I present my husband, the Admiral Commanding" et cetera et cetera – followed by much shaking of hands. And then, on to the scene comes the lady accompanying the Minister. On closer inspection she proves to be rather highly coloured as to hair and complexion – but not by the hand of nature. Lady F., never put about for how to make the next move, smiles deliciously at the newcomer, introduces her husband and closes with the telling phrase:

' "And the lady, I presume, is his highness's mother." '

'Now, Faith, you know that Lady F.'s voice generally silences all other conversation in a room for a radius of several yards. So it was on this occasion: all turn to regard – through monocles, pince-nez and lorgnettes – the mother of the rich, distinguished and no doubt handsome Italian prince and government minister.'

'Oh, Jack – how *awful!*' I exclaimed. 'I just *know* what happened next!'

'You're very prescient, Faith,' he replied. 'And it was as you anticipate. The lady in question (who, by my friend's account, could out-shout Lady F. by far and must have learned to do so selling oysters in the Naples fish market), responded in stentorian tones that reached right across the reception room:

' "You have the relationship wrong, *signora!* Not mother – *wife!*" ' '

We laughed until the head waiter brought the bill and coyly apprised us of the time by requesting to know if we were staying for tea.

*

Jack walked me back across the park. I, in turn, walked him to Westminster pier to catch the Greenwich steamer. We stood by the embankment wall and quite unselfconsciously held hands – looking, I suppose, for all the world what we were: a couple apart from the humdrum workaday and totally immersed in each other; a couple, in fact, enjoying the entirely satisfactory state of a commonplace human condition.

'I shall require a very convincing explanation from Father regarding this luncheon engagement,' I said with mock severity.

'Don't be too hard on the Skipper,' said Jack. 'He's certainly a better hand at bringing girls and chaps together than poor Lady Freakley.' At which sally we more or less collapsed into each other's arms in paroxysms of laughter, so that a Salvation Army lassie handing out temperance tracts felt constrained to press one into my hand.

'How is the Skipper, anyhow?' asked Jack, as we went together down the steps to the pier, where the steamer was warping alongside. 'What's he doing with himself – apart from looking out at the world from the smoking-room window of the Naval and Yachting?'

'He's working as an assistant in a tripe and cowheel shop in Lambeth,' I said.

'I'm sorry, Faith, I must have misheard you,' he said.

I said it again. . .

'As an assistant?' he repeated.

'Yes.'

'I bet he's a bloody good one,' he said.

It was the first – and only – time I ever heard Jack Cummings utter an expletive.

*

The steamer went out from the pier; paused a little as she met the incoming tide; gathered speed with a flurry of white wake at her stern; moved out across the broad river and went out and on, trailing a curling black plume of funnel smoke.

Jack was standing in the stern: a tall figure in a formal black coat and top hat, every inch the naval officer ashore. I waved to him and he waved back, until the bend of the river took him from my sight and I from his . . . until there was only the spindrift of memory to keep him to me.

I turned to go, and doing so I met the eyes of the little Salvation Army lassie who stood at the bridge end. When I came abreast of her, I dropped a coin into her box and we exchanged a smile.

'Are you Saved?' she whispered.

'Oh, yes!' I responded. '*Yes!*'

'Do you hear that, Archie?' she said. This to a pleasant young man in their Army uniform whom I had not noticed before. He was handing out tracts with her and had the eager, zestful looks of someone rather like Dickie Jobling. He met her gaze; they were so obviously, blatantly, uncaringly in love. Also Saved.

*

I had no great feelings of guilt about having neglected my post at the

Cawnpore from midday until tea-time. As my father often said, the difference between a well-run and ill-run ship is quite simply that the latter needs constant attention, while the former practically looks after itself, like a lone goldfish in a bowl who only needs a sprinkling of ants' eggs every day and will continue his peregrinations round and round without raising any complaint. Thanks to the distant influence of Mrs Cornwall and the light but dextrous hand of Beatrice Carradine, the hotel functioned on lines not unlike this – and I liked to think that my own modest presence as temporary chatelaine had not done much to upset this happy balance of affairs.

'Afternoon, Miss Dangerfield.' From Arthur the doorman.

'Good afternoon, Miss.' From the captain of page-boys.

Suzie, now in her longed-for position at the flower stall – waved and grinned.

Stanley was holding the fort at the reception desk, along with two girl assistants. He looked unconscionably pleased to see me, and beckoned.

'All well?' I asked. 'I was detained on some family business.'

'The bracelet!' he cried, eyes dancing. 'Mrs Chalmers' bracelet has turned up.'

'Well, that's a blessing,' I said. 'My father was never in any doubt about that. Where was it?'

'*In Lord Bathchurch's room!*'

'Aaaaah!' I exclaimed.

He looked from left to right and assumed a prim expression; it had always struck me that there was something very old-maidish about Stanley.

'Not to put too fine a point on it, Faith,' he added, 'the cleaners found it on the floor behind the bed. It must have slid down the crack between the pillow and the head-board!'

'Oh, dear,' I said. And there we left the matter.

'What is the best thing to do, do you suppose?' he asked. 'Send it after Mrs Chalmers by hand of special messenger, perhaps? The liner will almost certainly have sailed, though.'

'Yes, but the shipping company will send it after her, under custody of the Purser, in the next ship to sail,' I said. 'Let's get it off our hands.'

'We have her forwarding address,' said Stanley. And to one of his assistants: 'Miss Conway, where's the forwarding address for Mrs Chalmers and Lord Bathchurch?'

'Here it is, Mr Waterford,' she replied, searching through a file.

'Read it out to me,' said Stanley, taking up one of the heaviest of the hotel's crested business envelopes and waiting with pen poised.

'White Star Line – Liverpool.'

'What vessel?'

'It doesn't say, sir.'

'Well, get on to the White Star Line office in Piccadilly and find out on which of their ships the passengers Chalmers and Bathchurch are booked.'

'Yes, sir.'

Stanley and I exchanged glances. I had a premonition that all would be well, that one or other of Father's options would intervene to prevent that woman and her new lover from destroying the only thing I had ever done, had ever built of my own in all my life.

'Thank you,' said Miss Conway into the mouthpiece of the telephone instrument a minute or two later. 'I've got it, Mr Waterford.'

'Name of the ship?' asked Stanley, poised.

'The *Titanic*.'

'Oh, yes. It's her maiden voyage, of course.' He added to me, *sotto voce*, 'Your friend and her companion do themselves very well, Faith. I heard that first-class cabins were going at a premium for the *Titanic*'s first trip to America.'

*

I approached my coming encounter with Father rather after the manner of a cat encountering a bowl of cream – slowly and with caution, half-convinced that trickery and deception were in the air.

Unexpectedly, we had a particularly heavy evening at the hotel and not a few minor problems. It was late when the tramcar dropped me off on the Embankment, and the lights were on in our front sitting-room. Father rose from his favourite armchair, put down his paper and kissed my proffered cheek.

'Nice luncheon?' he asked, straight-faced.

'You never turned up,' I replied, tit for tat.

'I . . . had another engagement,' he said.

'A board meeting at the tripe and cowheel shop?' I suggested.

'It's odd that you mention it, but in fact Arthur Frost has offered me a partnership in the shop. What you might call the board meeting, which took place at the counter, was swiftly terminated by the arrival of our midday customers.

'I repeat, my dearest Faith – did you have a nice luncheon?'

'Very nice,' I said. 'And thank you for engineering the encounter in your inimitably machiavellian manner.

'What led you to do it, Father?' I added.

The cat – after a little hesitancy – was poised over the bowl of cream. . .

Father, eschewing his favourite and expensive cigars, had taken to smoking cigarettes, the cheap Egyptian variety. He lit one now and puffed out a cloud of aromatic smoke before replying.

'It has not escaped my notice, dear, that whenever Cummings' name arises, you take on a certain attitude.'

I laughed. 'Oh, come now, Father – you're not suggesting that I colour up like some lovelorn schoolgirl? I won't have that, that doesn't sound like me at all.'

'I wouldn't insult you by implying it, Faith,' he replied. 'No, your attitude to Cummings – or so it seems to me – is informed by a certain defensiveness. You are still of the opinion that he let me down at my court martial and you are most gratifyingly protective towards me on that score. On the other hand, you tend to overplay your resentment towards the fellow to such a degree that one is inclined to think you are really seeking around for some means to justify what you imagine to have been his ungentlemanly conduct. Am I right?'

I shrugged, avoiding his eye. 'I suppose you must be, Father. You so very often are.'

'The corollary of which, or so it seemed to me, is that you are stuck on him. Are you stuck on him, Faith?'

'Yes, Father, I'm stuck on him.'

'And he?'

'He feels the same.'

'Has he told you so?'

'He doesn't have to, Father – neither of us has to.'

My parent reached out and threw the unexpired half of his Egyptian cigarette into the fire. 'These things are really disgusting,' he said, 'and quite confirm my opinion that poor deluded Gordon died in vain at Khartoum.' He sat back in his chair. 'Faith, there is something else that, in the light of your declaration (which I may say comes as no surprise to me, hence my somewhat heavy-handed method of arranging a rendezvous for the pair of you) you must now know.'

'You were there at my court martial. You heard all the evidence and the submissions. In particular, you heard Cummings admit to certain truths relating to the collision. You heard him say under oath that my orders to increase speed to the virtual maximum and reduce the distance between columns by one-third were not, in his opinion, prudent.'

'And in doing so, he destroyed you, Father!' I cried. 'No matter what there is between Jack and me, nothing can ever change that!'

Father continued mildly, as if I had not spoken.

'Cummings also said under oath that he had expressed his opinion of my orders many times, and that I had ignored his comments.'

'That, if anything, was the point which finally swung the Court against you, Father,' I said. 'The part about the bad visibility simply hammered the last few nails into the coffin which they had already fashioned for you.'

'You're probably right, my dear,' he admitted, 'though I am bound to say that I did not appreciate it at the time. I was so convinced, you see, that in my own evidence I should be able to swing the Court to my theory that, as in war the Navy must dare all for success, so in peace must we take acceptable risks in our training for war.'

'As it turned out,' I said bitterly, 'the prosecutor cut your philosophy of attack to ribbons on that very issue of safety which Jack Cummings floated when he said that he had warned you of the dangers.'

'Cummings said what he had to say, since he was under oath', my father responded. 'What he stated was the truth and nothing but the truth. . .' he broke off.

'And?' I prompted him.

'But it was not the *whole* truth, Faith.'

I stared at him. 'Are you saying, Father, that he – the man for whom you arranged a rendezvous with your own daughter today, who you freely admit gave evidence against you – actually withheld other evidence that might have *saved* you? *Are* you telling me that, Father?'

He smiled. It was a sad smile, the saddest I have ever seen on that well-loved face. Nor did he reply for quite a while and when he did, he avoided my gaze and stared steadfastly into the fire.

'Cummings deliberately withheld one piece of evidence,' he said, 'which I am convinced he would have continued to withhold even if the direct question had been put to him – almost certainly to the ruination of his own career if it ever came out.'

I was suddenly full of a great fear. 'What are you trying to tell me, Father?' I asked.

'In a slight mood of ebullience,' he said, 'I had been drinking rather heavily the evening before the accident. . .'

'Oh – *no!*' I breathed.

'No more than I would normally take when at dinner in harbour,' he said, 'but it was a break from my habitual mode of avoiding drink when on active duty at sea.

'Oh, it was nothing to write home about. Jolly Jack Tar Danger-field, the four-bottle man who could drink any of his young officers under the table and still dance the whole night through, is not one to be put down all that easily. But it was . . . enough. Enough so that when I woke up in the morning, it took a couple of stiff whiskies to set me straight on my feet and quench the nausea.'

'Father . . . Father . . .' I moaned.

'Cummings found me out,' he said. 'Oh, he did it so tactfully: suggested that I was looking unwell, and would it not be better if I went below and got my head down while he conducted the mock attack upon the *Darmstadt?* And all done well out of earshot of any-one, just the two of us.'

'And you refused his offer,' I said. It was not a question.

He smiled bitterly. 'I stand guilty as accused,' he said. 'But I think, given the chance all over again, I might have behaved exactly as I did.

'Put it this way: the commodore of an attacking fleet, heading for the enemy's capital ship and under heavy fire. The bridge is hit. The captain is hit. He is legless, perhaps – bleeding to death, and with the dead and dying all around him. . .'

'No more, Father – no more!' I cried, trying to stop up my ears against this evocation of a vision that was so at odds with the gold lace, the proud bunting fluttering in the wind, the charm and civil-ity, the rather stuffy protocol – that part of the Navy which, as a Navy daughter, I knew so well.

His voice dinned on. . .

'There is no escape for such a man in such a situation. He must endure. He must live – long enough to give the order: "*Hard a-starboard! Fire torpedoes!*" '

Then I was on my knees beside his chair and pillowing my head in his lap, overwrought with the mental image that he had presented and utterly defeated of any argument.

'What use?' he asked. 'What hope of emulating the conduct of such a man, if a couple of drams of Mr Haig's universal panacea could lay one low, down below?'

*

As Father pointed out to me, Jack's action in concealing their encounter on the bridge of the *Hecuba* that fateful morning must have saved him from a far worse sentence than the one he suffered. Dismissal with ignominy and disgrace might only have been the beginning of it; if any of the injured men had died (happily all recovered from their injuries), the dread words 'criminal negligence' might have entered into it.

'For a man who would do so much for me, place his own career in jeopardy, I would go that extra mile,' said my father. 'Even to the extent of bringing him and my daughter together again – since it was quite obvious even to a blind man on a galloping horse that she was stuck on the fellow.'

I clung to him still. 'Oh, Daddy, I wish you had told me all this before!' I cried. 'I have thought so ill of Jack; I was so insufferably rude to him after the court martial. And he never so much as hinted, never offered a word which could have entirely justified his conduct, but just let me go on thinking that he had betrayed you.'

'He never would have told the whole truth about the way things were that day,' said Father. 'Nor ever will, I fancy. You have yourself a good man there, Faith my love. Take my tip and do what I did when I met your mother: hold tight and hold hard with both hands!'

*

I had arranged to see Jack as soon as he returned from Devonport, where his new command, the *Juncta* – one of the new types of fleet destroyers – was then being fitted out.

Before that happened, of course, came the dreadful news of the *Titanic* tragedy, which burst upon a horrified world on the morning of April the fifteenth.

I was supervising the pre-luncheon arrangements in the main restaurant lounge when Stanley Waterford rushed into the room with a jumble of telegraph tape in his hand and horror written large over his homely countenance. His stumbling words soon had him surrounded by guests and staff. At the first mention of the disaster and the suggestion of casualties – though their number was then uncounted – a woman at the edge of the throng began a loud and heart-rending sobbing: it seemed that her only son had been travelling aboard the ill-fated liner which was deemed to be 'unsinkable'.

It was only after many days that the final death roll was published. And among the hundreds unaccounted for were my enemy Mrs Natasha Chalmers and her paramour Lord Bathchurch. Her hideous passing in the icy waste of the North Atlantic provided me in no sense at all with a feeling of revenge; I could think only of her final moments, as they must have been: alone in darkness and terror, vainly struggling to live, while the great vessel took its final plunge and the orchestra was silenced for ever.

This whole chapter of my life, encompassing the passing of Mrs Chalmers, my reunion with Jack, my father's confession, closed with the spring of that year.

I then thought that Fate had perhaps brought me to my safe haven at last, and that everything which lay ahead would only promise new fulfilment, fresh dreams come true and a tranquillity I had not known even in the days when I had only to snap my fingers for the material things of this life to be mine to command.

But I was wrong. As a continuum of the cynical philosophy that Jack had once offered for my consideration, I was to learn that one cannot buy serenity with mere happiness.

TEN

That summer – the summer I had designated as the first of my new life – began promisingly enough.

Due in part to his own hard work and thrift (and no gambling!), but mostly to the unexpected improvement in a parcel of Australian mining shares which had lain around disregarded for many years and escaped the notice of the Official Receiver – and indeed of everyone else, including my father – he was able by the intervention of Lady Luck to pay out 20/- in the £ to his debtors and was accordingly discharged from bankruptcy. This of course left him free to seek out and accept a whole spectrum of positions formerly barred to him. In fact, he sensibly began his new life modestly by accepting a post as director of a small yacht brokerage in Wapping, negotiating the sale and purchase of sailing and motor craft and incidentally spending a most pleasant and profitable time afloat in the Thames estuary and beyond – showing off his wares to prospective wealthy customers.

Father's departure from the tripe and cowheel shop was fraught with both sadness and gaiety. Arthur and Alice Frost reiterated their offer of a partnership in the retail business and I really believe there was an imp of compulsion in my parent's subtle, wayward mind that half-prompted him to take up their offer. However, as he pointed out, his heart lay with the sea and with all things nautical; the brokerage job, while being only a modest beginning, could lead to greater things in that line.

They gave a street party in true Lambeth tradition to mark his departure, which I also attended. Beer and tea flowed freely, with jellied eels, faggots and pease pudding and – of course – tripe and cowheel in abundance. Mr Arthur Frost delivered a speech of farewell to his friend and late colleague the 'Toff', and was then gently laid down to sleep off his excesses in the scrupulously neat little parlour behind the shop. Over the two long trestle tables that accommodated the guests, a banner was strung right across the street, from house to house, bearing upon it the legend: GOOD LUCK TO THE TOFF. He was always known as the 'Toff' in Lambeth. They guessed that he was someone out of the ordinary, of course, but with the natural gentility of the Cockney in such matters his anonymity was always respected; if Mrs Bloggs of Lambeth Walk knew or guessed that she had been served at the counter by a lord in a striped apron, she certainly never let on.

And in that almost perfect summer Jack and I became engaged – and I the proud wearer of his diamond ring: a tiny glittering piece of precious stone, modest enough in all conscience, as befitted someone who existed entirely on the exiguous pay of a naval officer. But greatly treasured as a gift beyond price.

*

'Jack! This cannot really be yours! Have you come into a *fortune*?'

It stood outside the house in St George's Square. It was short and fat, with a lot of brasswork gleaming in the sunlight, and painted a bright green. Beside it, clad in Norfolk jacket and knickerbockers, a cap on the side of his head and a pair of motoring goggles raised on his forehead, stood my smiling intended.

'Hop in, Faith – we're going for a picnic!'

'But – what shall I wear?' I cried.

'Bring a coat, it gets a bit draughty. And a scarf to tie your hat down. And hurry, darling! If the motor stops, it could take all afternoon to get her started again.'

It was the pop-pop of the motor which had brought me to the door. The engine – wherever it lay within that green and brass contraption – had the sound of an expiring monster, missed a beat now and again and emitted loud bangs and puffs of dark smoke from a pipe at the end. The name limned in silver paint on the side of the car read: MRS FREQUENTLY

So we drove northwards, my love and I, through sunshine and shadow, with the clean wind of Epping Forest in our faces and our heads held high. Insofar as it was possible to hold a conversation in 'Mrs Frequently', I learned that she had been bought second-hand at a knock-down price by a syndicate including three fellow officers because the former owner couldn't make her go – a shortcoming quickly overcome by one of the syndicate who was an engineer.

Presently we came to an opening into the forest, a grassy lane that led into the promise of bosky solitude. The car lumbered gallantly in between the whispering tall oaks until she could go no further, and there we stopped and laid out our rug on a mossy bank, under the spreading branches of a tree which had been ancient when Nelson won at Trafalgar.

'For tea we have Bath Oliver biscuits with a choice of Gentleman's Relish, potted meat, brawn or Stilton cheese,' said Jack. 'In the sweet line, there are strawberries and cream, seed cake and French fancies. Hock and seltzer water for drinking purposes. All by courtesy of Greenwich College wardroom . . . Faith, you look so beautiful,' said my corsair, stooping towards me.

We kissed through an infinity of time and emerged breathless.

'This will not do,' I admonished him. 'The hock and seltzer will be warm and the strawberries mushy. What a wonderful idea this was, darling!'

Jack poured the drinks and I made up the savoury biscuits. We pledged our joint health in wine and more kisses. It was then, when we pledged again – and our toast was 'the future' – that I detected in my beloved a certain restraint, a faint but discernible disinclination to meet my eye as he stabbed at the soft turf with the heel of his boot, as if it was doing him some kind of harm.

'Out with it, young Jack,' I said lightly. 'What is it you are dying to tell me, but just cannot bring yourself to say? Met a nicer girl when you were down in Devonport last week?'

He squeezed my hand. 'Little idiot,' he murmured.

'Well, what is it? And you can fill my glass again, please. I have a notion I shall need to be fortified.'

'It started in Devonport,' he said, refilling our glasses. 'The ship's nearly ready for commissioning, Faith. You'll love her.' His wonderful eyes danced a caper of enthusiasm.

'And you'll be joining her soon?'

'At the end of the month. We have a week to provision, arm and so forth, followed by a short working-up cruise so that the gunners don't feed shells into the bread-ovens nor the bakers slop their dough into the torpedo tubes.'

'And after that?' I had a premonition, and now it was I who was avoiding *his* gaze.

'We are ordered to the Eastern Mediterranean. The Dardanelles.

Some sort of war is starting up – in the Balkans.'

'War? Oh, Jack!' I sought his hand.

'Not our war, love. I don't know the ins and outs of it, but according to this morning's *Post* the Greeks, Serbs and Bulgars are going to knock seven bells out of poor ramshackle old Turkey. The Empire's not involved, but as usual the RN is going to make a show of strength there and fly the flag, to show these foreign Johnnies who really rules the roost. The Tenth Cruiser Squadron is already on its way and *Juncta* is to join them as part of the destroyer escort. We shall be home for Christmas, I don't doubt.

'But I shall miss you, Faith – oh, how I shall miss you!'

'And to think,' I said, 'that I have been a Navy daughter all my life – all in peacetime – and have never given a thought that my father did other than steam in and out of harbour, give parties, balls and receptions aboard and ashore. It wasn't until something he said some weeks ago – the day you took me to luncheon at the Ritz – that I was really brought face-to-face with what lies behind all the pageantry that I had been brought up with from the time I left school and first joined Father in his peregrinations.

'Oh, Jack, you won't be involved in any fighting, will you?'

'I shouldn't think so,' he replied and grinned. 'I wouldn't know which side we'd be fighting against, anyhow. For choice I'd have the Turks, whose navy wouldn't shame Fred Karno from all accounts.'

I clung to him. The hock may have made me more than usually emotional, for I felt very weepy. 'Jack, whatever happens, promise me that you won't go out of your way to be brave,' I pleaded. 'Be a *little* brave, by all means. But not much.'

'The first Turk who shows his head, I'll run!'

'Don't tease, darling, I'm serious. I don't want to be a widow before I've even become a wife.'

'Correction!' he said. 'As I understand it, one can't be a widow before one has first become a wife.'

'Be serious!' I admonished him. 'I don't want to be a dead hero's widow *or* fiancée. I want you, Jack Cummings, to end up as a fine distinguished admiral like Sir Jasper Freakley, with rows and rows of medals for opening fêtes and regattas, sucking up to foreign royalty and so forth, but never having had even the opportunity to be brave. You have your lovely genuine medal – be content with that!'

'Perhaps you fancy yourself in the role of Lady Freakley,' he said. 'Want me to make you a Lady, Faith?'

'There's no need,' I murmured, laying back and gazing up at him. 'You have already made me a woman – anything else would be superfluous.'

So we ended on a light note. But as I lay in his arms on that mossy bank in Epping Forest, that lovely summer of 1912, I looked up and through the trees saw a cloud no bigger than a man's hand against the cerulean blue of the sky.

It seemed like an omen. . .

*

Jack delivered me at St George's Square in the early evening; he had to return to Greenwich for the valedictory dinner marking the end of his staff course. Before long he would be joining his command – and all that was to come after.

The postman had just made the late delivery when I ascended the steps to the front door; he touched his helmet to me and wished me good night. There were only two letters and one of them was a boring buff-enveloped bill. The other – the kind which always roused a certain excitement in me – bore on its flap the impress of the foul anchor and was addressed to Captain Lord Dangerfield, DSO, RN (Retd.). And I wondered what *that* was all about.

I bustled about and made some supper; it was Sunday and my free day; Father had gone coarse fishing up the Thames with one of his old cronies from the club. After that, I went down into the basement to find a steamer kettle which I knew we once had. In finding it, I came upon more detritus of our former life, particularly the large tea-chest which surely filled up more space than it was worth, but promised to contain some long-forgotten, intriguing items. I resolved to sort through it at an early date.

Father came in punctually half an hour before our Sunday supper-time of 8.15 pm. He was in splendidly high spirits, and after pouring his then customary single measure of pre-prandial whisky, modestly informed me that he had heard on the 'old boys' network' that he was to be offered the chairmanship of his brokerage firm. Nor was that all: he opened the Navy letter and after reading it through to himself with many exclamations of manifest delight, repeated it aloud to me; the burden of the missive was approximately that 'Captain Lord Dangerfield was requested and required by their Lordships of the Admiralty to submit his name to a list of retired senior officers who might, in the expectation of a future war, be willing to give their unpaid, temporary services in such capacity as their Lordships might determine . . .'

'Which means,' said my father, 'that their lordships are trailing their cloaks after some expert free labour, to help carry out the many tasks in preparation for the time – and it cannot be more than a couple of years hence – when the Fleet mobilises to go to war against the Kaiser. Well, I'm at their command, so help me.'

'Oh, Father, not you as well!' I said. And I told him about Jack's latest orders.

Predictably, he knew the main drift of the situation.

'The Balkan incident – it will be no more – will soon be over,' he declared. 'Your Jack will be back in home waters before you know it. Turkey, for all that the armchair strategists dismiss her potency, will make mincemeat of the jackals who seek to eat off her plate, and be ready to play her part in the big fight yet to come.'

I sighed. 'Father, if you don't mind I've had quite enough war talk for one day. Do you think we might relax a little while you finish your whisky? Have a quiet chat about cabbages and kings until suppertime?'

'Of course, my dear, of course,' he responded. 'Very remiss of me. But I assure you that your Jack is in no hazard. He will show the flag in the manner born, and will be back in home waters in the New Year, I'll wager a thousand guineas on it. Ah! Sorry, m'dear! Mustn't say that!' He winked at me, picked up the evening newspaper and browsed through it while I laid the table for supper, my thoughts turning to what I must do to occupy my mind outside my work at the hotel, to fill in the empty hours while Jack was away. I always had my embroidery, and that was of more special interest now that Jack and I would be setting up a matrimonial home in the near future. There would be chair-backs to make and cushions to cover, and shop-bought embroidery was so tremendously expensive. Might I not turn my hand to some petit-point work, also?

And there was the basement to clear out. Tomorrow evening, after I came back from the Cawnpore, I would give my attention to that task.

Just then Father said, 'I see they have discovered the remains of a 50,000-year-old man in Sussex. I had always regarded Sussex as a place largely inhabited by geriatrics, but this is beyond all belief.*

'Supper's ready, if you will take your place, kind sir,' I informed him.

*

That night, I dreamed that I was flying about a dark and vengeful sea whose spindrift, rising from mast-high waves, lashed at me as I skimmed high over it. Ahead and below me, I saw the dark lean shapes of warships scudding through the combers and deep troughs, white plumes cutting from their sharp stems, white water streaming behind them in long tails of wakes. As I watched, there blossomed from them the pretty, pinky-yellow flames of gunfire shrouded in burgeoning white smoke – the way I had delightedly watched it as a child from a score of places of safety, when my father and his ships had been playing war out on the horizon within range of my telescope.

I had no control over my dream, nor over the direction that it might take me – though aware all the time that I *was* dreaming, as one so often is, so that when the experience becomes unpleasant or terrifying, one strives to wake up and make an end to it. But for the while complaisant, I allowed myself to be led along over wave-crests, deep into swirling troughs – straight towards the nearest ship ahead of me, which had taken on the appearance of *Hecuba*, my father's last command. And it seemed she was under fire from the grey shapes ahead through the wind-thrown spume: after every pink gun-flash there appeared an eruption of white water, kicked up close by the *Hecuba*. And twice or thrice, an orange glow and a tangle of splintered steel thrown sky-high denoted a hit.

As I drew closer, *Hecuba* was being hit continuously along her whole length and seemed to be moving more slowly and lying lower in the water. Nor was there any sign of life aboard the surely stricken ship; no one, quick or dead, upon the open decks; no one manning the guns.

No one . . . save a single dark figure hunched by the compass platform on the bridge: the man in command, the Captain.

His back was towards me as I came down upon the streaming, shell-scarred deck of the dying ship; unmarked by the splinters of

* So it was: 'Piltdown Man' was proved to be a hoax – if not a scientific fraud – 40-odd years later in 1953.

steel that cascaded all round me, nor blinded and deafened by the holocaust of exploding fire, I presently climbed up on to the bridge to join the hunched figure at the compass platform. And I knew a great fear.

'Father . . . is that you?' I cried above the tumult.

No answer; the figure did not turn.

Approaching nearer, I reached out to touch his shoulder, as an equally appalling possibility struck me regarding the identity of the doomed Captain of this ship which steered inexorably on towards the enemy line.

'Jack . . . Jack . . . if it's you, turn back – please!'

My hand closed about the hunched shoulder and under the thick greatcoat it was as hard as stone.

Then the figure turned slowly to meet my gaze . . . and I was not looking into the countenance of either my father or of the man to whom I had given my heart.

Under the braided Navy cap was the face of Death himself.

I awoke screaming.

*

Jack wrote me every other day from Devonport, and it was only pressure of work which prevented me from going down to join him for a few days. The ship, he said, was in splendid state and the crew were arriving in dribs and drabs of drafts. His officers were first-class and his First Lieutenant, Robert Pearse (formerly of the *Hengist*) sent me his very kind regards – a nostalgic harking-back to that last, memorable if much-flawed ball aboard the *Gloria* which all seemed so very long ago; the characters in the play were now all dispersed, Natasha Chalmers drifting fathoms deep amidst the icy sea-wrack of the wild Atlantic, and many dreams either dead or new-born.

A week or so later he wrote to inform me that he was coming to London to spend a few days' leave before departure. It would be his last chance to see me.

Happily, Mrs Slyte had a spare room available at the top of the house, which she rented by the week to commercial travellers and the like. Though small, it was neat and cosy. I brightened it up with some cushions, a couple of pictures from our store of former treasures and a vast bowl of chrysanthemums in readiness to greet my love's arrival.

He came in 'Mrs Frequently', now renamed 'Mrs Slightly', because the engineer officer had made great inroads upon the lady's internal shortcomings and, indeed, it was with only the greatest difficulty that – once started – the engine could be persuaded to stop.

The day was fine. We decided to go to Epping Forest, but on second thoughts persuaded ourselves that one should never look back upon perfection; but instead make new tracks across unknown places and strew blissful recollections like everlasting flowers as widely as possible . . . later to be gathered in tranquillity.

So we went, instead, to Kew.

'What are you going to do with "Mrs Slightly" while you're away!' I shouted, as we bowled along Thames-side with the wind fairly hissing past our ears.

'What, darling?'

'Do with her . . . with the car?'

'She's yours.'

'What did you say?'

'I bought the other chaps out of the syndicate – and since they are also going overseas they were both glad to let her go for a snip. And I'm giving her to you!'

'I can't hear you – it sounded as if you said you were giving her to me.'

'That's what I *did* say!'

'But, Jack, I can't drive!'

'You'll soon learn. I'll give you a lesson on the way home and you will have the hang of it by the time we're back at St George's Square. The rest's simply a matter of practice.'

'Well, if you say so, darling. I really am most extremely grateful to you. But – do you think I shall be safe *out*?'

'Of course,' he assured me, turning our vehicle to cross over Kew Bridge with all the practised insouciance with which he no doubt handled his own ship at full speed. 'The police are very tolerant of motorists because we're so few and pose less problems than horse traffic. They are particularly tolerant towards lady motorists, especially those who obviously haven't quite got the hang of it yet.'

'I'm much reassured,' I replied, feeling far from it.

'Kew!' he shouted, pointing. And there ahead was the exotic land-mark of the Chinese pagoda, soaring on high above prosaic suburban Surrey like an orchid rearing its alien head in a field of buttercups and daisies.

Somehow he brought 'Mrs Slightly' to a silent halt near the entrance to the Royal Botanical Gardens. The peace and stillness were quite extraordinary after the din. Five minutes later we had established ourselves on a pleasant knoll with a clear view to the Palladian elegance of the Orangery. There were not many people about on that quiet mid-week afternoon; we had the place almost to ourselves.

Immediately we sat down and unpacked our picnic tea, a constraint fell upon us; it was Jack who broke the silence.

'You'll want to know when we leave, darling,' he said. 'We sail on Monday next. Destination Portsmouth, then westwards back down Channel. By then – barring teething snags – we shall be deemed to be in a fit state of readiness to proceed to our station in the Eastern Med.'

'And there will be no more leave, for sure?' I asked, ever hopeful.

'Not a chance,' he said. 'We have these few days together, no more.' He grinned, that familiar lop-sided grin I knew and loved so well. 'Hungry? I could eat a horse!'

'Or Mrs MacIntosh's grilled lampuki with tomato sauce and sweet potatoes?' I asked, remembering our first meal together as if it had been only yesterday.

'Could I not – could I not?'

The exquisite lobster sandwiches which I had ordered from the hotel kitchens tasted like straw in my mouth, and the rose congol tea from the quart flask like warm washing-up water. And I noticed that Jack laid aside his second sandwich, half-eaten.

We smiled sadly at each other.

'This was to have been an occasion to lay between the leaves of memory,' I said, 'to treasure like pressed flowers in the family Bible. We really must cheer up.'

'Would you have been happier if we had married before I went away?' he asked, with the earnest direct bluntness that was so much part of his attraction for me.

'I don't know,' I replied. 'And you?'

He looked relieved. 'I had a notion that possibly you might have preferred it,' he said. 'But I have come to think, on balance, that we are more sensible to wait until I return. Are we in agreement on this, Faith?'

I nodded. 'Yes, on balance I am sure we are, Jack. It's not as though you will be away for long – at least, that's Father's opinion – and . . . I'm afraid you will think me very boring, but all my life I have set my heart on a white wedding, beautifully planned right down to the last detail, at one's leisure . . . Was that the kind of wedding that you and Stephanie Trafford had planned?' I added, dropping my gaze and drawing my finger along the lined pattern of the tablecloth.

'Stephanie would have settled for any sort of wedding on offer,' he replied. 'I daresay she had had the same lifelong, girlish dreams as yourself, Faith. In the event, it turned out to be Hobson's Choice for poor silly, tragic little Stephanie – as regards both wedding and groom.'

'What are you trying to tell me, Jack?' I asked him.

'She came to me in tears,' he said. 'Either someone must marry her or she must kill herself. Her mother, the widow Trafford, is very prominent socially in Leicestershire and hunts with all the best packs. It would have killed poor Mummy, the shame of it.'

'She was going to have a baby?'

'Or thought she was. Not mine, I hasten to add. We scarcely knew each other, and only because her brother and I were once ship-mates.'

'And you . . . offered to marry her? Just like that?'

As he looked at me squarely with those deep blue, honest eyes, I remembered how he had risked his career to keep silence for my father. 'Pity is not a very good basis for a marriage,' he said, 'but it might have served in this case. And she was very grateful – so that would have helped things along. And in any case, Faith, following your father's court-martial and what came after, I had no hopes or expectations of ever finding another you. However, as it turned out my gesture was futile. She had panicked unnecessarily and so we called off the wedding. I was quite sorry at the time, for I was really looking forward to being a father – even if only by proxy.'

I drew a deep and shuddering breath before I could trust myself to speak again and then, reaching out and taking both his hands, I said, 'Jack Cummings, the more I learn about you, the more it seems to me that I must be the luckiest woman alive.

'In addition to what you have just told me, you see, I also know about the sacrifice you were willing to make – indeed, made – to save my father from ultimate disgrace.'

'He told you that?'

'Only when he knew for sure the way things were between us. After he had contrived to bring us together again.'

'In St James's Park,' said Jack. 'Third bench on the right. . .'

'Facing the duck-pond. Oh, how I love you, Jack! Hurry back from that horrid little Balkan war and marry me. I want to fill a house with children for you.'

As we sat together, hand in hand, eye to eye, a little girl in a tam o'shanter sped round the path from the Orangery on her scooter. She stopped facing us and stood grave-faced, all-regarding.

'I think,' said Jack, 'that she's expecting me to kiss you.'

'Don't disappoint either of us,' I whispered.

Nor did he.

*

In the few golden days we had together, learning more about each other with every hour, I enjoyed the rhapsodical headlong delight of confirming that my heart had chosen well. Here was a man who might conceal something of the martinet beneath the swagger of the corsair – though this was neatly offset by the gamin; what lay beneath the many-faceted exterior that he presented to the world was an unbending, unquestioning 'rightness'. For without any hint of the prig, Jack Cummings was simply unable to perform a mean or selfish act, though he never gave this quality of his any thought and was thoroughly embarrassed to have it pointed out to him.

He was also an extremely good teacher when it came to driving a car!

Before Jack's departure, the other man in my life received news that his chairmanship of the brokerage firm had been confirmed. The three of us had a celebration dinner at home in St George's Square on the Saturday evening – Jack's last Saturday – at which Father stood up and made a charming if rather embarrassing speech extolling the virtues of his daughter and her intended. We three got rather tiddly on non-vintage champagne and my parent was with some difficulty restrained from trying his hand at what he described as 'driving Mrs Slightly up to Buck House in my old uniform and getting a salute from the sentries'!

The few days passed like fine sand dribbling away between one's fingers, and there was no slowing down the speeding hours. All too soon it was Monday morning and Jack drove the car to Paddington Station . . . just the two of us.

We parted at the barrier, for since the days of my childhood and Father's many departures I have never been able to watch a train carry a loved one out of a station without breaking down.

I stood and watched the tall figure in the Norfolk jacket walk down the long line of carriages behind his porter. He paused only briefly to wave as he got into his compartment.

It only remained for me to make what shift I could of driving 'Mrs Slightly' to work at the Cawnpore.

*

One day I had a letter from Beatrice Carradine which cheered me immensely. It was addressed to me at the hotel from the sanatorium in Derbyshire:

> My dear Faith,
> Thank you so much for your kind letter. It must sadden you very much to be parted from your fiancé so abruptly after your reunion and engagement. From what I read in the papers, the Balkan war cannot last long, and it's clear that the British are only playing a diplomatic role in the proceedings. I join you in praying for your Jack's swift return.
> Speaking of roles reminds me to tell you that I was asked to direct 'A Midsummer Night's Dream' for a performance by a cast of staff and patients. It was very well-received and so much praise was heaped upon me that I felt like Max Reinhardt!
> I should love to see you and hear all the Cawnpore news from your own lips. Do you think you could manage to come up here? Buxton is very beautiful, particularly now that the leaves have fallen and the mountainous landscape is touched with frost. Do come if you can, before the snows make the journey a hardship. I am so much improved in health that they will doubtless send me home before the spring.
> Write and tell me, do, that you will come. . .

Behind her buoyancy there seemed to be a touch of wistfulness, and I determined to make the journey up to Buxton and see her. In the meantime, it was necessary to clear away the accumulated work that had piled up on my desk at the hotel and to organise a busy round of late-season balls, parties and other functions. After that, there would be a slack period before the Christmas rush began. Three weeks, I told myself, and then things would be quiet enough for me to take a weekend off and visit the strange and compelling woman who had done so much for me.

And in that three weeks, also, I would get our home in good shape for Christmas. The loose covers of the drawing-room sofa and easy chairs needed to be cleaned; a lick of paint on the kitchen walls would not come amiss; the light fitting in the hall had to be taken down and washed – I would get Father up there with a step-ladder. And there was the basement . . . a constant, nagging reproach; I really must get down to clearing it out. And would do so. Not today, but tomorrow. Or very soon.

*

The event which turned my whole life upside down happened on the Saturday afternoon when I put on my coarse apron, wrapped a bandanna around my intractable hair and addressed myself to the task of putting to rights the Augean stable down below. Father had gone to the Naval & Yachting to play billiards and I didn't expect him back before evening. With a certain wry, dogged-as-does-it determination, I addressed myself to the unenviable task of sorting out the mess in the basement and cleaning up what lay beneath. But first – to make some room in there, so that I could actually move around. . .

Our precipitate departure from Grosvenor Mews Place, when Father went to live at his club and I at the Cawnpore, had meant our bundling together a whole collection of personal belongings which we had managed to rescue from the bailiffs and put into storage. When we rented the St George's Square apartment, all that gallimaufry of gear was hurriedly dumped in the empty basement by the removal men, before we had the opportunity to clean the place out. Hence the state it was in.

As a typical Englishwoman faced with such a task, I took one look at the mess and first made myself a cup of tea.

And then began. . .

Heaven knows that if I had guessed what I should find there, I would have as lief put a match to the place and burnt down the whole of the Square, as live through the agony that followed.

But how was I to know what was in store from the cruel fates up there in the clouds, looking mockingly down at me? The passage of time has softened the blow, but nothing in my life thus far – not even my father's disgrace and our subsequent struggles – could ever compare with the shock I suffered then. If I seem at this distance to make light of the grubby circumstances that attended my discovery,

233

it is because there are some things in life which transcend common feeling and can only be expressed in terms of the unreal – or, in an expression much bandied about nowadays in the world of *avant garde* art, the surreal. As an illustration, there is the tale of the poor man who visited his doctor complaining of the most profound, suicidal depression. The latter prescribed that his patient went to see the great comedian Grock, then appearing at the Alhambra, who would almost certainly raise the sufferer's spirits, as on the previous evening he had raised those of the doctor and his lady. Replied the patient: 'Doctor, I *am* Grock!'

But to the task! First I lifted out the more portable pieces, such as an elephant hoof log-basket that had graced the fireplace of the great hall at Mondisfield; next was a mildewed bag of hockey sticks, cricket bats, billiard cues, golf clubs and suchlike sports equipment, some of which must have dated back to my father's schooldays; there followed sundry items of minor interest, mostly broken, such as statuettes minus heads or arms, clocks without hands and so forth. These and many other items I piled outside in the corridor until there was scarcely any room to move out there. But presently I had an open space in the centre of the basement room that could be said to provide me with an area in which to move around and take stock.

This I did. And was impressed by the considerable inroads I had made into the problem. In fact, so it seemed to me, the only two major items barring my path to success were a stuffed moose's head that my grandfather, the first baron, had shot in Canada, and the big tea-chest.

I decided to tackle the latter first. Since it was quite out of the question for me to drag its enormous weight out of the chamber: I must first empty it where it stood. And this I began to do.

Virtually the first items I came across confirmed my earlier impression that, during the frantic haste to clear our gear out of Grosvenor Mews Place, it was I who had filled the chest in a hurry for the removal men to carry out to their cart. Here was the bolt of now rather moth-eaten Donegal tweed which I had intended to have made into a skirt, coat and flat cap to match, for wearing on the grouse moors. Here a pair of dancing pumps, worn only once and upon heaven knows-what-occasion. Next an old teddy bear of mine, with whom I had never had the satisfactory kind of friendship I had managed to achieve with a golliwog of the same vintage, now alas no more.

234

And much else of a like ilk . . . all, as I remembered, from the bottom of a little-used cupboard in a corner of my dressing-room.

Next I came upon some items belonging to my father; and here I remembered that I had cleared out an old chest of drawers belonging to him and containing mostly discarded things. There were old shirts; old invitation cards relating to dinners, balls and parties long gone; fancy striped neckties presented by every yacht club of every harbour to which the *Gloria* had put in for the night over the last fifteen years; a Glengarry bonnet with – of all things – a bullet hole put through it! . . . and much else.

And then – the attaché case. . .

It was quite small, of good leather much battered and mildewed, as if it had spent decades in bottom drawers in damp places. As I picked it out of the chest, the handle broke off and the thing fell to the floor where, upon crashing, the single retaining catch and lock burst open, spilling out the contents: all papers, all of the stuffy legal sort that require to be fastened with pink string and sealing wax.

I was stooping to scoop them all back into the case when my eye lit upon a name written in a clerkish hand upon the face of the uppermost document: *The Hon. Mrs Myles (Marie Hortense) Dangerfield – Her Last Will and Testament.*

Thus passes the glory of the world, I thought; a fine place for my poor dead mother's will to end up. But then Father never held dusty parchments in very high regard; being of the living, loving, earthy sort, he would never have connected this line of crabbed handwriting, nor whatever lay within, with the woman whom he had loved to her grave and beyond. In a sense, the neglect with which he had laid aside, mislaid and presumably finally lost my mother's will was all of a piece with his workaday philosophy.

Gathering up the rest of the papers, I noticed my mother's name repeated again – and yet again.

It was upon the last document, with her name staring up at me and the appalling superscription to it, that I stared for an eternity of time until I was able to reach out a wavering hand and, picking it up, read the dreadful words written there.

*

By the time I had read all – over and over again – the wintry sun had died and the thin light remaining being inadequate for more reading, I gathered up the documents and left the basement.

Any moment now my father might return. I was in no state to meet him, for I had to digest and re-digest the information which had so appalled me before I could assemble a formula for dealing with him. Accordingly, I wrote a short note pleading a headache and the beginnings of a cold, and left it on the kitchen table where we regularly ate our supper – together with instructions on how to heat up the steak and kidney pie which I had prepared. The last bitter tear of my day plashed upon the sheet of writing paper; after that, my night was bitter and dry-eyed.

I washed and prepared myself for bed, drawing the curtains against the night and lighting only a candle, so that Father should not see a light from the street when he came in and, guessing that I was still awake, come knocking on my door to ask if there was anything he could do for me.

He arrived about 7 pm, firm of tread, his key steady in the key-hole, whistling as he entered the sitting-room and then went into the kitchen. I could almost see him reading my note and clucking his tongue in sympathy; surely his head cocked to one side and he looked up at the ceiling, to pick out the faintest sound which might signify I was still awake. He heard nothing, for I lay as silent as a mouse, even holding my breath. Presently I heard the oven door open and his faint whistling was resumed; all was well.

I readdressed myself – and surely for the twentieth time – to the documents. . .

The first in the series chronologically was the Will which had been drawn up by a London solicitor, signed by my mother and duly witnessed. In this, she left all her unspecified worldly goods to her husband, my father. It was dated about eighteen months prior to my birth.

Nothing remarkable there. But more followed of a very different nature.

The second document – which had so caught my eye and sent me scurrying through it and the rest – had been written shortly after my mother gave birth to me. It is a truly terrifying paper, the title on the outer fold bearing evidence to the horror that the sight of it had aroused in my mind:

A Medical Report bearing upon the mental condition of Mrs M.H. Dangerfield, arraigned before the Suffolk County Court on the charge of feloniously wounding Annie Leggart, a spinster and maidservant, with the intent to kill.

It appeared that the report within, signed and attested by three medical practitioners, had been ordered by the County Court to determine if my mother – accused of attacking and gravely wounding her kitchen-maid at Mondisfield with a hunting-knife such as is used to dispatch wounded game – was of sufficiently sane mind to plead guilty or otherwise to the charge.

The finding of these three learned gentlemen will remain forever scored upon my mind. This was its content:

> The subject Dangerfield, having been examined by we the undersigned, is deemed by us to be suffering from a state of homicidal dementia, sometimes called schizophrenia, a condition which is not, nor is likely in the foreseeable future, to respond to any treatment whatsoever.
>
> Accordingly, we adjudge that the subject Dangerfield was, at the time of committing the crime, labouring under such a defect of reason from disease of the mind as not to know the nature and quality of the act, or if she did know it, as not to know what she was doing wrong. (*Ref.* Reg. *v.* Macnaughten (1843).
>
> Signed . . . . . .

Horror piled upon horror. . .

The third document in the hideous quartet was equally brief and devastating. It stated that Mrs Marie Hortense Dangerfield, having under the Lunacy Act of 1890 been deemed to be a lunatic not under proper control, and having been directed by a magistrate to be examined as an alleged lunatic by two medical practitioners who, having given of their opinion that the said person was of unsound mind, the said magistrate directed that the patient be detained in an institution.

And last of all was a death certificate, stating that the Honourable Mrs Marie Hortense Dangerfield died in the Heathfield Private Insane Asylum, Reading, Berkshire on a date shortly after being committed there. The cause of death was given as multiple injuries following self-defenestration.

I looked up 'defenestration' in the dictionary: The definition is as follows:

> **défĕnĕstrá'tion** *n.* The action of throwing (partic. a person, or self-d.) out of an open window. (From the Latin *fenestra* – window.)

So it added up to this, I told myself, dry-eyed with shock and robbed of everything but a terrible numbness: my mother, an adjudged homicidal maniac, having been committed to a lunatic asylum, had shortly afterwards committed suicide by throwing herself out of a window.

*

A week later, I came by appointment to the house in Wimpole Street where the door was opened to me by a young woman in a nurse's uniform of pale mauve. She showed me into a waiting-room, where a long-cased clock ticked ponderously in a corner, the view from the window looking into a mews. A whistling ostler was rubbing down a horse out there, watched by a barefoot urchin.

Presently the door opened and an elderly lady came into the room. Her berry-bright eyes swept me from head to foot and appeared to approve; she smiled.

'The doctor will see you now, Miss Dangerfield,' she said. There was a gentle edge to her voice, as one finds in people who have encountered suffering and death and formed a warm carapace around themselves against its intrusion into their own lives. When she introduced herself, my impression was confirmed. 'I am Sister Hawarth,' she said, 'former matron at Heathfield. I knew your mother well, poor lady. Will you come this way, please?'

She led me down a long corridor that smelt agreeably of beeswax and, pausing outside a door at the end, she laid a hand upon my arm and murmured in my ear, 'Doctor's very old, you know, and not as strong – nor as agile in his mind – as he used to be. He no longer practises, of course. Merely sees a few of his older patients from time to time; chats with them; makes them feel that someone still cares for them.'

She tapped on the door and a faint voice called out for us to enter.

Doctor Mainwaring sat behind a vast desk, the muted light from a curtained window throwing his fine shock of starkly white hair into a halo about his hunched head. He wore a dark coat and – despite the unseasonable warmth outside and the presence of a blazing coal fire in a wide grate – a thick plaid shawl drawn about his bowed shoulders and fastened across his narrow chest.

'This is Miss Dangerfield, Doctor,' said Sister Hawarth.

'Miss Dangerfield – ha.' His voice, though that of a very old man, carried clear overtones of a firmness and authority that had not been entirely dissipated.

'She wrote to you, you'll remember. . .'

238

'Of course I remember, of course!' He was not querulous, merely concerned that the woman might think he had forgotten. Searching among the papers before him, he picked up a letter – my letter. 'See – I had it with me all the time! Method, Sister. Method! My old mentor, B.A. Morel, was of the opinion that method, method, method is the key to clear thinking, and I have always adhered to this principle. What did you say the young lady's name is?'

'Miss Faith Dangerfield, Doctor.'

He smiled at me, and it was a heart-warming experience to see the old, creased face take on an expression of almost child-like amiability. Behind thick-lensed glasses, his pale blue eyes were gentle.

'How do you do, ma'am?' he said. 'Do please forgive me for not rising. And be so kind as to take a seat.' Then to the other woman: 'Sister, I should be obliged if you would stay, for you may be of help in certain aspects of this case.'

Both Sister Hawarth and I sat down. The old man fidgeted with my letter for a few moments, appeared to read it through and finally looked towards our companion with some irresolution.

'Ah, perhaps you can give us a lead here, Sister?' he suggested.

Sister Howarth appeared to have been waiting for just such a question and had the answer pat: 'Miss Dangerfield's mother was admitted to Heathfield about twenty-five years ago, Doctor. The actual date is on one of the documents that the young lady enclosed with her letter.'

'Quite so, quite so. And? . . .

'As you will recall from the letter, Doctor, Miss Dangerfield wishes to know more about the circumstances surrounding her mother's tragic death.'

He looked at me over his glasses with a slight hint of severity.

'Can the young lady not obtain this information from her family?' he asked. 'There was no secret surrounding the patient's demise, surely?'

I spoke up: 'There is only my father, Doctor Mainwaring, and he is not aware that I know that my mother was insane – let alone that she killed herself in a . . . in a lunatic asylum!'

He continued to look disapproving. 'I see,' he said, but obviously did not. 'Well, you will appreciate that I no longer attend at Heathfield. Indeed, the nursing home as such no longer exists. And that even if I had kept my case notes on the patient all these years – which I have not – it would be most improper for me to divulge. . .'

'I'm not asking much!' I cried and heard my voice teeter on the brink of hysteria. 'I – I simply want to know what was wrong with my mother and why she killed herself.'

Again the old man looked towards the woman by my side – questioningly.

'You will remember Mrs Dangerfield, Doctor?' she prompted.

'Of course, of course.' He looked vaguely towards the ceiling.

Sister Hawarth turned her head and shoulders to address me. 'Your mother was in a sorry state when they brought her to us,' she said. 'To begin with, the enquiries made by the police, the examinations which the doctors had put her through, only served to convince her that the entire world was involved in one big plot to destroy her and that everyone in it was a party to the conspiracy.'

Doctor Mainwaring cleared his throat and said, 'A classic paranoid reaction, of course. Characterised by unrealistic, illogical thinking, with delusions of persecution. I published a paper on the syndrome in '89, and Eugen Bleuler concurred. . .'

'It was terrible to watch her,' continued Sister Hawarth. 'And frightening to listen to her – so convinced was she that we were all plotting to destroy her mind and her body. The woman she had attacked – the housemaid. . .'

'Annie Leggart,' I supplied.

'She had proof, your mother said, that this girl had been sent by her enemies to kill her. So she was forced to defend herself with a knife.'

'The paranoid type of dementia praecox, undoubtedly,' interposed the doctor. 'I discussed it with Freud at the last Vienna conference I attended, but we were not in agreement over the regressive symptoms being explained away by a retreat to less mature levels of the ego. . .'

Sister Hawarth went on, 'I tried to get closer to your mother, but it only made her worse. I began to occupy the same place in her mind as the girl she had attacked with a knife. We allowed her no dangerous articles, of course, but they have this terrible cunning, you see? Somehow she managed to lay hands on a knife and when I came to her, she attacked me. The male nurse managed to wrest it from her – and that took some doing. And then she . . . she rushed out on to the balcony and threw herself over.'

I bowed my head, closed my eyes and wished the image away before it was burned indelibly upon my mind – but the thing was already done.

As if from far away I heard the doctor mumbling, half to himself: 'Or was it Meyer, and not Freud, with whom I had that slight disagreement? Surely not, since Adolf refuses to separate the mental from the physical. . .'

'There was no stopping her, Miss Dangerfield,' said Sister Hawarth, laying a sympathetic hand on my arm. 'She was like a child with a broken rattle; she would thrust it in anyone's face – including her own.'

I raised my head and looked towards Doctor Mainwaring, who was regarding me as if we had never met. My question, when it came, was directed towards the woman – and I clenched my fists until the nails hurt the palms of my hands as I waited for an answer.

'Is this thing – this . . . what do you call it? . . . paranoid dementia praecox? – is it *hereditary?*'

Sister Hawarth was watching me closely, but she did not reply.

'As to that,' said the doctor presently, 'there is no doubt. No doubt at all. Not in my mind. I have postulated that the disease is transmitted in a family by recessive genes in the form of a pre-disposition. Oh, yes. Familial. Yes, definitely.'

He looked at me vaguely. 'Sister, who is this lady?' he asked.

She rose and fussed around him then, arranging a cushion behind his head against the high-backed chair, straightening the shawl across his chest.

'We have tired you out this afternoon, Doctor,' she said. 'Time for your rest. Sleep for a while and I'll have nurse bring you a cup of bouillon when you wake up. You'll like that.'

'Bouillon – ah, yes.' He closed his eyes.

Taking my arm, she led me out and quietly closed the door behind us.

'Well, you have the answer you came for, my dear,' she said. 'And I'm so sorry, I really am. He doesn't remember your mother, of course; the poor old gentleman's memory for names and faces has very nearly gone. But you can be sure his diagnosis of her case was correct. That, at least, he has never lost. They say he was the most brilliant man of his generation in his field.'

She offered me the solitude of the unused waiting-room and the offer of a 'nice cup of tea'. I declined her offer and went out into the dying sunlight of Wimpole Street with the knowledge that all my hopes of future happiness with Jack Cummings had died back there in that overheated room on the lips of the old doctor.

Where, and to whom, could I turn?

Not to Father, for certain. In the first place, I needed guidance as to how I should broach the subject with him – *or even if I should raise it at all*.

Jack? Out of the question to write to him and burden him with the terrible dilemma that kept me sleepless and haunted my daylight hours.

Then it came to me that only Beatrice Carradine, with her earthy and slightly cynical wisdom, could be of any possible help to me in the situation in which I found myself. Accordingly I sent off a telegram to the Buxton sanatorium, telling her to expect me. With Stanley Waterford's help, I worked late for several nights in order to so arrange the various schedules that the complexities of two Wedding Breakfasts, a Masonic Ladies' Night and a 21st Birthday Ball could be fitted in on two successive days. This being done, I felt free to absent myself to Derbyshire during that time.

Father accepted my decision to go and visit my sick friend in the Midlands as a typical manifestation of my inherent kindness – as he put it. I particularly asked him not to come and see me off at King's Cross.

*

'Buxton – Buxton!'

My train drew in with great gushings of steam, in a valley that was virtually alpine in appearance, high dark crags already topped with winter frost. A carriage conveyed me to the end of the small town, up a winding drive to a turreted building faced with verandahs upon which, even in that chill air, there were patients strung out like white and coloured beads, in wheelchairs and beds. All of them were looking down at me, silent and regarding, as I alighted. I felt like an interloper and half-ashamed to be whole and healthy.

The regime at the Holly Hall sanatorium was informed by a brisk, affable efficiency that strongly put me in mind of naval routine. A pretty little nurse, upon hearing who I was and why I was there, checked through a list.

'Ah, come this way, Miss Dangerfield, we have been expecting you.'

Beatrice was not out on a balcony, but in a shaded room which was nevertheless abominably cold – all the windows being wide open. She was sitting up in bed, swathed in shawl and blankets and wearing a quite becoming woolly night-cap. Her eyes – bright and eager and burning with life – widened with delight to see me. And I was relieved to see how well she looked; her complexion was positively blooming with apparent good health, though it did seem to me that her bone structure, particularly her cheekbones, appeared more prominent than I remembered.

'Faith, my dear. How lovely to see you!'

'Beatrice. How are you?'

She clutched at my hands, held them tightly between hers for a long time. 'I'm well, so well,' she said. 'I don't know why they keep me here, and I can tell you that if they don't discharge me by Christmas, I shall discharge myself. But tell me about you. . .'

*

Later the nurse brought us tea. By then I had given Beatrice a complete word picture of life and times at the Cawnpore since the day she left. Her mind was so clear, I had forgotten how clear; her retention of detail regarding things that had been in abeyance at the time of her departure was really uncanny, and she put me right on quite a few points that I had overlooked, orders that I had omitted to give, decisions that I had shirked.

In the end, gradually, evading it for as long as I could, we came to the grist of the matter. . .

'Now tell me more about your beautiful heroic man whom you wrote about,' she said. 'And I see you are engaged.' She stroked my ring finger wistfully.

'It's all over,' I said. 'At least, I think it *has* to be.'

And then I broke down and wept for the first time since hearing my life sentence from Dr Mainwaring.

Beatrice gently soothed me, but not until I had shed all the tears there were to be shed. Then she coaxed the whole story out of me, beginning with the facts of my mother's early death – as I had understood them from Father; leading on to my discovery of the documents, my tracing of the doctor who had attended her at Heathfield, my visit to him . . . and the outcome.

When I had done, she put her finger on the nub of the matter in one short sentence. 'And now, because this condition is hereditary, you are doubtful of marrying Jack?'

I nodded.

'Does he want children?'

'Oh, Beatrice, you can't believe how much!' And I told her about Jack's poverty-stricken but blissfully happy childhood, with the houseful of siblings, the mystical wonder of small pleasures that most folks pass by unnoticing, his ethic of family life. How he was willing to marry a silly, wayward girl for the sake of an unborn child.

'And I promised him a houseful of children, Beatrice!'

She held my hands very tightly for a long time and then said, in a very matter-of-fact voice: 'Now, let's consider what you are to do, or not do. It would be best to go through all your options, my dear. There is a notebook and pencil on the table over there; bring it to me if you will, please? I always find it clears the mind to put one's thoughts down on paper.'

I knew it well, this method of hers, and had seen her do it often at the hotel when the affairs of the place seemed in a hopeless tangle.

'Tell me first,' she said, pencil poised, 'you have told no one but me about this – not your father, Jack or anyone?'

I shook my head. 'No one else.'

'Good,' she said. 'This leaves you with the option of continuing to keep silent about it. Saying nothing to your father about your discovery (and we can presume that he has either forgotten about the documents or is under the impression that he destroyed them years ago), marrying Jack as if nothing had happened, producing progeny and hoping for the best.

'How does that strike you?' Her burning eyes were upon me.

'I can't do that, Beatrice. You *know* I can't!'

She struck out a line of writing in her notebook.

'We proceed,' she said. 'The next possibility – you tell Jack the truth and agree between you never to have children. Do you think that would work?'

'No,' I said. 'Oh, yes, Jack would agree because he loves me. On another level, he is such an honourable man that he would never go back on his promise to marry me, nor would he ever reproach either me or himself for marrying under those conditions. But it would simply, quietly break his heart.'

Beatrice drew another line across the paper.

'What if you should go to him?' she suggested. 'Tell him the truth and say that, under the circumstances, you cannot – and will not – marry him? While you are about it, you also tell your father about your discovery. Bring the whole matter out into the open – and to hell with it.'

'And destroy two men?' I asked. 'Remembering that Father loved my mother to the end – and beyond.'

'Then tell only Jack,' she proposed. 'Explain why it is impossible that you should marry, but ask him – for your father's sake – to conspire to some other reason for breaking off the engagement.'

'That changes nothing from the previous option,' I said, 'save that it puts an extra burden on Jack – the burden of silence. No, that won't do either, Beatrice.'

Two strokes more across the page.

'Then you seem to be left with only one other choice, my dear,' she said quietly.

'Yes,' I said.

'Can you bear to do it?'

'I don't know, Beatrice – I simply don't know if I'm strong enough.'

She laid aside the notebook and pencil, almost as if they had become too intolerably heavy for her to hold. 'I am quite satisfied that you're strong enough, Faith,' she declared. 'If there was any weakness in you, you would have chosen any one of the easier options I suggested.'

'Beatrice – can I? Do you really think I'm capable of carrying it through?'

'Yes,' she said. Just that.

*

We spent the rest of the dying day together and had a plain and simple supper at about 7 o'clock. By that time she was visibly tiring, and seemed not displeased when the nurse came in to tell me I must leave and allow the patient to sleep.

I had a booking for the night at an hotel in the town and was planning to catch an early train back to London on the morrow. We held hands and both wept a little.

'See you soon, Beatrice,' I said.

'Christmas – no later,' she promised. 'Just keep my seat warm at the Cawnpore, dear, I shall be back around Christmas. And – Faith. . .'

'Yes?. . .'

'The hard option . . . don't take it, don't attempt it if you feel that you cannot carry it through right to the end. And that means the end of your life, Faith.'

'I know that, Beatrice,' I replied. 'And I shall keep your advice before me – always. Good-bye, dear Beatrice, until we meet again around Christmas.'

Downstairs in the hall, I was met by a very pleasant looking lady who introduced herself as the Matron. Was I Miss Dangerfield who had been visiting Mrs Carradine?

Yes, I was, I told her. And how heartening to see my friend so well. We should all be looking forward to seeing her home around Christmas.

The woman's answer was delivered with all the tact and gentleness which one has grown accustomed to receiving from the members of her dedicated profession:

'I'm very sorry, Miss Dangerfield,' she said, 'but there is no hope, no hope at all, of your friend being discharged for Christmas, or ever. It's only a matter of time, you see. And Mrs Carradine has long overstayed her time. We think here that she has hung on as long as she has – against all medical likelihood – in the hope of seeing you again before she dies. It cannot now be more than a matter of a few days at the most.'

*

Plymouth Hoe. A chill dawn. . .

'Mrs Slightly' parked close by the dockyard gates, where I had arranged to meet Jack.

The return of the British fleet from the Mediterranean upon the cessation of hostilities against Turkey had brought me a telegram, stating in very specific terms that my lover's first wish on making his home port was to see me. And here was I, high on Plymouth Hoe, searching the southern horizon for the first sight of my man's ship as so many women before me have done down the centuries. There were others with me, that dawn: a small group of women and a sprinkling of children, some of the very young ones still asleep in perambulators or in their mother's arms.

I shivered. My resolve was not very strong, but I told myself it would be enough to see me through the immediate test. The hard part would come after : the lifetime of might-have-been.

A stir ran through the people there and someone pointed out to sea beyond the breakwater. A sturdy sailor's son lifted his little sister high on to his shoulder.

On the far horizon, to the south-west, a faint smudge of funnel smoke quickly resolved itself into a lean grey shape coming on towards Plymouth at a fast rate. And I knew that it was the *Juncta*.

The rising sun broke out through the clouds, flooding the wooded hills to my right with a mystic light that touched every leaf of every branch and caught its shimmering movement. The very wave-crests beyond the breakwater seemed so clear and close that one could have reached out one's hand and touched them with a finger-tip. The toy ship that sped towards us with white water creaming at her sharp stem was only . . . a toy ship.

Through my sudden tears, I watched her pass the Mole and shape course to pass close by Drake's Island, which lay below me, almost at my feet. I could see the sailors on deck. At the shrill sound of a bosun's whistle, they ran to their correct stations for entering harbour – two straight ranks on the fo'csle and more aft, where the proud White Ensign snapped in the wind.

Now they were as close to me as they ever would be. In a few moments, the ship would begin a gentle turn to take her upriver to Devonport and home.

I lifted my binoculars; trained them on the open bridge and the figures grouped there.

One stood out above all. He was the tallest there and stood at the compass platform, conning his ship. As they drew abreast of the Hoe and must have heard – as well as seen – the small cheering, waving throng gathered there to greet the homecomers, the men on the bridge waved. And Jack waved with them – though he could not have picked me out with the naked eye.

My tears washed away the sight of him. When I had dried them, he had gone from me.

*

I took the train back to London. Sometime soon, as soon as his duties allowed, he would come in search of me and would find the little motor car parked close by the dockyard gate in the charge of the naval pensioner who manned the gatehouse. The old fellow would then hand him the letter which it would break his heart to read – as it had broken mine to write:

. . . please don't question my decision. Don't write to me or attempt to see me, or my father, I beg you. It would bring a terrible unhappiness on us all.

Just forget me, as I must forget you. . .

I knew he would come. A man so determined as he would not be fobbed off with a few lines. He loved me and knew that I loved him. My first attempt – the letter – had been no more than an act of cowardice: a means to deliver the first blow in the dark with my eyes averted, away from him, so as to avoid seeing the sudden agony and astonished deprivation in his wonderful eyes.

He came to me at the Cawnpore – still in uniform, as he had left his ship and taken the first train to follow me. I had been more than half-expecting him and had prepared my ground for an encounter which I faced with the utter conviction that I would greatly have preferred to cut off my right hand.

'Commander Cummings, ma'am.' The bellboy ushered him into my office – Beatrice's office.

He did not mince matters, but held out my letter. His voice was firm and even, not inflected by passion.

'I think you need to explain why this should be, Faith,' he said. 'I don't say I deserve an explanation, and I will not point out that simple civility, if nothing else, cries out for one, since you know – none better – that this is so.'

I drew a deep breath. 'Jack, I cannot marry you,' I said. 'What is more, I cannot *tell* you why it is impossible. Add to that, my dear . . .' and here I had to fight against breaking down, 'if you have any love left for me after the way I have treated you, I want to ask you – *beg* you – to let it rest at that.'

'You can't mean this, Faith,' he protested.

'It's the way it must be, Jack,' I told him. 'I am asking you to walk out of that door – now – and leave my life for ever. And if you have any regard left for me, never to question further – of me or anyone else – as to the reason why it has to be so.

'I would explain if I could, Jack – believe me. But the outcome would destroy us both in the end. And others.'

My whole being ached to reach out, to take his hurt and puzzled face in my hands and rain him with kisses. Instead, I looked away.

'Please go – now!' I whispered.

'Faith – Faith. . .'

'No! Don't say anything. Nothing you say can make the slightest difference and will only hurt the more.'

'Well, then. Good-bye, Faith.'

'Good-bye, Jack.'

He left me – as I knew he would. No man, he, to turn the knife in the wound. And it must have been hideously obvious to him that I was wounded to the heart.

ELEVEN

'Miss Dangerfield, your father telephoned, ma'am. He can't meet you for luncheon, but will you come to this address any time this afternoon, at your convenience?'

The hall porter greeted me with this message as I came downstairs after supervising the quarterly inventory of silverware and crockery. He handed me a slip of paper with an address scribbled upon it. I went through into my office, which the previous year I had shifted down from the room in the rafters inherited from Beatrice, to a room behind the reception desk where I was, in naval terms, right on the bridge of my ship.

I passed by the photograph that I had caused to be put up on the wall behind the reception desk – to meet a pair of humorous and inscrutable eyes. I winked at her. Under the portrait was a single printed line: *Beatrice Carradine – Housekeeper 1909–1913*.

How like my father, I told myself. Today, on my birthday, he had arranged to take me out to luncheon at no less a bastion of male supremacy than the very Naval & Yachting itself; for the previous year, the bastion had so far been breached as to permit the institution of a ladies' dining room, where personages of the frail sex were allowed on sufferance to be entertained by members. It was reliably stated that twelve of the older members had resigned upon this decision being passed by the house committee – and that at least one of the dissenters had passed away of apoplexy in his habitual armchair in the smoking-room!

Be that as it may, at the eleventh hour I had been denied this dubious privilege and bidden to meet my parent elsewhere. But where?

The address was unknown to me and distinctly lacking in promise. I supposed – correctly as it turned out – that it was some

250

small hole-in-the-corner dockyard in one of the seedier purlieus of the London river area that my noble father (in the pursuit of some rather mysterious business that he had been conducting the previous twelvemonth on behalf of their lordships of the Admiralty) had taken to frequenting: *Tink's Wharf – Rotherhithe Street.*

Stanley Waterford knocked and came in. Since the death of his aunt six months previously, Stanley had seemed to acquire additional stature. He had been elected to the Board and had out-manoeuvred the sinister Lord Barnworthy on several occasions. It was he also who, upon poor Beatrice's passing, had had my position as housekeeper made permanent. In every way we acted as left hand and right hand in the running of the Cawnpore.

'Happy birthday, Faith,' he said, and came over to kiss me. 'A little something for you!'

The 'little something' was a quite delightful and obviously quite expensive brooch set with pearls – my birthstones.

'But, Stanley, you shouldn't have. . .' I began.

'Not solely from me,' he said, 'though I will seize the credit for originating the idea. No, Faith dear, it's a present from the Board, in token of the wonderful job you are doing for the old Cawnpore. As to my own small offering – well. . .' he held out a long, thin box.

I opened it. Inside, nestling in a cushion of black velvet, was one perfect red rose.

'Stanley, you are such a dear,' I said. And I kissed his cheek.

He grinned and went pink. 'I've never changed at any rate,' he stated. 'Proposed to you the first time I took you out. And the offer's still on the table, Faith – you know that.'

'If I were in the marriage market, Stanley,' I assued him, 'and you know I'm not, there's not a gentleman in all the land to whom I would give more earnest consideration than your good self.'

'That's as nice a declaration as I have come across this year,' he replied. 'I don't require that in writing, but you may be sure that I shall file away the same in my mind and trot it out as evidence should the situation arise.'

We both laughed.

'What are you doing for your birthday anyhow?' he asked.

'Meeting my father – for some activity best known to himself,' I replied. 'At a place called Tink's Wharf. . .'

*

The cab driver had never heard of Tink's Wharf, but he took me to Rotherhithe Street and asked around. It turned out to be a fairly typical riverside dock: all rusting piles of metal, overturned boats on the jetty, a large covered boat-shed, seagulls screaming overhead and swooping down for scraps that drifted by on the oily tide.

'Anyone at home?' I cried when I had paid off the hansom, and almost immediately wished that I had retained its services. Father, by no means a stranger to practical joking, had surely not lured me there on my birthday on some elaborate whimsy?

There being no answer to my hail, I walked towards the boat-shed, which was a substantial building and might well contain offices and people.

In fact, when I entered it I found the place to contain very much more. With a sudden, heart-warming moment of new encounter, I found myself looking up at one of the dearest artifacts of my life.

Set upon a slipway in a cradle, her masts unstepped out of deference to the roof of the building . . . was the *Gloria*!

But she was much changed. Instead of her brave finery of gleaming sides and her gold-leaved scrollwork at bow and stern, she was painted all over in battleship grey and had an alien name limned upon her sternpost: *Unbending*. Notwithstanding all this, I would have known her a mile off.

'Coming aboard?'

My father called me from the top of the gangway and I saw that he was not alone; a stocky figure stood by his side who, when I ascended onto the holystoned deck, gave me a naval salute and a bright smile.

'Able Seaman Hopwell!' I cried.

'Now Leading Seaman,' corrected my father. 'And this time we hope he'll stay sober and keep his rate, eh, Hopwell?'

'Do me best, me lord,' responded the other. 'Nice to see you again, ma'am. Hope as 'ow you're keeping well.'

'But what is all this?' I asked, gesturing. As well I might, for in place of the formerly empty area in front of the bridge and wheel-house, there was an exceedingly businesslike gun.

'She's now His Majesty's patrol vessel *Unbending*,' said Father. 'Or, at least, she will become so officially in the very near future. Come below, birthday girl, and I'll tell you all about what I've been up to these last months.'

The descent to the main saloon was like re-entering a familiar old home that has been turned over to some kind of institution such as a particularly austere school. Gone the delicately fashioned birds'-eye maple panelling and the faience tiles, the Art Nouveau lanterns, the trio of naked naiads pouring water from their conch shell into the alabaster basin at the foot of the staircase. And the enormous Persian carpet which once had stretched the length of the big compartment – that had gone too and in its place was some kind of functional rubberised flooring. I could have wept.

'Oh, darling *Gloria* – what have they done to you?' I asked.

'*Sic transit gloria mundi*,' intoned my father. 'Don't cry for the old girl, my darling. She'll do as proudly in her sombre rig as she ever did in her finery, never fear. But now – the champagne, Hopwell!'

'Comin' up, me lord!' cried that worthy.

There was champagne and caviar and a whole nursery of flowers displayed on the long table. They pledged me, the two of them, and we pledged each other and the dear old yacht. It was then Father explained that his brief from the Admiralty had been quietly to buy up, through his yacht brokerage, suitable seagoing vessels of around the thousand to fifteen-hundred gross tonnage mark to be converted into patrol craft for the English Channel in time of war.

'Only, like many others up to similar tricks,' he ended, 'I have had to play "softly softly catchee monkee" – for there's the "peace at any price" faction in the House, not to mention the Kaiser, who is forever on the lookout for an excuse to rattle his sabre.'

'Father, do you think there is going to be a war?' I asked.

'I do, my dear,' he replied soberly. 'And not long hence. If this year, it will come after the harvest's gathered in.'

'But 'twill be over come Christmas, ma'am,' interposed Hopwell. 'Just you see.'

*

They showed me over the converted *Gloria* (I could not bring myself to think of her by any other name) and what I saw saddened me greatly – even allowing for the champagne, which always makes me maudlin.

My delicious little stern cabin and its private egress on to the secluded poop deck had been rudely ripped away to make room for yet another heavy gun and its cylindrical mounting.

As I stood there and marvelled, scenes both of sunlight and the deepest shadow came back to me: among other episodes, I remembered the night when I had stood there and overheard Natasha Chalmers and her inamorata exchanging their vile confidences — and recalled with a shudder how inexorable Fate had repaid her in hard coin.

On the happier side, I imagined the lilt of waltz-time coming from the broad deck above, the tinkle of ragtime being played on the piano.

'Father, despite all, I am so glad you found her again,' I said. 'I know she'll bring luck to all who sail in her.' The conventional declaration (which I had heard so many times at innumerable launchings during my girlhood) slipped lightly off my tongue; why, then, did I seem to hear the whispers of unhappy ghosts all about me?

I shuddered and went back down to the saloon with Father, while Hopwell departed to fetch more champagne.

'Did you see that Cummings has been promoted Captain and given his own flotilla?' asked my father.

'Oh, really?' I responded with elaborate carelessness, which I profoundly hoped would deceive him; I knew very well about Jack's new promotion, for I avidly followed the progress of his career in the *Gazette* and the *Post* — yet I would as lief have admitted as much to Father as shout it from the roof-tops. 'I always knew that he would prosper,' I added with an assumed air of judicial appraisal. 'Make an admiral yet, I shouldn't wonder.'

My father cocked a shrewd eye at me over the top of his champagne glass. 'Always thought you two would make a splendid go of it together,' he commented. 'Never could understand how it was you came to split up.'

'Oh, it was over a very small thing, Father,' I murmured, 'and it's all forgotten and past us now.'

That was my birthday. Two days later, the newspaper sellers strung out along Oxford Street were crying their wares and displaying posters that told of the shocking assassination of an Austrian Archduke and his wife.

*

I was out in the streets the day war was declared and the scenes were unbelievable, like Doré engravings of the inner circles of the damned; when night came and flaming torches illuminated the faces of the cheering, singing masses, I was quite sickened; yet perversely was part caught up in the patriotic jingoism, the righteous wrath against the Kaiser – good Queen Vicky's grandson – with his sabre-rattling and his ebullience; the feeling over the unspeakable outrage against gallant little Belgium, the firm assurance that we should have it all over by Christmas, and that any man who didn't take the King's shilling right away was going to miss the bus for the great victory.

I was in my office early the following morning. The hotel was in a turmoil. Cancellations were coming in at one door – for functions, for room bookings – while frantic requests for accommodation seemed to be flooding in through the other; from all over the land, from the shires, from quiet country hamlets throughout the British Isles, officers of the Reserve were pouring into London to join their units.

'Judith, can't you get hold of Mr Waterford?' I asked my secretary. 'I've phoned his office half a dozen times and can get no reply. We shall simply have to get one of the smaller commercial hotels to absorb our overflow.'

The girl coloured up and stammered. 'I . . . don't think Mr Waterford will be available, ma'am,' she said.

'Not available? What *do* you mean, Judith?'

'Well, ma'am, he told me not to tell you, but he's . . . gone to join the Army, ma'am!'

'Join the *Army*?' I was appalled. 'What in heaven's name does he want to go and do a thing like that for? Who does he think is going to run this hotel while he's away playing at soldiers? Does he think I can cope with this mess all on my own? When did he go?'

'Straight after he came in, ma'am,' said Judith. 'And young Alfred Slyte went with him.'

I stared in disbelief. The thought of my landlady's infant child donning the khaki was ludicrous. 'But he's not of age to join up!' I cried. 'What on earth is his mother going to say?'

*

Stanley was back before midday and looking very lugubrious. He came straight to see me.

'Hello, soldier,' I greeted him. Having simmered down slightly, I was inclined to take the whole matter as an elaborate joke. 'I'll wager the Kaiser's really worried now.'

'They wouldn't have me!' he cried, bereft.

'Why ever not, Stanley?'

'The doctors say I have a weak chest,' he replied brokenly. 'It's damnably unfair.' He punched the palm of one hand with the balled-up fist of the other. 'I want to do my bit, I want to knock hell out of the Hun!'

I had the wry notion to advise him to join one of the bands of patriots who were roaming around Oxford Street and district smashing the windows of shops with German-sounding names, but restrained myself from the cruel irony.

'What happened to young Alfred Slyte?' I asked.

'*He's* in!' replied Stanley, glowering. 'The young blighter added a year to his age. Told them he was eighteen. They didn't argue the toss. I had the very clear impression that they're taking anyone with two arms and two legs who can stand upright.' He slumped down in my office armchair. 'All except *me*!' he added bitterly.

I crossed over to the cupboard where I kept the wherewithal for a little occasional entertaining. 'Have a sherry and simmer down, Stanley,' I said. 'After all, if it's going to be over by Christmas, you would scarcely have had time to learn to shoot straight before you'd be back here.'

'That isn't the point, Faith,' he responded. 'War separates the men from the boys, and when victory comes I want to be in uniform, to demonstrate which side of the dividing fence I stand. And yes, please, I will have a sherry!'

I had pressed him to another sherry – without much difficulty – when his secretary knocked and came in. She had a letter which she said had been delivered by hand from our chairman, the odious Lord Barnworthy. It was a round robin to all the directors.

Stanley read it through in wide-eyed silence and then exclaimed. 'Good God, Faith – just listen to this! It says:

The Home Office has informed the Board that, in pursuance of its plenary powers embodied in the War (Emergency) Powers Act 1914, the Board is to place the entire property known as the Cawnpore Hotel, South Audley Street, Mayfair, into the hands of the London Garrison Military Authority, for conversion into a military hospital. Detailed instructions of the turn-over will follow, but it is expected that the present staff of the hotel will remain in their present employment.

'What do you think of *that*, Faith?'

I thought for some seconds before I replied. 'It doesn't sound to me, Stanley, as if the government shares the view of the man in the street,' I ventured. 'I mean – would they turn us into a military hospital if they thought the war was going to be over by Christmas? It seems to me that they're anticipating long-term hostilities.'

Stanley pulled a long lip and looked doubtful; but I had never spoken a truer word in my life.

*

Of all things, Dickie Jobling heralded in the war by marrying!

I received a very elaborate invitation card from the parents of his intended – titled Scottish aristocrats – inviting me to attend the wedding in Glasgow Cathedral, followed by a reception at some stately home overlooking the Clyde. There followed a note from Dickie, addressed from a Royal Naval Air Service base in Scotland, begging me to make the journey if I could. He ended with the words: '. . . and you're excused the traditional monthly offer – at least for the foreseeable future. . .'

I sent the happy couple a gift of a piece of silver from our slender stock of possessions which had escaped the bailiffs. Anticipating much that came after, I have to add that I have never seen my former suitor again to this day; he survived the war and remained in Scotland to manage his in-laws' wide estates in the Highlands.

Father dropped his bombshell a week after the declaration of war. It was on the afternoon of the same day that Mrs Slyte returned in triumph from the War Office; she had laid siege on that hallowed place, day and night, until she was allowed to see a red-tabbed staff officer who, having heard her complaint, meekly agreed that her son Alfred Slyte, private soldier designate, was indeed too young to volunteer to serve King and Country. The glowering Alfred returned to work at the Cawnpore within the hour!

Father took me to dinner at the Ritz that evening. He too, like Mrs Slyte, had been haunting the seats of power – in his case the Admiralty, as a result of which he had been removed from the retired list and bidden to await orders.

'I suppose I shall be given command of some shore establishment or made to count paper clips in some office in Whitehall,' said my parent, 'but at least I have one foot in the door, and I have plenty of friends in the Service – if also quite a few enemies – and this is going to be a long war, so I shouldn't be surprised if they don't give me a real job before it's all over!'

257

To surprise me, Father had donned his old uniform, which stood badly in need of a good press and smelled vilely of mothballs; but he looked so tall, so straight, so handsome . . . and I felt immeasurably proud of him and went to have a little cry in the Ladies' room.

Through tears and laughter, we had a brilliant evening and danced together until past midnight. On the way home, walking arm-in-arm through the silent streets, he talked about the situation on the continent as he had heard it – the up-to-the-minute situation – in the Admiralty that day.

Those of us like myself, who read the newspapers, were aware that the situation on the Western Front was grave, with the German advance within gunfire sound of Paris, with the French and British in retreat to the River Marne, and every expectation of the conflict indeed being over for Christmas as anticipated . . . but with the Allies having lost!

The next twenty-four hours would be critical, said Father. Our people were going to stand and fight on the Marne, he said. There were reports of reinforcements being driven to the front in Parisian taxi-cabs, twelve men to a cab! Oh, how he wished he had command of a gunboat on the Marne, he cried! And how glad I was that he had not!

How I hoped and prayed also that Jack – wherever he might be – was safe that night – as countless women all over Europe, in Germany also, must have been doing likewise.

*

As history records, the line was held on the Marne and the enemy fell back and began to dig ditches. They remained in these ditches – the trenches – facing our own, through the months and years that stretched in front of us all; while the finest blood in Europe watered the fields of Flanders and Picardy, Burgundy and all the way down to the Swiss frontier . . . and the Europe of old, the Europe I had been born to and had grown up in, disappeared for ever.

At the Cawnpore, we also went to war.

There arrived Sister Emily Gravestoke. . .

She came, all unannounced, on a Monday morning. I have always held it to be an immutable truth that most of the worst things in life begin on Monday mornings, and that this is so obvious as not to require examples by way of illustration. Sister Gravestoke was a prime example of that truth.

She was not tall, but carried tallness within her; she was not young, as one counts youth in years, but there was a taut alertness about her that one more often sees in athletes, and also a strange liveliness; she was not beautiful as the world reckons beauty, but her face was like that of a tutelary matron-goddess of some sacred grove of Attica . . . carved out of granite.

She entered without the grace or courtesy of a knock.

'Are you Dangerfield?' she demanded.

'I – I am,' I responded, rising.

'Gravestoke,' she said, holding out a hand. 'You will have heard of me.'

Now, I *had* heard of Sister Emily Gravestoke; the hotel having been empty of guests for weeks and the public rooms shut down by order of the authorities who now guided our existence, I had had several communications from those on high. One of the most recent was a memorandum informing me that the charge of the hospital (to be designated Military Hospital, London District–24) had been given to Sister Emily Gravestoke of Queen Alexandra's Imperial Nursing Service, and that I might expect her arrival imminently. Imminence – as I had quickly discovered in my dealings with authority – being a purely relative term with such folk, I had filed away the memorandum and resigned myself to await events. Meanwhile a month had slowly passed.

Having wrung my hand, she looked about her imperiously.

'Yes, this office will do for me,' she announced, 'being near to the centre of things. You will wish to find yourself other accommodation, Dangerfield. I shall move in forthwith. My baggage is in the hall.

'Now – as to logistics. . .'

While I was standing and staring at her, this astonishing woman by some means deftly interposed herself between me and the desk and neatly slid herself into my swing chair; there she settled down with the air of a sleek cat who has discovered the best sofa in the house and apportioned it to herself.

'Do sit down, Dangerfield,' she said, indicating the chair opposite, 'and I will instruct you on our relative duties.' She sat back, placed the finger-tips of both hands together and eyed me with a certain chill benevolence.

'Sister – I. . .' My intervention availed me nothing. . .

'Later, Dangerfield – later,' she said. 'I will give you ample opportunity to make your observations when you have been apprised of the facts' – another chilly smile – 'for what are observations un-backed by facts? To resume: I shall be in complete charge of the hospital and will be addressed as Matron. Your function, as former housekeeper of the hotel, will not greatly differ from before, since as I understand it you were manager of the establishment in all but name.

'You will attend to the workaday running of the hospital in matters relating to the procuring and provisioning all non-medical supplies, organising of meals, cleaning and supervision of non-nursing and military staff. . .

'Subject to *my* sole direction.'

I took a deep breath.

'Sister Gravestoke. . .'

'Matron,' she corrected me mildly, but with a certain edge.

'Matron,' I said, 'I would remind you that I am under no obliga-tion to the military authority, being a paid servant of the company that owns the hotel. I must tell you, therefore, that I shall have to consider my position in the light of what you have told me – and I shall certainly consult Mr Stanley Waterford, a director of the com-pany and a close associate of mine. I have no doubt that he, also, will wish to consider his position.'

She fixed me with a granite stare.

'I have to tell *you*, Dangerfield,' she said, 'that Mr Waterford's wide experience has earned him today the offer of a commission in the Royal Army Service Corps, in command of field kitchens attached to the British Expeditionary Force in France. He will almost certainly accept it.'

'Oh!' I exclaimed, the image of my only ally vanishing before my very eyes.

'However, feel free to consider your position,' said my tormentor. 'Sleep on it, do. Call to see me first thing tomorrow morning and give me your decision on the matter. On the other hand, if your decision is to resign (which you are perfectly entitled to do), you may save us both time and trouble by telephoning such a decision to me.

'You already have the telephonic number. Good day to you, Dangerfield.'

*

I picked up my few portable belongings and walked home as if in a trance, unbelieving that my state could possibly have changed for the worse so suddenly and seemingly irrevocably; that my achievement in lifting myself up from a sudden nobody to being a somebody by my own effort should have been so uncaringly swept aside.

To be subject to the 'direction' of that woman Gravestoke!

My father was not at home when I arrived and I made myself a cup of tea, but was unable to sit down and drink it; I merely walked up and down, up and down the kitchen, fuming with fury. I was still in this state when Father came in.

'Hello, dear. What are you doing home at this hour?' he asked.

I told him the whole sorry story.

'Well, the war's caught up with you and no mistake,' was his somewhat rather less than sympathetic comment. 'You will have to make what shift you can of the situation, won't you?' And before I could interject, he went on, 'The business of turning a luxury hotel into a military hospital overnight will surely be enough to tax the organising genius of a Florence Nightingale. I'm not surprised that your Gravestoke lady is pretty formidable; she's likely to need all the formidability she can muster.'

And then he added something which totally demolished the last of my defences and made me realise how selfish and uncaring my attitude had been: 'I should think that the two of you together will make a splendid job of it. And there'll be a lot of poor, wounded chaps who will come to be grateful to you both. Oh, come now – why all the sudden affection on a wet Monday morning?'

I clung to him and held him tightly. 'Oh, Daddy, what would I do, where should I be without you?' I asked.

'Well, m'dear, you will have to try your hand at doing without me, I'm afraid.'

I stood back from him, searched his face.

'What do you mean?' I murmured.

'They've given me a sea appointment,' he replied. And his face was as creased and pink with joy as that of a little boy on Christmas morning. 'I've got a ship – and that ain't all. . .'

'A ship? You're going to sea – to the *war*?'

'And guess what, Faith – she's the *Unbending* – our dear old *Gloria*! It took a lot of wangling, a lot of to-ing and fro-ing amongst my chums at the Admiralty. A massive exercising of the old boys' network and quite a lot of finagling at the Naval and Yachting! But it's all fixed and I have my written orders.'

I was back at the Cawnpore just as soon as Father and I had had a scratch luncheon interspersed with reminiscences of the past, hopes for the future.

Emily Gravestoke looked up from my desk – *her* desk – as I entered. My hair was coming down, for I had run most of the way in the rain, all the tramcars being full. I felt like some woman up from the country selling eggs – but didn't seem to care.

'I – I've considered my position, Matron,' I said. 'And I shall be pleased to stay.'

'I thought you might, Dangerfield,' she said impassively.

*

Father departed to join his ship a week later; he left for the railway station with two hansom cabs – one for his sea-chest and gear, the other for himself. I didn't go with him, for the protracted parting would have been too much. We embraced on the front porch, while Mrs Slyte stood tearfully watching us from her upstairs window.

'Look after yourself, Captain,' I said. 'Please don't be heroic.'

(I recalled with a stab of sudden anguish how I had once said something of the sort to someone else, in another place, at another time.)

'Nothing to be heroic about, more's the pity,' was his reply. 'All we'll be doing, Hopwell and I and the rest of the deadbeats manning the old *Gloria*, will be pottering up and down the Channel on patrol, getting in the way of the real, fighting Navy.'

'You keep it that way,' I admonished him.

Then he was gone from my sight, his second hansom following after.

Back in the sitting-room, my eyes strayed towards the thick envelope which he had given me the night before, still lying where he had put it on the occasional table. And his words came back to me:

'Just in case anything happens to me, Faith – a ridiculous notion, considering the luck of the Dangerfields – I'd like you to keep this. Give it back to me when the war's over. On the other hand. . .'

He had not needed to say more, the implication was quite clear. And knowing what I did, the contents of the envelope called for no great exercise of the imagination. My father had given into my hand the true account of my mother's death, with which he had not wished to burden me.

But he wanted to make sure that, if he was killed, the secret did not perish with him.

*

I heard from Father every week. His return address – HMS *Unbending*, c/o GPO London – betrayed no hint of his whereabouts to enemy spies and suchlike who might have designs upon Captain Lord Dangerfield and his shapely little patrol vessel as they ploughed up and down the English Channel. Father's laconic weekly postcards, on the other hand, made no such pretence; all of them carried, on their reverse side, some view or other of Dover and the white cliffs.

The Christmas which should have ended it all came and passed. With the New Year came mutterings of a big offensive that the Allies were planning to launch, to break the hideous stalemate which had frozen the opposing armies in a war of attrition. The terrible battles of the Marne, and later at Ypres, had passed by the Cawnpore Hotel, for we were not ready to be considered as Military Hospital, London District–24 until well into 1915. By then, we knew that we should soon learn something of what war was all about.

My relationship with Emily Gravestoke continued to be that of headmistress and untried – very much untried – head girl. If she wanted to see me, she summoned me. I was never invited to sit down in her presence, but was briefly issued with my instructions, either verbally or in writing. And that was that.

She was certainly a person of tremendous energy, and with the talent to delegate. Once having given me my orders, she never interfered in my method of carrying them out; but woe betide if they were not carried out to her entire satisfaction!

Quite simply, the lower three floors of the hotel, plus the ground floor and basement – which were all connected by modern electric lifts – had been turned into twenty- or thirty-bed common wards by the simple process of knocking down intersecting walls. This was not the drastic task that might be thought, since the hotel itself had originally been built as a private town mansion with enormous rooms, and only later divided up into much smaller units by light panelling.

The kitchens, laundry, still-room and other utility rooms were, of course, ideally suited for conversion to a hospital. The public rooms likewise were translated to canteens for walking wounded, messes for medical and nursing staff and so forth – with hardly any construction work.

I returned to Beatrice Carradine's original little office under the rafters. And in the turmoil that accompanied the changeover, it was a refuge indeed to retreat to my eyrie under the roof, unconnected by lifts and with only the telephone to bother me.

It was on the first of March that the Military Hospital, London District–24 was deemed to be in being, and a signal to that effect was dispatched to the powers-that-be. This occurred at a meeting in Matron's office attended by Sister Gravestoke herself, the medical director Dr Crooks, his senior doctors, my principal assistants and myself; Stanley had long since departed for his field kitchens.

We of MH 24 were ready for war.

We had not long to wait for the war to come to *us*!

*

The news of March 10th–11th was that the British Expeditionary Force had begun an offensive in the Neuve Chapelle area, had over-run the enemy trenches and taken many prisoners. The heady sense of victory inspired by this communication, however, was soon eroded by a long period of significant silence, followed by reports that all was not going well, that the enemy had closed the breach in his line and that the attack had failed. There had been, we were told, heavy casualties on both sides.

This last utterance was most significant for MH 24.

I shall never forget the night when we had a telephone message to prepare for the wounded. The air was deathly still; threats of attack upon London by German Zeppelin airships had led to a drastic reduction of street lighting. I alternated on night duty at the hospital with my secretary Judith Marks, and at that time was doing my rounds of the kitchens and still-rooms. The medical staff had just finished their supper, the nurses also. We of the civilian staff ate in what used to be the old muster room.

Within minutes of the message being received everyone was at his or her post: the surgeons were ready in the operating theatre – formerly the ballroom; beds were turned back in readiness; porters grouped in the lobby by the main doors, lifts ready to move; everywhere there lurked an atmosphere of tension, of nerve-searing expectation. I myself took up a position by Matron's office door, ready to give aid wherever it was required. It seemed a lifetime away from the workaday peacetime tasks of organising balls and wedding breakfasts, supervising the counting of silver spoons and arguing over the telephone with recalcitrant meat and fish merchants in Smithfield or Billingsgate.

'*Watch yourselves – here they come! Here they come!*'

The shout from the street door made the adrenalin flow. Rushing to one of the long windows and peeping round the heavy curtains to look out into the night, I saw the first of a long convoy of Red Cross motor ambulances pull up at the foot of the old Cawnpore's marble steps – lacking on this occasion the red carpets which were put out in happier days and for happier events.

The first vehicle having been emptied of its burdens, it moved on. The second followed. Presently a long file of stretcher-bearers were swaying across the foyer with their charges. Our own porters and nurses – one nurse to every two porters – moved forward and took over from the khaki-clad bearers, who doubled away to rejoin their ambulances and return to the railway station for yet another load of wounded.

It was the lifts which provided us with the first hurdle to the smooth running of the operation. Six persons they carried; but, as quickly transpired, only two stretchers could be accommodated at a time. And the stairs were long and winding.

Next the condition of the wounded – and the most appalling state of some of the worst wounded – cut to ribbons the resolve of some of the younger and more impressionable of the hospital staff.

'Gawd! How can a feller be in that state and still be alive?'

I shall never forget the sheet-white face and staring uncomprehending eyes of a porter – no more than a boy – who lowered his burden and then fled from sight, sobbing hysterically. There being no one else available, I took up the abandoned end of the stretcher and helped carry it into the nearest lift.

As we emerged on the first floor, I met the eye of Emily Gravestoke. She had with her a porter whom she directed with a nod and a curt order to take charge of my end of the dying soldier's stretcher.

'You shouldn't be wasting your time on work like that, Dangerfield,' she snapped. 'How are things in the kitchen?'

'All in order, Matron,' I replied.

'Hot soup, hot tea for all?'

'Yes, Matron.'

'Supper for those who can eat?'

'Yes.'

'Prepared to serve breakfast for five hundred?' The question was delivered with a narrowing of the gimlet eyes in that granite countenance; this, I discerned to be my acid test.

'Yes. From 7 o'clock in the morning onwards.'

'Good work, Dangerfield. Follow me.'

I followed that woman through the three upper, the ground and the basement floors of the old Cawnpore, as the wounded poured in and were laid first on beds; and when the beds ran out, on the floors, and when there was no further room in the makeshift wards, on the parquet flooring of the reception lobby; on desks, counters, sofas, tables . . . anywhere.

I followed her everywhere she led; and she alert and assiduous as if she were doing her daily rounds to seek out the single patch of dust, the neglected grease mark, which would bring down her fury upon the person responsible.

I followed her – through hell. . .

Any words of mine, my own outrage, my whole being, my inclination to the life-loving civility of human congress – are totally inadequate when I try to describe what horrors descended upon the old cawnpore on that March night in London's Mayfair.

The wounded were wonderful. There were a few who, in their transports of agony, cursed God, man and the mothers who bore them. Many others, superficially better off, drew on the cigarettes that were tenderly placed between their lips by the attendants, cracked a joke or two, smiled and died a credit to their race – to the human race.

It was odd – I noticed it everywhere – that the soldiers, however badly wounded, or wounded and dying, were for the most part less affected than those of us who witnessed their agonies. I know that I discovered hitherto unsuspected sources of weakness in my own self during that long night of horror, when the wounded and dying came teeming in with every convoy of Red Cross ambulances. Many was the time – particularly towards dawn, when the spirit is weakest, when it most readily slips away from the body and takes refuge in infinity – when I would gladly have thrown aside my bloodstained apron and run for obscurity and silence.

But how could I – with Emily Gravestoke beside me all the time? She with her granite countenance, her maddening alertness when everyone about her was becoming limp and enfeebled by the accumulated physical weariness and the constant hammering on shocked sensibilities by the scenes about them.

Then came my personal crisis. There was a boy soldier, surely not many months older than the egregious Alfred Slyte, who had suffered such wounds – and subsequent neglect in the chaos – that both his legs had to be amputated in our makeshift operating theatre, and all with the most basic amenities as regards anaesthesia and disinfectants. The amputations done, the surgeons moved on to the next table, the next case; and I was left with the boy – a farm-hand from Suffolk who, so he told me in the coming hours of dawn when he recovered some sort of drifting consciousness, remembered Mondisfield well, and my father, and indeed had some recollection of me when I rode my pony Bimbo at the gymkhanas.

He died holding my hand. I had no recourse but to flee downstairs to a quiet place where I could weep alone. The only place I could think of was my former office, since apportioned by Emily Gravestoke for herself.

I burst in. The single electric light above the desk was on and by its illumination, I saw the bowed figure of the Matron seated there, her head in her hands.

She looked up when she heard me enter. I never saw anguish written so clearly on a human face as I saw there that dawn. And the granite cheeks were streaked with tears.

'You've caught me out, Dangerfield,' she said. 'The Gorgon, you will be surprised to know, feels the pricks of pain just like everyone else.' She smiled, a wry, self-mocking grimace. 'But then I'm not a sailor's daughter, nor the daughter of a fine lord, so I don't have the upbringing to bear the unbearable with fortitude, as you have. I knew from the first time I set eyes on you that you were the woman I should need at my right hand, Faith Dangerfield.'

When I stepped into the circle of the light, she must have seen my tear-streaked face and she reached out her hands towards me. 'What happened to you, child? What have you been through now?'

There was no need for explanation; with suffering and death all around us, there were a hundred sights, a hundred experiences which could have brought us both so low as we were. I took her hands and we clung to each other for a few moments in silence and mutual support. And then she lifted up my chin between finger and thumb and met my eyes.

267

'We know each other now, Faith. That was good,' she said. 'Now we must dry our tears and try the game again.'

*

The Neuve Chapelle casualties were MH 24's baptism of fire, as the saying goes. This was only the beginning. After that first holocaust the hospital – which had won itself an immediate reputation with the powers-that-be – never had an empty bed; a steady stream of sick and wounded soldiers passed in through the plate-glass doors.

In recognition of MH 24's effort that March, our Matron was commended by the War Office and Lord Barnworthy was awarded his OBE for the same reason.

As for my relationship with Emily Gravestoke: that first unforgettable night when we had mutually sought and found, our strengths and weaknesses marked the beginning of an association which I was able to compare only with the relationship I had had with Beatrice Carradine. But there was this difference: there was no real affection between Emily and I as there had been with the latter. We were professional associates, deeply committed to each other's support. I never came to know the essential Emily any better than I had that day she marched into my office and took over. And still she continued to make me stand in her presence on formal occasions.

A delightful surprise: Stanley Waterford came to see me . . .

'Stanley, you look every inch the gallant officer!' I declared. And so he did. The well-cut tunic, the pale lemon riding-out breeches, the tall boots boned to mirror brightness, two 'pips' of a full lieutenant on his cuffs, swagger stick and jaunty cap – he was fit to turn any girl's eye.

'No point in being in command of a battery of field kitchens and *looking* as if I am!' he said, grinning. 'Give us a kiss, Faith.'

He was off to the Middle East, to Palestine, Mesopotamia and beyond, to 'attend to the Inner Man of the chaps who are going to knock hell out of Johnnie Turk'. But before that we talked about the old days at the hotel. We went into fits over the abominable Lord Barnworthy's OBE; and he took me to the picture theatre to see Charlie Chaplin in a bioscope called 'Tillie's Punctured Romance'. Fortified to the point of unaccustomed assurance by his splendid uniform, no doubt, he proposed to me again outside Charing Cross Station, but with more earnestness than before. With equal earnestness I refused him and watched my would-be swain walk on into the station to catch his train to Dover, the Middle East and on. I never saw him again.

There was no word, no news of Jack. . .

He had disappeared into the anonymity of war, though blessedly his name did not appear on the constantly lengthening casualty lists which were published every day in the press and posted outside police stations, town halls, post offices and the like. But there was not a passing day, nor a sleepless night, that I did not pray for his safety and mourn my precious scruples which had prevented me from snatching at immediate happiness no matter what the risk of future heartbreak.

*

It was in May that young Alfred Slyte, having attained the age of eighteen, made fair to break his poor mother's heart by again attending the recruiting office in Piccadilly and enlisting. This time he was accepted, and put in a brief appearance as Private Slyte of the 'Ox and Bucks' before being rushed off to France and the trenches. It was in May also – on the 26th, if my memory serves me right – that a German Zeppelin made the first aerial raid upon the capital city of the British Empire.

The drone of the contraption's engines woke me in St George's Square and Mrs Slyte's frenzied cries brought me up and out into the street; the inhabitants of the entire square must have been out there, pointing up into the cloudless night where, clear in the moonlight, we could see the huge cigar-shaped thing that was slowly moving across our vision; it was enormous and seemed to dominate the whole sky, travelling so close and so low down that one could see the lighted compartment underneath with figures inside, watching us perhaps; and the slowly-turning windmills of the engines; and the black crosses emblazoned on the side.

Mrs Slyte clutched at my arm. 'Is it going to bomb us?' she asked me.

It occurred to me that the Germans could not possibly have come to London on a reconnaisance trip; furthermore they had dropped bombs on villages in Norfolk earlier in the year.

'I think we should go down and take shelter in the basement,' I suggested.

And so we did. Minutes later, we heard the thunder of exploding bombs as we cowered down there in the darkness and lived through a piece of history. They dropped a ton of the fiendish devices, killing seven harmless civilians. War had come to the very doorsteps of the island race.

*

The Greeks, as usual, had a word for it and that word was 'hubris', being the presumptuous pride that generally goes before a fall. The substance of my pride was the success of Military Hospital, London District–24, and my part in it.

As to the fall. . .

There were several offensives in Flanders, after the Neuve Chapelle fiasco, some large, some small, and MH–24 played its part in most. By then our first fumbling attempts had smoothed out into an organisation which – as I sometimes told myself – worked like a beautifully made clock.

That was the hubris talking. . .

The incident which so very nearly laid us low began without any sign of trouble. We had information that an ambulance train was arriving at such-and-such an hour, full of walking wounded from an attack which had taken place a few days previously. All the soldiers had been attended to at the field dressing-stations and there were no gravely wounded. It was simply a matter of accommodating them for a few days, generally caring for them, and changing their dressings until they could be shifted out to convalescent homes. Simple.

Emily Gravestoke sent for me as she usually did before the arrival of a big influx – in this case about 350 men. And as usual, seeing it was a formal occasion, she did not invite me to sit down.

'They will need a meal immediately they arrive, Dangerfield,' she said. 'I had a call from the Railway Transport Officer just now. Apparently someone slipped up at Dover and there was no breakfast for the walking wounded. It appears moreover that they have not eaten since they left the railhead in Flanders, which could have been twenty-four hours ago or more. I trust you can cope?' She gave me her granite goddess look.

'I'm short-staffed in the kitchen,' I told her, 'but the girls will rally round and knock together a nourishing soup, with bread and cheese and pickles. We can give them something more substantial this evening.'

'Good. There never was a hungry soldier who would turn his nose up at a bowl of soup and some bread and cheese!' She gave me one of

270

her rare wintry smiles. 'See to it, Dangerfield. I'll be down later on to see how things are going.'

I went down to the kitchens with no expectation of trouble. We had had a certain number of staffing problems in this department; many of the old Cawnpore kitchen staff had gone to work in munitions, attracted by the high wages, which left us with the scrapings at the bottom of the labour barrel. It was not that the girls were unwilling or particularly inept cooks and kitchen hands – simply that they were young, for the most part uneducated and very badly paid. The military had imposed their own scales of pay when they took over. These rates were at Army level, which was why the old hotel staff had opted for munitions.

I put my head into the kitchen and called out to the duty head cook – a girl named Hattie – who was not the most amiable of creatures and had a strong tendency to mutter behind my back, yet not quite beyond my hearing.

'Three-hundred-and-fifty walking wounded due in at midday,' I told her. 'We'll feed them something easy. Do a soup to the Mrs Beeton recipe. Bread, cheese and pickles. And cocoa. All right?'

She made no reply, but then she was the sort who seldom did more than glower when given an order. Then I went to tell the maids in the muster room to lay tables for the 350: knives, spoons, plates, mugs, and I returned to my office to write out my supply requisitions for the following day.

*

They came dead on twelve midday in London omnibuses: three hundred and fifty-odd khaki-clad figures, still with Flanders mud adhering to them, their moderately clean bandages whitely contrasting with the drab. They all walked, some with the aid of crutches. Some were blinded or partially-sighted; their eyes bandaged, they walked with one hand resting on a sighted comrade's shoulder. All had that strained, pale-faced and slack-mouthed look of men who had suffered and were suffering still.

All were from the same brigade, most from the same regiment. The majority of them, despite their troubles, were in high good spirits at being back in Blighty.

'I'd quite forgot – the world's full of beautiful women! Hello, darling!' This to me from a boy soldier on crutches, who trailed a bandaged foot.

'Bring on the dancing girls!'

'And the steak-and-kidney pud!'

The porters ushered them down to the muster room, where places were laid out on the scrubbed table tops.

'Thank Gawd – we *eat*!'

A cheer went up.

I went into the kitchen to see how things were progressing, but to my surprise I did not catch the pleasurable aroma of Mrs Beeton's justly famous 'Soup for Benevolent Purposes', nor did I see small mountains of sliced bread cut thick, little 'bricks' of cheese piled high and innumerable giant jars of mixed pickle. Moreover the kitchen staff – Hattie and her six assistants – were gathered in a glowering group by the vast stove-top, where there should have been a huge kettle of simmering cocoa – but was not.

'What are you doing?' I demanded. 'And where is the food? The men are all waiting.'

'We ain't doing nothing,' Hattie informed me. 'We're on strike.'

'You *can't* be on strike!' I cried. 'There's a war on.'

'Well, we are and that's that!'

'But,' I cried, pointing back the way I had come, 'there are 350 wounded soldiers out there. None of them has eaten for twenty-four hours and more. You can't even think about *striking* at a time like this!'

Hattie appeared unmoved by my protestation; her followers, who glanced at her for a lead, nodded and appeared to think likewise.

She – apparently the ringleader – opened her mouth to speak, but was drowned by 350 British infantrymen's voices raised in chorus in the next room:

> We're here because we're here
> Because we're here,
> Because we're here. . .
> We're here because we're here
> Because we're here,
> Because we're here . . .

This was sung to the tune of, 'Should Auld Acquaintance be Forgot'.

'What were you going to say, Hattie?' I demanded when the racket had finished. 'Can you argue against *that*? Those boys are hungry and you're just standing around.' I folded my arms. 'Might one ask what you are striking *about*?'

'We want better wages,' she responded.

'That's right — more money!'

'Slave rates, that's what we're on!'

Her companions echoed her sentiments loudly and vociferously.

'All right, all right!' I cried, holding up my hands. 'You've made your point, girls. This afternoon, I suggest you form a deputation and go to see Matron. Put your points to her and she'll make out your case to the powers-that-be. Then maybe something will be done about it.'

'And maybe not!' sneered Hattie.

'In any event,' I said, 'this is neither the time nor the place to make your protest. Get to work like sensible folk and feed those poor fellows. Argue the toss afterwards.'

They all looked at Hattie and none of them moved.

'No!' she mouthed savagely, glaring at me.

'You can't do this, Hattie,' I said. 'Those soldiers have fought and bled for you!'

'Not for *me*!' she spat.

'Then for who else?' I challenged her.

'For *your* sort!' she cried. 'For the la-di-dah boss class and their stuck-up daughters, so they can lord it over the likes of us when the Germans is beat — like what they've always done. *That's* why them silly mugs out there has fought and bled, *Lady Dangerfield*!'

Three strides separated us. I covered them before she had time to raise a hand to defend herself and struck her full across the cheek with my open palm.

She staggered back, her face a mask of mingled fury and triumph.

'You've gone a bit too far this time, milady!' she hissed. 'Come on, you lot — let's get out of here!'

And before my horrified gaze they threw down their aprons and caps, picked up their coats and hats and stalked out of the back door.

I drew a deep, shuddering breath. 'Oh, my God — what have I done?' I breathed.

> Why are we waiting,
> Why-y are we waiting?
> Why are we way-ay-ting,
> Oh, why do we wait? . . .

The chorus dinned in my ears . . .

I elbowed my way out of the door and into the muster room. Three hundred and fifty-odd faces turned to regard me, and a round of cheers rose from three hundred and fifty-odd of throats.

It was then that Emily Gravestock stalked in. Took one look about her at the empty plates, the grinning soldiers, and at me standing by the kitchen door, half in tears I don't doubt.

She looked at her watch. 'Dangerfield, it's nearly half-past twelve and no food on the tables,' she said. 'What's holding you up, pray?'

In the silence that followed – you could have heard a pin drop, and every ear in the room was tuned to my answer – I replied: 'Matron, the kitchen staff have walked out.'

'Walked out? Walked . . . *out*? What *do* you mean?'

'They refused to prepare a meal for the soldiers.'

A growl of fury arose from the men at the tables.

'Why, Dangerfield?'

'Because they want more money.'

'But that's ridiculous. You told them, of course, to complete their task and then come to see me in order to lodge a formal complaint?'

'Yes, that's more or less what I told them.'

'And?'

'They refused and were rude to me, Matron.'

'Well, Dangerfield, your shoulders are broad enough to carry that. What did you do?'

'I smacked the ringleader's face – so they all walked out!'

A hoot of laughter and sporadic cheers greeted my statement; but Emily Gravestock did not share the soldiers' approval of my action.

'You struck one of the staff?' she cried. 'You – a trusted senior member of my hospital – degraded yourself and put our whole organisation to disrepute by using physical force upon one of your subordinates? I have never in my whole life. . .'

'I'm sorry I did it,' was my response. 'But, given a like circumstance, I'd do it again! I'm sorry, Matron, but that's the way I'm built. It's not in my nature to turn the other cheek. I knew it was wrong of me, but . . .'

Another cheer from the soldiers further incensed Matron.

'We will speak of this later, Dangerfield!' she said in a voice of Arctic frigidity.

And then the small miracle began to happen. . .

'Oh, come now, ladies! This ain't the time nor the place for fighting – there's enough of that over in France.' He rose from his seat close by us. He was tall and carried himself with an air of easily-worn authority, with the chevrons of a sergeant sewn upon his sleeve. His eyes were heavily bandaged and the two hesitating steps he took towards us, hands extended, were those of the freshly blind.

'Give me your hand, miss,' he said, touching my shoulder. 'And yours, Matron.'

We obeyed him. He said no more, and there was no refusing his gesture as, our hands in his, he joined us both together, hand in hand, Emily Gravestock and I. And she obeying, like me, as meek as a lamb.

The sergeant had not finished. . .

'Right, you 'orrible little men!' he bellowed in a parade-ground bark, 'I want volunteers for the cook-house. No scrimshanking! Private Barnes of six platoon; Welsh of number seven; Hawkins of three – you was all in the catering trade in civvy street. You're all volunteers. Take as many others as you need. Get in that cook-house and knock up a meal, double-quick.

'On your feet! Double-march! One-two! One-two! One-two!'

He put his hands on our shoulders. 'And you, ladies, will be the Army's guests today, will sit with us and share our meal.' And there was no refusing him.

The sergeant thumped the table. 'Right!' he bellowed. 'The slight hiatus – *hiatus* is what I said, you ignorant little man! – between now and dinner will be filled with some sparkling entertainment. First off, Corporal Hemmings will oblige with one of his incomparable recitations. On your feet, Corporal!'

A small soldier at the far end of the room stood up; climbed upon his chair.

'Recitation!' he announced. ' "The Green Eye of the Yellow God", by J. Milton Mayes. . .'

He paused, sawed the air with his one good arm in the manner that Shakespeare's Hamlet said he shouldn't.

There's a one-eyed yellow idol to the north of Katmandu,
There's a little marble cross below the town;
There's a broken-hearted woman tends the grave of Mad Carew
And the Yellow God forever gazes down.

In the applause that followed the rendition of that lurid ballad, I looked about me in wonderment at the thought that people like

275

myself should stand upon our small dignities in the face of men such as these: hurt, bruised and beaten men – beaten, but unconquered and unconquerable.

To my surprise, I found that I was still holding Emily Gravestock's hand tightly, and she mine.

Our glances met and she smiled. We were both weeping quite unashamedly.

*

'Miss Dangerfield! It can't be you – but it *is*! What a surprise!'

I was just coming out of Gamages' emporium in Holborn, where I had been to order some goodies for a party that we were holding in the staff canteen for war orphans of Paddington (party hats 2d each, novelties and jokes 8½d to 1/- each), when I ran straight into little Miss Angela Dearing, sometime quasi-fiancée of our secretary Charles Knight aboard the *Gloria*.

'Well, Miss Dearing, how very nice,' I said. 'How are you?'

After the conventional greetings, she asked me if I would care to join her in a cup of tea at Gamages, where she was bound, but I replied with truth that I was on duty at the hospital in half an hour's time.

There the conversation might have flagged and died, but for a casual remark I made: 'Odd the way things worked out, isn't it? We never did keep that rendezvous for tea at Gauchi's in Jubilee Street!'

'Oh yes, and I did so need a wise person like yourself to act as confidante. It was when I had broken with Charles, of course.'

'Yes, I remember,' I said. 'How is Charles – do you ever hear from him?'

She looked abashed; she was the kind who did that very well. 'Oh, didn't you know? He was killed.'

'Oh, no!'

'Yes – at Ypres. He joined the Territorials immediately after he returned to England, and went to France with the second batch. His mother wrote me . . . afterwards, you know. It was very sad. I was . . . very fond of Charles, until the real Mr Right came along.'

Already we were well into confidences. I was greatly grieved to hear about Charles Knight, whom I had always regarded as a splendid person and, it has to be said, totally wasted on Miss Dearing whom I considered to be a shallow and somewhat snobbish girl.

She added, rather archly, 'Of course, you were the one really to blame for Charles and I breaking up. The ball on the *Gloria*, you know.'

I stared at her, puzzled. 'I'm afraid I don't. . .'

'Commander Cummings!' she cried. 'Jack Cummings – you put me next to him and I fell in love with him at first sight. Just like a silly schoolgirl!'

'Oh, I had no idea,' I heard myself say.

'Oh yes, the true love of my life,' she said. 'It was hopeless, of course, quite hopeless.' She tapped my arm knowingly. 'He was . . . well, not one of us, you know, Miss Dangerfield. His father was a stoker in the Navy and Jack came up through the lower deck. So of course, I couldn't entertain the idea of marriage to him. Mother was one of the Rutland Cavanaghs, you know, and *her* mother was related to the Marquess of Evesham.'

'What a pity,' I responded dully. 'So what did you do – was there an affair between you?'

She looked affronted. 'Oh, dear no! How could you think such a thing? I never so much as showed him by look or gesture where my feelings lay. Nor ever would.' She added wistfully, 'But at the time I could have done with the advice of an older and more experienced woman of my own class.'

Greatly relieved, I asked, 'And what now – did you ever contemplate marriage to some other gentleman?'

It's very odd, the way things sometimes fall out. If anyone had told me that Angela Dearing – whom I confess I always tried hard to like, but with no success whatever – would with a few empty phrases encapsulate and illuminate the depth and truth of my own feelings, I would given them the lie.

But there it was; on that afternoon in Holborn, with the crowds drifting past all uncaring, Angela Dearing showed me myself in reflection when she answered my question.

'I shall never marry anyone else, Miss Dangerfield,' she said. 'When you have loved someone the way I loved him from the very first, and with all your heart and soul, you can never look at anyone again. Ever. I shall never marry. I shall love him all my life.

'Goodbye, Miss Dangerfield. Nice to have seen you.'

And then she was gone – lost from my sight for ever in the milling throng of heedless people.

*

And so it was, with the war closing more nearly about us all every day; with the daily casualty lists bringing anguish, dread anticipation, broken lives, broken marriages and broken dreams, I lived like the rest of the women in love . . . in constant fear of the knock on the door, the line in the newspaper, the casual word.

For though I had tried to shut my mind to it, I had given not one but two hostages to fortune: my father and my lover.

*

ST PAUL'S CATHEDRAL

1916

TWELVE

THE SECRETARY OF THE ADMIRALTY REGRETS TO INFORM YOU THAT CAPTAIN LORD M J R DANGERFIELD DSO, RN, IS MISSING BELIEVED KILLED IN A NAVAL ACTION OFF THE BELGIAN COAST ON THE 14TH INSTANT STOP THE CIRCUMSTANCES OF THE ACTION GIVE NO HOPE THAT CAPT DANGERFIELD SURVIVED THE ACTION BUT THIS WILL BE CONFIRMED IN DUE COURSE — ADMIRALTY OF THIS DATE STOP ENDS

The sudden emptiness of one's life, when a person who has been for so long an integral part of it has gone, is like the severance of a limb, the cutting out of a heart; but it is the small change of things that hurt the most. . .

As when I went into Father's room to walk around and try to conjure up a living presence (I never supposed for one instant that Father had survived the action) and turned over his belongings.

There was his dressing-table and his best pair of monogrammed and crested silver-backed hair-brushes (he had a simple ebony-backed pair for service use); the cufflink and stud box, also silver, in which he kept all his best little pieces of male jewellery, including the half-hunter that I was sometimes allowed to wind up when I was a little girl on his knee. There were small, silver-framed photographs of himself and me, of me on my own, of me on my pony Bimbo with a winner's rosette.

But my father was no longer within the compass of my touch and was gone for ever.

Slowly, tentatively – in the way I have when I am fearful of what might be revealed to me – I approached the last letter that he had left for me to read on the occasion of his death.

There was no date, no preamble; he had simply dipped his pen in the inkwell and started to write in his swift, slanting script:

Dear little old Faith, I'm not good at this kind of thing, and I should have gone right through it with you, face to face, long before you and Cummings finally got around to marrying, but I funked it, God help me. And then for no discernible reason, you chucked him. Or he chucked you. I never knew the truth of it, so I kept quiet about it.

I met and married my wife Marie when I was a junior lieutenant and she the belle of Portsmouth, her father being a local landowner and MFH, now deceased. I had not been married to her for more than a month before it became painfully obvious to me that my beautiful bride was insane. On my honeymoon, indeed, I woke up to find her trying to strangle her pet dog – a long-haired dachshund which she had insisted on bringing with us to Menton.

After that things went from bad to worse and Marie had several attempts at killing me. She had the notion, you see, that I had been employed – paid! – by certain undefined enemies of hers – to insinuate myself into her life with the intent of destroying her. Thank God I had the Service for consolation, a means to escape the hell of my home life with the lovely woman I had married in such good faith and who, through no fault of her own, was so dreadfully flawed in her mind.

Then came my short and idyllic leave in Venice. I have already told you about this, the happiest episode of my life. The girl I met there, and loved until she died tragically early, was your mother, my dear Faith. We were never able to acknowledge either our love or your birth, because she was a royal princess, a member of a European dynasty.

Somewhere between heaven and earth, I lost or destroyed the evidence of my wife's tragic end. If ever you unearth it, my dear, I beg you to destroy it. The best you have, the finest assurance I can give you, is that you are whole, that the bluest blood in Europe runs in your veins and that you are free of any taint save that of illegitimacy.

This, my darling girl, will have to remain your secret. For reasons of State it was necessary to register you as the child of the woman I married. The day may come – and may it be soon – when the taint of bastardy will no longer blight the lives of the innocent. You will then be able to declare your proud birthright to the world.

I'm off now to join my ship. If you read this, I hope to God that I have managed to get it right. And have wiped the slate clean. . .

There is a second document which I treasure as another precious souvenir of my father: a report printed in the *Gazette*:

DEATHLESS GALLANTRY OF LORD DANGERFIELD

In posthumously awarding Captain Lord Dangerfield, DSO, Royal Navy, the Victoria Cross, their Lordships of the Admiralty issued the following citation:

'Ld. Dangerfield, as Commanding Officer of the patrol vessel HMS *Unbending* on duty in the North Sea on the 17th of last month, sighted in fog a German heavy cruiser escorted by two destroyers steaming south-wards along the Belgian coast, and immediately withdrew into the fog, unseen by the enemy.

'Throughout the night, *Unbending* most skilfully shadowed the enemy squadron until they put into the enclosed harbour of Cèvres for refuelling. At dawn, Ld. Dangerfield approached the harbour entrance and after ordering his crew to the boats, himself steered the *Unbending* at full speed into Cèvres, taking with him as his only aide Leading Seaman Alfred Hopwell.

'Ld. Dangerfield then with great skill rammed his vessel across the harbour entrance, all the time under fire from the German naval units in the port and from gun batteries ashore.

'As a result of this action, in which both men lost their lives, a heavy unit of the German High Seas Fleet and its escorts are imprisoned within Cèvres for the foreseeable future by the sunk *Unbending*.

'For his part in the action, Leading Seaman Alfred Hopwell is posthu-mously awarded the Conspicuous Gallantry Medal.'

Father had, in his own words 'Managed to get it right'. And had wiped the slate cleaner than driven snow.

*

One evening a seaplane, flying across the Channel from the Belgian coast, swooped in low over Ramsgate and dropped a package attached to a long, coloured streamer; and then was gone back the way it had come before anyone had really noticed that the craft bore the black crosses of Imperial Germany.

The package contained a set of photographs and a brief type-written note; another souvenir of my father that I shall cherish all my life, and my descendants after me.

The photographs show a military cemetery in Belgium and a coffin draped with a tattered White Ensign being born on the shoulders of six officers of the Imperial German High Seas Fleet – one of whom was once known to me personally. A firing party of sailors stand by the open grave.

The note reads:

'To a brave enemy, sometime comrade and friend in peacetime. Salute!
(signed) Alois von Schleicher
Captain of HIMS *Zollern*
(formerly of the *Darmstadt*)

283

It was strangely chill in St Paul's when I took my place in the front row, facing the high altar. High above, the interior of the great dome with the swirling baroque figures forever gesticulating; immediately below the centre of the dome's lantern, in the silent crypt, encased for all time in a simple catafalque, lay the 'Little Admiral' whom my father had joined as a not inconsiderable member of that great company of heroic men who have held the seas for England.

The organ swelled in the sonorous cadences of the 'Dead March' in *Saul*, and the Senior Chaplain of the Fleet, officiating at this memorial service for my father, walked in procession of banners and candles and chanting choristers to the altar. I, blinded by tears beneath my heavy veiling, tried to cast my mind back to memories of my brave, noble father – but could think only of the bearded, beloved figure in the Norfolk jacket, knickerbockers and funny flat cap, alighting from the train in Newmarket station, towards whose arms I always ran with such joy of release and relief to see him again.

The prayers. The psalm. The hymnody. And then the Senior Chaplain rose from his great chair and walked towards the steps of the pulpit to deliver the eulogy, bowing towards the altar as he passed.

The packed congregation settled in their seats. There was a brief chorus of coughs, and then silence.

Then, from out of the silence, the tread of a pair of footsteps coming silently. They paused close by me. From the corner of my eye, I saw a tall blue-clad figure take the place next to me.

He knelt for a few moments in prayer and I rejoiced to see the calm, clean cut of his bowed profile, the steadiness of his sun-bronzed hand. Then he sat back in his seat and our eyes met. I drew back my veil, so that he should see the joy in my eyes which I could not hide.

High above, in the ornate pulpit, the Chaplain of the Fleet pronounced the resounding words of Alfred, Lord Tennyson's *Ulysses* which my father had quoted years before at the graveside of his brother, and which were particularly apposite on both occasions:

It may be that we shall touch the Happy Isles,
And see the great Achilles, whom we knew. . .
That which we are, we are,
One equal temper of heroic hearts,
Made weak by time, but strong in will
To strive, to seek, to find. . .
And not to yield.

  By mutual, unspoken accord, our hands reached out — mine and
the man whose love I shared — and met in a compact that we sealed,
there and then, in a communion of silence, to last until our lives are
ended.